T0090436

MINDANAO GOLD

D.W. Chambers

Order this book online at www.trafford.com
or email orders@trafford.com

Most Trafford titles are also available at major online book retailers.

Printed in Victoria, BC, Canada.

ISBN: 978-1-4269-2880-2 (sc)

ISBN: 978-1-4269-2881-9 (hc)

Library of Congress Control Number: 2010906914

Our mission is to efficiently provide the world's finest, most comprehensive book publishing service, enabling every author to experience success. To find out how to publish your book, your way, and have it available worldwide, visit us online at www.trafford.com

Trafford rev. 6/30/2010

 www.trafford.com

North America & international
toll-free: 1 888 232 4444 (USA & Canada)
phone: 250 383 6864 ♦ fax: 812 355 4082

To my brother Bob, who took the time to read a very poorly, written novel with patience and understanding; without his support I doubt if this story would have made print!

PREFACE

In 1996, I was offered a position as a manager of mining in the Philippine Islands. I'd never thought much about the Philippines or for that matter Southeast Asia; however, being a person noted for risk, I accepted the project and was off to Manila with more of an attitude to visit than to make it a permanent move. It's now thirteen years later, and I'm still enjoying the visit!

Research on the book's factual information was gained while working with the Filipino people and the expatriates over the past 13 years while in the country.

Mindanao is one of the largest islands in the Philippines and is located within the southern archipelago. The government has, over the past one hundred years, chosen to view Mindanao as a secondary priority in regard to growth and development, even though the island has been recognized for its vast natural resources (of which gold mining plays a major part). The Philippine geological fault has produced huge amounts of gold, silver, and other precious metals through mining operations; during the early 1990s, the Philippine islands were among the top six gold producers in the world. It should be mentioned that the black-market gold produced by the small-scale miners throughout the islands was not part of the disclosed gold produced. Some analysts have speculated that, if added, the gold that the small-scale miners produced would have placed the Philippines higher in world gold production for the period mentioned.

During the Second World War, the Japanese armed forces took control of the Philippines, forcing the United States and their allies from the islands. While in control of the islands the Japanese confiscated and stockpiled immense amounts of gold and silver with a plan to transport the goods back to Japan after the war. The valuables were hidden in caves, vaults, and private homes throughout the Philippines in anticipation when the war ended to ship to Japan. However, as history reveals over the past 65 years, very little of the ill-gotten gains ever reached Japan but remained within the Philippine Islands. The story of the hidden fortune has been passed on; consequently, many treasure hunters have roamed the islands searching for the hidden plunder. Although some of the treasure has been found, and it has been suggested that the Marcos regime took an undetermined amount, it is agreed that the majority still remains hidden throughout the islands.

This story is about a group of treasure hunters in search of the hidden gold. The saga takes the adventures from the safe confines of Elko, Nevada, to the treacherous jungles on the island of Mindanao. Follow the group as they attempt to find and retrieve the gold; follow them as they attempt to escape from the Muslim bandits; find out what price they must pay while searching for the gold!

Characters

Americans
John Barrington, thirty-five, 6', 175 lbs. Junior mining executive
Gary Enright, thirty, 6'2" 180 lbs. Clean-cut mine geologist
Jerry Kerns, fifty, 5'8", 210 lbs., slightly bald / Fortune hunter
Charlie Taylor, fifty-two, 6'4", 250 lbs. Hard-knocks mining engineer/ adventurer

Filipinos
Ramon, seventeen
Mila, twenty beautiful Filipina
Omar, thirty Muslim bandit
Primitive Tribal chief, sixty
Magellan, twenty-three Filipino fishermen

The Old Man's Map

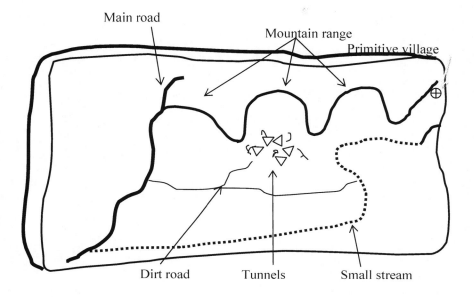

CHAPTER I

The Village

Ramon continued to dig as the sweat soaked his shirt, but he had no intention of stopping until he found the gold.

Carlos looked at him and said, "Ramon, I am going home. We have been here all day; I am hungry and tired. You will never find the gold, it is a myth!" Carlos had asked himself many times in the last couple of weeks why he had let Ramon talk him into this ridiculous plan. Three months he had helped Ramon dig—digging and digging for nothing. What made him decide to agree to this nonsense?

"It is here my grandfather has told me; we must keep digging," Ramon responded. Ramon was on his knees, digging the soft soil with his hands, frantically throwing the dirt in every direction, trying to open yet another tunnel. Carlos started to leave the dig site and began walking toward the village, but before he could leave the dig site, Ramon turned from the tunnel face and grabbed Carlos by the shirt. "You will not leave; you will help me find the gold!"

Carlos was shocked. Ramon had never, in their fifteen years together, ever done such a thing. Carlos pushed Ramon away and said, "Ramon, your grandfather was very old and did not always speak with reason; you must understand that you can not trust an old man's tales. Now let us go home; we will return in the morning." But Carlos had no intention of continuing this foolishness. He had decided a week ago that there was no gold to be found, and he would not continue this waste of time. When Ramon had first approached him about the gold, Carlos was excited to find the cave where the old man had said the gold was hidden. He had dreamed of the riches and could not wait to begin digging for the treasure; But now, no more. The villagers are laughing at us, he thought. The rebels watch us and the Muslims are always asking questions. This is not good for us!

"Ramon, I will not do this anymore! It is time to quit this crazy thing and go home for good!"

"Then go! I do not want you here anymore! But when I find the riches, you will not get any! It will be all mine! So go home, Carlos!"

Carlos started walking away from the dig and soon was out of sight. Ramon sat down on the soft mound of dirt, thinking of his grandfather and the wonderful stories he had told Ramon as a boy about the vast riches the old man had helped the Japanese hide during the war. In 1941, as a young boy, Ramon's grandfather had been forced to carry gold into caves that had been confiscated by the Japanese soldiers. For over a year his grandfather had worked with the Japanese and other Filipinos hiding the gold. Each day the men and boys would go with the soldiers to unload trucks containing the gold then carry it into the cave. The Japanese had told the Filipinos that once the gold was buried the Filipinos would be marched to the prisoner of war camp in Davao. On the last day, one of the soldiers yelled to him, "Boy, you will not continue to the camp! You will go home, now run!" Ramon's grandfather stood looking at the soldier in confusion. The man said again, "Run!" The soldier raised his rifle and pointed the barrel at Ramon's grandfather; "Run!" he yelled again. The boy began to run when he heard the rifle fire. He could feel the bullets hitting the ground around his feet as he ran for the jungle cover. He hid in the jungle for a week, fearing for his life. Later, after returning to his village, he learned that the Japanese soldiers had not marched the Filipinos to Davao but had murdered all of them and thrown the bodies in an open ditch. Ramon's grandfather was the only survivor! For over fifty years the old man had kept the secret of where the gold was hidden.

On his deathbed he now told Ramon where the gold could be found. The old man pulled a map from an old wooden box hidden beneath the floor of his house. All during day his grandfather explained to Ramon about how to find the gold. He carefully explained the map to Ramon late into the night, but finally the old man was too tired to continue. He looked up at his grandson and said, "The gold is a curse, my grandson.

I will tell you now never to search for it, but you must make your own decision. I am dying and no longer want to worry about the gold and its secret hiding place."

A week later the old man was gone. After his grandfather's death, Ramon spent several weeks agonizing over his secret. Each day he would look at the old man's map and consider if he should look for the treasure or, as his grandfather had said, "Leave it alone. It is a curse." After many agonizing hours, Ramon decided to search for the gold. He thought of his grandfather and the life he had had with him. When Ramon's father had died in the mine, Ramon had moved into his grandfather's home. During his years as a boy and then as a young man, Ramon watched his grandfather become a master map designer for the foreigner's mine. After the mine closed, the old man would help the small-scale miners with their mine claims and mine design. All the local miners would come to his house and have him help them. The locals called him "the map man."

Carlos had been his boyhood friend. They had grown up together; now Ramon had decided to trust Carlos with the secret. He thought, who can I trust other than Carlos? The night before Ramon decided to tell Carlos about the hidden gold he tossed and turned in his bed. He had a terrible nightmare of Carlos stealing his gold and leaving him inside the cave. Ramon woke in the early hours of the morning, his bed sheet covered in sweat. Once the sun peeked over the mountain, Ramon sat up in bed and peered through his window at the mountainside where his grandfather had told him the gold was buried. He thought, Why, Grandfather? Why did you tell me of this curse!

After breakfast, Ramon washed his face then opened the door of his hut to the outside. It was time to find Carlos—the decision was made; now he could hardly wait to get started and find the gold. Ramon found Carlos sitting outside his family's hut cutting away the husk of a coconut. Once the story was told the two had swore an oath to secrecy.

As time passed, however, and the search proved fruitless, Carlos began complaining, telling other villagers about the wasted time looking for the old man's gold. Now the story was out, and everyone began digging around the mine site and in the nearby mountains. They would watch Ramon each day, waiting until he began to dig. Once they were convinced he was nearing the buried gold, they would move into the area and start digging, pushing Ramon away and frantically throwing rocks and debris in all directions. In the beginning, many of them were digging alongside

Ramon; however, as months of work passed, less and less of the villagers joined Ramon, and now even Carlos was quitting.

Ramon was disturbed; what would he do for help if Carlos left? But he came up with a plan—he would go to Davao and talk to the American mining engineer, that's what he would do! The American engineer had been to their village a year ago looking for mining claims and walking around the old abandoned mine that had been shut down for many years. Ramon frowned and thought, the engineer had not returned; maybe the man had forgotten the mine and the village? Ramon was determined, though. He thought, if no one will help me, I will find the American and tell him of the gold! After all, the engineer would want the gold, wouldn't he?

CHAPTER 2

Elko

"That's enough! In the last year we've invested over a quarter-million dollars on the mining claims, and what do we have to show for it—nothing!" John Barrington was tired of losing money at the mine. Two years they had fought the big boys for the rights to the mining claims, only to have injunction after injunction filed against them. Gary Enright had gotten them into this mess and now he was saying if they invested another $100,000 they could get the mining rights!

"Listen," John said, "we are wasting our time in Nevada. Every mining claim is either taken or not worth filing on. We have to find something else or go broke!"

"John, I talked to one of the major mining companies last week and they said they are willing to go along with us in a partnership if we will only allow them to operate the mine—that seems like a good deal!"

"Yeah, Gary, they want to go into partnership with us, seventy–thirty! We find the mine, we invest over a quarter-million, and now they want to work with us? Bullshit! My dad founded this company twenty years ago, and I am not going to let him down! Before he died, he built a nice little mining company–and he would roll over in his grave if he thought I was going to give it away."

Jerry Kerns had been listening to the argument and decided he had better say something. "Guys, arguing isn't the answer; we need to decide what to do. I'm not a mining engineer, I'm an investment man with $250 thousand in this deal—and something has to be done. I agree we are in a tight spot and cannot afford to lose any more money! Let's take a look at other investments or get in bed with the big boys—but let's do something!"

John walked over, sat down at his desk, and looked out his window onto the street, thinking, I have always wanted to make it happen for the old man's sake but I guess we should have done a better job of looking this set-up over before we got in too deep; it probably would have helped us with this deal. The old man always told me to stay on top of things. I guess I just forgot or just didn't listen to him.

"Listen John," Gary said, "I looked this project over from every angle. Everything was fine until some SOB sent the major mining companies the reports; if I get my hands on the bastard—."

"Talking like that gets us nothing," John responded. "We need to do something, and I am not sure what that is! Gary, you start looking at some other options. Jerry, you and I are going to the banks and see what can be done on refinancing." He paused, looking dejectedly at the two men, and stood silent with his hands in his pockets for a long time. Finally said; "End of meeting."

Gary Enright graduated from the University of Idaho as an exploration geologist two years before meeting John Barrington in the Nevada gold fields. John was operating a small gold mine that his dad had operated for several years before his death in 1990. He hired Gary to do the geology work and help run things in the office. He had a little money left from his dad's estate, and Gary had a few dollars; however, it wasn't long before the two men were in trouble—no money. Although John had worked at the mine with his dad during summers, he was no miner and neither was Gary. Finally it became impossible for the two men to continue the mining operation.

One afternoon after finishing a shift in the mine, John looked at Gary and said, "Gary, it's time we gave up on this mess and moved on."

Gary nodded his head in agreement and answered, "You're right, John; the grade is lousy, and it's costing us a fortune to put timber into the damn drift. It will take us a year to get back into some decent gold at this rate." He paused and continued, "If it's even there!"

So in the summer of 1992, the men shut down the mine, sold the equipment, and started looking for other opportunities in the gold fields of Nevada. After settling down in Elko, the two started looking for an opportunity. They would soon learn that opportunity comes with a cost and lots of disappointments!

CHAPTER 3

Taxi?

Ramon arrived in Davao very late at night. He had been there only once as a boy and did not like the city. There were too many people, and it was dirty and unfriendly. But what could he do, he must find someone to help him find the gold. Ramon thought how I will find this engineer the city is very big and the people are not friendly.

Ramon had seen the mining engineer in his own village six months before. The villagers watched the man inspect small-scale mining sites, tour the old mine workings, collect samples, and leave for Davao. The mining engineer had not returned to Ramon's village, and soon everyone had forgotten about him. Now Ramon must find the engineer in the big city but where, where would he be?

The next day, after sleeping in an alley, Ramon walked the streets of Davao, not knowing where to look or how to find the American engineer. He asked a stranger on the street, "Do you know the mine engineer, the foreigner?"

"Go away, boy! Are you crazy, there are many foreigners in the city, which one are you looking for?"

"The mining engineer that came to my village, do you know him?" The man he had asked walked away, shaking his head.

All day Ramon traveled the city looking for the engineer. Finally he stuck his head inside a parked taxi and said to the driver, "No one will help, sir taxi driver. Do you know where the American engineer is?"

The driver started to run the boy off, but hesitated and thought, Hmm, a sucker? Then he said, "I am not sure if I know this man, but you may find him at the Estrada street tavern. Many foreigners go there to drink in the evening. I have taken many to the bar."

"How do I get to this place?" asked Ramon.

"What do I look like, my little friend; do I not look like a taxi driver?" Then the driver laughed, thinking, pretty clever!

Ramon ignored the laughter and said, "Then would you take me to this place?"

The driver answered, "For a small fee I will take you anywhere in Davao."

Ramon hesitated. He had only a few pesos to spend until he could find the engineer. "How many pesos will you ask from me to take me to this place?"

"From here, one hundred pesos."

"I do not have one hundred pesos to spend on such a trip. I can give you just twenty pesos but no more; I must have pesos to eat and sleep until I find this man."

"Twenty pesos!" the driver exclaimed. "I cannot take you from here all the way to the tavern for just twenty pesos!"

"Then will you show me the way, and I will walk there."

"My friend, it is very far and it is very hot, my taxi has cool air and I can take you there very fast! Give me fifty pesos and I will take you to this place."

"Please, sir, I mean no disrespect, but I must not spend my pesos. If I can walk to the tavern, I will do this instead."

"My little friend, you drive a hard bargain. I will take you for twenty pesos."

Ramon looked at the taxi driver and asked, "Would you take me for 15 pesos?"

"What!" The driver exclaimed, "No, I will not take you for fifteen pesos and I will not show you the way!"

Ramon turned and began walking away. No, he thought, I will not wait. He turned to the taxi driver and said, "I will pay you twenty pesos to take me to this place."

"Very good, my little man; you will not regret that you decided this."

As they drove away, Ramon could feel the cool air blowing inside the taxi. Yes, he thought, this was a wise decision."

However, in a very short time the driver stopped the taxi and said, "Here you are, we are at the tavern."

Ramon's eyes widened. "But this is only a short distance from where I entered your taxi!"

"The fare is for twenty pesos and I have driven you to the tavern! Get out of my taxi or I will crack your skull!"

Ramon thought for a moment but he knew he could not prevent this man from forcing him from the taxi. Ramon said to the taxi driver, "You are not an honest man, but I must find the foreigner so I will leave your taxi. But understand, I will not take a ride with you again, and I am not your little friend!"

As he climbed from the taxi, the driver said, "All of you from the provinces are idiots! You should stay away from the big city!"

Ramon stepped onto the sidewalk and looked up at the big sign. He could not read it, but there was a picture of a man drinking a bottle of beer and a glass sign above the door. Ramon had seen the glass signs when he was younger when he had visited the city with his grandfather. At night the signs were very beautiful but now this sign was not shining. Ramon approached the door of the bar. This was a strange place; he did not want to go inside. He thought I have never been to a place like this. What will I do inside? How will I know how to find the engineer? He walked back and forth in front of the door wondering what to do next. Finally he decided he must go inside; it was his only choice.

As he entered the tavern, he could not see anything inside; it was very dark, and the lights were very dim. A man standing behind a long table said "We are not open for business yet, go away!" Ramon stepped back into the street, and now the sun was blinding! He thought, I must wait I will stay and hear until the engineer comes, but he felt lost and alone. In his heart he was not sure if he could wait. He yearned to go home and forget this nonsense!

CHAPTER 4

Three's a Crowd

Jerry Kerns was a risk taker, no doubt about it. He had moved from New Jersey to Nevada in 1986 looking for an easy opportunity to make a buck. Nevada had been the Mecca of gold mining in the United States for over 150 years. If you wanted to get into the business, this was the place to be.

Mining began during the gold rush days in the 1800s and continued to grow through the 1960s. As time passed, the major mining companies began to take control of the small operations, and by 1970 they had forced the smaller mining companies out of business. In the 1980s, the environmental laws had increased mining costs, and the government had developed strict mining laws that virtually ended the changes for small-scale mining in the United States. Some of the seasoned small-mining companies managed to eke out a living; however, the newcomer had very little chance of survival. The government looked at mining as a messy business. The country was trending to cleaner ways to drive the economy. The computer industry was dominating the world economy. Banking was thriving on Wall Street. The service industry was everywhere with good old McDonald—big Mac—leading the way! The steel and logging industries were headed down the same road as mining throughout the United States. Legislation was being driven by the environmental surge: Clean-up the mess and shut down the mining operations was the champion of the day. The industrial modern age was on its last legs.

Jerry Kerns felt there were still some opportunities in the Nevada goldfields, if he played his cards right. He had a knack when it came to making a quick buck. All he needed was a way to get his foot in the door. He was a risk taker; there was only one way to the top as far as he was concerned—jump in with both feet and do whatever was necessary to make it big! He would not be satisfied working for anyone except himself. He was not a nine-to-five guy; if it took twenty-four hours a day to get what he wanted then it was twenty-four hours a day. But with a slight grin across his face he thought, Better to let someone else do the twenty-four hours a day grind. He would prefer to be the thinker, the money man, and he considered himself the point man. I can get the money; let someone else do the grunt work was his way of thinking.

He had tried his hand first in Vegas but never seemed to get to the top. After spending six months wasting his time trying to get into the gold mining business, he put a few dollar into a small nightclub in east Vegas to make ends meet, still waiting for a better opportunity in gold mining. However, after a year it was evident that the big money was on the strip, or downtown and he finally had to face the facts: There wasn't a chance in hell he would ever get a piece of the action if he stayed in east Vegas. In 1989, after fighting the system and losing, he decided it was time to make a change. He headed north to Elko and the gold mines.

During 1990 and 1991, Jerry managed to open a small mining-investment firm in Elko. Most of his business was a hustle. He would look for potential mine sites or old mining claims, and then generate investors from the eastern U.S. There was always a sucker who was looking for the big deal! Jerry would send out investment opportunities using the old shotgun method of investment. He would saturate the newspapers, journals, mining magazines, and adventure trade papers, claiming big gold discoveries and the chance to become a millionaire overnight! At first he hit the jackpot; every get-rich-quick poor bastard sent him hundreds of thousands of dollars. However, it wasn't long before the word got out about Jerry Kerns. His investors began to question his ethics and wanted more information before giving him any more money. Jerry had no real information or properties, so the investors' well began to dry up.

While having lunch one afternoon at the Commercial Hotel, Jerry overhead John and Gary sitting at the adjacent table discussing mining although he didn't know either of the men he was very interested in their conversation.

"We need to get going right away, John," Gary had said. "We can't wait on this deal."

"I know, this could be big, real big, but we don't want the big boys to get wind of it," John replied.

"I know, I know, keep your voice down!" Gary answered.

Jerry had heard this before; a couple of young guys thinking they had the inside on something big—which usually meant it was a risky deal, especially if it was being discussed in a restaurant. Jerry continued to eavesdrop; after all what was there to lose?

The two men continued their conversation. "I'm going to the land office today to follow up on the claims and start getting things going," Gary said.

John looked at Gary and said, "Don't make a big deal of it; keep a low profile. I mean what I said—we have to go about this the right way!"

Although Jerry's back was to the two men, Gary noticed him again and nodded toward him to John. John acknowledged Gary and said, "Let's finish this back at the office."

Later that day Jerry did some background checks on the two men he had been listening to in the restaurant and wasn't long before he had the information he needed. Not much goes on in the mining business in Elko that doesn't end up on the street! The two men had opened up a small office about a year earlier and had been looking at possible mining operations. They had a small bankroll, but the word on the street was that their money was getting short. Jerry also found out that the two men had a couple of prospects near Elko and were about to file on one of them. He also knew that the big boys were already watching and were now debating whether to move on the two men's claims.

Two days later Jerry walked into John's office. He looked at Gary sitting at a desk and said, "How's business?"

Gary looked up from his desk. It didn't take him long to recognize the man. Before answering, he turned around in his chair and motioned to John, who was sitting in his office. Gary turned back around and said, "I beg your pardon; do I know you, my friend?"

Jerry walked across the room to Gary's desk and sat down in front of him. Before Gary could say a anything "No, I don't think you know me, but I am sure we'll know each other in a bit."

John emerged from his office and approached the two men. "My name is John Barrington, and you are?"

"Jerry Kerns."

Jerry stood and shook John's hand then sat back down. Gary wasn't sure he wanted to shake the man's hand but decided it was best to get it over with. "Gary Enright, and what can we do for you, Mr. Kerns?" he asked.

"Gentlemen, I am an investor and am looking to spend some money in the right place."

"Well, you have come to the right place," responded John.

Gary's eyes widened as he thought what the hell is John doing? This guy is as crooked as a dog's hind leg!

Jerry continued, "I heard you boys had your hands on a couple of good prospects. Is that true?"

"I guess it depends on what you are talking about when you say 'prospects.'" John replied.

Gary had listened to enough and said, "John, I have to leave for a meeting, but I would like a couple of minutes of your time in your office before I go."

"Okay, Gary."

John looked at Jerry and said, "Will you excuse us for a second? I will be right back."

Jerry nodded his head in approval, and the two men walked back to John's office. They were not inside the door for a second when Gary exploded.

"Don't you recognize this jerk? He's the sneaky bastard eavesdropping on us a couple a days ago in the restaurant!"

"I saw your high sign when he came in, Gary. What's your point?"

"I don't like the looks of this guy, that's all. He looks like a shyster!"

"Go and check out the claims; let me handle the shyster, okay?" Gary stood for a moment looking at John.

"Gary, how much money do you have in your wallet?"

"What do you mean?"

"I said how much money you have in your wallet, damn it!"

John's burst of anger took Gary by surprise but he responded, "About a hundred; but why are you asking?"

"Well, I have about twice that. Gary, we have three hundred dollars between us and about $10,000 left in the bank. If we don't generate some cash flow soon we'll be back where we were a year ago! I'm going to feel this guy out, and see what he's up to—and you're going to check on our claims, is that clear?"

Gary had a feeling of desperation and said with a hint of panic, "John, we don't need this guy! I'm telling you there are some investors around town we can depend on; don't do this!"

"Gary, I'm tired of wasting time and money and I'm not waiting any longer. Let me talk to the man, and then we can decide what we're going to do!"

Gary knew he was going to lose this argument and decided to let it go for now. "John, please don't make any decisions until we talk later, okay?" Gary left the office, giving Jerry a hard parting look.

"Okay, Mr. Kerns, why don't you tell me what you really have in mind," John said as he walked back into the room.

"I'll be up front with you. I've been doing some checking around town and people tell me that you may have something worthwhile; problem is the big boys are watching and nobody beats the big boys, if you know what I mean."

"That's true, but we have some friends of our own and just maybe the big boys have a surprise coming to them." John knew he was lying through his teeth but he wasn't about to let this guy know he was in trouble with the claims.

"That's interesting," Jerry replied, "because I've been around Elko for a while and haven't seen anyone beat them yet. What makes you think you can?"

"My friend is on his way to confirm the claims as we speak, that's why! We just got the phone call, in fact—there are two other investors ready to turn loose some money once the claims are signed and registered."

"Registered claims are not mining claims, my friend," Jerry answered. "Just because you have the claims doesn't mean they are ready for mining. Do you realize the legal nightmare you are going to have just to get the proper permits and what it will cost to fight off the injunctions that—and I guarantee you—will be filed against you? These guys play rough. Don't you understand that they will never let a junior in? They are determined to control mining in the state of Nevada and there is nothing you or I can do to prevent that!"

"I don't agree," said John. "I was in the mining business for ten years with my old man in Nevada and we fought off the same bunch; Gary and I will get it done!"

"Well, you get the claims approved and the rights to mine and then we can talk," Jerry said as he got up from his chair, shook John's hand, and left the office. After stepping outside, Jerry paused. Better do some more checking on these two. They aren't tellin' the whole story. Besides, I have to generate some money if I decide to jump into this deal. I'm going to have to make some phone calls. He put his hand into his pockets and started down the street.

CHAPTER 5

The Engineer

Ramon waited outside the tavern for several hours, but the engineer did not come. He wondered if he would ever show up. As time passed he began to question himself, could the engineer—or would the engineer—help even if Ramon did find him? The bartender turned on the sign outside the bar and people began to enter the tavern, but still the engineer did not come.

Ramon had not eaten all day and decided to leave his spot in front of the bar and find some food. He passed in front of the bar, walking just past the tavern door. The sun was dropping over the mountain, the light glaring in his eyes. He shielded them with his hand but without warning he walked straight into someone going into the bar, someone very big. The encounter knocked Ramon to the sidewalk.

"Hey, watch it kid!"

Ramon looked up, and there stood the engineer! He was a big man, over 6' tall and must've weighed over two hundred and fifty pounds!

"What the hell's the matter with you? Don't you look where you are going?" the man continued.

Ramon got to his feet and looked up at the engineer. He was going to say something but was unable to open his mouth; he realized he had not used English for a very long time. He struggled to say something to the man but nothing would come out. A girl standing next to the engineer said in Tagalog dialect, "Go away or my man will beat you!"

Ramon looked at her. He knew about the young Filipina girls being with foreigners. The girls were always looking for the good life with the rich foreigners from the United States and other countries; this girl being with the engineer did not surprise him. Filipino men were disgusted with women that lived this way. The foreigners used the women then left most of them behind when they returned to their home country.

Ramon took an instant dislike to the girl. He thought why do our women not see that these men are using them? He started to leave, but then stopped and said out loud, "No, I will not let this woman stop me from finding the gold!"

Ramon waited until the engineer and the woman entered the tavern then followed them through the door. It was very dark inside, and because of the bright sunlight outside his eyes had not adjusted; he could not see. He could hear the music and the people talking but could not tell where it came from. The air was cool on Ramon's skin; it felt good after standing outside all day.

"Hey, close the door!" someone hollered from inside the bar, "you are letting in the hot air, you idiot!"

Ramon quickly closed the door and walked a few steps inside the room. Finally his eyes adjusted to the dark tavern and he could see men and women sitting at the bar and tables. He glanced around and found the big engineer sitting at the bar with the girl beside him. Carefully crossing the floor toward the engineer, he decided he would talk to the girl first in dialect.

"Excuse me," he said, "but I must speak to the big engineer."

The girl gave him a look of disgust and answered, "Go away! You will make trouble for me!"

But Ramon repeated, "I have to talk to the big engineer. I have something important to say to him."

"I will have the manager throw you out, you little pig!" she yelled.

Ramon ignored her and said to the engineer, "Gold!"

Charlie wasn't interested in the conversation; he had witnessed Filipinos arguing and knew it could go on for hours; but when he heard the boy say gold, he was all ears!

Charlie Taylor was a mining engineer from Montana. He had worked the mines around the state until mining had fallen on hard times during the eighties. Once Butte closed down, he made the decision to move to Nevada, where he met Art Barrington. The two men immediately became friends, working Art's small mining operation outside Elko. Art had a son about twenty-five years old, however, the kid preferred to stay in Elko while the old man and Charlie stayed at the mine and worked it with a couple of local miners. They weren't getting rich but they made a decent living producing a few ounces of gold. That paid the bills and enough for a small bank account to keep the operation going.

After working the mine for a couple of years, Art began having health problems. He was sixty-two years old, now with a bad heart. One night after his shift Art complained to Charlie, "Damn chest pain is real bad tonight, partner."

Charlie hadn't been in bed for more than an hour when he heard Art call out, "Charlie, I can't breathe!" He rushed into Art's room just as the old man rolled onto the floor, clutching his chest. Five hours later, Art Barrington was dead.

Charlie didn't have much to say to Art's kid after the funeral. They had met a couple of times, but the most said between them was, "Hi, how are ya?" Once Art was gone, Charlie figured there wasn't much use in stayin' around; anyway, the kid didn't know minin'. Besides, he hadn't said much to Charlie other than "Thanks for helpin' my old man."

Charlie was back at the mine site a couple of days after they buried Art. He was packing his clothes, getting ready to head back to Elko, and had just closed his suitcase when the door opened. In walked the son, John Barrington. He had called earlier and told Charlie he was taking over the operation. Charlie knew the kid had no idea how to run the mine and he was in no mood to show him, so Charlie had decided to move on.

Charlie had been to the Philippines while in the navy in 1966, during the Vietnam War. He liked what he had seen, so in 1988 he decided to leave the states and head to the Philippines. Two weeks after he left Nevada he was in Davao, and been there ever since. He was able to get work throughout the islands during the eighties and early nineties, but the last year had been tough due to the damn Muslims! They were raising hell in southern Mindanao and had just about stopped all foreign mining in the southern Philippines.

The only income Charlie had was a little money coming in from a savings account he had in Manila. He was able to survive thanks to the low cost of living in the islands, but money was running out and he was starting to feel the crunch. A man could buy a beer in the province for twenty cents US, and a decent meal for a couple of dollars, but still, his cash was running low, so Charlie turned around on his bar stool and said, "Gold, what do you mean, gold?"

The girl turned and looked at the big engineer and said in English, "He is a fool; he does not know about any gold!"

Even though Ramon had studied English in school, he was having a hard time understanding what she was saying to the engineer, but he knew it wasn't good!

"Yes," Ramon repeated, "gold. Engineer, I have seen you in my province, you came to my village six months ago."

"What is he saying?" The big engineer said to the girl. He was having a hard time understanding Ramon's English.

"Nothing, he is crazy! Do not listen to him!" She answered; however, Ramon would not let her stop him this time.

"My grandfather knows where the gold is, engineer."

Charlie looked at the Filipino boy standing there and wondered if what he had said made any sense.

"Tell me about the gold, my little friend." He looked at the girl and said, "I want you to translate for me." Charlie waved his hand and told the bartender to give him and the girl another drink. He told the girl to ask Ramon what he wanted. When she asked Ramon he told her "Water, please, give me some water." He was very thirsty after standing outside in the sun all day!

The engineer pointed to an open table near the back of the bar, motioning for them to sit down. Charlie thought it's only going to cost me a glass of water; besides, what else am I to do?

Ramon decided he must trust the girl; he would never be able to tell the engineer the story in English. He realized he was taking a risk, but he had no other choice.

After the three were seated, Charlie said, "Okay, son, tell me a story about gold!"

Ramon asked the girl if he could tell the story in dialect then she could repeat it to Charlie. The girl said, "I don't care how you tell it, but get going or this conversation is over!" For the next two hours Ramon told the story.

"My grandfather was a boy during the American war with Japan. When the Americans started winning the war, the Japanese decided to hide the gold they had confiscated in caves throughout the Philippines."

"Hey, kid," Charlie interrupted, "I know all about the Japanese gold. I also know that very little of the gold has been recovered—in fact, Marcos got most of it!"

Ramon had to have the girl translate what the engineer had said. He waited a minute to make sure he said the right thing back to the engineer.

"Yes, you are right. Although I do not know what our President Marcos did, I do know what my grandfather has told me. Many Philippine men and boys were used to bury the gold in many places here. Once the gold was hidden, the Filipinos were killed in order to keep the secret of the gold. My grandfather was shot at but did not die and was able to return to his home. For many, many years he did not tell anyone where the gold was hidden, but as he was dying he decided it was time! For two years now I have been looking for the gold but I cannot find it!"

"So what do you think I can do, my little friend? If you cannot find the gold, what makes you think I can?" Charlie asked.

"My grandfather made a map, but I cannot understand all of it; I cannot read all of what he has written!"

"Where is this so -called map?" asked Charlie.

Ramon looked at the man for a very long time. Can I trust this engineer? But again what choice do I have? He slipped his hand inside his shirt and slowly pulled out the map, laying it on the table in front of Charlie.

Charlie leaned over and said, "Let's take a look at what you have here,"

It was a map all right; it had several markings on it that Charlie didn't recognize. It looked like it may have indicated some cave sites. The only thing he could determine from the map that might be a reasonable landmark was the twin mountains, side by side. They looked identical; however, Charlie thought that might just be due to the crude drawing the old man had made. There was what looked like a small stream crossing in front of the mountains—but again it was difficult to determine from the drawing. Charlie asked, "What part of the Philippines are we talking about, young man? I don't recognize the area."

The color in Ramon's face paled. He said, "But you are an engineer! You must know where the gold is; it is on the map!"

"Listen, little man—you have to have more information. The map shows places where the caves are located, but are they in Mindanao, Cebu, Luzon, Latye, Zamboanga, or some other place within the islands?"

Ramon was shocked; he had never considered the engineer might not have the answer to the map! "But Mr. Engineer, the gold is on the map! You must know where it is! I have traveled a long way to show you!"

"Settle down, kid, I didn't say we can't find it, but this map has to be studied, and I gotta do some figurin' before we can find the gold!"

Ramon relaxed a little, but he was still very nervous—had he made a mistake with the engineer?

"Listen, let me have the map for a couple of days, and I'll see what I can do," said Charlie.

Ramon grabbed the map off the table. "No! I promised my grandfather on his deathbed that no one would have the map except me!"

"All right, settle down; you can keep the map. Meet me here tomorrow and we'll take another look, okay?"

Ramon put the map back into his shirt and agreed to meet the engineer the next day.

After leaving the tavern, Charlie began to consider what he was going to do. He started to think about where he was six months ago. He had been working for Chaparral Mining Corporation back then. They had hired him to evaluate some properties in the mountains of Mindanao, but he couldn't remember how many he had seen. He thought, Christ, I must have looked at twenty different properties—hell, they all looked the same to me. Was the map for real? Could he locate the caves from the map? Should he take the map from the boy—and for that matter, was the kid for real? Charlie could not think any more; the girl wouldn't shut up.

"He is just a peasant, he knows nothing! Forget this fool!" she kept repeating.

"That's enough! I'm tired of listening to you! If you don't like it, take a hike! There are other women around that will keep their mouths shut!"

The girl knew she had gone too far and decided it was dangerous to continue protesting. She would wait until Charlie regained his senses before she would say more.

Charlie knew it would take some work to find the locations on the map, but, more importantly, he knew he would need money to make this thing work. I can do the work, but I will have to get the money. Either way, I have nothing to lose!

CHAPTER 6

Trouble in Paradise

"In the last three months, guys, I have come up with over a hundred thousand dollars for this project, and we still don't have the mining permits!"

Jerry had been listening to John and Gary argue over the mining claims, and he was fed up. He continued, "John, I know how hard you and Gary have worked to make this deal, but unless I see something positive, I am going to pull the last hundred and fifty thousand out."

"Wait," Gary said, "remember I didn't want you in the first place, but you and John decided to make the deal, so you don't have a damn thing to complain about!"

"Yeah, you are right about that, asshole, but you sure accepted the money!" Jerry answered.

"Stop the arguing, it will not get the job done!" John interrupted. He knew both men had a point, but that didn't solve the problem. Gary had run into trouble with the claims and mining permits. They had been fooling themselves when they believed that the majors would let them mine the claims; now some major mining companies had filed injunctions against the mining operation and had tied them up in court.

"I guess it is time to make a deal with one of the majors," Gary said.

"No way in hell!" John yelled. He looked at the two men. "I told you I would not do anything my old man would not approve of, and I meant it!"

"John, I agree with Gary on this. These guys have the money to keep us out for as long as they want! Remember, they have the clout!"

John got up from his desk and walked out of the office. As he opened the door to the street, he turned and said, "No way, no deals with the big boys!" As he headed down the street with his hands shoved into his pockets he said out loud, "Dad, ya gotta help me here. Send me some kind of a message—I'm outta ideas!"

CHAPTER 7

Who's Calling?

John was sitting in his apartment watching The Late Show when the phone rang. He thought, Damn, I hope this isn't Gary. I need to relax! He hesitated, looking down at the ringing phone. Finally he picked up and said, "This is John."

"Hello, John."

John hesitated for a second then answered, "Hello. May I ask whom I am talking to at this time of night?"

"It's Charlie, John."

John hesitated for a minute then said, "Charlie Taylor?"

"You've got it," Charlie answered then continued, "John, you are a tough man to find. I have called all over hell looking for you! I thought you might have left Nevada! Lucky I was able to track you down. An old buddy of mine in Elko gave me your number out of the phone book. I figured when you were not at the old mine site you had left the state."

"Well, you're right on one thing and wrong on the other, Charlie. I did leave the mine—it was mined out—but I didn't leave Nevada. Enough of me, where in the hell are you?"

Charlie answered, "The Philippines; been here ever since I left your old man's mine."

"Charlie, it's late, and this must be costing you some money, so what can I do for you?"

"Gold, John, how does that sound to you?"

"Sounds good, Charlie; do you have some?"

Charlie laughed and said, "Yeah got a couple of tons here in my kitchen!"

"Okay, okay, Charlie, what do ya have for me?" John replied.

Charlie spent the next half hour telling John the short version of what the Philippine boy had told him of the hidden gold. At first John thought Charlie was drunk and was rambling on, but as the story unfolded he became more interested. After Charlie finished, John said, "What do you want from me, Charlie?"

Charlie never hesitated. "Money, John, money."

"Money," John said, "that's hard to come by right now. How much are you talking about and for what?"

"About twenty thousand, John; that covers all the expenses we will need."

"Listen, Charlie, why don't you give me your telephone number and I'll get back to you tomorrow night; will that work?" John thought for a minute then continued, "Charlie, can you fax me a copy of the map? That sure would help me out."

"John, the kid won't let go of the map. He told his grandfather he would not let anyone have it, so I'm stuck for now."

"No problem," John said. "We can decide later on what needs to be done—if we move on this deal. Nice talking to you."

Charlie hung up the phone wondering if he had done the right thing; had he explained the set-up well enough for John to buy in? He decided he would have to wait until tomorrow to find out.

The next day John let the partners know what Charlie had told him over the phone the night before. Gary listened for a few minutes and said, "Where the hell is Mindanao?"

John replied, "After I got off the phone with Charlie, I took a look in the encyclopedia. Mindanao is one of the big islands in the southern Philippines. It's one of the largest agricultural and natural resource areas in the entire Southeast Asia region.

Gary interrupted, "So, what does that mean, do we just take off and forget everything we have here and head for the Philippines? Let's get real here; we don't have enough information to just pack up and leave. Besides, we are close to getting this thing done. John, I have a meeting with one of the majors today, and I think we are going to complete the deal."

Jerry glanced over at Gary and said, "Okay, I'm willing to wait another day, but this might be something we can do if the deal falls through."

"It won't fall through!" Gary retorted in a high-pitched voice. He was very tense, and he was getting tired of John and Jerry questioning his every move!

"Okay, Gary, settle down," John continued. "You have until 12 o'clock tonight to get it done, but if not we are going to make the call to the Philippines!"

Jerry had listened to the two men and thought, The Philippines. Not a bad idea, gold! Jerry loved this kind of deal: quick fix, big money, and more importantly, adventure! Yeah, this is my kind of operation!

Gary left the office; he was desperate! He thought *No way was he going to walk away from a deal of a lifetime!* He was going to make the deal on the claims today, no question about it! He walked into the restaurant and spotted Tom Anderson.

Tom looked up from the table and said, "Hello, Gary, what's the good word?"

Gary looked at Tom and put on his best promotion smile. He was aware this might be the most important meeting of his life! Tom was the investment manager for Anderson Gold, a major operator in Nevada. The company had two operations going outside Elko, the Two Ton and the Over the Top project. Gary took a deep breath and continued toward the man's table. He knew he must make the deal today! He pulled out the chair across from Tom and said, "Good." He didn't hesitate and continued, "No sense beating a dead dog anymore; let's do something with the claims. I'm ready to make a deal. Tell me, what do you have to offer?"

Tom almost started laughing; he knew he had the kid. Gary was ready—he was going to be easy pickins'! Anderson didn't need the few claims that Gary had, but since they were near the boundary the VP had told him to get a hold of them and run the small outfit out of the area.

"Whoa, Gary; let's order something to eat first."

Gary realized how tense he was and also knew he might have put himself in a bad spot by jumping the gun. Tom would guess that Gary was desperate to make the deal. He thought, Damn it; settle down!

After ordering lunch, Tom said, "Well, we are interested in the claims, that's for sure, so here is what I have been given permission to propose.

We will invest half a million in the claims for the next five years. We will operate the mines. If it is decided there is potential, your group will receive 10 percent of the net after the first full year of production. We reserve the right to buy you out on or before the third year of deal at an agreed value of the property. How does that sound?" He looked across the table to see if he could determine Gary's reaction to the offer then continued, "I have the contracts with me; all it takes is you and your partners to sign."

Gary thought about the offer, Ten percent of the net; will John accept it? He looked across the table at Tom and replied, "Listen, it sounds good to me. Let me take it back to John and I will let you know by five o'clock this afternoon, okay?"

Tom said without hesitation, "You need to understand this is the final offer. If your people say no, don't bother coming back. You understand what I mean, don't you, Gary?"

"Are you saying there is no compromise?" Gary asked.

"You said it, no compromise!" Tom answered.

"Come on, Tom, let's be reasonable."

"That's the deal; take or leave it, Gary. I like the way you work; we have plans for you. If this thing goes through, you can write your own ticket with our company—if you can get your people to go along."

"All right, let me get it done, Tom. Five o'clock, okay?"

"Five o'clock, no later," Tom answered.

Gary left the meeting thinking out loud, "Write my own ticket," he grinned, "I can make this work!"

Fifteen minutes later he entered the office with a smile on his face. "Well, I think we can live with their offer."

"What do they want, Gary?" John asked.

"We get ten percent of the net, and they will invest half a million into the mine the first year."

Jerry looked at Gary and said, "Ten percent of what? If we don't net anything then we get nothing!"

"Come on, Jerry, everything has some risk!" Gary answered.

John looked at Gary and said, "What else, Gary?"

"What do you mean?" Gary answered.

"I said what else, just that simple."

"Well, they want a buyout within the first three years, but by then we are rich!" Gary responded.

"Yeah, or we are broke!" Jerry retorted. "No net means no money!"

"That's what I thought you might say," Gary answered. Gary looked at Jerry and said," I thought you were willing to take a chance, Jerry, but I guess I was wrong."

John stood up and looked at Gary. "What else, Gary?"

"What do you mean, what else, that's it! Why do you keep askin the same question?"

John looked at Gary and said, "We have been partners for how long?"

Gary looked back at John for a moment and said "About what, three years, Why?"

"There is something else that you are not telling us, Gary."

"Bullshit, that's it!" Gary exclaimed.

"Well, whether that's it or not, no deal, do you agree, Jerry?"

"You bet I agree, John," Jerry replied.

Gary jumped to his feet and said, "Wait just a minute! I worked my ass off for this deal! It's a good one and we have to take it! They said no compromise!"

The two men looked at Gary, neither one saying anything.

When the two men remained silent Gary hollered, Damn it I say yes! Gary had lost it!

"Remember who runs this company," John replied. "No deal."

"Yes, and remember who has the money, my friend," Jerry added.

Gary stormed out of the office and slammed the door behind him.

John looked at Jerry and said, "Should we make the phone call tonight?"

"That's the best thing you've said today, John!"

CHAPTER 8

For Real?

Charlie was standing outside the bar. It was four in the afternoon. He thought where is the kid? If he doesn't show up in the next ten minutes, I am out of here! Charlie walked back into the bar and sat down next to the girl. He was still pissed at her, but she had kept her mouth shut, and he decided to let things go. Besides, he wasn't in the mood to argue with her over the kid.

Charlie sat looking at himself in the mirror behind the bar and thought, *Man, I have got to do something about my weight I'm fifty pounds overweight!* He rubbed his hand across his rough, day-old beard and shook his head. The girl sat next to him sipping her beer, not saying a word; she had been quiet since the run-in the day before. Charlie continued thinking, *Good; she's keeping her mouth shut for a change!* He was about to take a sip of his beer when he heard Ramon say, "Hello, Mr. Engineer."

Charlie turned on his stool and looked down at the Filipino boy. "Good afternoon, how are you?"

Ramon struggled to speak English "I have decided to find the gold with you, engineer, but you must understand that the map must stay with me."

Charlie reached out, grabbed Ramon around the shoulders, gave him a big shake, and said, "No problem, kid, let's do it!"

Ramon was startled and almost fell to the floor when Charlie turned him loose.

The girl never bothered to look at Ramon; she was not going to let this idiot take her man away from her, but this wasn't the time to say anything; she would wait! She had worked too hard to catch Charlie and no one was going to take him away from her. She was going to marry Charlie and become his American wife!

Charlie had located every historical map and documentation of the Philippines that he could find and had spent all night trying to figure out where the gold may have been hidden. He would close his eyes and attempt to visualize the map but knew he was wasting his time; he had to have the map! He needed the damn thing to match it with the geology maps and other information he was working with. Charlie clinched his fist and thought, the kid's map was critical! Finally he decided he would have to convince Ramon stay with him and work on the map but again thought, Would the kid agree would to stay with him and the girl?" If the girl was going to be a problem then she would have to go!

"Listen, what is your name again?" Ramon opened his mouth but before he could answer Mila sarcastically said, "Ramon." "Yeah Ramon, Charlie said out load, he continued, you stay with me we can compare the maps and maybe locate where the gold is hidden, what do you think?"

The girl froze. She knew what this would mean. She had treated the boy with disrespect, and he may not want to stay with the engineer if she were there. She waited for the boy to say no, however, she was surprised when he agreed and to her relief, did not mention her.

Ramon had agreed, even though he did not like staying with the girl, but he understood that he would need her to translate to the engineer when he was not able to speak the English.

"Good, let's go," Charlie said. Forty-five minutes later, they entered the apartment. Charlie looked at his watch; it was eight o'clock in the evening just about time for John's call. A half hour later just as Charlie opened his second beer the phone rang. He sat down next to the phone, picked it up, and said, "Hello?"

"Charlie, this is John, he continued. Sorry—the damn phone bill is higher than hell to call there so ya need to tell me in a hurry what you have over there?"

"Okay John, I have the map, and the kid is here at my place."

"Good, does the map look authentic?"

"Yeah, it's the real deal!"

John responded, Good, good! Charlie, if it's a go, I'll be bringing two other guys with me. One has the money, and the other is my partner; any problem with that?"

"No, John. If there is as much gold as I think there is, we will have plenty for everyone, so bring them along! Just one question; can you trust them?"

John thought for a moment. He knew he could probably trust Jerry, but for the last couple of weeks he wasn't so sure about Gary, but decided not to mention it and said, "Yeah, we can trust them, Charlie."

"Okay, John, when do you plan on being here?"

"We will be on a plane in the next couple of days and in Manila by the end of the week. That's an extra day to you, Charlie, considering the time change. I will fax you our itinerary; can you can give me a number?"

Charlie gave John the fax number for the hotel and hung up the phone. Charlie looked at the two and said, "Well, we are on our way, gang!"

Ramon wasn't sure what Charlie meant, but Charlie had a big grin on his face, and that seemed to be a good enough for Ramon.

CHAPTER 9

Adventure Time!

Gary stayed drunk the entire night after the meeting with John and Jerry. He had decided not to call Tom Anderson with the bad news; after all, what good would it do; the deal was off. Gary thought as he drank I will get even, no matter what it takes. I will get even with those two, but how, how can I get them to pay for what they have done? I will bide my time; it will come sooner or later, but it will come! Where did Jerry come from? How did he end up between John and me? Three years shot to hell!

The next morning Gary returned to the office. He said nothing about the meeting the day before other than asking them if they were sure they were not going ahead with the Nevada deal. John let Gary know in a hurry, "No deal, and that's the end of it!"

"All right, John, you know me; it's over as far as I am concerned, but what's next?"

"We are headed for the Philippines. Are you in or out, Gary?" John replied.

"I'm in, John, no sweat," Gary answered. Gary could not control his shaking; the booze and the stress of losing a once in a lifetime deal was too much. Jerry noticed Gary's condition and mentioned it to John while they were together in John's office.

"Hey, he don't look so good. Did you see the look on his face when you told him no for the last time?"

"Yeah, but Gary's been like this before. He gets over it quick, don't worry, Jerry, he is with us now."

By one in the afternoon the next day, the men were at the Elko immigration getting their passports updated. "I guess you boys know that this is going to take twenty-four hours to get there, and we lose a day, don't you?" Without waiting for the men to answer John continued, "We will catch our flight from LA to Tokyo at seven thirty AM Friday, so don't waste any time getting ready! They travel agents got us arriving in LA at six fifteen; that doesn't give us much time to catch the international flight."

It took them the remainder of the week to get their passports, cloths and other gear for the trip but by Friday they were on their way. After takeoff, John and Jerry talked about the trip and how it was going to be a hell of an adventure. Gary sat in his seat with his arms folded across his chest looking out the window. He was thinking this is a big mistake; the whole deal is stupid! You don't jump into something like this in a week! John threw it all away for this SOB, but I will get them, I will get them good!

"Gary, you are awful quiet; what you thinking about, partner?" John asked.

"What?" Gary replied, startled. He had not been listening to them, and the question surprised him. He became nervous he felt that John was able to read his mind.

"Gary, what are you thinking about?" Jerry repeated the question.

Gary forced a smile and said "Gold, Jerry, gold!"

Jerry laughed and winked at John. John smiled and said, "See, I told you he would come around!"

When they arrived in Manila it was hot, real hot. The humidity was terrible; all of them were sweating profusely within minutes of leaving the plane. The airport was loaded with people, and the lines to the immigration desks were long and confusing to say the least! Once through immigration the men encountered four luggage belts howling away and dumping bags in every direction. The three men were running from one belt to another trying to figure out which one was carrying their baggage. They stopped at the number one belt and waited.

Jerry commented, "Damn! Why the hell did I bring a black bag; they all look the same!

Gary stood back from the rat race with his arms folded across his chest, smirking at the disorganized nightmare unfolding in front of him. Well, boys, welcome to success! he thought. Yep, we got ourselves a real winner! Gary was starting to enjoy this! He was about to burst out laughing when from nowhere a woman slammed a cart into the back of his legs. Gary let out a piercing scream as he went to the floor. The woman paid little attention to him; she backed up her cart and went around Gary's crumpled body lying in the walkway.

John and Jerry had no idea what had happened behind them. Both were busy looking at the bags as they traveled by. Finally, Gary struggled to his feet; he was sure that the dumb broad had cut open the back of his legs. The pain felt like someone was holding a cigarette lighter next to his legs! The sweat was boiling off his brow as he took a deep breath, bent over, and pulled up his pant leg to discover that the hide was scratched away, exposing oozing blood. He became sick to his stomach. After twenty hours of flying he was too weak to do much but grab onto John's shoulders and steady himself. He thought, Damn, I'm gonna puke!

"You all right, partner?" "John asked. "You look a bit pasty-faced!"

Gary was about to say something when the load speaker barked out, "Those passengers who arrived on flight 804 from Tokyo can pick up their baggage from carousel number 3, flight 804, carousel number 3, thank you." Before Gary could react, the whole damn bunch broke into an uncontrolled riot and began pushing, shoving, and knocking people out of their way as the moved toward carousel 3.

John and Jerry turned to face Gary, each with a big grin on his face. Jerry said, laughing "Ain't this great, man!" Gary was about to tell him what he thought about this being great when down he went again! He was backing up to let someone by when the person pushed him violently backward over a pile of bags! His elbow slammed hard against the floor, then a bright light flashed across his face; the pain was unbearable, again! He yelled at the top of his lungs because someone had just stepped on his vulnerable exposed crotch. He was done!

Gary was waiting for someone to help but—he rose to a sitting position and looked around—no John and no Jerry? Again the intercom came on, "Ladies and gentlemen, there has been an error and we would like to apologize. Flight 804 passengers can pick up their luggage at carousel number 1, thank you." Gary folded his arms across his chest and leaned back against the luggage behind him, when he realized what had just been said. "Oh my God!"

And he was right; here they came pushing and shoving everything in their path which included Gary! A few minutes later he was limping around the luggage belt looking for John and Jerry.

"Hey!" someone hollered, "Where the hell ya been? We got the luggage; do you have your stubs?"

Gary looked up and saw his two buddies standing next to their luggage; both had excited grins on their faces. John took one look at Gary and said, "Shit, partner, you look like shit!" Jerry started howling; he couldn't help it—shit, you look like shit!

Once through customs, the men exited to the outer terminal where the carnival continued. It seemed everyone was yelling about something!

"Hey, Joe, where are you going?"

"Hey, Joe, best ride in town! I speak good English and know all the girls!"

"Hey, Joe, come on, jump in!"

John stood with his briefcase in hand, taking it all in, while Jerry talked to an airport service attendant.

Again someone asked, "American?"

"What?" John answered in surprise, but before he realized what was going on, a middle-aged Filipino man was pulling on his briefcase, trying to drag him toward his taxi.

John looked at the man in anger and said, "Hold on their, friend, don't pull on my luggage!" He turned to see Jerry still talking to the terminal agent. John managed to pull his briefcase away from the taxi driver then asked, "How much?"

"Only two thousand pesos; I will take you anywhere in Manila for two thousand pesos!"

John realized they hadn't done their homework—they were at the mercy of a bunch of pros! Hell, they hadn't even bothered to get any Philippine money!

"How much is that in American dollars?" John asked.

"Very little, my friend, it is a very good price!"

Gary looked at John and said, "Let me exchange some money, John. Don't let them do anything until I get back!" John nodded in agreement.

Gary approached the currency exchange and looked at the rates—forty pesos to the dollar—and thought Now what the hell does that mean, forty pesos to the U.S. dollar? He sighed, and said out loud, "Piss on it; I'm tired of all this!" He looked around at the line and thought there has to be at least thirty people waiting! He kept looking around. The airport was a madhouse; people were everywhere, pushing and shoving. Gary just shook his head and whispered, "I'll get even for this!" Damn, his legs hurt; bitch!

It took him ten minutes standing in line, but finally, finally, he was at the window! Just as he was about to pull his wallet from his pocket, someone from behind jammed up against him, and down went the wallet onto the floor! No "excuse me"? He thought as he stepped out of line to pick up the wallet. After bending over to pick up the wallet he turned around and realized someone had taken his place, he was back to square one!

Gary turned toward the person to say something. It was unbelievable— it was the same old bag that had been knocking him around for the last hour! He didn't hesitate— sweat was running down his face, his legs were on fire—"Listen, you old bag, I'm gonna give you two seconds to get the fuck out of my way, or I'll knock you on your ass!"

The lady understood every word he had said. Her face turned red, and she said in broken English, "I am a daughter of God and will not allow a heathen to speak to me in that way!" She turned around and at the top of her lungs started hollering, "Help! Help! I am being attacked!"

Gary never wasted a second; he took his right shoulder, and with just the right move, he elbowed her in the lower back and knocked her on her ass! He was ready to catch hell for it but by now he didn't care; however, to his amazement no one bothered to say or do a thing. She lay on the floor with her dress over her head screaming to high heaven, but still no one seemed to notice or gave a damn! Gary stood looking down at her and said out loud, "And life goes on!"

He turned to the teller, "I would like to exchange some American dollars."

The young lady behind the counter answered, "Yes, sir, how much would you like to exchange?"

"Can I get five hundred dollars?"

As the teller counted out the exchange money, Gary asked her "How much should we pay for a taxi into Manila? We're new in the country."

The teller asked, "Where are you going?"

"The New World Hotel," Gary replied.

She answered, "Three hundred pesos and fifty pesos tip is the going price."

Gary thanked her and returned to the curb where he found Jerry and John still fighting with the taxi drivers. Gary said to the taxi drivers, "Three hundred pesos, boys, no more!"

John turned to Gary and asked, "Is that the going rate?"

"Yep, not a peso more!"

"No, no, one thousand pesos!" said one of the taxi drivers, "That is the price!"

While the men were arguing about the price, a police officer started walking toward the group. The first taxi driver saw the him and immediately started to walk away.

"What seems to be the problem, gentlemen?" the officer asked.

The second driver was caught off guard and said, "Nothing, sir, I am taking the Americans to Makita for three hundred pesos."

"Yeah, that's right," John said, "he is taking us into the city."

The policeman stood looking at the driver and said something to him in dialect. The driver shook his head and answered him, "Oh, oh."

Once inside the cab, the driver headed away from the curb and they were on the way into Manila. Jerry looked at Gary and said, "Do you smell that?"

"Yeah, what the hell is it?" Jerry replied.

"I don't know, but it is sure different!" John answered. John looked at Jerry and said, "Did you put money in the bank?"

"I put forty thousand in the Hong Kong bank in Manila in all our names. I will call the bank after we check in," Jerry answered.

"We had better get our heads together before we end up broke, if this is any indication of what these people are like!" Gary responded.

"Yeah, I'm not thinking too well right now; I need some sleep!" Jerry replied.

After twenty minutes, the men arrived at the hotel. The driver jumped from the cab and opened the trunk. Before the three men could move their luggage, a bellhop was jerking the bag from John's hand. A second bellhop was saying, "Good afternoon, sir, let me take that for you," and without hesitation he too jerked the bag from Gary's grasp. They started walking toward the entrance when the taxi driver hollered, "That will be one thousand pesos, sir!"

Gary, who was walking in the rear of the luggage convoy, turned around and doubled up his fist. The show was over! "You little twerp," he shouted, starting after the driver. Jerry stopped walking and started running back toward the two men, yelling, "Hold it, partner; take it easy, I'll handle this."

The driver had backed up against the cab, his eyes bulging, his mouth hanging open. Jerry stepped between the two men and put his hands on Gary's chest. "You go in and help John check in; I'll handle this, okay?" Gary was open and closing his fist, his face was crimson red, and it was obvious his temper matched his face!

John hollered from the hotel entrance, "Come on, you two! I'm beat, let's go!"

Gary took a shallow breath, looked over Jerry's shoulder at the driver, and turned around and started heading for John standing at the door.

Jerry turned to the taxi driver and said, "Now how much was that?"

The man stood away from the car, looked over at Gary walking toward the entrance, and said in a meek quiet voice, "One thousand pesos, and sir."

Jerry didn't hesitate. He turned around and hollered to Gary, "Say, partner, do you have a thousand pesos for the taxi driver? "

The driver immediately turned around, grabbed the door of his taxi, opened it, started the engine, and sped away from the curb.

Gary yelled back, "What do you want, Jerry?"

"Nothing, partner; it's been taken care of!"

Finally the men and the bellhops entered the hotel and approached the check-in desk. After setting the luggage down the bellhop stood looking at the three men. Gary sighed and said, "How much? "Sir?" the bellhop replied. How much said again?" Jerry interrupted the conversation and handed the bellhop a 100 pesos. The young man gave Gary a nasty look and walked away. Gary said to Jerry, "They're going to break me I'm tellin ya their going to break me!"

"May I help you, sir?" asked the young lady at the desk.

"Yes," John answered, "we have three reservations, John Barrington, Gary Enright, and Jerry Kerns."

The young girl looked at her reservation list and replied, "Yes, I have a Mr. Barrington and a Mr. Kerns but no Mr. Enright?" Gary went into a tirade he threw his coat across the lobby and crust to high heaven, I'll kill somebody, I'm tellin ya I'm going to kill somebody!" he finally ran out of breathe too much the trip and the last week was just too much! He fell to his knees and lowered his head into his chest and began gasping for air. The young lady was standing behind the counter with her mouth wide open the fear on her face was evident to both John and Jerry. Jerry said to her, "it's ok sweetheart he's had a bad day." The manager approached the group and after some discussion Gary was given a room with apologies being bandied around from everyone in the lobby while Gary stood leaning against a roof pillar in the lobby a resigned look of despair on his face.

After getting their keys and heading toward the elevators, Jerry remarked, "Did you see how pretty she was?"

"Do you think I'm blind?" Gary responded. "I know I have jet lag, but I'm not that jet lagged!" All three laughed.

John said to the other two, "Let's get settled in our rooms and meet in about a half hour in the lounge, okay?" The two nodded their heads in agreement as they stepped into the elevator.

CHAPTER 10

Manila

While at breakfast, Charlie said to Mila and Ramon, "I have to meet these people in Manila tomorrow and I want you two to get along until I get back."

Charlie was worried about the two Filipinos; they had been fighting between themselves all night. He wasn't sure why, but the two did not like each other. They constantly argued in Filipino. He wasn't able to understand much of what was being said, but it wasn't good, that was for sure! The little bit he did catch was the girl telling the boy, "You will not take the American from me; he is mine!" The boy was trying to convince her he was not going to do what she was accusing him of, but with little success.

Charlie looked at the two and said, "I mean it, don't cause any trouble! If we are going to get the gold, I will need both of you!"

"I will do as you ask, Charlie; I love you!" Mila answered.

Ramon added, "I also do not want to have trouble with the girl; I want to find my grandfather's gold!"

Charlie left for the Davao airport but he still felt uneasy. These two were important in finding the gold and he could not afford to have them fighting. The girl was his interpreter and the boy had the map and was the best bet in finding where the gold might be. All he needed when he met John Barrington was trouble with these two!

Charlie arrived in Manila about eight in the evening and checked into the Courts Inn hotel. It wasn't the Peninsula five-star hotel, but it had a clean bed and shower. He decided to go out for dinner and maybe check out the action on Burgus Street. Burgus was where most of the expatriates hung out; it was where all the action in Manila was. The street was lined with bars on both sides. The expats moved from bar to bar looking for action—this was where the young Filipino girls were hanging out.

After dinner as he strolled down Burgus street he stood and looked across at, Magumbos, The Pearl, Ivory Coast, Jewels and all the rest. Charlie smiled and thought Things never change down here! This is where he had met Mila a few years back; she was working at one of the clubs. He had had a couple of drinks with her and ended up taking her back to his hotel. At the time she seemed like a nice kid and hadn't given him any trouble. Boy did that change after a couple of months! She told him she did not have any money and needed help; she said would do anything to get out of the club. Charlie didn't see any problem with her at the time and decided to keep her around; besides, she was from Mindanao, and he had been debating for some time about moving to the island and after a couple of weeks with Mila, Charlie finally decided to head for Mindanao. He would take her along, and if things didn't work out, he could send her back to her village.

A year later, he was wondering if he had made the right decision. At first things were fine, but after a couple of months she started asking if he would marry her and take her to the United States. It was the normal way in the Philippines—lots of expats had found wives in the islands, but after a while Charlie was tired of her nagging about marriage. He was irritated by the constant questioning and finally told her, "No more! I have had enough of this bullshit I have no intentions of going back to the states, so knock it off or find someone else!" Since then she had stopped hounding him about marriage and the United States—but Charlie was sure she would not forget or give up!

The next morning Charlie got out of bed, went down to breakfast, and read the paper. He was sure the boys would sleep late, so he was in no hurry to head for the New World. He would do that after lunch. Around one o'clock, Charlie grabbed a taxi and said, "New World, young man, take me to the New World Hotel."

John recognized Charlie right away once he entered the into the main lobby but could see that he had put on some weight, quite a bit of weight. He also needed a haircut and a shave. Charlie looked as though he had slept in his clothes all night. John thought Charlie's got a few more years on him; he looks a little rough around the edges.

"Charlie," he hollered, "over here!"

Charlie turned and saw the group sitting at a table in the lobby. John was sitting next to two men, one thirty or thirty-five, clean-cut; the other was a little older, maybe forty-five or so, with an overnight beard showing. Charlie walked over to the table where John introduced everyone.

"Charlie this is Gary Enright and Jerry Kerns. Guys, Charlie Taylor."

Both men stood to shake Charlie's hand. The younger man was first. Charlie felt Gary's soft hands, which matched his demeanor, tall and clean-cut, but not much physical labor in this man's past, he thought. The other man's hand was rougher, a little more worn; however, he wasn't exactly a ditch digger either! John had not changed much other than there were a few more years on him; he still was slim with dark brown, wavy hair and a healthy look; strong features much like his old man.

Jerry looked at Charlie and said, "Man, what kind of a country do you have here? I haven't seen this many people in one place in my entire life!"

Charlie laughed and said, "Guys, in 1940 there were about twenty million people in the entire country; today there are over million and a half in metro- Manila alone! In fact, there are over two million in Davao and almost eighty million in the country, so you had better get used to it!"

The four men sat back down at the table and pondered Charlie's remarks. Finally John asked, "What are you drinking, Charlie?"

"Beer is fine, John."

Gary was nervous and said, "Let's get this thing going, guys; no sense in wasting time and money, right?"

"Okay, Gary, keep your pants on. A couple minutes won't make that much difference. What's the big hurry?" John answered.

"Yeah, I don't think taking a little time now is going to screw the deal," Jerry added. "Besides, I want to know this man a little better. He's going to make me a millionaire!"

Charlie laughed. "Well, let's talk a little before I make you a millionaire!"

"Okay, Charlie," Jerry laughed. The two men seemed to hit it off and enjoyed each other as they continued to talk; however, Gary was not as happy about Charlie as John and Jerry. He thought, this is getting worse by the minute! This guy is a mess, a dirty, filthy mess. He's a broken-down old man!

After a couple of hours listening to Charlie, John turned to his two friends and said, "Boys, what do you think?"

Gary had been waiting for his chance and said sarcastically, "I think it's time to get back on a plane and head for home! This is a harebrained idea. We are better off in Elko; at least we have a mine to work with!"

Charlie smiled, "Yeah, I guess you are right, young man; this is a risky business, to say the least. No one knows where the gold is, and a lot of people have been looking for it for a very long time!"

"Wait, wait, let's not get in a hurry; we've only been here a day," John interrupted. He continued, "I think we need to relax, get something to eat, and decide after we take an afternoon nap to get adjusted to the time change. I'm still jet-lagged; remember its one AM in the morning back home!"

Jerry leaned across the table and said, "The rest of you may need some sleep to decide, but I'm in. We will never beat the big boys back home, and I am willing to spend a little time and money on this deal."

"What, are you crazy?" Gary interrupted his face red with rage. "We talk to a man for a couple of hours, and you are convinced he is straight; but I don't believe it!" Gary folded his arms and sat back in his chair with a look of disgust.

Jerry looked at Gary and replied, "I listened to you for a year, and what did it get me; a hundred thousand in the hole!"

Gary jumped to his feet with clenched fists, and in a very tense voice said, "Remember who came to who, so don't sit there crying the blues and blame John and me!"

"Hold it, both of you!" John yelled.

People in the lounge were watching the men at the table. Some were whispering among themselves, while others around the lobby had stopped talking all together and were watching the men arguing.

John took Gary by the arm and set him down. "I said we would think on it and decide later, and that's what we are going to do!" In a low voice he said, "Look around you—you have every SOB in the place watching us!"

Charlie started asking himself if these were the right men he wanted on the deal. John was a question just because of his first encounter with him in Nevada while they were working together at the old man's mine.

Gary was bad news, not only a risk to the project, but he seemed to have something else on his mind. Charlie could tell that Gary had more to say than what had been said already; besides he had an uneasy feeling about this kid! On the other hand, Jerry seemed okay, but what did that mean? Okay is okay, but would he come through if things got tough?

After lunch John looked at everybody and said, "We are headed for Davao in the morning. While you were eating, I booked us a flight at seven. Anyone that has a problem with it, say it now. After tonight there won't be another chance."

The statement caught everyone by surprise, but no one said anything. Gary knew he was on thin ice with John. Charlie had nothing to lose. And Jerry was for the deal all along. John raised his beer and said, "Cheers!"

CHAPTER 11

Home Alone

She had been complaining ever since the engineer left! "I will kill you if you try and take my man from me! Why did you come here and ruin my life? I am going to marry Charlie and go to the United States! I will not let you stop this!" she screamed.

Ramon had heard the stories about the United States, that everyone there had money, wonderful houses, and food to eat; however, he did not want to go there. He was happy in his village; he did not need the United States. If he could find the gold, he would build his family a new house and buy some new clothes for his children—but that was all he wanted.

Right now Ramon had other concerns. When the engineer told him about the Americans coming to help find the gold, he thought, Why do we need these other men? The engineer and I can find the gold. The others are nothing but trouble. However, Ramon also knew if he had not agreed with the engineer, Charlie may not have wanted to help him. But then again, would that be such a bad thing? Maybe he would not need these Americans!

Ramon tried to stay away from the girl; each time he was near her, she started screaming at him. Should he tell the engineer when he returned? No, he decided, nothing must get in the way from finding the gold!

Mila thought Charlie was gone and was not coming back. She paced the floor for many hours worrying about him. Although Charlie had been angry with her before, now that the boy had came into their lives, Charlie had changed; he was angry with her all the time; she did not like this! I will bide my time, she thought and when the time is right, I will convince Charlie to get rid of this boy. Be patient, she told herself, but she knew this would not be easy to do.

Just then the phone rang. The girl picked it up.

"Hello, baby, how are you two doing?"

"Okay, Charlie; when are you coming home? I miss you very much!"

He answered, "Tomorrow. I need you to meet us at the airport about nine in the morning. There is some money to rent a car in my packsack. Take only what you will need, okay? Now let me talk to the kid."

She thought for a minute. Would the boy tell Charlie bad things about her? She hesitated for a minute and then said, "He is not here, Charlie; he has gone to find something to eat."

"Well, he had better be there in the morning or you will be in big trouble! Do you understand what I am saying?"

This scared the girl. "Wait. Charlie; he just came into the apartment," she lied.

Mila set the phone down and walked outside where the boy was sitting on the steps and said, "Charlie wants to talk to you, but if you say any bad things about me I will have my friends get rid of you before he comes back from Manila, do you understand?"

Ramon looked at her and said, "I do not have anything bad to say about you; why do you say this?" Ramon had decided not to cause trouble with this girl and he meant it.

"Okay then, you can speak to him on the phone."

Ramon's eyes widened. "Speak to him on the phone?" he asked in surprise.

"Yes, he is waiting for you on the phone inside the apartment."

Ramon got to his feet very slowly. He had never talked on a phone!

"Will you help me? I do not know about this phone."

She laughed with a cruel smile crossing her face. "You peasants know nothing, you are stupid!" She led Ramon into the apartment and handed him the phone.

Ramon took the phone from her; she showed him how to hold it next to his ear. "Mr. Engineer, this is Ramon," he said tentatively into the phone.

Immediately a loud voice exploded into his ear, "Hi, kid, how's it going down there?"

Ramon almost dropped the phone onto the floor. Again he spoke into the phone, "When will you come back, Engineer? I do not like it here, and I want to go back to my village." The girl glared at Ramon and he got her message.

As if Charlie were right in the room, he said to Ramon, "Is the girl giving you a hard time, kid?"

"No, everything is good, but I want to go home to my village," Ramon responded.

"Be patient, I'll be there in the morning. Now hand the phone back to Mila."

Mila took the phone from Ramon. Charlie spoke with a stern voice, "I mean what I said. Don't cause any trouble with the kid, and be sure both of you are at the airport by nine AM."

Mila answered, "I will be there with the boy, Charlie. I love you." She waited for Charlie to answer her, but he had already hung up the phone. The girl returned to the chair she had been sitting in. She thought back to when she had met him in Manila. Mila had come from a poor village in Mindanao and from a family of ten children. Her father was a farmer, and the family was always struggling to survive, not enough food or cloths for the family it had been a day to day existence. However this was normal most of the provinces were low income most families lived off the land eking out an existence using carabao and manual labor to harvest their crops. Money was not a priority. From the time she could remember she wanted out, Mila had seen the wonderful things on the barangay local television and she wanted them!

She thought of the many young girls from her village that had left home, traveling to Manila, where everyone said there was lots of money and nice clothes. Three of her friends had returned from Manila, and yes, they had new clothes. Many told her of the wonderful things they had found in the city. Later, when one of the girls was preparing to return to Manila, Mila asked her to let her go back to the city. At first the girl had said, "No, it is not what you think, Mila; there are bad things in the city!"

"Bad things?" asked Mila. "How can you say that; look at your wonderful clothes and the money that you have!"

The other girl became very angry and said, "You do not know what I had to do to get these things, so do not talk about this again, do you understand?"

Mila would not let the girl alone and continued to badger her. Finally the girl agreed and said, "Do not blame me for what will happen to you, you will see!"

Mila left her village, with the intention to never return. That had been three years ago. At first, Manila was wonderful—the lights and excitement of the bars made it like living in a new world. The food was good, and the people treated her very well, especially the bar owner. He made sure she had a place to stay and plenty of nice clothes. He told her she was pretty and that he liked her very much. Two months later, however, things began to change. He told her to be extra nice to the men who were spending money at the bar and to make sure she convinced them to keep coming back to see her. She did not understand what he wanted until one of the men told her he wanted her to come back to his hotel room. She tried to explain to him that she was not to leave the bar, but he grabbed her by the arm and insisted she leave. She pulled away from the man and went to the bar owner. She told him she did not want to go with the drunken man and expected the owner to help her, but instead he struck her across the face and screamed, "You had better start earning your living, baby, or I will take it out of your hide! Where the hell do you think you are? This is Manila and this is Burgus Street!"

Mila was terrified. The bar owner continued, "Now get your pretty little ass out there and earn your keep." From then on, things changed. She was forced to dance on the stage with little or nothing on. The men grabbed at her body and stroked her breast! She was treated like a prostitute.

One night, the girl who had brought her to the city said, "We are all the same, Mila. We are nothing but meat to these bar owners; we have no dignity. I tried to tell you, but just like me, you insisted on coming to this place."

Mila took her friends hand, squeezed it, and said, "I know now what you were trying to tell me, but I do not blame you. But I will not stay here any longer. I am going home.

The girl's face changed; she looked frightened. "No, Mila never say that out loud! If they hear you, they will beat you! Sometimes the girls who try to leave disappear; please, Mila don't talk like that!"

Things became worse for Mila. Every night she was forced to go with the men and do as they asked. Some of the men were good to her but most were drunk and made her do terrible things with them in their hotel rooms. Again she talked with the girl who had brought her to Manila and said, "This is not what I wanted! Why do they make me do these terrible things?"

"I tried to tell you in the village, but you would not listen. Now you must do as they ask you, or like I said, bad things will happen to you and then they come after me!"

Six months later, Mila met Charlie. She knew that she must find a way out of this terrible life, and this man seemed to like her better than most. She gave Charlie what he wanted; she had learned her trade very well in six months! One night while they were together, he mentioned that he was going to Davao. She told him that she was from Mindanao and wanted to go with him. She was desperate and begged Charlie to take her. She told him he would not regret it, and that she would help him find a place to live in Davao. She thought if she spent enough time with Charlie, he would marry her and take her to the United States. What she did not know was that Charlie had no intention to return to the United States in the near future, much less take her with him if he did go home.

After Charlie had hung up the phone, Mila went into Davao and rented a van to pick up Charlie at the airport. She did not want to be late!

CHAPTER 12

Davao

"What a nightmare!" Gary exclaimed as they came down the stairs into the parking lot at the Davao airport. People were pushing and arguing, trying to locate their cars or find a taxi. This was even worse than the Manila airport; there was absolutely no control over the mass of people!

"Stop pulling on my luggage!" exclaimed Jerry. "We already have a driver!" The taxi driver immediately turned loose of Jerry's luggage and grabbed John's.

John pulled at his bags and said, "I'm with him!"

Charlie seemed to take it all in stride and was not paying any attention to the chaos going on around them; He continued pushing through the crowd looking for the girl. The other three men realized that they were better off following Charlie and soon were in line with the big man as he made a path through the mass of people.

The girl came from nowhere and threw her arms around Charlie. "Where is the van?" he asked her.

"Over here, Charlie," she said, leading them to the van in the parking lot. The boy was sitting in the back seat.

"Hi, kid, how's it going?" Charlie asked Ramon.

"I am okay, Engineer," Ramon replied.

After loading the luggage, everyone climbed into the van. Charlie instructed the driver to go to the Davao Hotel. It had been agreed that Charlie's apartment was not big enough for everyone; they decided to stay at the hotel until they left for the province the next day.

Gary looked at the girl; he could not believe his eyes! She's a beauty, he thought. How can this old, fat, dirty bastard have a woman like this? He could not take his eyes off her during the trip to the hotel. She was aware of his stare but was used to it from working in the bars in Manila. At first she ignored him and held onto Charlie's arm in desperation.

Charlie did not pay much attention to either her or Gary; he was pointing out the sights to John and Jerry as they traveled through the city. The streets were full of shanty houses stacked next to each other up against the roadway there was just enough room for the cars to travel one mistake and they would end up in some ones house! Jerry was amazed—you could stick your hand out the window and touch the houses! The driver seemed to ignore the centerline; the traffic was four wide in a two-lane street! The Americans were waiting for the cars to hit head on at any time, but drivers paid no attention to the traffic, traffic rules, or, for that matter, the stoplights! People were running back and forth across the street between the cars; dogs were everywhere; it was a miracle that no one had been run over!

Again Charlie seemed unaware of the chaos, even as John was waiting for a terrible accident to happen. He asked nervously, "How much money will we need, Charlie, to get going on this deal?"

"Well, I figure we will need about ten thousand to get what we need for now. That takes into account the rigs, food, general supplies, and a few dollars to take care of the officials if need be, John."

Just at that moment all the cars came to an abrupt stop. Horns began to blow and drivers started yelling out of the windows.

"What the hell is going on, Charlie?" Jerry asked.

Charlie seemed confused at the question at first and said, "What do you mean, Jerry?"

Jerry continued, "The traffic is stopped and everyone is yelling; that's what I mean!"

Charlie looked at the others and said with a laugh, "You'll get used to it. This is a normal day in Davao; there aren't enough roads for all the traffic, so these jams happen all the time. We'll start moving in a few minutes."

The few minutes ended up being thirty before the traffic began to move. During the remainder of the drive to the hotel, Jerry remained quiet. He was in deep thought about the project. *This is for me; this is what I have been waiting for all my life. God, this is great!*

Gary, on the other hand, could not get used to the poverty all around him, the dirty shacks lining the streets, the smell of rotten food, and the heat, the appalling heat of Southeast Asia! The only thing he was remotely interested in was the girl. *She could win a beauty contest back home! My God, what a woman*—and she seemed to be in love with this lush! However, as more time passed even Mila's beauty was no longer a distraction; Gary was over the top with disgust!

After arriving at the hotel and checking in, John told Jerry to work with Charlie to get everything ready for the trip the next day. Gary and he would start talking with the boy and Mila to get more information about the gold.

It didn't take Charlie and Jerry long to locate the vehicles and equipment for the project. Davao was surprisingly well equipped with everything they would need. Charlie was very familiar with the city and knew where to look for everything needed for the trip. He led Jerry to the Hong Kong bank branch in Davao where Jerry checked on the bank account; to his relief, everything was in place! Since they had finished early, Charlie suggested that they have a beer and relax for a while.

"We can go to my old hang-out, Jerry, you'll like it."

"Okay by me, Charlie. I am getting to like this place. I'm ready for a cold one, if you know what I mean."

"Yeah, a person can get to like it here after a while. It doesn't cost much and the life is easy going," Charlie answered.

After arriving at the bar, Charlie looked at Jerry and said, "I'm going to be straight with you, Jerry, simply because time is running out."

Jerry answered, "I like that, Charlie. I feel the same way, so let's get things out front now. After tomorrow we won't have much of a chance."

Charlie began, "John is a good man but lacks experience. I worked with him and his old man, I guess you know that."

"Yes, I do, Charlie, and you are right. John is a little green behind the ears, but he has a good heart. Gary is my concern, my friend, it isn't John!"

Charlie sighed in relief and looked at Jerry. "Well, I'm glad you said that. I was wondering what you thought about the guy."

"You know, Charlie, he doesn't want to be here. He thinks the whole deal is a waste of time."

"I can tell you this, Jerry—we need people we can trust or we may find ourselves in deep shit!"

"Tell me about it! I have had trouble with this kid ever since I got into business with him. I think he screwed John a couple of months ago in Nevada, but I can't put my finger on it."

"It looks like John trusts him, Jerry; is that true?"

"Yes, it is, but I think even John is getting a little tired of his complaining!"

"One thing is for sure—we need to watch him close!" Charlie replied.

The two men raised their beer glasses, touched them together, and each took a long drink. It had been quite a day!

John and Gary sat down with Ramon and the girl. They had decided to have her there for an interpreter in case it was needed.

"Do you have the map, young man?" John asked.

"Yes, Mr. John, here it is."

The map was like Charlie had said: crude. It didn't give much information other than some general outlines, a mountain range, a stream, and some cave locations. John and Gary looked at the map in silence for a few minutes. John thought it seemed authentic, despite its crude and faded appearance.

"Do you know where this area is located, young man?" John asked.

"I do not know all of this map, Mr. John, I—"

Gary interrupted, "Well, that's great! We have an old map with some chicken scratches and a few landmarks on it, and he doesn't know where it is!"

The boy was intimidated. He lowered his head and thought I do not like this man!

Mila saw her chance. She turned to John and Gary with a look of anger and said, "I have told Charlie many times that he cannot trust this boy; he does not know anything! He is from a poor village and has no idea where the gold is hidden."

John raised his hands over his head and said, "Let's settle down for a minute we don't want to jump to any premature conclusions until we've heard everything. Let's give the boy a chance. Go ahead, son."

Ramon regained his composure and continued. "I do not understand the entire map, but I talked with my grandfather for many hours before his death and he told me where the gold is hidden. He gave me the map the day of his death and told me it would lead me to the gold."

"This map is of your village?" Gary asked.

"I do not know for sure. Like I have said, I cannot read the map and do not understand it," Ramon replied.

Gary shook his head in disgust and turned to John. "John, I know you want this to go, but for God's sake, let's call it a day and go back home! We can still make the deal in Elko!"

John stood up from the table and motioned Gary to follow him. He motioned to the café waitress and said, "Bring the two young people something to drink." He turned around to Mila and Ramon and said, "You two stay here. We will be right back."

John directed Gary outside the café to a bench on the street. "Sit down, Gary; I want to say something."

Gary sat down and waited for John to speak.

"Gary, I want you to get a ticket back to the U.S. and—"

Gary interrupted, "Now you're talking! I wondered when you would regain your senses! Enough of this garbage; I'll call the boys back home and set up a meeting and—"

John raised his hand and said, "Hold it-hold it!" He stared at Gary and continued, "Don't jump the gun, Gary. I said you get a ticket back to the states! I have listened to you for a week about this plan. I understand you don't want any part of it, so let's take care of it right now. Jerry saw it coming, and I guess so have I, but I ignored it because we've been together for a while—but it is over, Gary, so let's let it go at that."

"Wait a minute, John! My concern has always been in the best interest for both of us. We are a team. I have always been up front with you. I told you when Jerry entered the picture we might have a problem, but you insisted that he come in with us so I let it go, didn't I?"

"Gary—"

Gary's voice started to rise, "No, no, let me finish, John. I have stood behind you all the way in the past, and if this is what you want, let's forget this conversation and move on. I have said the last word about the downside. I am with you one hundred percent!"

John stood looking at Gary for what seemed to Gary like an eternity. Finally John said, "I mean this, Gary, so listen to me very carefully. The next time you start kicking this project around, I will run you off in a heartbeat. You have been a good friend and partner for some time now, and I want it to continue, but you know I mean what I say!"

"Enough," Gary said. "Let's get back to the kid and the map." Gary was ready to explode inside; he knew John had the upper hand. The company was broke and John had to approve all business agreements since he was the president of the company. Yes, Gary thought, he's got me over a barrel and he knows it! But what goes around comes around, and I will never forget this!

CHAPTER 13

Let's Take a Ride!

At six the next morning, Charlie showed up at the hotel with the girl, Ramon, and two vehicles. It had been decided to drive to Ramon's village and begin the search there since that is where Ramon's grandfather had given him the map. They would be able to compare the map with the area and determine if the gold was located near Ramon's village, or at least try to verify the map locations.

On the way to Ramon's village, the caravan passed through several small agricultural and fishing villages. As they traveled north from Davao, the poverty became more evident, the roads began deteriorated, and driving more difficult. The girl and Ramon seemed not to notice the changes; however, even Charlie was uncomfortable with the surroundings as the two vehicles sped along the highway.

After about two hours on the main road the lead van, with Charlie on board, signaled a right turn and swerved off the highway onto a single-lane road. For the first couple of miles the road was built of concrete, which was similar to the main highway; however, an abrupt end to the concrete surprised John, Jerry, and Gary. The van lurched out over the concrete and hit the dirt road with a bounce. Everyone's head hit the roof, causing an outburst of complaints! Once the driver straightened up, he continued down the dirt road without any concern of the protests coming from his passengers.

The two vans bounced violently down the road after leaving the smooth concrete. Dust filled the vans, causing the occupants to roll up the windows and turn on the air conditioners. The second van had to drop back due to the heavy dust; it was impossible for the driver to see the road. However, they continued to drive at a frantic pace and hardly noticed the change in road conditions. The farther they traveled along the road, the more the road went too hell, but again, the drivers seemed not to notice and continued on at a frantic rate of speed! Every once in a while a chicken, dog or some other varmint would race across the road in front of the roaring vans which usually prompted a long irritating blast from the horns.

Rice fields stretched along both sides of the road. Caribou pulled the ancient plows through the fields under the hot sun. Women were seen irrigating the rice fields as the men followed, tilling the soil. The farmers seemed oblivious to the small caravan as it drove by rice farms which had been cultivated the same way in the Philippines for hundreds of years. The only new technology incorporated in the last fifty years was the foreign companies' plantations. Large banana, coconut, and pineapple plantations had sprung up throughout the islands since 1949 after the end of the war. The import companies used modern equipment: tractors, balers, and separators. The rice farmers, however, as their ancestors had done before them, and before them continued to till their fields using the beast of burden.

"How much farther, kid? We're running out of road!" Charlie exclaimed. The road was now just wide enough for one way traffic the tires were running on the edge of the road which ran down to a river 50 feet below.

Ramon answered, "We are very close, Engineer. Do you see the mountain ahead of us with the corn planted on the hillside?"

"You mean the one on the right side?" Charlie motioned with his right hand. He was looking in amazement at the mountain. The terrain was very steep, yet there were massive stocks of corn planted across the mountain face! Charlie thought, How in the hell can these people farm on the side of a mountain? Then it hit him, and he shouted, "I remember this place!"

Ramon looked at Charlie with surprise; the comment had caught him off guard.

Charlie thought, Yes, I there's an old mine up ahead. He remembered that Chaparral had been interested in the old mine and directed Charlie to take a quick look at the place. Charlie had spent a couple days at the mine, but it didn't take long to figure out that it wasn't worth much. When he returned to Davao he sent a report back to Chaparral on his findings in the area but never mentioned Ramon's village and the mine; they just weren't worth the time as far as Charlie was concerned.

As the two vans approached the village, Charlie remembered commenting about the houses during the first visit and that they were built on stilts to compensate for the steep terrain. The rest of the crew were more interested in getting the hell out of the rigs, enough was enough!

"Yes, my village is below the mountain," Ramon commented.

In the second van, John took a long look at the surroundings and said, "I don't know about you two, but why would the Japanese hide the gold up here in this godforsaken place?"

"Beats me, John; we'll just have to wait and see," replied Jerry. Gary seen his chance to get back into John's graces and said, "maybe not John they might have figured the further away from civilization the better, what do ya think?" He waited. John just nodded a bit and let it go at that. Gary was disappointed with the John's reaction; this is going to take some time to get back on John's good side.

The road was now just a path leading into the village, just wide enough for the tires of the two vans; however, the drivers continued driving as though there had been no change. The occupants' heads bounced as the vans ran over ruts and boulders in the roadway. Everyone was holding on for dear life!

What came next was a complete surprise to everyone except Charlie and the Filipinos. As they turned the last corner into the village, the caravan encountered a fully established mining site!

"Well, would you look at this!" exclaimed Jerry.

The mine site set just below the base of the mountain, with modern milling and mining facilities, including a major power plant. The jungle had grown up around the plant, but anyone could see that at one time it had been a major mining operation. Several company buildings surrounded the main mine site, and a dozen bunkhouses for the employees were built along the road to the mine. From what the group could see from the van, it was apparent that at one time this was a major operation.

A guard wearing a worn-out uniform stood in front of a dilapidated gate. As the vans approached the gate, he put up his hand and signaled them to stop. He approached the first van and leaned inside the window, speaking in Filipino to the driver. The driver turned to the girl and spoke to her. A long conversation with Mila and the two men ensued, back and forth, on and on.

After ten minutes that seemed like ten hours Charlie said, "Mila, for Christ's sake, what the hell is happening!"

She turned to Charlie and said, "He wants to know what we want, and who told us we could come here."

Charlie acknowledged with a shake of his head and got out of the van. He gave a friendly wave to the security guard and walked back to the second vehicle. John rolled down the window and said, "What's up, Charlie?"

"I'm not sure, John; the kid didn't tell me about this. I guess I am going to have to do some fancy talking to get us through here."

Charlie asked Jerry, "Can you give me a couple hundred pesos? I might need it."

Jerry handed Charlie five hundred pesos, and Charlie returned to the first van, the security guard following close behind. Charlie looked at Mila and said, "Ask him who owns the mine, Mila."

She talked to the guard for several minutes. Charlie could never get used to the way the Filipinos communicated. Simple questions or conversations usually lasted for several minutes or even hours; in the states the same conversation would be over in five minutes. Obviously, the culture was different here. Filipinos believed in a full explanation right down to the last detail—which could, in some cases, take half a day to get one simple questioned answered!

"Mila!" Charlie said in frustration. "What is he saying now?"

"He is telling me that the company officers are in Manila and no one is allowed to pass without a letter from the manager who is also in Manila."

"Tell him we want to use his telephone to call Manila, and we will pay for the call."

She looked at Charlie with a confused expression. "Charlie, there is no phone at this place!" she said.

"Then ask him if there is someone we can talk to here at the mine," Charlie responded.

She started to say something to the guard when Ramon interrupted. "Engineer, this is my cousin, and I am sure he will let us in if you let me talk to him."

Charlie turned around and to Ramon. "Okay, kid; it's up to you to get us in."

Ramon climbed out of the vehicle. The minute the guard recognized Ramon, he smiled widely, showing his mouth with several missing teeth. He immediately began speaking to Ramon in Filipino, and finally he pointed to the mine office. Ramon shook the guard's hand and got back into the van.

"We can go now," he said.

Charlie grinned and said, "That's the fastest conversation I have seen since I came to this country!"

Ramon smiled and sat down in the seat. The driver drove the van forward; Ramon spoke to him in Filipino, pointing toward the mine office.

"What's going on?" Charlie asked.

"We will go to the mine office and talk to my uncle, Engineer," Ramon replied.

Charlie laughed. The drivers pulled the two vans into the parking lot in front of the main office. Everyone climbed from the vans; after four hours of steady driving, they were stiff, and ready for a break

"I can't feel my legs. God, what a trip!" Gary exclaimed.

Charlie turned to the group and said, "The kid says we have to talk to his uncle about what we are doing here, guys."

Jerry was not listening; he was looking around in amazement. Here was a major mine operation cut out in the middle of nowhere, completely surrounded by jungle. Unbelievable! He thought.

The four men proceeded to the office with Ramon in the lead. It was obvious that he knew where he was going; they would have to depend on him to get them past this obstacle. John was thinking I hope to hell I haven't made a mistake; this is definitely not what I was expecting. Maybe Gary was right—maybe we were a little quick in getting ourselves into this deal. John knew he needed to keep his opinion to himself until he had a chance to look things over a bit more; no sense in giving Gary ammunition to start complaining again!

Charlie nudged John and said, "I recognize the place, John; I was here about six months ago."

John looked at Charlie and said, "What the hell is the deal, Charlie? What kind of place are we looking at?"

Charlie answered, "The place was mined out thirty years ago. Other than that, I don't know much about it; I was only here a couple of days I guess the Japanese mined during the war and the Americans afterwords. He continued, never really made much always shutin down."

As they entered the office Ramon said, "Hello, Uncle." An older Filipino, sitting behind a worn out desk, looked up at the group entering the office. He was a short, heavy set, partially bald man, with a cigar hanging from his lip. He looked over the group and leaned back into his chair. After a couple of minutes, he spoke in Filipino to Ramon then turned his chair toward the other men standing in his office. In excellent English he said, "My little Ramon tells me you are here to find the gold."

The men were taken by surprise, not only because of the man's excellent English, but also because of what Ramon had told him. The man could see the surprise on their faces and understood.

"Don't worry, gentlemen—we are used to Ramon and his foolishness. He has been looking for this gold ever since his grandfather told him about it last year. We are well aware of his escapades. The man laughed out loud. "I am afraid you have been, as you say in English, taken for a ride; a long, long ride! However, since you are already here, and it is four hours back to Davao, we welcome you to stay. I am sure you will enjoy our village hospitality. We have not seen strangers for some time and the change will be good for us."

Finally, John regained his composure and spoke. "I guess there is no sense in trying to hide anything. Do you have any objections if we take a look around?"

"Of course not; in fact, I would like to show you the mine, if you have the time. We have been looking for someone to invest; maybe it would be more advantageous to you than searching for the foolish hidden gold. Are you gentlemen in the mining business, by any chance?"

Gary answered, "Yes, we are, sir. What type of mine is this?"

"Gold, my friend, gold! The mine has been operated since the Japanese were here in '39. Lots of gold has been mined from here, gentlemen, and there is plenty still in the mountain!"

"When was the last time the mine was in operation?" Jerry asked.

"Nineteen-ninety," the man answered.

"That can't be!" Gary blurted out. "It looks like the mine hasn't operated for thirty years!"

"The jungle, my dear sir, it is unforgiving," Ramon's uncle continued. "Yes, it is too bad what the jungle does to the mine. It eats away at the buildings and equipment very fast." He raised his hand and said, "Enough of this. You must be tired, so let us find something for you to eat and a place for you to stay."

With that, the old man stood up from behind his desk and led the men toward the door. He escorted them to a small building near the main office that had been used in the past as a barracks for the miners. "Will this do?" he asked.

"This will be fine. We appreciate your hospitality," John answered.

"All right then. I must attend to other business. If you need anything else, tell Ramon he knows where to find me." The heavy set man gave them a wave and left the building.

John turned to the group and asked Charlie and Jerry to have Ramon lead them to the mine site, unload one of the vans, and set up a work camp. He also suggested to the group that Gary and he make a visit to Ramon's village and introduce themselves to the village people. The village was located next to the mine, which was convenient for the miners to travel to work each day.

It was obvious that an international company had set up the operation. The mill was a quarter of a mile from the mine entrance. The portal to the mine was one hundred feet above the mill, which was designed to allow the mine ore to be dumped directly into the mill rock-crushing circuit.

After they had settled in and Charlie and Jerry began to unload the vans, they sat down to relax for a minute. The old man was right; it was a tough trip from Davao to the mine site. Ramon looked at John and asked, "Would you like to see my home, Mr. John?"

John smiled and said, "Of course, Ramon, lead the way."

As Ramon and John started walking away from the camp, Gary yelled, "Wait, John, I will go with you." Ramon did not like this. He did not like this Gary, but said nothing and led John and Gary to his house.

The house was a dilapidated two-room concrete building next to an old tailings pond. The pond had been used to pump wastewater and material away from the mill when the mine was in operation. Again Gary was visibly shaken by the obvious poverty in the village. A common garbage dump was within one hundred feet of the houses; there was no visible plumbing to speak of, except a small one-inch plastic pipe running from the mountain into the village, which he assumed was the fresh water source. An old woman sat in a chair in front of the house, chewing what appeared to be tobacco. Ramon spoke to the old women in his native tongue then turned to John and Gary and said," This is my grandmother, but she is not well and does not think clearly. I told her you would be here for a while, but I am sure she does not understand or care."

John smiled at the old woman and said, "Ramon, you have never mentioned your father or mother, why?"

"The mine took my father many years ago and my mother died of a strange sickness when I was just a boy; that is why I am the only child in the family."

John decided to change the subject, "Ramon, why do you think the gold is buried near here?" he asked.

Ramon looked at the men and said, "As my grandfather was dying, he asked me to take him to this window." He pointed toward a window inside the house. When we were standing at the window my grandfather said to me, 'Ramon, I have not told you where the gold is hidden because I believe it is evil and will bring trouble to our family and the village. But now I am dying, and I am going to give you the secret. After I tell you where the gold is, you must then make your own decision; but before you choose to dig for the gold you must understand what it will bring. There are people who will kill for the yellow metal. It will cause greed and bring treachery to you and others; therefore, you must understand the danger. I have learned over the last seventy years that wealth does not always give you what you want. But I am an old man and will die soon, so now you will have to decide what to do with the gold." Then he asked me to hand him an old box, hidden under his bed. I handed the box to my grandfather. He opened it and took out a yellow piece of paper and said, 'This is the map, my grandson; no one has ever seen this. When the Japanese soldier let me go, I returned to the village and many years later I drew the map on this very piece of paper."

Ramon told John that the old man then asked Ramon to help him closer to the window. He pointed toward the mountain and said, "The gold is there," and collapsed into my arms.

John looked out the window. "Are you sure this is where he pointed, Ramon?"

"Yes, Mr. John. My grandfather stood at the window and pointed toward the mountain. The map was in his hand when he fell to the floor. My grandfather said, "Ramon, I am very old and could not remember everything, but the map will help lead you to the gold.'"

"Why do you say that, Ramon?" John asked.

"Mr. John," Ramon began, "the map does not show the same as my grandfather told me, and it does not look like the mountain on the map and the one he pointed to."

"I have the map, Ramon. Let's take another look," John responded. John laid out the map on the old handmade table. He walked over to the window and looked at the massive mountain in front of him then returned to the table. "You're right, Ramon, it doesn't look much like the map, does it? Could your grandfather be talking about something else? Are you sure he was looking out this window?"

"Yes, he pointed to the mountain, Mr. John."

John looked at the mountain again and said, "Well, Ramon, let's go see what you have been up to and let's find your grandfather's gold!"

The three men said goodbye to Ramon's grandmother and headed for the dig site.

After arriving at the site, John was amazed at the amount of excavation Ramon had done. Several old tunnels had been exposed along the base of the mountain.

"Ramon, what are these tunnels you have opened up?" John asked.

"My grandfather told me that the Japanese had hidden the gold inside the mountain and that they had used mining tunnels for the hiding place."

John thought That makes sense; the Japanese would probably do that instead of making a new tunnel besides time had to be a factor. "How many old tunnels are there?" he asked.

"There are many, many, Mr. John; the miners have mined gold from this mountain for over one hundred years!"

"But which ones did the Japanese hide the gold in, Ramon; that is the question," Gary added.

As John looked over the dig site he imagined hundreds of old tunnels along the mountain base. What now? He thought.

After returning from the dig site, John asked everyone to sit down outside the barracks. He began, "Well, boys, we have a problem. The gold is buried in a tunnel, but we don't know which one. I would guess there are over one hundred old mine workings along the base of the mountain, but which one is the gold hidden in? Ramon has dug out about four tunnels near the place his grandfather pointed at, but guys; we don't have the time to continue this type of work. We could be here another one hundred years before we find the right tunnel!"

The group was silent for some time until Jerry spoke up. "Let me get this straight, John. We have no idea where the gold is buried, and there are hundreds of possibilities?"

"Yes, that's about it." John replied.

"That's just great," replied Gary, "we have to uncover every tunnel in the mountain. If we are lucky, it could be the first one, or if we are unlucky, it could be the last one, right?"

"Since we are into this, let me point out a couple of things," Jerry interjected. "One, why would the Japanese hide the gold in an area where everyone in the village plus the miners would know where it was? Second, why would they bring it all the way up here? We've made the trip; it doesn't make sense to me to haul the gold into this remote site. And finally, if they planned to move it before the end of the war, this is the worse place in the Philippines to move it to." He leaned forward and looked straight into the eyes of the men sitting in the circle. "We had better find the answers to these questions soon, or we will find ourselves broke and out of business!"

Charlie hadn't said a word during the meeting until now. "Boys, I think we are getting a little ahead of ourselves. First, we haven't done any digging; second, we haven't sat down together and really looked everything over. I believe there are people in this room who have no interest in seeing this thing be successful! Also, remember the mine was a gold mine, right? So it does make sense that they would hide it here! So before we jump into our vans and drive off, I think we need to do a little more research and decide what the best thing to do is."

"Okay, Charlie," John said, "let's break up into two groups. Charlie, you and Gary look into the mining operations, engineering, and geology. The mine engineering office should have some information about this area. Try to find out what tunnels were driven after the Japanese left—maybe we can eliminate some of them, Also see if you can find out which ones were still in operations just before or during the Japanese occupation. In the meantime, Jerry and I will hire additional miners to open some of the other tunnels that are in the area where the old man indicated. Any questions?"

The men stood up, but everyone still had the look of frustration and dejection on their faces. Gary and Charlie returned to the mine engineering office and began reviewing the maps and mining activities from 1940 to 1945. The information revealed that the mine was in full operation during the war and produced significant amounts of gold; however, the areas where the old man had apparently pointed to were not mined until after the war, except for a couple of exploration tunnels driven by small-scale miners. The tunnels driven by the small-scale miners were not located in the exact area where the old man had indicated. Although this helped in limiting the search area, it was also disturbing that the locations did not match.

The next two weeks were disappointing, to say the least. Charlie was heading up the projects to open the tunnels and had hired several miners from the village to help. John and Jerry had returned to Davao and withdrew money to finance the project and purchase additional supplies, while Gary continued to review old mining data. None of the projects were going well.

Jerry approached John one evening and said, "John, have you noticed Gary?"

"What do you mean?"

"He seems to have given up. He looks terrible; he doesn't change his clothes, and I don't think he has taken a bath for a week!"

"Yes, I have noticed he has gained weight and hasn't been shaving; he's looking worse than Charlie, if that's possible!" John replied.

It was true Gary was in a deep depression and had no interest in anything associated with the project. Yes, he continued to research the mine documents, however, his heart was not in it. He began to drink with the villagers during the day and long into the night. The villagers didn't mind since they had little money, and the American was doing all the buying!

John said to Jerry, "I will have a talk with him, Jerry. Maybe he needs a break from here; what do you think?"

"Good idea, John. Let's send him out for a couple of days, maybe back to Davao."

Later in the day, John approached Gary while he was relaxing in the barracks.

"What's the good word?" John asked.

"What's the good word? Gary replied. We are going on our third week in this godforsaken hole, and we are no closer to the gold than the first day we got here, so I guess there isn't a good word!" Gary grabbed a bottle of beer from the cooler and asked John, "Do you want one?"

"Hitting it a little hard, aren't you, Gary? It seems like that's all you have been doing the last couple of days. Is there a problem?"

"John, I promised I would go along with this deal and not complain, so let's leave it at that, okay?"

John took a hard look at Gary and said, "Tell you what, Gary—why don't you take a little break and get out of here for a couple of days?"

"What makes you say that, John—you have a problem with me?"

"No, I just thought you would like to get out of here and see some other part of the country, that's all. We've been on the run since we got here; in fact, I think we all need a break. After you get back, someone else will go for a couple of days. How does that sound?"

"And where do you suggest I go, John, in this dreadful county?"

"I don't know, Gary. Ask Mila; maybe she can help you find someplace. Remember, she is from Mindanao. She will know where there are some resorts along the coast or a nice hotel in Davao, but I am sure you will come up with something. You never know, you may find something you like."

"All right, John, enough said. I agree I need a little vacation. I'll talk to the drivers and Mila and find some quiet place to go."

At dinner that night John casually mentioned that everyone needed a little time off, and Gary was going to be the first one out. The rest of the group agreed but were suspicious about what was going on—but agreed all of them needed a break away from the site!

"Mila," John began, "do you know where Gary can go to get some peace and quiet away from here?"

Mila had listened to the conversation during dinner and wondered what was really going on; why did everyone want Mr. Gary to leave? She had grown tired of staying at the mine site and was ready for a change. She also was upset that Charlie was spending most of his time at the dig site and not with her. She had noticed a change in Gary and had seen him looking at her at the camp as well as when she was interpreting when he talked to the engineers and manager. She was sure he was interested in her, and she had decided to get closer to him, not only to see if Charlie would notice but also to insure her position with the Americans. She also understood that she must be very careful and not create a problem between the two men, but Mila was sure Charlie would not care anyway! He had left her alone as if he didn't care what she did as long as she stayed out of his way and this angered her! So when Mr. John asked her if there was somewhere they could go, she was more than willing to suggest a place.

"I will take Mr. Gary north to Butuan and Surigao," she continued. "The cities are near the ocean and very nice; there are many hotels and resorts that I am sure he will enjoy."

"Okay, then it is settled," John responded. "Let the driver know, and you can leave in the morning."

The next day Gary, the driver, and Mila left for Butuan. After turning north onto the main highway, Gary became more somber. He was not interested in the trip and was depressed that he was going, but as expected Mila continued to talk excitedly as they drove.

"I am so excited, Mr. Gary! I have friends in Surigao; I cannot wait to see them! You will like the places we are going!"

On and on she talked, hour after hour, but Gary was not listening. He wanted to go back to the U.S. He had had enough of this bullshit, but how was he going to convince John? He had to come up with a plan—he had to get the hell out of here! The driver began talking to the girl, but Gary wasn't listening he was thinking of other things.

"Mr. Gary, Mr. Gary," she poked Gary's shoulder, "the driver says he must eat something and go to the comfort room."

"What?" Gary said. He was daydreaming again and not listening.

The girl repeated, "The driver wants to eat something and go to the comfort room."

Gary looked around and asked, "Where are we?"

"We are about fifty kilometers from Butuan. There is a small fishing village near here where we can eat," she replied.

"Okay, I'm a little hungry too." Gary decided to pay more attention to where they were and began looking at the landscape as they drove along. The girl continued to talk a hundred miles an hour, but by now Gary managed to ignore most of her comments.

As the neared the fishing village, Gary felt he recognized the area, but that was impossible; they had not been here before, and the road from Davao was in the opposite direction. He thought why do I feel that I have been here before? This place looks familiar, but I can't put my finger on it.

As the driver turned off the main road and drove around a sharp corner, Gary was able to see a small oceanfront fishing village. He had not been able to see the fishing village from the main road because the hillside had obscured it from view. The driver drove the van up next to a small restaurant and shut off the engine.

"What do you want to eat, Mr. Gary?" the girl asked.

"Do they have a bottle of pop and some potato chips?" he answered.

She looked at him dejectedly. "You must eat more than a soft drink and potato chips!"

The driver continued into the restaurant and began looking for the comfort room. Gary could not get rid of the feeling that he recognized the area along the main road; the place looked very familiar, but why?

The girl and the driver selected some food from the buffet, while Gary drank his Coke and finished his potato chips. The Filipino food was not to his liking. Fish, pork and some vegetables but not much in western food, besides he questioned the kitchen sanitation and the freshness of the food. The woman behind the counter was using a cloth to keep the flies off the food.

While he sat next to the window sipping his coke and looking out at the mountain, it hit him.

My God, he thought, this is the map, for Christ's sake! There it was right in front of him like a vision, the twin mountains, just like on the map—and the road along the highway almost exactly matched the map! Everything started to make sense to him; the old man was not pointing to the mountain at the mine site, he was pointing north! The fishing village was not on the map because it was hidden from the road by the low mountain range between the road and the ocean! Wait, wait, he thought, take it easy, don't get too excited. He would have to do more work on this, but it sure looked like the spot. How lucky can this be? It's too easy; there has to be a catch, but it looks almost exactly like the map! The old man did a better job drawing the map than anyone could have dreamed!

"Let's go," he called to the girl and the driver, "now!"

"But we have just started eating our food!" she replied.

"Let's go, I said, right now! We are going back to the mine!"

"What! I want you to see Butuan! Why must we return to the mine?"

Gary headed toward the door then turned and said, "Stay here if you want, but the driver and I are headed back to camp."

Mila grabbed her plate and drinks and followed Gary and the driver out into the street, eating as she went.

CHAPTER 14

Maybe it's Not For Real!

After Gary had left for Butuan, John had a short meeting with Charlie and Jerry.

"Guys, I am a little worried about this project. I know we have only been here three weeks, but all the indications are bad! We really have no idea about what we are doing or how long it is going to take! I may have gotten us into something we can't win. If you guys want out, I will understand."

"Wait a minute," Charlie said, "don't get down on yourself. Remember, I called you."

"That's right, Charlie, but you didn't force us to come here; it was my decision."

Jerry interrupted the conversation. "I've been thinking about our predicament, and I agree it don't look good, but hell, we have about thirty thousand still in the bank, and I think we can find a damn good project in this country. All we have to do is look around a little."

"Charlie," John said, "how much longer do you think it will take to clear the tunnel you are working on?"

"Oh, I don't know for sure, John; maybe a week to ten days at the most."

"Okay, guys; if we don't find something in this tunnel, we will call it a day. Make sense to you two?"

Both men shook the heads in agreement.

John continued, "Don't say anything to Ramon or anyone else, guys; let's keep this between ourselves!"

Jerry and Charlie grinned, and shook their heads in agreement.

It took Gary two and half hours to return to the mine. This time he wasn't concerned with the speed of the van! John, Jerry, and Charlie were at the new tunnel site when the van pulled in. All three were surprised to see Gary walking toward them. He seemed to be in a hurry about something.

"Stop the digging, guys, we have to talk," he said as he approached the group.

"Why are you here, Gary? You should be in Butuan by now," John remarked.

"Come with me into the tent; we have to talk right now!"

The four men headed for the tent with Gary in the lead walking very fast and motioning the others to follow.

"Come on, guys, get a move on!" he yelled in excitement.

After entering the tent he asked, "Where is Ramon?"

"I'm not sure; he was working with the miners a little while ago, but I have no idea where he is now," Charlie answered.

Gary started, "Gentlemen, we are looking in the wrong place!"

"What are you talking about Gary?" asked Charlie. "This is the place Ramon's grandfather pointed out and drew on the map."

"Is it?" Gary grinned. "All of us have questioned the map; it just doesn't look right. Admit it; we all have questioned the map time and time again—and the location, right? All of us at one time or another has said something about this place not looking right, so listen to what I have to say. If the Japanese were looking for a place to hide the gold, what would they need? Let's think about that."

The other three men were confused and waited for Gary to go on.

"They would need a port to bring the gold in from other parts of the island, wouldn't they? Remember, this was during the Second World War; the roads are bad now, what do you think they were like back then? Why would anyone haul gold up here? They would never be able to take it out in a hurry. Besides, there are too many people here to see what was going on! Don't you understand, the Japanese were looking for a place near the ocean, a seaport that would satisfy all their needs. Don't you see?"

"Okay, let's just say for argument that we agree with you, Gary. What are you getting at?" Jerry asked.

"I know this will sound crazy, but I think I found the place where the gold is hidden."

The other men still were wondering what Gary was up to. How could he know where the gold was hidden?

"Listen, the old man knew what he was doing when he drew the map. When he went to the window and showed Ramon where the gold was, he was not pointing to the mountain, he was pointing north!"

"How did you come up with this conclusion?" Jerry asked.

"On my way to Butuan, we stopped by a little fishing village along the road. I kept having the feeling that I had been there, but couldn't place it. I kept looking at the mountain range across from the port, and it hit me! The old man drew an exact sketch of the twin mountain range, the roads, everything; it was unbelievable! I was looking right at it from the restaurant, and it matched perfectly with the map! There is no mistake in the detail, I'm telling you! It was like an exact picture of the place."

"Okay, before we go crazy, guys, we need to look this place over," said John.

"That's great!" Gary responded, "let's go!"

"Hold on," Jerry said, "we need to clean up around here first, just in case we don't come back. Let's get the place cleaned up and put it on standby, and then we can head out; okay with the rest of you?"

John interrupted Jerry. "Here is how we'll do this." "He paused for a moment then continued, "Jerry and Charlie will stay and straighten things out here, and Gary and I will take Mila and check out the new site. John looked at the men standing in front of him and said, "Now listen, people. We made a mistake in telling everyone what we were up to when we arrived here. Let's not do it again. Every Tom, Dick, and Harry knows what we are up to, so let's keep this among ourselves this time, okay? We'll tell Ramon, but no one else—and let's make sure he understands that we don't want this told to anyone, not even his best friends!"

"Wait," Gary interrupted. "Why are we bringing Ramon in on this? We gave his idea a chance; now we are on our own, as far as I am concerned he's out, along with everyone else. Besides, Mila can do the interpreting, so what do we need him for?"

John looked at Gary in surprise. "What about the map and all the help the kid has given us, Gary; don't you think he has helped?"

Charlie did not wait for Gary to answer but said, "What the hell is the matter with you, Gary, you SOB! This kid is the reason we are here and why we may find the gold!"

All of a sudden Jerry grabbed Gary by the shirt collar, yelling, "I have had about enough of your shit! You've been nothing but trouble since I met you! You are a first-class prick!"

"Hold it, hold it!" John pulled Jerry away from Gary. "This is getting us nowhere! Ramon is in, and that's the last word on it!"

"Is that so?" Gary replied. "I am the only one who knows where the gold is, remember? I didn't tell Mila, so I think you boys had better think about what you are saying."

That's all it took for Charlie. The big man hit Gary square on the nose with a right hook, and then followed up with a left between his eyes. Gary dropped to the floor, blood gushing from his mouth and nose. Charlie bent down and pulled Gary to his feet; he struck him again, down Gary went again!

"You broke my nose," he yelled, as he lay on the floor.

John and Jerry moved in and grabbed Charlie. Jerry looked at Charlie and said, "I think you made your point, Charlie, and I'm sure Gary got the message."

John looked down at Gary in disgust. "Are you sure you want Ramon out? We can take Mila back to the place where you ate, and I am sure we can figure out what you found, Gary, but that's up to you. I can let Charlie finish the job if you insist."

"All right! Ramon stays. I didn't think it was such a big deal, for Christ's sake!" Gary answered.

John, Jerry, and Charlie stood over Gary while he raised himself into a sitting position. It was obvious what each of the men was thinking. Leave the bastard here, pick up Ramon and Mila, and head back toward Butuan.

Gary slowly got to his feet. He took his fingers and squeezed his nose and managed to stop the flow of blood. Charlie motioned to Jerry with his eyes, and the two men headed outside. Jerry glanced at John and said, "Charlie and I are going outside to have a beer, John. I think you and Gary need to talk."

Once outside Charlie said, "I am telling you this, Jerry. If that SOB keeps up his shit, I am going to put him in the hospital!"

"You won't have to, Charlie; that will be my pleasure," Jerry replied. "We had better watch him—I'm telling you, he acts like he is going off his rocker!"

"This is the deal—if he looks like he is up to something, we are going to take action, and I mean action!" Charlie warned.

"What do you mean action?" Jerry asked a look of concern on his face.

"That depends on Gary. If he stays in line, it means nothing. If he doesn't, I'll handle it. Don't ask me anymore, Jerry."

Jerry looked at Charlie and knew there was no need to continue the conversation. "Okay then; let's tell John we will get started closing the tunnel. We want to be ready to head out in a couple of days."

Neither man was aware that John was standing behind them, and neither one knew how long he had been there. There was uneasiness for a moment. Finally, John said, "Charlie, you and Jerry better get moving." The two men looked at each other and headed toward the mine site.

The next morning is after breakfast John had told Mila and Ramon the news. Although Mila was excited to leave the site Ramon was hesitant and wondered if he should leave his village however after talking with John and Charlie he had decided to go along with the new plan. He had made his mind up to find the treasure!

John, Gary and Mila loaded into the second van and headed for the new site. Gary's face was a mess; his right eye was completely closed and the left not much better, however, no one mentioned the incident and continued to pack as though nothing had happened.

Before John left camp, Jerry had a chance to talk to him for a few minutes. "John, the situation could get out of hand real quick if we don't watch it. Charlie is ready to do something to Gary, and it doesn't look good, if you know what I mean!"

John answered, "Are you telling me? I am well aware of what can happen if we don't get this situation taken care of. I agree we need to keep those two apart, that's why I am taking Gary with me. You have a talk to Charlie and get him settled down."

"Easier said than done, John, but I will work on him and have him under control before we get there in a couple of days. Just make sure we have the right directions, and for Christ's sake, talk to Gary!"

"Are you sure you can find us?" John asked.

"Yeah, the driver knows where the place is we can find you don't worry; now get going."

"Okay, see you in a couple of days."

Gary had already gotten into the back seat of the van next to Mila. He looked at her and asked, "Do you want to get out of this country?"

Mila looked at him in total surprise. "I don't understand, Mr. Gary; what do you mean?"

"You heard me. If my plan goes as I expect it will, I will take you with me to the U.S."

"Oh, thank you, Mr. Gary, thank you!"

He looked at her, his eyes dark, swelled with circles under them. Mila could see he was out of control with rage! His knuckles were white, his hands clasped together between his knees, squeezing them repeatedly. He said, "If I hear you mention this conversation to anyone, I will make sure you don't go anywhere. I mean what I say!"

Mila threw her arms around Gary's neck and kissed him on his cheek. Gary quickly removed her arms, just as John opened the door to the van. He put his finger to his lip and let Mila know to keep her mouth shut and to relax. Mila could hardly believe what she had heard; she was going to the United States! But what did he mean when he mentioned his plan? Never mind, she thought, he said if she would do whatever he wanted; if only she could go to the United States!

John turned around to face them and said, "Are we ready?"

"Yes," Gary replied, "let's get moving."

Gary knew he was taking a big chance with Mila, but he also knew he might need her help later. He had no intention of taking her to the U.S., but she would never know that until it was too late. He had depended on John to back him up at the meeting, but when John did nothing after Charlie struck him, Gary knew he was on his own. They had all turned against him, and now they would have to pay! He had already set a plan into motion. While everyone else was asleep, he had a long conversation with a couple of miners who were working with him in the engineering office. He told them just enough to get them to agree to his plan. He knew he could count on at least six of them to get the gold from the others if it became necessary—and it looked like it would be necessary! When they found the gold he would have the six miners tie up the others, and he would take the gold to the port. One of the miner's families had a fishing boat and, for a price, they would load the gold onto the boat and take it to a small island near the Malaysian coast. If things went as planned, the boat owner would never know that the cargo was gold! Gary knew he would need John and the others to find the gold—but from that point on he was on his own, and they could go to hell!

For the first time since Gary and John had met, John felt uneasy. Things between the two had gone from bad to worse. He was preoccupied as they drove from camp toward the new site. Gary was not the same man he had known for the past couple of years; he seemed distant and hostile with everyone. John attempted to start a conversation with him as they drove along, but Gary failed to respond and sat staring out the window. John thought, Had Gary always been like this? After two years, do I really know this man? No, something had happened to Gary, he had changed. But why? John by now had made the decision that he would have to watch Gary every minute; he could no longer be trusted!

What Gary did not know was that John was awake last night and had seen Gary leave the tent. John had followed him until he entered the village's bar, and then John returned back to camp. He was awake when Gary returned—it was late! John wondered what Gary was doing at the bar, especially after everyone had agreed to keep everything quiet and stay near camp. Had Gary said something to the villagers, or was he just having a beer? Whatever the reason, John was convinced that he must keep Gary in check from now on!

Two hours later they were at the turnoff to the port. "Stop the van," Gary said to the driver.

"Gary," John asked, "does this driver understand English?"

"A little but not enough to know what we are talking about don't worry he is smart enough to catch on! I have tested him several times, and he doesn't understand what we are doing. The money we are paying him is good, so he minds his own business."

"Just the same, I would suggest that we don't say too much in front of him, okay?"

Gary was mistaken; the driver understood English very well. Most of his customers were from other countries, and he realized as a driver he must be able to understand and speak English in order to get the best fares. However, he also realized it was better if his passengers didn't know he was fluent in English. He had been listening to these fools for almost a month, laughing to himself about their crazy scheme to find gold! After all, the Filipinos knew that the gold was a myth; it was what old women talked about. If there was any gold, the Marcos regime had taken it.

Still, as long as the money was good, he had no complaints. Many, many greedy men had come to the Philippines after the Great War, looking for riches—and now these fools! He shook his head and thought again, greed! What also was very good for him was that the other driver could not speak English and had to depend on him to tell him what was going on. As he sat in the van while the Americans climbed out, a wide grin crossed his face, and he nodded his head as John stepped outside. The driver was right; the other driver was hired on the spot due to the rush of the men to head for Ramon's village. Ramon and Mila had spoke with him in dialect and continued to interpret for the group. The driver liked the feeling of control over the other driver, so much the better, he thought, but for now he would continue to speak in Vasyan.

The minute the two men stepped out of the van and looked at the map, John could see it just as the old man had drawn it!

"My God, Gary, this is amazing! It's the exact contour of the twin mountains, the roads, everything we have been looking for!"

"Didn't I tell you, John? See, the road from the port is just a couple hundred yards from the main road. The old man never seen the port because of the rolling hills between the ocean and the main road; besides, the Japanese didn't want them to see the port—that's why none of the Filipinos would know the entire operation!"

"Yes, you are absolutely right, Gary. Let's go ahead and drive down to the restaurant. We'll have something to eat, and we need to get some supplies; we're almost out of everything." The two men got back into the van and told Mila to have the driver continue to the fishing village.

While Charlie and Jerry closed up the tunnel at the mine site, several of the villagers began asking questions. They teased Ramon, "Why are you leaving, Ramon? Have you found the gold? Have you hidden the gold in the van?" they asked in jest. "Why do you not give us some of the gold?" The villagers were laughing at Ramon. Ramon was very nervous; he had never lied to his family and friends. He did not like this deception. Mr. Charlie had told him to tell his people that they were giving up; they realized that the villagers were right, that the gold was not hidden here and they had decided to go back to the United States.

What Ramon, Charlie, and Jerry did not know was that Gary had told some of the miners and villagers about his plan and what he had found at the fishing village. So as Ramon told his story to the villagers, the ones who had talked to Gary became more distant from Ramon. They would settle with Ramon when they met him next time! The miners that had agreed to help Gary knew there was no gold here, or any place else in the Philippines, but Ramon lying to them was unacceptable. He was a Filipino, and now he was taking sides and lying to them for these foreigners!

"We must leave the village very soon," Ramon told Charlie. "I do not like the way my people are treating me!"

"What do you mean, Ramon?" Charlie asked.

"They tease me, Mr. Charlie! Some of them only say a few words and seem angry. They continue to ask me why you are leaving, and when I tell them, they act as though they do not believe me!"

Jerry looked at Charlie and said, "What do you think, are they on to us?"

"How can they be? No one has said a thing to them about the new site; we are the only ones who know about it." The two men paused and looked at each other. "Gary!" They both blurted out at the same time. Jerry grabbed Charlie by his arm and said, "Better get the hell out of here; John has to know what is going on, and that Gary is up to something!"

Ramon stood next to the men with a confused look on his face.

"Never mind, Ramon. Get into the van; everything is all right. We are leaving right now."

"But we have not finished the closing of the tunnel and loading all the tools," he said.

"Don't worry, Ramon. We will buy new tools. The miners can use these tools to mine for gold," Charlie answered.

The three men left the tunnel site and headed for the village. Two of the miners were helping close the tunnel watched as the three left the site. One of the miners looked at the other and said in Filipino, "Our brother has betrayed us. We will get our revenge when the other American tells us it is time for his plan."

"What about the Americans?" another miner asked. The first miner just grinned and continued working on the tunnel.

Ramon looked through the rear window of the van as the villagers stood in a group watching the van drive out of sight. He thought, I did not want this! I wanted the gold for all of us and now I am no longer welcome in my own village. This is very bad!

CHAPTER 15

Get Ready

John, Gary, and Mila sat in a corner table at the restaurant while the driver stood at the bar across the room. John looked across the table at Gary and said, "After we eat, we will buy additional supplies and see if we can set up a camp near the road heading toward the twin mountains. I want to be far enough off the main road so we don't attract attention, if that's possible."

"And listen, Mila," John said, "If anyone asks, we are mining engineers looking for properties in the area."

Gary added, "We are exploration people for a large mining company in Manila and have been looking at old mine sites in Mindanao, okay?"

"Yes, Mr. Gary," she responded. Mila would do anything he asked; after all, he was taking her to the United States once they found the gold!

It had taken most of the day to find the supplies. John had just loaded them into the van when Charlie, Jerry, and Ramon pulled up next to him. John was surprised and asked, "What are you doing here?"

Charlie responded, "Where is Gary, John?"

"He is down the street getting some more supplies at the hardware store, why?"

Jerry looked John straight in the face and said, "We have a problem!"

"What do you mean a problem?" John responded.

Charlie interrupted, "We think Gary has something going on John who is definitely not in our best interest." The two men explained what had happened back at the village. John thought for a minute and began putting two and two together. He told the others what he had witnessed the night before.

"Well, that tears it as far as I am concerned," responded Jerry. "This dirty bastard has done nothing but give us hell ever since we left the U.S. John, if we don't do something about it, we will end up regretting it. I am convinced of that."

Charlie added,"Listen, guys, I totally agree, but is this the time to kick him out? You both know he would not tolerate it for a minute; he would find someone else, and we would end up fighting off, God, who-know-who before it was over!"

"Then what the hell are we going to do, John?" Jerry asked with disgust.

"Listen, I hate to do this, but we will have to take turns watching him until the deal is done. Also, Charlie, you should know the girl and Gary are getting awful close lately!"

Charlie laughed out load. "Hey, don't you think I know that? As far as I am concerned, he is doing me a favor! She is okay for what I need, but believe me, guys; I am not in love with her, so more power to him!"

"Okay, that clears that up, so let's move on. One other thing; our driver seems to be listening but not listening, if you know what I mean," John said.

Charlie again answered, "Listen, I will bet you a hundred bucks that guy speaks better English than Mila!"

"Why do you say that, Charlie?" Jerry asked.

"Guys, I have been in the Philippines long enough to see what is going on. Don't say anything in front of this guy—in fact, I suggest we get rid of him if we can."

"Wait a minute," Jerry said. "What are we going to tell Gary when he sees us here today instead of tomorrow?"

"We tell him we got excited to get over here and decided to pay the miners to finish the job, that's all!"

Charlie spoke. "Yeah, but what about the tools? He is going to get suspicious, I'm telling you!"

Jerry looked at Charlie and said, "Let me handle Gary; I will convince him. Don't worry if he gives me any shit, I will finish what I started back at camp!"

Just about that time, Gary hollered from down the street. He was walking along with Mila as they approached the two vans.

"What the hell are you two doing here? Shouldn't you be back at the village?"

"Yeah, and let you have all the fun? What the hell do you think we are, stupid? Jerry exclaimed. "Two more days at the village and we would have gone nuts thinking of the gold down here. This gives us two extra days to help look for the gold instead of spending time at the village."

"What about the villagers, what did they say when you left the site?" Gary asked.

"We told them they were right; there was no gold. We were giving up and heading home. We told them to keep the tools for helping us, They seemed happy with that, so we left."

Gary knew something was up. He had told some of the village miner's part of his plan. They knew this was not why the foreigners were leaving, so why were Charlie and Jerry here?

John interrupted and said, "Hey, it's a done deal! Let's get going and forget about it! Besides, the villagers don't know where we are and why we are here, so forget it."

Gary knew he couldn't say any more for fear the others might start asking questions, so he left it alone and loaded the tools into the van.

John looked at Charlie and said, "Charlie, take a look around town and see if there is another van and driver. If we can, we will get rid of this guy."

"What are you talking about?" Gary asked.

"I will tell you later, Gary," John responded.

Gary again decided to keep his mouth shut. He wasn't sure what else had been going on, but he didn't like the way the others were acting.

Two hours later, Charlie had found a new driver and van. The team loaded the new van and got ready to head out. The driver from the first van had not complained at all; he had simply accepted his money and drove away, which made Charlie very nervous. After word he had asked Mila what the van driver had said when he was paid off. She told Charlie that the driver had said he wanted to go home that he was tired of these foreigners. That seemed to satisfy Charlie for the moment but still felt uneasy.

CHAPTER 16

The Site

The two vans left the fishing village and turned onto the main road. Half a mile later they turned off the main road and onto a dirt road leading into the mountains.

"We need to find some place to camp right away; it's getting dark," John said to Gary.

Gary commented, "This road is in poor shape doesn't look like anyone has used it for some time."

"I think you're right, Gary, but that's good for us. We don't want anyone coming around, right?"

After driving a couple of miles up the road, John noticed a cutout wide enough to set up camp for the night. "Mila, tell the driver to pull over. This is it."

She spoke to the driver, and he pulled the van into the wide spot, the other van followed.

"We can't stay here, can we, John?" Charlie asked, after getting out of the van. "We will be in plain sight if someone comes along."

"I think it is getting too dark to go any further, Charlie. Tomorrow we will look for someplace else less conspicuous—with some decent water if possible."

"Okay, but let's just unload the sleeping bags and call it good; is that fine with the rest of you?" Charlie asked.

Everyone nodded at Charlie and began unloading the sleeping bags, water, and cooking utensils. The next morning, John awoke to find both of the vans missing, along with Charlie and Gary. Now what the hell?

A fire had been started and the coffee was hot he poured himself a cup and debated whether or not to wake the rest of the people. He decided to wait. He was just pouring himself a second cup when he heard a vehicle coming down the road. It was Charlie, in the first van.

Charlie got out of the van and walked toward John standing near the campfire. He bent over, picked up the coffee pot, and poured himself a cup. "I guess you want to know where I have been."

"No, I know where you have been. I saw the other van missing, along with Gary."

"That's right. He left this morning about four-thirty without the driver, so I gave him about a ten-minute head start and followed him up the road. About five miles above here, the road starts to get real bad, so I turned around. I didn't want him to know I was following."

Just as the two men were finishing their coffee, the other van appeared, coming down the road from the same direction Charlie had driven earlier. Jerry had just gotten out of his sleeping bag and immediately headed toward John and Charlie standing near the campfire. "What the hell is he up to now?" Jerry asked.

John and Charlie grinned at each other and looked at Jerry. "We have it under control, Jerry. I followed him this morning, but he doesn't know it," Charlie answered.

"I am telling you two that this guy is up to no good!" Jerry responded.

"We agree, Jerry, but all we have to do is keep an eye on him," Charlie answered.

"Hi, guys I've been doing a little scouting up ahead. I couldn't sleep." As Gary passed by the first van, he noticed that the engine was hot but didn't mention it to anyone. Charlie caught Gary's observation and made a comment. "Yes, I know. I was worried and went looking for you, but didn't want to go too far on the bad road."

Gary ignored Charlie and proceeded toward the campfire and coffee. While pouring his coffee, he said to the group, "We need to look over the map before we go ahead. This road goes all the way up to the base of the mountain, and if I am not mistaken, I believe the map doesn't show the gold being hidden that far up."

John pulled the map from his coat pocket and laid it out. "Yes, you are right. It shows the tunnel down from the mountain quite a bit. This morning we will break up into two groups and start looking for an old road or an indication where the old tunnel might be, all right, guys?"

Charlie scratched the back of his neck and said, "Hey, before we get started, let's get something to eat!" Charlie was hungry and wasn't about to move until he was fed!

Mila startled everyone when she said, "I will get something started for breakfast." No one had seen her walk up behind them since they were busy watching Gary while he walked toward them from the van. Jerry thought, "Damn, she's spooky; didn't even hear her." Charlie set his coffee cup down and looked at her with strange look on his face. Jerry noticed the look and asked Charlie, "Hey partner what's the problem?" Charlie grinned and said, "been around her almost a year never seen her cook a thing!" Mila directed the two drivers and Ramon to help her get breakfast ready for everyone.

Ramon was still upset about lying to the villagers and was preoccupied while the food was being prepared. From out of nowhere, Gary grabbed Ramon by the arm and yelled, "What do you think this is a free ride? Get going and help the others!"

Charlie was like a cat. He grabbed Gary with his left hand around his neck, drew back his right fist, and was ready to strike him when Jerry stepped in. "Careful, big guy I think we had enough of that back at the village!"

Gary had thrown his hand over his face and prepared himself for the blow. John stood up and said, "Calm down, all of you. We are close to being rich beyond our belief, and already we are fighting between ourselves, again! Get a hold of yourselves and now!"

Everyone relaxed and continued preparing breakfast. Charlie eased over next to Gary and without anyone hearing him said, "If you as much as brush up against the kid again, I will break your fuckin' neck!" Fear etched across Gary's face and he realized he had done it again. He said to Charlie, "I'm sorry, Charlie; I don't know what got into me. I promise you it won't happen again." After Charlie walked away Gary thought, Just wait, all of you will get what is coming to you, and I will personally make sure the kid is taken care of!

CHAPTER 17

The Jungle

After breakfast the group gathered around the hood of one of the vans and looked at the map, deciding on a plan. Gary and John would start near the mountain base and work their way back toward the camp, while Jerry and Charlie would search from camp toward the mountain. Gary protested at first and said he would prefer to search near camp, but John made the decision and that was that.

The first van with John, Mila, and Gary drove up the road a couple of miles. The road began to deteriorate, and the jungle began to close in around them, just as Charlie had mentioned earlier. Jerry, Charlie, and Ramon followed the first van, then stopped a couple of miles up the road from the campsite and watched the others disappear out of sight into the heavy overgrowth.

It took John's van a couple more hours to reach the end of the road at the base of the mountain. John touched the driver on the shoulder and motioned him to pull over. Once outside the van, Mila commented, "Mr. John, someone has been here recently."

John walked over to her and peered down at a footprint in the mud. "Yes, it looks that way." He glanced over at Gary and said, "Gary, take a look at this."

Gary walked around the van and looked down. "It's a print of a bare foot, John." Then he turned to Mila. "Are there people living way the hell up here, Mila?"

She put her hand to her chin. She seemed confused and finally said, "There are many tribes in the jungle that no one knows about; this could be one of them, but I do not know."

"Well?" John asked, "Should we go back and tell the others or press on?"

Gary didn't hesitate. He answered, "Let's take a look. Why go all the way back to camp?" Gary was still steaming over his confrontation with Charlie and Jerry. The less time he spent with those two, the better!

So the group moved on. The farther up the trail they traveled, the better the trail became. It was obvious that someone used the trail and used it frequently. As they rounded a turn and crossed a small stream, they encountered a village. It sprang up out of nowhere!

The group slowed to a stop, huddled behind a short coconut tree, and looked at the village. It was extremely primitive; grass-thatched huts were scattered in a semicircle around an open, central area. Trails ran from the main door of each hut and zigzagged around the main encampment. The group was standing next to the main trail leading from the village—not a good place to be!

Finally John whispered, "No sense in just standing here. Sooner or later they are going to see us, and that might not be such a good idea if they figure we are spying on them. They just might not take kindly to that!" He looked at Mila and whispered, "Go ahead, Mila; we will be right behind you."

Mila looked up at John; it was clear she didn't like this idea one little bit. She thought *Why not send the driver? Why me?* But she was sure John wasn't about to change his mind, so she moved back onto the trail and walked slowly into the village. Before she was in full sight, several villagers saw her and the rest of the group. They immediately ran back toward the center of the encampment, yelling something in their dialect.

Mila quickly turned back to John and said, "This is no good; we must leave this place now!"

Gary was starting to get concerned. He hadn't expected this kind of a greeting. The people in the village seemed very upset. He looked at John and said, "Yeah, best move back, John; I don't like the looks of this!"

Before the group could retreat, the driver said to Mila in dialect, "No, we cannot leave now; they will feel we are afraid and chase after us. I know a little of this language; let me speak to them." The driver had no interest in being chased and possible killed and was willing to take the chance to convince the villagers that the group meant no harm.

Mila turned and spoke to the driver, "You know this village?"

The driver slowly nodded his head yes.

"Are you sure you can speak the dialect?"

The driver told her he had heard of the village but had never been there; however, but met one of the men at the fishing village and was somewhat familiar with their native tongue; he wasn't sure how much he would understand but would try and talk with them. Mila related the conversation to the others. John thought, Thank God I hired this guy from the local fishing village!

The driver walked around Mila and moved toward the center of the village. The further into the village the group moved, the less visible the villagers became. The driver began to yell in a dialect Mila could not understand. She looked at him and became very uneasy; he seemed to know more than he had told her. Eventually a villager came out from his hiding place and cautiously walked toward the group. Once the man stood next to the driver the two men clasped arms and started talking in a low whisper. Finally the driver turned and motioned to the group to come forward. Once they did, he said, "This is my cousin. He is the chief's counselor and advisor."

Mila became very angry and asked in her dialect, "Why did you not tell us this?"

The driver responded in a heated voice, "I do not know you! I am not going to let you hurt my people!"

John sensed this wasn't going the right direction and stepped forward. "Mila," he said, "what is the problem?"

She answered, "This is his village!"

John thought I have two choices: Give him hell for not telling us, or play along. He looked around and saw at least twenty-five men that he believed were warriors standing just inside the jungle foliage. He decided on choice two! He grabbed the driver's hand and said, "Great, we picked the right man!" John had a big smile on his face and kept shaking the man's hand vigorously up and down.

The driver's mouth fell open, and his face told the story of a very confused individual! After several seconds pumping the man's hand, John said to him, "Well, my lad, why don't you introduce us to your village?" Gary started to say something, but John shot a quick look of don't say a thing! Gary stood back and kept his mouth shut, but Mila started to say something. John gripped her arm and squeezed. Mila winced in pain and closed her mouth.

After a moment, the driver began to talk to his cousin and eventually motioned to the others to come out from the jungle's cover. When the other villagers had joined the driver, he began speaking to them. When he finished his conversation he turned to the group and said, "The village had been here for many, many years. They have not seen many strangers and are in fear of you." He had a slightly twisted look on his face and said, "I told them you are my friends." He hesitated and then said to John, "Is that true?"

John again grabbed his hand and said, "You can count on it!"

The driver turned back to the man and continued to speak. As the two men talked, villagers cautiously began to return from their huts and from their jungle hiding places. The driver turned to the group and said, "Come with me. It is our custom to invite guests to eat with us." He directed them to the center of the village, where they were they were seated at a large table.

Gary looked at the massive table and realized it had been constructed from one huge mahogany tree—it was amazing! The native women began placing various fruits and vegetables onto the table while others added wood to the nearby fire. After the fire began to burn and the hot flames flared into the sky, large pieces of raw meat were placed over the flames.

It seemed as though people emerged from the smoke; they were everywhere. Children would run up and touch John and Gary on the face then run away laughing. In no time the village was alive with activity, as though nothing had changed. Once the food was in front of the group, John and the others started to reach for it. The villager who had led them to the eating place whispered to the driver. The driver turned to Mila and passed on the message to her. Mila turned to John and said, "We are not to eat until the chief has joined us, Mr. John."

A few minutes later, an old man dressed in simple attire emerged from a hut located at the end of the village. The villagers stepped back from the table as he approached. The old man stopped at the head of the table. The women serving the table bowed their heads to him then one of them placed a woven blanket onto a large crude chair at the head of the table. The chief sat down and raised his hand to the visitors. The driver nodded his head to the others, and the group began to eat.

John turned to Mila and said, "Tell the chief that we appreciate his hospitality, Mila." Mila turned to the driver and told him what John had said; however, the driver explained to Mila that no one was allowed to talk to the chief until the meal had been completed. The group continued eating in silence. After everyone had finished, the women removed the food from the table.

John had noticed a necklace around the chief's neck, made of many shell-like ornaments, but more importantly, he noticed a gold coin of some type attached to the necklace.

After the food was removed from the table, the chief nodded at the driver and said something in his dialect. The driver turned to Mila and said, "The chief will listen to what we have to say now." John, using the driver as interpreter, introduced everyone from his party and thanked the chief for the wonderful food. The chief smiled and nodded his head in agreement. John then asked the chief about his necklace and wanted to know about the gold coin around his neck. The chief seemed pleased that it had been noticed. He spoke to the driver for some time, and finally the driver turned to John and explained. The driver told John that it was a gift from many years ago. Other strangers had visited their village and had given the coin to the chief's father and it had been passed down to him.

"What do you mean, strangers?" John asked.

The man responded, "The chief says that others from the past had come to his village when he was a small boy. The strangers had given his father the coin when his people helped them."

"What strangers?" John insisted. He had a hunch and wasn't about to let it go!

"The chief says many years ago foreigners in clothes with many shiny things hanging from the chest came to their village and asked his tribe to help them carry yellow metal into the mountain. The coin was given to his father when all the yellow metal was buried inside."

"Ask the chief if he will tell us where the strangers put the yellow metal. If he will tell us, I will give him two coins for his necklace." The driver repeated to the chief what John said. The chief jumped to his feet and began yelling in a high-pitched voice. The villagers surrounded the group and raised their machetes. The chief was enraged; he continued to instruct the villagers, talking very fast, making it difficult for the driver to understand everything he was saying.

The driver stood up, turned to John, and said. "We must go!"

"Why, what has happened?"

The chief called to his people, and several men holding spears pointed them toward the group. The driver was in a state of panic and yelled, "We must go now!"

Gary did not waste any time. He got to his feet, grabbed Mila by the hand, and headed for the van.

The chief continued to yell to the other villagers, pointing toward the group. John decided that the situation was out of hand and also started walking toward the van. After everyone had climbed into the van, the villagers surrounded them and began beating on the van, yelling at the occupants inside.

"Get the hell out of here, now!" Gary yelled.

After turning the van around, the driver headed down the road in the direction they had come from. After driving a half-mile from the village, John told the driver to stop, and to pull to the side of the road. The driver was still very upset; he ignored John and continued driving down the road. He kept turning around in his seat to look over his shoulder through the rear window of the van.

"Stop, I said!" John repeated.

The driver stopped the van but continued to look backward.

"Mila, find out what the hell just happened back there!" Gary said.

Mila talked to the driver for a few minutes then finally turned to John and Gary and said, "The old man said that the other strangers had told his father never to tell anyone where the yellow metal was hidden. If anyone came to find the metals, and the villagers told them the secret, all of the villagers would be killed! The chief also said we must all go and never return; if we returned, he would have all of us killed. The strangers also told the villagers if anyone ever spoke of where the yellow metal was hidden, the village would be cursed and famine would destroy them all!"

After Mila finished relating the story to John, John instructed the driver to immediately return them to camp. John had to caution him several times to slow down before he ran off the road and killed everyone!

Meanwhile, Charlie, Jerry, and Ramon had been looking along the side of the road for hours without any luck. They were looking for any indication of a road or trail that might lead them to a possible opening into the mountain. The men's clothes were drenched; however, Ramon seemed to be fresh and was always a step ahead of the others. Finally, covered in sweat and exhausted, Charlie and Jerry hollered at Ramon, Stop! Jerry wiped the sweat from his brow and sat down on a tree stump. Charlie stopped next to him, leaned against a small coconut palm, and started wiping his face with the back of his hand. Ramon turned around and without warning ran back toward the two men, shouting loudly.

Ramon was excited, yelling in dialect; both men looking at him with confusion on their faces. Charlie looked at Jerry and asked, "What the hell has got him riled up?" But Jerry couldn't answer Charlie—all of a sudden he was covered with biting red ants! They were all over him, biting into his flesh, around his eyes, and up his nose!

Jerry jumped to his feet and began running back up the trail, slapping at his face and neck. Charlie started running after him and finally tackled Jerry to the ground. But no sooner had Charlie started knocking the ants from Jerry's back than he began to feel the biting on his body! Ramon stopped shouting in dialect; he finally realized that neither man knew what he was yelling. Once he reached the two men who were kicking and rolling on the ground, he yelled, "Rub the coco branch on you! You must rub the coco leaf on you!"

Charlie was not as bad off as Jerry and was able to get to his feet and run to the coconut palm. He ripped the leaves from the tree and frantically began to rub his face, arms, and legs. Meanwhile, Ramon had grabbed a large leaf and was rubbing it on Jerry's neck and shoulders. In a few minutes the ant bites started to lessen. Jerry's face was a mess, and Charlie had massive welts on his arms and chest.

"Come," Ramon said, "there is a small stream just ahead. You must wash the venom off your body before it begins hurting you again."

Jerry never hesitated; he jumped to his feet and began to run ahead of the other two. He had no idea where the stream was until he tripped and landed head first in the middle of the trickling steam, God! He thought; this feels great! Just as he was about to turn around to say something, Charlie landed on top of him!

"Sorry, mate," Charlie hollered, "I can't take no more!"

Ramon stood next to the stream and looked down at the two. He couldn't help it and started to laugh; they looked like two drowned rats! Big welts, mud, torn clothes—the two were quite a sight!

Charlie was about to say something to Ramon when he turned and looked at Jerry. A massive lump had formed over Jerry's left eye and another on the end of his nose. Charlie slapped his knee and began to howl. "Damn, man!" he said, "You are the ugliest SOB I've ever laid eyes on!"

Jerry was already laughing at Charlie, whose ears were now double their normal size! Jerry finally was able to catch his breath and said, "You look like a damn monkey!" He threw his arms around Charlie and continued to laugh. The two men got to their feet, and Charlie said to Ramon, "That's it for today, guys. Let's get out of here before there's nothing left of us!" The men started walking back to the road when they heard the other van coming down the road.

John saw the second van and told the driver to stop; however, the driver was still shaken and was more inclined to head for the fishing village. He looked at John, fear flashing across his face—he was not going to stop!

John saw that the driver was going to pass the other van. He reached over and turned off the key, not realizing that the steering wheel would lock! The driver let out a scream as he tried to apply the brakes and swerve away from the other van.

Charlie, Jerry, and Ramon had no idea what was going on but they could see that the driver in the van was frantically trying to stop the vehicle. Jerry hollered, "Christ almighty, run!" The three men darted back down the path just as the other van bounced to a stop a couple of feet from Charlie's rig.

Once the van came to a halt John was in no mood to discuss the issue. He said to the driver, "Didn't you see the van? What the hell is the matter with you?"

Charlie, Jerry, and Ramon slowly walked back to the road and sat down under a tree. John and Gary climbed out of the van while the dust was still swirling around them and walked to where to three men were sitting. It was apparent to them; that John was upset. John did not wait for Charlie or Jerry to say anything he began speaking to them as he approached.

"Guys, we damn near didn't come back!" If it wasn't for the driver-------

Charlie interrupted him and said, "Yep, same here. That was us you tried to run over!"

John stopped in his tracks and said, "Huh?" Then it dawned on him what Charlie was talking about, and he continued, "No, no, not that!" He was about to continue when he saw the ant bites. "What in the hell? I thought we had a bad day, but you two!"

Jerry eased to his feet and said, "Forget about us; we just got a little too close to some ants. So tell us; what happened to you?"

John spent the next few minutes explaining the events of the day, every now and then stopping to take another look at his buddies and their angry -looking knots. After he finished, he wiped his brow and sat down next to Charlie. Gary had been quiet but decided he had better say something.

"Look, people, this is bad news. I won't try to down play down what happened this morning at the village, but let's look at it realistically. We are at least five miles from the village, and I doubt very much if the villagers are going to come looking for us." He stopped and looked at Jerry's nose, pondered for a second, then continued. "Besides, the village can't have more than fifty people in it, and half of them are women and children."

"What the hell are you talking about, Gary? Those people threatened our lives, for Christ's sake!" John yelled. "Besides, I don't want to talk any more about it right now. We need to think and figure out what has happened before we decide anything!"

After a few minutes, while everyone had a chance to calm down, John instructed the drivers to take the group back to the camp. He remained quiet during the trip. When they arrived back at camp, John told everyone to find a place around the campfire.

Charlie said, "Okay, it's time to make a decision. Are we going to stay, or are we going to get the hell out of here?"

Jerry looked at everyone and said, "I don't want to die, but hell, we all know we are close to the gold. I say we get some weapons to protect ourselves and keep looking."

Charlie nodded his head in agreement, and, of course, Gary nodded a yes.

John slowly rose to his feet. Everyone looked up at him waiting to hear what he had to say. He began, and it was apparent to everyone that he was very upset.

"I want to find the gold just as much as the next man, but people, we are talking about a good chance of us being killed! This chief means it; he believes if anyone finds or tries to find the gold, it will bring bad luck to his village. Let me tell you, these primitive people believe in this kind of bullshit and are very superstitious; they are not going to back down!"

"No one said that they had to back down, John; we are only suggesting that we protect ourselves. I am convinced that if we fire a couple of rounds above their heads, they will be gone in a heartbeat. Remember, all they have is spears and machetes," Gary replied.

Jerry was next. "I can understand how some of you might feel about this, and I can guarantee you that I am not happy either. If I had any sense I would get the hell out of here right now. However, no one, and I mean no one, is going to make me leave now, we are too close!"

Surprisingly, Ramon was the next to speak. "I do not know these people in the village, but I do know that I cannot go back to my village without the gold. My people do not trust me anymore; therefore I must bring back the gold or never return."

Charlie spoke. "The hell with these people! Are we going to walk away, damn it, when I can taste the gold?"

"Then that's it," John said. "We will stay, but if anything at all looks like trouble, I am leaving—with or without the rest of you, understand!"

Later John sent Charlie and the new driver into the port village to see if they could find some hand guns for protection. Meanwhile, the rest of them began to organize the camp for a longer stay. They cleared an area and camouflaged as much of it as they could from the road. John assigned lookouts around the camp and set up a twenty-four hour rotation for everyone. Later that night, Charlie returned with two pistols and a half a dozen boxes of ammunition for each weapon.

"They won't try anything now; I can guarantee that much, or somebody is going to get their asses shot off!" he remarked.

"Okay, Charlie, you have the three AM watch, so you had better show the rest of us how to use those things before you try to get some sleep," John responded.

"Nothing to it, guys," Charlie said, "just point and pull the trigger." With that, Charlie fired two rounds into the night. The sound of the gunfire echoed through the jungle. Mila jumped and ran to the van. She wanted the gold and a future in the U.S., but this was very bad she thought, very bad! These men did not know the jungle people; they did not understand their ways! If they did not leave this place someone would die!

No one except Charlie had fired a pistol so he explained to everyone how to hold it, point it, and pull the trigger. After everyone had finished with the weapons, Charlie put one away behind the van seat and kept the other in his belt. He would make sure Gary had the pistol for the first watch that way someone would be awake to watch Gary! Before Charlie headed for bed to get some rest he approached John.

"John, you had better know the rest. While we were in the fishing village, I noticed our old driver is still there. He was talking to a couple of bad-looking boys at the bar and seemed to be motioning toward me. I don't know if it means anything, but I thought I had better tell you."

"It figures. It seems like everything is going in the wrong direction since we've been here," John replied. "I guess we had better let the others know, and make sure we keep a lookout for these guys you seen at the fishing village."

CHAPTER 18

The Find!

Charlie didn't sleep a wink he didn't trust Gary for a minute. By the time he had taken over at three o'clock and finished at five o'clock, it was too late to try to sleep; he was awake for over twenty-four hours! He was beat the next day at breakfast thanks to good old Gar! He looked over at Gary and Jerry he could see the look in their eyes said, "This is it!"

The group ate breakfast and began to get organized for the day. Gary said, "It seems to me that we need to concentrate near the road. I figure that the Japanese needed a decent road to use to transport the gold. Did you notice that the road from here to the village was more of a trail than a road, John? If I were the Japanese, I would want to unload the gold at the port and hide it as soon as possible. I wouldn't want to transport it too far from the port, just far enough to keep people from knowing what they were up to."

"Makes sense, Gary," Jerry interrupted, "I would agree. Back in the forties, the roads were not quite what they are today; therefore they would keep their trips as short as possible. Let's concentrate a mile from the main road to where we are now, what do you say?"

Charlie looked at everyone and said, "That sounds good. Let's get going; we're wasting time sitting around camp!"

John added, "Same groups as yesterday. Our group will start looking on the lower end of the road, and the other can start looking from the camp working toward us. After we meet, we will evaluate what we have found."

All day the teams searched both sides of the road. Charlie and Jerry were about to quit for lunch when Jerry called out, "Charlie, over here!"

Jerry was out of sight from the road; Charlie had to holler to find him. "Where the hell are you?"

"Keep coming! You're headed in the right direction."

Charlie finally found Jerry in a small clearing thirty feet from the road. It was easy to see why Charlie could not find him at first; the jungle was very dense along the road and almost impossible to navigate. The tall vines, heavy brush, and trees stood in the way. Every inch had to be cut away before moving forward. When Charlie found Jerry, sweat covered both men's bodies.

"I found this, Charlie, what do you think? Jerry handed Charlie a rusty can. "It looks like a can for food at one time, doesn't it?"

Charlie looked at the can and nodded his head in agreement. "Let's look around here a little more," Charlie replied.

"Charlie, take a look at this!" Jerry was standing over something protruding from the ground.

Charlie approached and looked down. "What are you looking at now, Jerry?"

"This, Charlie. Isn't this a piece of rail for railroad cars?"

"By God, you're right!"

Ramon interrupted the two men and said, "What is rail, Mr. Charlie?"

Charlie could hardly control his emotions but answered Ramon. "Kid, this is what they used to load the rail car onto and push it into the mountain. See, the wheels are on a car kinda like our van, only they run on steel rail. So they would load the stuff, like I said and—

"Over here!" Jerry yelled.

Charlie and Ramon ran to where Jerry was standing. He had cleared some underbrush and exposed a rail tie. Jerry continued pushing back underbrush. "Here is another one! Damn, man, it's the railroad!"

"Listen, Jerry," Charlie said, "I'm going to find John. You and Ramon stay here and mark the place so we can find it, but for Christ's sake, don't make it too obvious. We don't want everyone and their brother to find it; get my meaning'?"

"Yeah, yeah, go find John!"

An hour later all of them were at the new site searching the area for clues.

"Hold it," John yelled, "we are running around like a bunch of chickens with our heads cut off! Let's regroup. We will start with Charlie; what have you got?"

"Well, it's all the same things we've been finding: old cans, rusty tools, and old rotten timber, it's the same stuff."

"Okay, so what does this mean?" John continued. "One, someone has been here— but was it the Japanese? Two, if it was the Japanese, where would they put the tunnel into the mountain? And three, what should we be doing to find it?"

"Let me make a suggestion," Charlie commented. "We need to relax for a minute and look at the alternatives, then decide what the Japanese would have done. Make sense? Let's try to find out where the original road came into the site and go from there. Remember, they wanted things to go fast but be well hidden from view."

For the next couple of hour, everyone looked for something that might indicate where the main road turned into the clearing. Later, when everyone had gathered back at clearing, Gary spoke up.

"I have thought about this several times in the last hour, and it seems to me that they would not have built the road directly into the site from the main road. I would have put some kind of twist on the whole deal. We know from what Ramon has told us that only his grandfather was spared from the group of Filipinos. That leaves only the primitive natives up the road and the Japanese soldiers who would know the location, right?"

Everyone nodded his head in agreement.

"We also know we cannot ask the villagers, and the soldiers are long gone, so let me think about this for a while. The rest of you can continue to look around, but I am convinced that there is a twist to the hiding place."

Mila and Ramon had been ignored for the most part the past couple of days. Especially when the group had begun making plans, both had been excluded, and this bothered them. Although they had not discussed it between themselves, there was worry on their faces. Mila was becoming very concerned. She knew deep down that if the gold was found, she would not be given a share, or if she was, it would be very little. It was apparent to her by now that Gary never intended to take her to the U.S. She was convinced he was using her to his advantage! She had decided that she must play along with the group and be ready to make her own move when it was time. She also realized that she had no loyalties to anyone in the group, including Ramon; she was on her own! Ramon had similar worries; he also believed these men would take his gold and leave him to fend for himself. However, this did not bother him as much as returning to his village empty-handed. Ramon had also decided, when the time came, to take advantage of any situation that would get him his share of the gold, no matter what!

After the first day at the new site, Mila found a place away from the others and began to sketch a drawing of the site. After she had completed it, she carefully hid the map inside her clothing. She thought; *I will keep this map. When the time comes, I will sell it to the highest bidder!*

Gary had been preoccupied the last couple of hours while he considered where the tunnel might be. He began to regret his involvement with the miners from Ramon's village. He had told them to meet him at the fishing village in a week—and the week was up! He thought *what now? I have betrayed the group; they will never let me get away with it, no matter what I tell them. I will have to take care of the miners before it gets out of hand!*

"John," Gary said, "I think we need to make a run into the fishing village for more supplies. Besides, it will give me a chance to clear my head, what do you think?"

Everyone else was concentrating on the site and not listening to Gary. "Yes, it makes sense, Gary. Why don't you take Mila with you? She can help you in the village more than helping us here."

Gary didn't want anyone except the driver with him, but he realized that it might create suspicion if he argued the point. He would simply have to distract her for a while when he met with the miners. So while the others continue the search Mila and Gary headed for the village.

After they arrived at the fishing village, Gary gave Mila some money and a list of goods and told her to start buying some supplies and equipment. He also told her if anyone asked why she was buying extra supplies, to tell them they were prospecting near the mountain and needed more supplies. Gary knew small-scale mining was common in the area and this explanation would keep suspicion to a minimum. He explained to her that he was going down to the tavern to have a decent meal for a change. He would pick her up something to eat while she finished the shopping.

Although she agreed, Mila would have preferred to go with him, but decided not to protest. She sensed Gary wanted to be alone.

After arriving at the tavern, Gary immediately looked around and spotted the miners. They were sitting at a table near the back of the room. He tensed as he approached the table; two men he did not know were with the miners, along with the van driver they had fired. Gary took a deep breath and said, "Hello, boys, how was your trip?"

The men at the table had not seen Gary approach their table and were taken by surprise; they became edgy. Once Gray sat down at the table, everyone relaxed a bit. However the van driver and the two strangers got to their feet immediately, nodded their heads in respect, and left hurriedly. Gary used his thumb to indicate the direction the men were walking and calmly said, "Who were those men with our driver?" Gary was anything but calm; he felt the floor falling out from under his feet. He thought, now I've done it! Who the hell are these jerks, damn it!

One of the miners responded, "We met them this morning while we waited for you. They are fishermen from the village. But enough of that; what have you got to tell us, Mr. Gary?"

"Well, it's not good. We haven't had much luck. It doesn't look like this is the place where the gold is hidden, I'm afraid."

Again, one of the miners who seemed to be the leader, said, "What do you want to do? We are here to help you if we can."

Gary knew he had to be very careful from here on; he did not want to let this get out of hand. "Tell you what, guys; let me give you some money so you can stay awhile in the village in case something comes up. But right now you need to stay out of sight. He reached into his pocket and pulled out some money. "Here is five thousand pesos; that should hold you over for a week, okay?"

Surprisingly, the men took the money without concern and seemed to be in agreement. Again the leader spoke. "We will wait for you to tell us what you want us to do. When do you want to meet next, Mr. Gary?"

"Gary replied, next week at the same time. Guys, listen I have to find my driver. Do you need anything else? Can I buy you a drink, something to eat?"

"No, Mr. Gary, we are fine."

Gary stood up from the table and realized that he was sweating—his clothes were soaking wet; he was more nervous than he thought. He hoped that the others hadn't noticed. As he left the restaurant, he turned and looked back at the miners at the table. He thought, this don't look good. They were too friendly! Why in the hell didn't they ask more questions?

Mila had completed the shopping list for the tools and equipment and was now looking for food and clothing. As she passed a dress shop, she thought, oh, this dress is beautiful! I have not had a new dress for such a long time! But should I buy it without asking Mr. Gary? She paused and put her hand to her face. I am sure he would not mind if I buy the dress he would like to see me wearing it.

Mila realized that the restaurant where Mr. Gary was eating was only a couple of buildings down the street. She thought, I will go and ask him if I can buy the dress. She told the driver to finish loading the tools and equipment; she would be right back to finish the shopping. As she entered the restaurant she immediately noticed the van driver from Davao and two strangers leaving the table where Mr. Gary and two others were sitting. Mr. Gary was talking with two men but she did not recognize either of them; the two men leaving the table with the driver looked very suspicious to her and made her feel uneasy. In an instant terror struck Mila. MILF! Oh my God, MILF! She thought.

MILF was a Muslim terrorist group that struck fear into the hearts of Filipinos throughout the islands. Southern Mindanao was the center of the Muslim stronghold in the Philippines. For the past twenty-five years the MILF bandits had attacked and killed innocent Filipinos, taking their meager belongings and destroying their villages. They were notorious for kidnapping foreigners and holding them for ransom! During the past three years, the MILF had become more vicious, killing and maiming their captives if their ransom demands were not met. Every year the bandits became more ferocious, if that were possible. They were feared for their brutality to their victims; cutting off their heads was a trademark of the MILF!

At first she did not recognize the men at the table with Mr. Gary, however, she was convinced she had seen them somewhere before. She started to walk over to Mr. Gary's table but something inside her told her not to, and to get out of the restaurant as fast as she could! Mila eased her way back out the door, trying not to attract attention, and hurried down the street to where the van driver was finishing loading the supplies.

Gary walked out of the restaurant, the sun blinding him as he stood in the street. He cuffed his hand over his eyes and looked up and down the street he thought he had seen Mila hurrying up the street toward the van, but because of the sun glaring into his eyes he wasn't sure. After his eyes were focused he was able to see her helping the driver load the van. He thought, Damn, that sure looked like her, but if it was what the hell was she doing down here? Did she see me with the guys? Gary stood for a few seconds looking at Mila and the driver. Maybe I should say something? No, better not start something; if she wasn't at the restaurant then I had better not start her thinking or asking questions.

Gary started walking down the street toward the van. He watched as Mila and the driver loaded the van then called out, "Are you ready for something to eat, Mila?"

"No, Mr. Gary, I am ready to go back to camp."

"But you both haven't eaten anything. Are you sure? We can get something at the restaurant; it won't take but a couple of minutes."

"No, Mr. Gary, we are ready to return to camp. As you say, we do not want to attract attention."

Gary thought Mila was a little nervous but decided it was due to the long day and let it go—but again, was that her walking away earlier?

John, Jerry, Charlie, and Ramon had started piling up things they found buried in the underbrush at the clearing in a central location near the site. It was obvious that this was a major work site at one time; partial building foundations were discovered, garbage had been discarded in a location near the outskirts of the clearing, but nothing was evident to the men where the tunnel might be.

"Damn it! It has to be here!" Charlie exclaimed.

"I agree," Jerry responded, "but we have looked all over this place, so what are we missing?" He raised his hands over his head in frustration.

"Wait," John said, "the map! "We have forgotten to look at the map. The answer is on the map; it has to be!"

The three men laid out the map once again. Jerry said in frustration, "We have looked at the map over fifty times and still can't find the damn gold!"

"I still can't decide what these small marks attached to the triangles are on the map; they don't make sense!" John remarked.

"Yes, they do, Mr. John," Ramon commented.

John turned to Ramon and said, "What do you mean, Ramon?"

Ramon continued, "The marks are the way my grandfather indicated the direction to the tunnel. When he drew maps for the miners at my village, this is the way he would mark the tunnel entrance to their claims."

"Show us how he done it, Ramon," Jerry said.

The men leaned forward as Ramon connected each corner of the triangles on the map using the strange lines attached to the triangles. Each triangle had a small mark on one corner. Ramon took each triangle and attached it to the others, and slowly a distinct line at the tip of each triangle started to form.

"I don't understand, Ramon," John said.

"See the very small marks on each triangle? The marks are my grandfather's. Each one tells the miner how to connect the triangle." Ramon continued connecting the triangles.

"Now I see," said Jerry. "Look here, John—the small marks are all different; only the old man knew which one went where."

Ramon handed the pencil to Charlie. Charlie continued to map out the direction to the tunnel entrance. "Yes, Mr. Charlie, that is it—see how the triangles show the direction to the tunnel? Only the miners who mined the claims knew of the marks; they did not want anyone else to find their claims. My grandfather would draw different marks for each mine in such a way that the miners would know their own mine site. It was my grandfather's code." Ramon took the pencil again and began drawing lines in conjunction with the ones on the map, but each time he drew he would skip two marks and move the third one in line with the first mark, and so on until he had completed a curved line into the mountain side.

The three men looked at each other. "How do you know this, Ramon?" John asked.

"My grandfather taught me this code. He told me that I would be a mapmaker like him one day and I must know how to use the code."

"Ramon, wait a minute," John interrupted. "This is too simple. If each miner was given a map with this code, each miner could figure out the others' claims by using the code your grandfather put on the map!"

"Look, Mr. John! See how the marks are designed? Not every map had the same type of marking; only my grandfather and I knew what each different mark was for each map, so if someone was to take another miner's map he would not be able to use it unless the other miner or my grandfather showed them the special code. Besides, if someone in our village stole another's map, there would be much trouble!"

"Well, what do we have to lose? Let's see if we can figure out where this railroad begins and where it ends!" John replied. "The first building looks like it was here on the map. Jerry, where did you find the piece of rail?"

"Right over here, John," Charlie replied.

"Okay, so if this is where the first building is on the map, and the rail was here, then the second building should be right over there next to the trees."

"Why do you say that, John?" Jerry exclaimed. "The rail was not attached to anything; it looks like it was an extra rail."

"Right, John," Jerry replied, "but think about it; they must have stacked the rail here and used it as they drove the tunnel. Each time they needed a piece of rail they would bring out a rail car, load the rail, and take it into the tunnel. They also knew that they must do everything they could to conceal the direction of the rail into the tunnel, but what they didn't plan on was Ramon's grandfather drawing a map! They figured once the gold was hidden, they were going to kill all of the Filipinos anyway, right? They knew the primitive tribe had no use for the gold and would be terrified of the curse."

"So where is the tunnel, John?" Charlie asked.

"It's right over there, people!"

Everyone looked toward the mountainside. Jerry remarked, "I don't see a thing except jungle; how do you know it is there?"

John directed his attention to the two men. "Guys, any mining engineer with any sense will tell you that you must have a certain amount of over-burden to start a tunnel; you simply cannot start digging into the ground and drive a tunnel, right Charlie? The tunnel would simply cave in as they removed the soft dirt."

Jerry looked at the hillside and said, "So that's why you say the tunnel is there, John?"

John responded, "It's a mining term, gentlemen: hard ground!"

Charlie hollered, "Damn, man, you're right! Holy shit!"

John continued, "Remember, we all agreed that they needed a place that was close to the port, quick access, and hidden from view, right? And right there, boys, is the perfect place to start a tunnel. The ground is stable, and the location is perfect if you intended to open a hole in the mountainside!"

"My God, I believe he's figured it out, Jerry!" Charlie said.

The three men stared at the mountainside. Charlie looked at John and Jerry and said, "Remember, guys—Gary wanted to leave the kid back at the village." He shook his head in disgust.

The men raced toward the mountainside and began to cut away the jungle growth. Soon Jerry exclaimed, "I found rail, guys!" And there it was, sticking out from the jungle underbrush like a work of art! The four men dug around the rail for an hour, looking for the main railway going into the mountain.

"John," Charlie said when the three men stopped digging and stood back from the undergrowth. "I have a question. Why isn't there rail leading back to the camp? Shouldn't we be able to trace the rail back to the buildings?"

"Charlie, if I were going to hide the gold, I would tear out all traces of the tunnel before I left; I wouldn't leave any sign. The only reason we found this is because they forgot to get rid of the spare rail over near the building and hadn't counted on the old man's map. But I would bet a million dollars—if we looked around the main road away from the site or maybe down at the fishing village, we would find the other rail they tore out."

"So what is next, John?" Jerry inquired.

"Keep digging toward the mountainside, guys. Eventually we will find the tunnel entrance."

"It's going to be caved in, John—remember it's been over fifty years, and the timbers have rotted," Charlie said.

"Charlie, it probably didn't matter. I'm sure they caved the tunnel in before they left. Anyway, they had no intention of keeping it open once they realized that the Philippines were going to be taken back by the allies. My guess is after they figured they were going to lose the war and had to get out they made a choice—try to get the gold out of the country or save their own asses! Oh, I'm sure some of the gold and other valuables were sent back to Japan, but most of it was from Luzon; remember that was the major stronghold for the Japanese during the war. The stuff we are after is from Mindanao and maybe some nearby islands. Probably the last place they would abandon was Mindanao due to its location in the Philippines."

"Yes," Jerry agreed, "I believe that the Americans controlled the seaways by the time the Japanese decided to move the gold. If that were so then they would be taking a big risk by trying to take it back to Japan. I would suspect their long-term plan was to retake the Philippines later on in the war and then get the gold."

"Whatever, guys—let's get going," Charlie said with excitement.

"Wait, wait Charlie, calm down. It's almost eight o'clock. We need to eat something and rest a while." John realized he needed to calm Charlie and Jerry down a bit. If they were in too much of a hurry they took the chance of missing something. He also realized that they were near exhaustion, which could lead to trouble. "We need to step back and think about this for a while. It's worked for us and gotten us this far; let's not start doing something different, not when we are this close!"

Jerry and Charlie were not about to stop now but knew John was right it was late and yes they were tired. Besides Gary would be back soon, and they couldn't wait to tell him the good news— especially about how Ramon had explained the map!

Gary and Mila arrived twenty minutes after the others had returned to camp. Gary's eyes were wide open after John filled him in on the discovery.

"By God, fellows, tomorrow we are in business!" He exclaimed with excitement.

"Yes, thanks to Ramon," Jerry added with a little sarcasm.

Gary ignored the comment and sat down near the fire.

CHAPTER 19

A Plot!

The two Filipinos and the driver from Davao returned to the table where the miners were sitting after Gary left. "What did he say?" asked the driver.

The miner from the village, who spoke for both of them, said, "They are fools. There is no gold, just as I told you. We will do as you suggested."

"Very good!" one of the Filipinos said. He grinned and continued, "We will kidnap these American idiots and hold them for ransom! Tomorrow we will return to our camp in the mountains and report this to Omar! You will wait here for the American to return in three days. We will meet with you again; then we will make our plan." The two men left the table and headed toward the door of the cafe.

One of the miners, who had been silent during the meeting said, "I do not like this plan, Armando—these men are MILF bandits! We cannot trust them. Besides, this is wrong; we are miners—we are not like these people!"

"Armon, did not Ramon lie to us? Do you think he will share the money he is getting from the Americans with us? We will let the bandits deal with the ransom money and only take our share, but we will get something for our time but we must wait one week from today. We will have money to take back to our village. In the meantime, we wait here!"

The second miner said again, "MILF, this is bad, very bad!" But his companion ignored him!

CHAPTER 20

Tunnel

John and the rest of the group worked for three days exposing the railroad going into the mountain. The task proved to be difficult due to the amount of jungle brush that needed clearing. It was slow going with only four men working the site. The two drivers were not interested in the venture and preferred to sleep back at camp under a shade tree. They never questioned anyone about what was going on; however, the driver who was with them at the primitive village, continued to complain about the chief's warning. He told the other driver repeatedly, "I am going to leave this place' these men are crazy! I cannot sleep at night! I cannot eat! This is bad, very bad!"

Later on during dinner, Ramon whispered to Jerry, "The driver is complaining. He is trying to convince the other one to leave us here and drive away!"

Jerry set his dinner plate down and walked over to John to fill him in on the conversation he had with Ramon. It was decided to let the driver leave. They agreed that one van was enough to complete the job; besides, everyone was tired of the driver complaining. He continued to tell anyone who would listen that the men in the primitive tribe were going to kill them all in their sleep! They did not worry about the driver telling anyone what they were doing simply because he never came to the dig site or showed any interest in the project. At least in this case, they had used their heads and kept the two men away from the digging and never discussed what was going on while the two were around them in camp.

Each day John would have the remaining man drive to and from the main road to within three miles of the primitive village to insure that no one was watching. Mila was stationed near the main road and was told to inform the group if she saw anything suspicious.

Finally, after three days of constant digging, the group exposed the hard ground into the mountain. As suspected, the tunnel had been caved in on purpose. The timbers were shattered due to some kind of a blast, probably dynamite.

"How far inside do you think we will have to go before we can open the tunnel?" John asked Charlie.

"From what I can see, we will be able to get inside by the end of the week," Charlie answered.

Gary could not get the miners off his mind. He thought; what were those other men doing at the table with the old van driver? Was there something going on? He walked over to the van driver and Mila and asked, "Have either of you seen any suspicious people around the main road during the last couple of days?"

Mila knew immediately what was bothering Gary but acted as though she was innocent. "No, Mr. Gary, no one has been near the road" she answered.

"How about you?" Gary asked the driver.

He answered, "Nothing, sir. I have seen no one except the people who are here."

"Well, keep watching. Sooner or later someone is going to become curious and decide to check us out."

By the fifth day of digging the men had opened up the tunnel and were removing broken timbers, replacing them with new support.

"Wait, I think I see an opening," Jerry said. "Give me a flashlight; I want to take a look."

"Be careful," Charlie yelled as Jerry forced himself into the small opening. "You don't want the tunnel to cave in on you! We don't want to get anybody killed or lose what we have gained."

Jerry tried to force his body through the small opening. Charlie grew concerned and said, "Back off! We have plenty of time, Jerry! Besides, the hole is too small for you."

Ramon spoke up. "Let me try! I am much smaller than Mr. Jerry; I am sure I can crawl through the opening."

Everyone turned and looked at Ramon. John grinned, "Yes, I suppose you deserve the first look. Anyway, we wouldn't be here if it wasn't for you, Ramon."

He gave Ramon a flashlight, and Ramon began crawling though the small opening. Finally he was able to move on his hands and knees. Eventually the tunnel opened up and the rock was very strong overhead. There was no need for timber supports; the tunnel was clear. Ramon stood up and looked behind him. It was not far to the opening, but he was afraid to be alone inside the tunnel. He had been in many tunnels near his home, but this was different; he was not used to being inside a tunnel alone he thought about returning to the opening but decided to continue on.

"Can you see anything?" John called after him.

"The tunnel is much better now, Mr. John. I can stand up and walk."

"Be careful, Ramon, we don't want to lose you!"

Ramon continued down the tunnel for another fifty feet until it made a sharp turn to the right. He pointed his flashlight directly ahead of him. What he saw made him catch his breath. The tunnel opened up into a large room. Ramon saw what at first looked like old boxes stacked one on top of the other, but as he approached the piles, he realized it was not boxes, but stacks of gold bars! The room was filled with bars stacked side by side! There must have been a hundred rows of gold, and the stacks stood almost to ceiling of the cave! There were other items lying around the cave: bags of coins, picture frames in boxes, some stacked on makeshift shelves.

"Ramon, what are you doing? Can you see anything?" Charlie hollered.

Ramon backed away from the gold bars. He could not believe what he was seeing. Grandfather was right—he was rich! Tears began to run down his face; he still could not believe it. He could not imagine the amount of riches in front of him! He began to back away from the gold; however, he was not paying attention. He stumbled and fell, losing the flashlight.

"Damn it, Ramon," John yelled, "Are you all right?"

Ramon got to his feet. At first he was terrified because he could not see, but he noticed the flashlight lying on the ground in front of him and reached for it. As he picked it up, he let out a terrified scream. The light was shining on the face of a skeleton, its jaw wide open, its arms stretched out on each side of its body. There was a hole in the middle of the scull. Ramon dropped the flashlight again and began to run. He ran directly into the cave wall and was knocked down. He lay there for a few minutes, confused not knowing what to do. He found the flashlight again, got to his feet, and ran for the opening he couldn't catch his breath.

Jerry was the first to see the light coming and could tell Ramon was running, tripping as he went. "Slow down, Ramon, you'll hurt yourself!"

Ramon climbed up the loose dirt into the opening and handed the flashlight to Jerry. The three men could see that Ramon was terrified.

"Well, kid, what did you find in there?" asked Charlie.

For a long time Ramon stood there silently then he finally said, "A dead man is in there!"

"What?" Jerry asked.

"A dead man with a hole in his head is in there, Mr. Jerry!" Ramon responded.

"Settle down, son; a dead man can't hurt you," John said.

"Tell us, is the gold in there, did you find it?" Jerry asked excitedly. Now all three men were looking intently at Ramon, all of them with the same thought: Did he find the gold, or was this just another wild goose chase?

Ramon looked at the men and said, "We are very, very rich. There is much gold inside."

There was a moment of silence while everyone took in what the boy had said. "How much is there, kid?" Charlie asked.

"The room is filled to the top with much gold! Also there are other treasures piled against the walls!" Ramon responded.

Jerry and Charlie began to dance around, holding each other, and John stood next to Ramon with a huge grin on his face. He looked down at the young man and said, "Thanks, kid! You know, you're all right!"

Ramon smiled at John for he knew at that moment that this man would not cheat him; he was his friend, and that made Ramon feel good inside!

"Let's go tell Mila and Gary what we have!" John said.

It was a wild run back to camp, all four of the men deep in their own thoughts. Jerry was thinking, Gold, good ole mighty gold! John was thinking of his dad, "Well, it's not conventional mining, Dad, but boy, are we rich! Charlie was laughing; every other step he would stop and laugh out loud. Ramon was in shock. His thoughts raced back to his grandfather and one of the last things the old man said to him, "The gold is a curse my grandson it is no good but you must make the decision." Ramon looked around at the men jumping around and at Charlie laughing, he thought,

"Please grandfather do not make this a curse, please!" Ramon was not happy, "why; he thought, why I am not happy?"

Once they reached camp John, although interrupted a couple dozen times by Charlie and Jerry, finally told Gary and Mila what they had found. Gary stood there in disbelief.

"Do you mean it is really there?" he asked. "I never would have thought—"

"Yes, it's there! We are rich, my friend! All we have to do is go in and get it!" Charlie hollered.

Confusion crossed Gary's face as he began to realize that he had never really believed until this moment that the gold was real. What had he done? He had betrayed the others! He could not deal with the situation and walked away in bewilderment.

Meanwhile the others were shaking hands and dancing around. The only person who noticed Gary was Mila; she knew then that he had done something bad with the men at the restaurant. There was going to be trouble, but she could not decide what to do! If she said something to the others, would they believe her, or would they believe Mr. Gary? Would they be upset with her for waiting too long to tell them what she'd seen? What will happen now? She thought.

"Okay, let's settle down; we still have a lot of work to do, guys. I know we won't get any rest until we see the gold, so let's get back in there and open the tunnel the rest of the way," John announced. He led the men back to the tunnel, and they began cleaning the remaining dirt and rock from the small opening. Gary was in a trance and was more in the way than helping, but again everyone was too busy and paid little attention to him.

"I can't go any more, John," Jerry confessed.

"Yeah, I've had it too," said Charlie.

"Okay, let's call it a day. It looks like a couple of hours are left, so let's leave it for tomorrow," John answered.

After dinner, everyone relaxed next to the fire and started talking about what they wanted to do with their share of the gold. John started with Charlie, "You first, Charlie."

"I haven't thought about it much, John—I've been concentrating on finding it and never really asked myself what I would do with the gold if we found it. I suppose I will do a little traveling at first and then decide from there. I really don't care too much about being rich—just rich enough to be comfortable, I guess."

John looked at Jerry. "Jerry?"

"Well, John, I have been a risk taker all my life, always looking for the big deal. I wanted to be recognized as a big dealmaker, one of the big boys, but you know something—I never, in a hundred years, expected to get there. I'm like Charlie; I'm going to have to take some time and find out what I really want to do. It's like trying to win the NBA championship your entire career, and once you have done it, you ask yourself, what's next?"

Gary got to his feet and walked away from the fire, turned and looked back at the group, started to say something but stopped, then continued walking with his hands in his pockets and his head down. John looked at the others and shrugged his shoulders in confusion. "Well then, Ramon, it looks like you are next."

"How much money is there, Mr. John?"

"Ramon, there is enough money to buy the Philippine Islands if you want!"

Ramon's eyes widened. "Oh, I do not want to buy my country," he exclaimed, and everyone sitting around the fireside laughed. "All I want is enough gold so I can go back to my village and help my people. I am ashamed that I told them a lie and want things to be the way they were before."

"John?" Charlie asked.

John paused for a moment and finally said, "My old man and I didn't have much of a chance to get to know each other, you know what I mean? I spent most of my youth with my mother and didn't do much with him until I was about twenty. One of the things that I respected about him was his hard work. He was honest and never cheated anyone out of anything; but he was tough! The one thing he loved most, other than my mom, was his company. He broke his back to build it; it was the one thing he gave to me before his death, and he asked me to take care of it. Until now I haven't done much of a job of it, so when this is all over I am going to make the business a success for him." John paused. "I don't know about the rest of you, but this has been a big day and I am tired, so let's try to get some sleep."

"Wait a minute," Charlie said, "what about Mila?"

"Yes," Jerry agreed, "what about Mila?"

Mila was caught off guard and wasn't able to speak until John said to her, "Mila, you are part of this crew and deserve your equal share of the gold. What are you going do with it, young lady?"

Mila stood, looking down at her feet and then at the men sitting next to the fire. Her emotions were on edge—she never dreamed she would get any of the gold. "Will I really get some of the gold?" she asked in a quavering voice.

"Of course," John replied, "did you help us find it?"

"Oh, Mr. John, I do not know how to thank you! I do not have any idea what I will do if you give me gold!"

Everyone laughed then stood up from the fire; it was time to go to bed. Even if they could not sleep, tomorrow would be a big day for all of them. Mila was the last to leave the fire, the light of the flames flickering onto the tears of joy glistening down her cheeks.

The next morning everyone was up at dawn and quickly finishing breakfast. There was no question what was on their minds! "You know something," Jerry said, "I was thinking last night. I wouldn't be a bit surprised that the Japanese might have left some kind of trap for anyone who got near the gold. What do the rest of you think?"

"It's a possibility," said Charlie, "they would probably do something, that's for sure, but after fifty years would it still be there or even work, with this much time passing?"

John looked at the group and said, "That's a valid point. Let's be damn careful when we get in there. In fact, don't anyone do anything unless we all agree and are satisfied that it is okay."

By eight-thirty they had opened the tunnel and were walking toward the gold hidden inside the cave. John was in the lead, Jerry next, then Charlie, and finally Gary. Ramon was lagging behind—he still remembered the corpse and was in no hurry to see him again! As they approached the sharp turn in the tunnel, John reminded everyone to take it slow and easy and not to make any mistakes.

There it was! It was unbelievable! The gold, just as Ramon had said, was stacked almost to the ceiling. Along the walls were the shelves with different items stored on them. The group didn't spend much time looking at the shelves; they were all staring at the gold!

"Did you bring the portable flood light?" Jerry asked.

"Yes," John answered, "its right here. Let me fire it up and get some more light."

It took John a couple of minutes to get the lamp running full, but after he turned it up the entire cave was illuminated. Portions of the tunnel were also lit, exposing even more of the storage area. It was apparent, once the floodlight was working, that the cave was much larger than everyone had thought. It was laid out in several chambers. The first held the gold, the second held silver, and the third was partially sealed; however, after clearing away some debris, the group discovered more crates stacked along the walls, one on top of the other. It was amazing how little damage the crates had suffered after over sixty years being stored inside the cave! The Japanese had picked the right place to store the crated treasure; it was dry and the constant temperature had kept the crates from rotting.

"Open one of the crates," Jerry suggested.

"No, not yet!" John hollered. "Remember what we said—check out the place for traps first!"

Just as John finished speaking, a large boulder fell from the ceiling, striking Gary on the shoulder. Dust filled the room, making it impossible to see.

"Is everyone all right?" John shouted. "Don't anyone move until we can see what the hell happened!"

After a few minutes the dust began to clear enough to see inside the cave again. The ceiling was covered with timbers; one of the corner timbers had broken loose and released the boulder that hit Gary, along with some loose rock and debris.

"What the hell is all that timber doing above us, Charlie?" Jerry asked.

"What do you say if first we find out if Gary is okay?" Charlie answered.

Gary was sitting up, rubbing his shoulder. He looked up at the rest of the group and said, "I'm fine; just shook me up a little."

Charlie studied the timbers above the cave where the gold was stored. The timbers were supported with ropes that were drawn tight and tied off along the walls of the cave, but there was more. The ropes appeared to be buried under the floor and under the stacked gold.

"No one and I mean no one move!" Charlie exclaimed. "I think we have found our first trap. John. It looks to me that the Japanese have rigged the floor the gold is sitting on to the timbers above, using these ropes. If you remove the gold or anything else inside the cave, the ropes will take slack and release all the timbers and material above the cave down on top of us."

John looked at everyone and said, "Everybody out! Don't make any sudden moves or touch anything, understand? Just get the hell out of here! Charlie, you stay here with me. We'll take a closer look at what other surprises they have left for us."

While everyone else returned to the clearing outside the tunnel, John and Charlie spent the next two hours looking over the cave for what they were sure were other traps. John called Charlie over to the wall behind the gold bars.

"Look here, Charlie—there are timbers bracing the back wall, what do you think?"

"I don't know; it's hard to see from here. Let me move a couple of rows of gold." Charlie began moving the gold bars, being careful not to disturb the ropes buried under the floor. As he removed the gold bars from the timbers' supporting wall, the timbers loosened, causing the wall to move.

John screamed, "Stop!"

"What's the matter, John?"

"Move back away from the gold, Charlie! Be careful, but get back!"

Sweat was running down both men's faces. "What did you see, John?"

"Take a look!" John carefully started scraping the walls around the timbers, exposing a fine line as he continued. "See here, Charlie—the timbers braced against the gold is holding the walls in place, and the gold is holding the timbers in place. I would bet that there is water or fine sand behind the wall. If we remove the gold, the timber braces will give way, and the whole place will be flooded!"

"It's time to get the hell out of here and think this over, John. You can bet these aren't the only traps in here!"

The two men left the cave and returned to the clearing. John explained to everyone what they had discovered.

"They have set traps in the ceiling and the walls. I am sure there are others we didn't find." Everyone stood looking at each other, wondering what was coming next. Ramon was standing back from the group and said, "The floor." They all turned and looked at him.

"The floor?" Charlie said.

"Yes, Ramon is right. I guess it makes sense," Gary answered. "That would cover all the angles."

"Then we had better go back in there and see what we can find." John responded.

John and Charlie started back toward the tunnel.

"Wait just a minute," Jerry spoke up. "You two took the last risk. Gary and I will go in this time."

"No, Charlie is the mining engineer, and he is the one that needs to be in there!" John replied.

"Then the three of us will go in, and you can stay with Mila and Ramon, John, but we are going in and that's final!" Jerry headed for the tunnel entrance.

John knew he had better let it go; he realized that everyone wanted to do his or her part in the project. Gary stood near the tunnel entrance but didn't volunteer for the dangerous job. After all, he thought, they have been playing games with me so let them take the risk. This is the time I get even with all of them. He said, "It's all right, Jerry. I will stay with Mila and Ramon. The rest of you can go back inside."

John, Charlie, and Jerry entered the cave and began carefully examining the floor and the rest of the cave. As Charlie dug down into the soft dirt under the floor the gold was stacked on, he discovered a second floor buried eighteen inches below the first.

"Wait guys—I think I have something here," he said. Charlie cautiously removed the dirt from on top of the second floor. After he had cleared a space of about four feet by four feet, he pried up one of the boards from the second floor. Underneath was a black hole.

"Give me the flashlight, Jerry," he said.

Jerry handed him the flashlight. Charlie pointed the beam into the darkness. "I can't see the bottom; I will drop a rock and see how far it goes." Charlie picked up a rock and dropped it through the hole in the floor. After a few seconds, the rock struck something and continued falling farther down into the hole. Charlie climbed to his feet and said, "It hit something close, but I will need another light to see what is going on."

Gary handed Charlie another light.

"Gary, hand me the flood lamp; it will do a better job," he said. Charlie lowered himself back onto his knees and dropped the flood lamp into the hole below the floor, using the cord to extend it as far as he could. "Shit!" he exclaimed. "You won't believe this!"

"What?" Jerry asked. Charlie answered, "We need to go outside; we can talk better about this in the daylight."

The men exited the tunnel. Gary, Mila, and Ramon were sitting near the tunnel and stood to their feet as they emerged. "Well?" Gary asked.

"The kid was right, Gary—we have a big problem below the floor."

"What do you mean Charlie?" Gary asked.

"The bastards have rigged the floor to cave in if the gold is removed, that's what!" Charlie answered. "The sides of the floor have been built so the weight of the gold will hold the floor in place. If you remove too much gold, the dirt will begin to loosen and fall into the pit. If that happens, the entire floor will collapse—sending the gold and anyone in there down a hundred feet to the bottom of the pit! Let me show you what I mean."

Charlie took a stick and began drawing a print on the ground. "The dirt is packed in around the floor like this, see? Now, as long as there is weight on top of the dirt, the boards of the floor will stay in place and hold up, but if we start moving the gold from the floor, the dirt will loosen under the floor, and the entire thing turns loose, see what I mean?"

It was now clear to everyone what he was talking about. If the weight was removed from the floor, the supporting dirt holding the boards in place would loosen and everything would end up a hundred feet below the cave covered in debris.

Charlie said, "The floor goes, then the ceiling turns loose, and finally the wall give way, and good night, Irene! This is going to take some time, people. We have to secure the entire area before we start taking out any of the gold."

John asked, "How long do you think, Charlie?"

I guess John," he hesitated for a minute and then said, "At least a week but right now that's a guess." "Okay then, the rest of us will do some clean-up around the camp and try to get some rest. We will talk about this after Charlie has had time to think."

Charlie sat down near the entrance to the tunnel and scratched his head, thinking, *this is going to be a tough one!*

CHAPTER 20

Muslims

Omar Mohammed Abdul was twenty-eight years old, the only son of a Muslim family. He was born on the far southern Philippine island of Jolo. His father was a quiet man who practiced his religion and expected his family to honor the Koran. He raised his son to be respectful to others and to honor his religious faith. In 1984 at twenty years of age, Omar left his family and traveled to the Middle East state of Jordan to continue his education in the beliefs of Mohammed.

While in Jordan, he became involved in a radical group known as the Freedom Fighters against Muslim Oppression. Although Omar focused on religious beliefs, he also attended terrorist training camps; he was fascinated with the energy of the young rebels. They were fierce fighters, feared throughout Jordan. After two years he returned to the Philippines and his family, where his father noticed a change in Omar. He was no longer the quiet son who respected his father and his family but a militant who constantly complained about the treatment of Muslims by the Christian leadership of the Philippines. He joined radical groups that planned ways to overthrow the government in southern Mindanao. One group, Abu Sayyaf, was a small offshoot of the MILF (Muslim Islamic Liberation Front) that wanted to secede from the Philippine government and form their own separate Muslim government and nation in southern Mindanao.

Omar was involved in many plots, involving ambushes of government troops and kidnapping for ransom Chinese Filipinos. At first the kidnappings were conducted to raise money for the cause of Muslim religious freedom in the country; however, as time went on, the kidnappings became a way of attaining money for the Muslim war Lords, and very little was used for the Muslim cause in Mindanao.

In the beginning, Omar was pleased with his role as a Muslim freedom fighter and advanced in rank and respect within the radical group. As time passed, however, he became disenchanted with the group as they became more interested in kidnapping and ransom and less interested in the cause of Mohammed. Omar complained to the leaders of the group and asked why they only were interested in the money, why were we abandoning the war against the infidels? His leaders would say, "You are a young man, Omar, and do not understand the long-range plan of the group, so do as you are told!"

Finally, after two years in the bandit group, Omar had had enough. He decided to leave the southern island of Jolo and seek out others who felt as he. Omar picked up his belongings and left for General Santos City where, he had heard, there were men that believed in fighting the Christian invaders to achieve their goals as free Muslims.

After arriving at General Santos City, Omar soon realized that these Muslims were not as he expected. Most had families and were not interested in an independent Muslim state but wanted to live in peace with their Christian counterparts. Omar continued to encourage them to fight for their independence, however, with little success. Finally after six months, Omar left General Santos City and traveled to Davao.

While in Davao, living within the Muslim community, he met another Muslim terrorist, Allah Mustafa, who was part of a new group of radical Muslims called the Abu Sayyaf. During one of their raids against government troops, six of the Muslim bandits were captured, while Omar and Allah escaped. The government troops executed the six men they had captured. The men were taken into a village square and shot; their bodies were hung in the square on display to warn others what would happen if any Muslim defied the government of the Philippines.

Although Omar swore revenge, Allah decided that this was not what he wanted and returned to his family in southern Mindanao. Omar became the leader of the group of radical Muslims. He was now committed to drive the Christians from his homeland! Quickly their terrorist activities were well known throughout Mindanao; everyone began to fear Omar and his men! He recruited the most hated radicals in Muslim society. Most of them were well known for their terrorist activities and their vicious treatment of innocent Filipinos. The terrorizing and torture of innocent men and women became well known throughout Mindanao.

Although Omar claimed to be part of the MILF group of Muslims, in fact, he was a bandit. Little of his time was spent advancing the cause of the Muslim faith in the Philippines, he too had changed! No more was the young man dedicated to create a Muslim state. He had become what he had considered in the past to be a disgrace, a rebel bandit kidnapping and extorting his fellow Filipinos. The true Muslim communities within the Philippines did not consider Omar and his men part of the Muslim enclave and did not approve of their terrorist activities.

Two of his most hated subordinates were living in the small fishing village when the Americans had arrived from Davao! The two now returned from the fishing village and told Omar about the Americans looking for gold. At first he was not interested in the Americans, but as the week went by he began to reconsider. He thought, Why not kidnap these infidels? We will show everyone that our group does not fear anyone; after all the Americans had supported the Philippine government, hadn't they? The American government would pay a very high ransom for their people! Yes, this is what we will do—we will kidnap the Americans!

He called the two men who had told him about the Americans and said, "Have all of our lieutenants report to me immediately!"

CHAPTER 21

Deceit!

"I think I've got it, John!" Charlie exclaimed.

"Well, let's hear what you have, my friend," John replied.

"I have planned it step by step, starting with the timbers overhead; it seems to be the easiest one to take care of. Then I worked on the water-seal problem, but the toughest one was the floor; however, I think I have it. We can use new rope and that will support the gold against the walls; at the same time it will support the floors. The new ropes will help hold the stacked gold. The second move will be to place long cross-poles under the second floor. If the loose dirt does fall, the poles will support the floor holding the gold. We can also use long timbers to support the walls. We can run them from wall to wall. This will eliminate the need for the gold in holding back the false walls; it will be difficult but it's do-able."

Charlie continued, "The floor was the difficult one. We are going to have to replace the same amount of weight onto the floor as we remove by taking the gold bars. I think heavy rock will do; we need just enough weight to hold the floor in place. If we put some heavy timbers or rock on top of the floor as we remove the gold, we should be okay. If that doesn't work, we will have to install a second floor under the existing one to hold if the old floor gives way. Either way we can handle the floor problem. What do you think?"

John looked at the rest of the group and said, "What do the rest of you think?"

Gary spoke first. "Whatever is the quickest way to get it done; remember, the longer we are here, the more chance someone will find out what we are up too."

Jerry spoke second. "I realize we need to get done in a hurry, but remember, we didn't come here to kill anyone but if we watch our asses we can make this work—so I am willing to give a try."

"Okay then, let's get started," John replied. "We will do it safe, and we will do it as fast as possible. Everyone agree?"

"I am telling you, the longer we take, the more chance we will be discovered. Can't we just watch what we are doing and start removing the gold?" Gary asked.

"No," Charlie replied, "removing the gold without taking care of the traps will end up killing someone, and I won't be involved it that!"

Jerry looked at Gary and asked, "What's your problem Gary? Ever since we set up camp here, you have been antsy. Why don't you tell us what is going on with you?"

"Nothing, I just am concerned with the primitive tribe. You never know when they might decide to check up on us."

"Bullshit," Jerry responded. "Those people will never come down this far. They haven't moved from their village or been seen in the port city in years. That's not the problem, so come clean, Gary—and I mean now!"

John looked at Gary and said, "Gary, if there is something that needs to be said, you had better say it now. I have backed you from the beginning, but I also believe you are not telling us everything."

Charlie laughed and said, "Come on, Gary, we all know you have been hiding something, so let's have it. I've been ready to run you off for a couple of weeks but John insisted that we keep you here. So talk to us, friend—before I kick it out of you!"

"All right, all right, it isn't a big deal! I figured we might need some help if we found the gold, so I had some of the miners from Ramon's village meet me at the fishing village last week. Okay, now you know! I met them and told them to wait until I had something. If we found the gold, I was going to have them help us get it out."

"You lying SOB!" Charlie grabbed Gary by the collar. "You were planning to take the gold from the rest of us!"

"No, I was only going to have them help get it out of the tunnel!"

Before anyone could stop him, Jerry tackled Gary from behind, knocking him to the ground. "You dirty SOB! I am going to break your neck!"

Charlie pulled Jerry off Gary and, laughing again, he said, "Careful, my friend; we need to find out what his plan was before we break his neck!"

Mila had been watching and listening to the men. Finally she could not help but tell them what she knew. "Stop!" she screamed. Everyone turned, startled, and looked at her. She was shaking out of control.

"Easy, Mila," John said, and took her into his arms. "We are not going to break his neck—just squeeze it a little."

But she was in no mode for jokes and said in a frantic voice, "They are bad men, very bad men!"

"Tell us what you mean by 'bad men,'" Jerry said.

"The men that Mr. Gary met with in the restaurant are very bad!"

Gary exclaimed, "No, they are not, Mila! Why would you say that? These men are from Ramon's village."

She answered, "Not the men from the village, Mr. Gary; the other men with the van driver. The ones I saw you talking with at the table."

Gary froze; he had forgotten about the strangers who were sitting with the miners at the table when he had arrived at the restaurant. "No, those men have nothing to do with the miners; they only met them at the restaurant—they are fishermen from the village!" Gary exclaimed.

"No!" Mila yelled. "They are MILF! Abu Sayyaf!"

Ramon was paralyzed; he could not move or speak, the words racing through his head. MILF! Abu Sayyaf!

It took several minutes for Mila to explain what MILF meant and what they were capable of doing. The entire group, including Gary, stood in total silence. Finally, Ramon was able to move. He stepped forward and said, "If this is so, Mr. John, we are in terrible danger! The MILF are very bad—they will kidnap you Americans and kill us Filipinos! The Abu Sayyaf are the most feared sect of the Muslim world they will kill and slaughter men, women and children they have no respect for anyone!"

John turned toward Gary. "Nice, Gary, very nice!" John looked into Gary's eyes and said, "Do you realize what you have done? These maniacs could show up any time, take the gold, and kill us all, you fool!"

Charlie interrupted John, "I think we had better get the hell out of here now! If these crazy bastards decide to come after us, we are done. Remember, there is only one road out of here!"

John asked Gary, "When are you supposed to meet these guys?"

Gary was shaken, and his voice quivered. "In a couple of days, I'm supposed to return to the fishing village and meet with them."

"So we still have a couple of days?" John continued.

"Yes, I guess so," Gary answered. He started to say something more but the look on Johns face was enough Gary was a complete wreck.

John looked at the rest of the group and said, "I know I was the first one to say let's get the hell out of here after we had the run-in with the primitive villagers, but that was before we found the gold. I will be dammed if we are this close and are just going to walk away!"

The others looked at John in dismay. "Well then, what is your plan?" Charlie asked.

"We are going to work our asses off for two days and retrieve as much of the gold as we can then get the hell out of here. I am sure Gary can stall them a couple more days. By that time we can have part of the gold loaded and be gone! Charlie, I want you to rig the tunnel to cave in quickly if need be. Set up some kind of system we can trip that will cave it in."

"That's no problem, John; it's ready to go now—all I have to do is set it up!"

For the next couple of days the group worked around the clock. They were able to support the cave and stabilize the floor holding the gold and planned to move the gold by Saturday, the third day since starting the work.

"Okay, Gary," said John, "it's time for you to head for the port city. We will finish up here and be ready to start loading the gold when you get back. But make sure you stall them a couple more days, understand?" John walked away from Gary in disgust.

"What if I can't hold them off, John?" Gary yelled after him.

"You had better—or I will put a bullet between your lying eyes, you son of a bitch!"

Gary thought, this is bad, real bad. John has never talked to me like that.

John never turned around to face Gary; he couldn't stand to look at him anymore! Everyone else in the camp stood silently as Gary tuned and headed for the truck.

Gary was sick to his stomach by time he arrived at the restaurant. He had asked Mila to go with him but she refused; she was afraid Gary might do something to her for telling what she had seen. John finally convinced Ramon to go with Gary. He explained to Ramon that he must go, but not go inside the restaurant; he would have to watch from the window. Also, the two men must find out who were the men with the miners and make sure if they were MILF. Ramon realized he had no choice. He knew that Mr. Gary could not be trusted, so he agreed to accompany him to the fishing village.

Ramon was let out of the van before they entered the village, as Gary and the driver continued on to the restaurant. He walked behind the buildings, trying to stay out of sight. Gary waited until he saw Ramon near the café before he entered. As he walked in, he immediately spotted the miners sitting at the corner table near the bar. Next to them stood the old van driver and, as expected, there were several more men in the group. Gary thought bad, real bad; in fact, he contemplated turning around and leaving! He took a second look and recognized two of the men who had walked away from the table the last time he was here. He glanced at Ramon near the window and noticed him motioning him to return outside. Gary was confused but decided he had better see what Ramon was up to. As he approached Ramon near the open window, Ramon whispered to him, "We must leave now." Ramon was visibly shaken. "This is very bad!" he said as he ran from the restaurant. Gary called to the van driver then climbed into the van and they began driving from the fishing village; on the outskirts of the village they picked up Ramon.

"What did you see, Ramon?" Gary asked.

"Omar," he responded.

"Who is Omar?" Gary asked.

"He has been to our village. He is very bad! They are killers of innocent people; our village pays him pesos to not harm us. All Filipinos fear Omar and his men; they are very bad—they are the Abu Sayyaf Mila spoke of!"

The van returned to the campsite and Gary told the group what they had seen. Mila began to cry when Ramon told them about Omar and Abu Sayyaf. John looked at the group and said, "We'll send Mila and the driver down to the entrance to the road. The rest of us will start getting ready to get the hell out of here. We are going to have to leave, and I mean now! Jerry, just in case we can't drive out of here I want you to set up some packs.

We might need to walk out to avoid getting caught in the van. Charlie, you had better close the tunnel, and do it now!"

John sent Ramon with the driver down the road. Mila was worthless; she stood wringing her hands and crying. Jerry had just completed packing the pack sacks when Charlie walked over to John and said, "It's ready anytime you are, John. All we have to do is tie the van to the ropes, pull the timber out, and down comes the tunnel."

At that moment the van came driving back into the camp, making an abrupt stop, as the driver and Ramon jumped out. Ramon yelled, "They are coming!"

"Charlie, you got the guns?" John asked.

"Yeah John, let's get moving!"

How many are there, Ramon?" Jerry asked.

"Many of them Mr. John I seen two truckloads!"

"Did they see you, Ramon?" Charlie asked.

"I do not think so, Mr. Charlie, but I am not sure!"

Charlie immediately hooked the van to the tunnel ropes and had the driver pull ahead. The van struggled against the weight of the tunnel timbers, but all of a sudden the timbers broke free, and the tunnel collapsed in a cloud of dust.

CHAPTER 22

The Chase

Everyone but Mila had a backpack. She was still in a state of shock and would be of little use to the group. John called everyone together.

"We will head for the primitive village. When we get within a couple of miles of the village, we will turn, circle around it, and return to the main road toward the fishing village. Does anyone have any questions or other ideas?"

"Sounds good to me, John," Jerry replied. "We sure in hell can't go directly back toward the main road with bandits on their way here!"

Gary led the group, walking up the road toward the primitive village. His pace was much too fast for the others, and John had to stop him, saying, "Listen, Gary, this is going to take some time. We need to pace ourselves and try to not leave a trail for them to follow, so slow down!"

Omar had not missed Gary standing at the door. The minute Gary turned and left, Omar realized his plan had a problem. He turned to the others and said, "No more talk; we go!" One of the miners said, "Wait, we cannot go; we have not planned for this!" Omar turned and faced the miner, who immediately jumped to his feet and started running for the door. Omar and the other men followed.

After leaving the restaurant, Omar directed the first truck to take the lead and drive toward the camp. "Once you have seen the camp, return to me. Do not enter the camp, understand? Report back to me!" The driver–bandit of the first truck drove slowly up the road. As he turned a corner, he could see the campsite and immediately stopped. One of the lieutenants in back of the truck directed three men to sneak up on the camp and see what was happening. After a few minutes they returned and reported, "The camp is empty; there is no one there." The lieutenant thought for a minute then instructed them to return to the camp and wait for instructions.

"You will wait inside the camp until I return with Omar. The rest of you get into the truck. We will return and tell our leader what we have found."

The first truck returned to the site where Omar was waiting. The lieutenant climbed out of the truck and approached Omar. "Commander," the lieutenant said, "there is no one at the camp. I have sent two of my men into the camp to secure it and wait for your arrival."

"What did I tell you?" Omar said to the lieutenant. "Did I not tell you to return to me? I did not give you instructions to go inside their camp!" With that, he removed his pistol and struck the man across the face. "Now they know we are here, you fool!"

Omar directed the two trucks to head for the campsite. "There is no chance for surprise now. Advance!" he shouted to the others. The two trucks sped toward the camp, with the soldiers hanging on for dear life! As they approached the camp, the trucks came to an abrupt stop. The men jumped from the trucks and ran toward the campsite with their guns at ready.

"Search the entire area," Omar commanded. The solders spread out and began searching around the immediate campsite as well as along the road. After fifteen minutes of searching one of the men hollered, "Commander, I have found something!" Omar immediately headed in the direction of the soldier. As he broke through the jungle he entered a clearing where it appeared the Americans had been working. Dust still filled the air where the tunnel entrance had been caved in; the van was still hooked to the ropes that were tied to the tunnel timbers.

Omar thought, what is this? They have done something which I do not understand. He paused and said out loud, "Bring one of the miners to me!"

The miner who had been the spokesman was brought to Omar, "What is this, villager?" Omar asked.

"They have been digging here, sir," the miner answered.

"I can see that, you idiot! What were they digging for?" Omar demanded.

"The fools believe that there is hidden gold in the mountain, but there is no gold," the miner answered.

"Why would they cave in the tunnel if there was no gold?" Omar asked again.

"If there were any gold in the mountain, they would have stayed and fought for it, Commander, but they ran so there cannot be any gold." However, the miner, after seeing the tunnel entrance thought, why did the Americans cave in the tunnel? Is there gold inside? He knew he must not tell Omar what he was thinking. If Omar knew, he would make them dig out the tunnel, and this would be very difficult and dangerous— especially with only two of them to do the work.

"How long would it take to clear the tunnel?" Omar asked.

The miner looked at the tunnel entrance for a few minutes and said, "Many days; the entire entrance is covered."

Omar had to decide what to do next. He stood looking at the tunnel, realizing that he knew nothing about mining and had to trust the miners to open the tunnel. "You miners will stay here and dig the tunnel out. I will leave four of my men to help." The lead miner started to protest, but thought better of it; he was convinced if he and his friend did not do exactly as Omar demanded, they would not live long. He knew of Omar and his men's reputations and was not going to question his directive. He thought, we must do as Omar tells us or die! I am afraid my companion was right; we should not have joined these bandits!

"We have to stop for a while, John," Charlie said. "The girl can't take much more."

"Stop?" Gary said. "Are you crazy? Leave her! She is going to get us all caught if we stop now!"

Charlie moved toward Gary. "Wait," John said, "it's my turn!" John hit Gary with such force that he knocked Gary's front teeth out. He straddled Gary's prone body and drew back his fist! It took both Charlie and Jerry to pull John off. Charlie added, "It's not the time John we need every minute to get the hell out of here." The muscle in John's arms relaxed; the two men holding him turned him lose. John looked down at Gary and said, "If we ever get out of this, I swear I will put you in the hospital!" After walking away Charlie leaned over and whispered to Gary, "Don't worry kid I won't let John do that to ya." Gary started to say something but Charlie raised his hand and stopped him. He said. "Because I'm gona do it!"

"John," Jerry said, "I think we are a couple of miles from the primitive village. We had better cut back now; no sense in taking any risk and getting too close."

"Yeah, you are right, Jerry. Why don't you take the lead?"

Gary got to his feet and wiped his mouth. He thought, first chance, first chance! He knew now that not only was his life in danger from the bandits but from his own people!

The group turned off the road and entered the jungle underbrush next to the road. The walking became very difficult, every inch of jungle had to be cut away in order to move forward. The men traded taking the lead slashing the jungle underbrush with the machete.

"Wait, John," Charlie hollered, "don't cut away too much jungle—it will make it too easy for them to follow. Leave some vines in place. We will just have to fight our way through until we can cover up which way we are going."

"I agree, Charlie, but we can't spend too much time in one place. These guys are pros and will find our trail no matter what we do. I think the best thing to do is move, and move fast!"

"I guess you are right, John. We can't fool this bunch. If what Ramon tells us is true, they are damn good at this, and trying to cover our trail is probably a waste of our time," Charlie answered.

The bandits had been at the camp for over an hour. Omar knew he must begin searching for the Americans if he planned to catch up with them before nightfall. "We will be back tomorrow, and I will expect the tunnel to be open. If it is not, I will make sure you never return to your village!"

"But Commander, the tunnel is caved in; we cannot do this by tomorrow!"

Omar smiled at the miners and said, "It is amazing what you can do when your lives depends on it!" One of his lieutenants returned to the clearing and said to Omar, "We have found their trail, Commander. They have headed in that direction," he pointed up the road toward the primitive village.

"Good!" Omar replied, "Send two scouts ahead. We will follow shortly."

The group had traveled another mile when they encountered a small stream. They immediately dropped to their knees and began to drink. All of them were drenched with sweat and began pouring water over their heads in an attempt to cool down.

Jerry was first to stand. He looked around to see where to cross the steam, suddenly, he froze! Upstream about fifty yards stood a young boy about ten years old. He was holding a spear of some kind and was watching the group drink from the stream.

"John," he said, "you had better take a look at this!"

John slowly stood up and looked up stream. The boy was still watching them drink.

"What now?" Jerry said to the others.

Gary wanted to tell them to kill the boy but he knew better. John motioned to the driver to step forward.

"Go talk to the boy. Tell him we are just hunting and are leaving now. Tell him we are not coming back. See what he says."

The driver walked slowly upstream until he was close to the boy. He began to speak in the primitive dialect. The rest watched and waited while the boy talked back to the driver while looking at the others downstream. The driver motioned to the group to wait and walked into the jungle with the boy.

"What is he doing?" Jerry asked, not speaking to anyone in particular. The group waited for a few minutes for the driver to reappear, but he did not.

"Shit!" Gary whispered, "He ran out on us!"

Charlie slowly walked toward the place the boy and driver had been standing. He disappeared out of sight for a minute and then stepped back into the stream. He motioned to the others and they walked to where Charlie was waiting. Once they got to the site Charlie said, "The SOB might be right, guys. There is no sign of them; we'd better get the hell out of here!"

"Move out! John commanded. "We probably are going to have two bunches after us within the next hour. The damn driver is going to screw us when he gets to the village; I just have a bad feeling about it!"

The group started across the stream. Charlie stopped and looked at John. "I've been thinking, John. If we follow the plan, we are going to get caught for sure."

"What do you mean, Charlie?"

"Well, remember these bastards are bandits, they do this for a living. They're going to figure out what we are up to the minute they find out that we left the road. The next thing they will discover is that we are circling around and heading back to the main road. John, they will cut us off!"

"Oh no!" Mila cried.

"He's right, John," Jerry added. "We had better come up with a better plan, or we have had it!"

Gary had made up his mind; the first chance he had, he was going on his own. He knew one man would have a better chance than a group, especially with a hysterical girl with them!

"Okay, I am open to suggestions," John said.

"Listen, if we cross the steam and backtrack, we can go upstream and go around the village. I know it's a dangerous idea, but it has to be better than the one we have." Charlie finished and waited for John to reply.

"Hey, it sounds good," John answered, "Let's give it a try."

The group crossed the stream and started into the jungle.

John asked Charlie, "How far into the jungle should we go, Charlie?"

"Well, we are running out of time, John. I would like to go about a mile, but we don't have the time, so about a half-mile is all we can do."

"Wait," Gary said. He now realized he might have a chance to separate from the group; this was a perfect opportunity! "I'm the cause of a lot of this trouble and it's time I do something for the rest of you. I tell you what, I will continue heading in the same direction for another half-mile. One person can cover a lot more ground than the group. Then I'll catch up with you—it might keep them off the rest of you for a while."

"What's the catch, Gary?" Jerry asked.

"What do you mean?" Gary replied.

"Well, let's face it; you haven't been exactly trustworthy, have you?"

"I know, but I need to do something to make up for what I have done. Please, guys—give me a chance! I'm sure I can slow their chase and give you some time to get into the jungle."

"We don't have the time to waste talking about it—let's let him do whatever, but we need to move now!" Charlie said in desperation.

Gary stood for a minute waiting for John to make a decision, realizing that his life might depend on what the decision was!

John thought of all the times he and Gary had been together, and thought that this might be the last time they would ever see each other. Maybe Gary was trying to help, but by now John doubted it. He said,

"Okay, Gary, get going. We'll head back to the stream. We'll meet you later tonight. If you can't find us, just keep heading back to the main road." He walked over and shook Gary's hand. Gary seemed surprised at first, but he took John's hand and said, "Good luck, John. I will see you tonight."

John's group continued into the jungle for another half mile and then decided it was time to turn back. John looked at Gary and said, "Okay, Gary, it's up to you, but remember, they will be waiting ahead somewhere like Charlie says, so keep an eye out and be careful. When you start back, remember they are following us, so move fast. Don't run, and for God's sake, don't let them catch up with you. If they do, they will make you talk; you can count on that. Stay alert; you will have to be ready, do you understand?"

"Yes," Gary answered. "Stop wasting time and get going! I will be fine!" Gary headed into the jungle while the rest of the group headed back toward the stream.

The two scouts found where the group had left the road. They decided that one of them must return to report to Omar while the other one continued tracking the Americans.

The first scout continued the chase and eventually found the stream where the group had crossed. He began looking over the terrain and could see that they had stopped to get a drink and rest; there were signs that someone had gone upstream, however, there were also signs that someone had crossed over to the other side of the steam! He wondered if they had split up. He carefully walked upstream and found the trail that the boy and driver had taken; now he had to make a decision. *I will leave a message at the stream, and I will follow this trail. The others can follow the signs on the opposite side of the stream.* He returned to the spot along the stream and left a special, coded message in the sand using rocks, weeds in a crude drawing.

The scout started up the trail that the driver and boy had taken. He had no idea that the trail he was following led back to the primitive village; if he had he would never had followed it! He was sure that when the rest of the bandits found his message they would follow the other trail across the stream into the jungle. As he traveled up the trail, he thought, the fools! Omar will cut them off before they reach the main road, and I will catch the others who have taken this trail Omar will be proud of me!

The scout had just begun tracking the boy and the driver toward the primitive village when John and the group returned to the stream. Ramon looked around and said, "Someone has been here, look!" He pointed to the message next to the sand along the creek. Although Ramon did not understand the message, he realized that it was there for it was a sign for the other bandits.

"Do you know what it means, Ramon?" Charlie asked.

"No, but it is there for the others, I am sure."

Jerry said, "Don't know how much good it will do, boys, but we should wash the message away, eh?" "Damn John exclaimed. If we wash it away maybe the figure it out but again if we wash it away they may just get confused enough to give us a little more time. He waited then said, the hell with it let's get going!"

Before anyone could say anything, John whispered, "Okay, let's move!"

The group headed upstream, trying to not leave any signs of their presence.

"Shouldn't we destroy the message, John?" Jerry asked.

I thought about it but I don't think so. Jerry. If we destroy the message, whoever left it for them will know we have been here and that will give our plan away. We have to leave it for whoever it was written. You never know; it might be an advantage—it might send them in the wrong direction."

Charlie doubted John but understood what he was saying. He thought it really doesn't matter too much either way; our chances are slim to none!

An hour later Omar and the rest of the bandits found the stream and the message left behind by the tracker. "They have split up," he grinned, looking at his men.

"It is only a question of time before we have them all!"

Before leaving the American camp, Omar had sent three of his men to cut off the group if they tried to return to the main road from the jungle. *The American plan is very simple*, he thought, *it will not be successful!*

Now he sent three of his warriors up the trail toward the primitive village to help the scout, while the rest followed the second trail across the stream. He realized he must split up again to follow the two groups. It was not something that he was concerned about, but he was now down to two groups of three warriors each to follow the Americans. I still have plenty of men to finish this, he thought.

Gary felt good for the first time in weeks. He would outrun the bandits, and in a couple of hours would be back to the main road. In a month or so he would come back and get the gold. He said out loud, "What a bunch of fools! They never caught on to what I was up to when I separated from them!" He stopped for a moment to catch his breath. "John; he's the only one I feel bad about, but he done this to himself, the hell with it." He started cutting his way through the jungle again.

The driver had decided that he must get away from the Americans. He was sure that once he had a chance to talk with the chief, he could convince him that he was only a hired driver and had nothing to do with the gold. He had told the boy to take him to the village; he must speak to the chief right away. The boy moved surprisingly fast, and it was not long before the driver told the boy he must rest. The boy agreed but after a half hour he told the driver, he must get back to the village, and he started walking up the trail.

"How far must we go?" asked the driver.

"Not far," answered the boy, "we are very close." But the driver could not go any farther; he was exhausted from fighting the jungle all day and could not continue. "I cannot stop again," the boy said.

"All right, you go on. Tell the chief I am coming." The driver collapsed next to the trail and watched the boy disappear out of sight; soon he was sound asleep. The tracker was moving fast and soon spotted the driver sleeping along the trail. He started to approach the man but stopped, thinking, where are the rest of them? Is this a trap? He hid behind a tree and watched the man for a few minutes, but no one else could be seen. I cannot wait any longer, he thought. He crept up to the driver and grabbed him by the neck.

The driver awoke in a panic and kicked the tracker away from him, then jumped to his feet and began running up the trail. The tracker got to his feet and started after the man. There was no need to hurry; he had done this many times, and no one had ever got away from him! The driver stumbled and fell; it was the last thing he would do! The tracker took his machete and with one stoke cut off the driver's head! He grabbed the head by the hair and placed it in a bag strapped around his waist. Now, he thought, I will find the rest of them!

He continued up the trail, expecting to find the Americans. As he turned a corner in the trail, he spotted a young boy running ahead of him.

He thought who is this boy? He must be with the others—is it his trail I have been following?

The boy never knew what happened to him. The tracker threw his knife and struck the boy in the back. "Yes!" he hollered. As he approached the boy's body in the trail, he pulled his machete from his waistband and picked up the limp body. "Two!" he cried, and he cut the child's head from his body and placed it into the bag.

A woman approached the chief and said, "My son is missing. This morning he left very early to hunt the small deer in the jungle near the stream, but he has not returned.

The chief looked at his sister with concern. "How long has he been away from the village?" he asked.

"He has been gone many hours, my brother. He never stays away this long."

The chief was worried. Everyone in the village knew that the jungle was not a good place to be after dark. Something must be done to find the child. He called three of his best warriors and told them, "My nephew is missing near the jungle steam. Go and find him, and bring him back to the village."

The three warriors started running down the trail toward the jungle stream. It was not long before they could hear the boy singing as he walked along the trail.. Just as they rounded a curve in the trail they heard the boy scream. The three men stopped in their tracks and listened—something was wrong! The first man motioned to the other to move forward with caution. As they continued around the bend in the trail they witnessed a horrible site unfolding in front of them. A stranger had just cut the young boy's heard from his body and was placing it into a bag strapped to his waist.

The men stood in horror at what they had seen. The first warrior pulled his blowgun from this waistband and aimed it at the stranger. In an instant he blew the dart which entered the man's neck just below his right ear. A look of surprise crossed the man's face as the dart struck him. He automatically reached up and pulled it from his neck; looked at it with disbelief and confusion and thought, what is this? He began to get dizzy and was unable to stand; he fell.

The group had traveled upstream for a couple of hours. Finally Charlie said to John, "John, I believe we are above the village. What do you think, should we cross over now?"

"Hell, I don't know, Charlie, I can't tell where we are! We must have come up the stream at least two miles. Let's cut into the jungle; trying to walk upstream is damn near impossible!"

Charlie was half carrying Mila by now; she wasn't able to walk more than a few hundred yards at a time without stopping to rest.

Jerry said, "Please, guys—I am almost done! Another couple of minutes of this, and I will drop!"

Charlie looked at Mila and nodded his head in agreement. "Listen, no matter what happens; we need to stop for the night. It will be dark in a half-hour and we won't be able to continue anyway," he said to John.

The group found a small opening in the jungle and sat down under a large tree. John leaned over to Charlie and said, "Charlie, I don't want the others to know, but I am afraid we are doomed. The girl is finished, Jerry is almost done, and I can't go much further either."

Charlie looked at John and responded, "The kid is doing okay, but it won't be long before he is had it too. Maybe we should split up; at least some of us might have a chance. If we stay together, we all will be caught."

"No Charlie, we started together and we will finish together. I am not about to break up the group; in fact, I don't think we should have let Gary go."

Charlie exploded, "The hell with Gary! What is it about, John—you are always defending him! Don't you realize what he has done to us? We're here because of that dirty bastard!"

"I know, Charlie, but I have been thinking if he is caught—and I believe he will be—he is going to screw the rest of us. It won't take much for him to start talking, and when he does, the little advantage we have will be lost, that's all I am saying."

"I'm sorry, John, I should have known what you meant. I guess I am tired too."

John looked over at Jerry and Mila and said, "We are going to stay here for the night, okay?"

"Are you kidding me, it's okay with Mila and me—I couldn't go another fifty feet. Thanks, John. I have to rest." Charlie gave a weak laugh and move away.

Mila was asleep within minutes. Ramon was nodding his head but refused to rest. He sat down next to John and said, "Mr. John, you know what this means—if we rest now, we will never get away from the bandits."

"I understand, Ramon, but take a look at all of us, especially Mila. We're done! It isn't a question if we should stop; it is a necessity. Do you understand, Ramon?"

Ramon lowered his head, got up and walked away. He knew John was right but that did not make it any easier for him to accept.

John said to those in the group still awake, without much enthusiasm, as he was also near collapse, "Tomorrow we will get started early, so try and get some sleep; If we get caught, we get caught!" With that John leaned back against the tree and fell dead asleep!

Omar led his men into the jungle. The trail was clear, and he knew it was only a matter of time before he would have his Americans. After an hour he realized that the trail was not the same; something did not seem right, but due to the darkness, he was unable to determine what it was. *Never mind*, he thought, *we will have them before dark!*

Gary was still moving very fast; the adrenaline rush was keeping him fresh. Each time he thought about stopping to rest, he would think about the gold and the bandits, and he would pick up his pace. He was starting to worry about the dark closing in; it got dark fast in the jungle and he knew he did not have much light left to travel. He was deciding where he would spend the night when, without warning, something, struck him across his forehead. The last thing he remembered was the feeling of warm blood running down his face.

The three bandits looked at each other and grinned. The lieutenant said to the others, "Omar will be pleased!"

Gary had walked right into the trap the bandits had set; he wasn't as smart as he thought! The three bandits had heard Gary coming through the jungle for several minutes and had set their trap! Two of them had hidden behind a large tree while the other had covered himself with vines and brush directly in Gary's path. As Gary approached the man lying in wait one of the men behind the tree stepped out and struck Gary across the head with a large tree branch. Once struck Gary staggered forward where the warrior under the leaves good grab his legs and force him to the ground however there wasn't much resistance as the branch had already done the job. Gary never realized what hit him. He was too busy focusing on getting out of the jungle.

The chief looked down at his young nephew headless body with the knife wound in his back. One of the warriors opened up the bandits bag and pulled the boys head out. He carefully laid it onto a blanket on the ground next to the boy's body. The bandit tracker was lying unconscious on the ground in front of the chief, his hands tied behind his back.

"Why did this man do this to my nephew?" the chief grieved. His anger began to rise up inside him. He told the men to tie a rope around the man's arms and hang him from a tree. He would find out soon why this man had killed this boy.

"Honorable One, we also found this head tied to his waist."

The chief recognized the face immediately; it was the translator who was with the strangers! The chief pointed his staff at the bandit lying in front of him and said, "String him up!"

When the bandit regained consciousness, his arms were in terrible pain! He realized he was hanging from a tree. Below him he saw several men in primitive clothing looking up at him; he did not recognize them and wondered what was happening. The chief took a hot iron poker from the fire and raised it toward the man hanging from the tree.

"Who are you?" he asked, "Why did you kill my nephew?"

The man had no idea what the chief was saying; the dialect was strange to him. The chief touched the hot iron to the man's leg, and the man screamed in terror. The chief repeated the question, "Why did you kill my nephew?"

The man saw the boy lying on a blanket and realized what the old man was saying, but he could not answer him because of the old man's strange dialect. At the same time, the chief realized that the man could not understand him, and he backed away from the tree. He sat for several minutes and finally called for two of his warriors and told them, "Go to the fishing village and bring me one of our tribesmen that can speak this language. I want to know why this man killed my nephew, before I take his life, slowly, very slowly! You will leave now and be back in the morning. Take ten warriors back down the trail with you. See if there are more of these men. If so, bring them to me or kill them!"

Gary woke up with a terrible throbbing around his forehead. He looked around and realized there was a fire burning nearby with men sitting around it. He slowly raised his hand to his forehead and felt a large welt across his brow; dry blood covered his entire face. He then realized he was not tied and was free to move, however, he realized there was no sense trying to run—they had him and he knew it! He did not want the men at the fire to know that he was awake; whatever was going to happen could wait until later. He was terrified of what that might be! One of the Muslim's at the fire said, Juan should have found Omar by now they should return soon. They had captured Gary over two hours ago and had sent Juan for Omar right after they made camp. Now Omar would take care of the American.

While Gary had fallen back to sleep Omar had arrived from tracking the others from the steam. Once Juan had told Omar that they had captured an American as Omar had predicted Omar could not resist the opportunity to see the American besides this man would tell him where the others were. Yes, Omar thought, he will tell me! He sat sifting the coals in the fire and asking himself where the others were. Why only this man? Had they missed the rest hiding in the jungle? No, it is something else. The Americans could not fool his men—they were here, and the captured American would tell them in the morning. He smiled this was the part of the chase Omar enjoyed the most making people do as he wanted was something he was very good at! He will be happy to tell me!

Gary lay half asleep all night; it was impossible to sleep with the injury to his head and the unknown waiting in the morning. Soon the men around the fire lay down near the coals and were sound asleep. Gary eased up onto his elbow and was trying to decide if he should make a run for it. However, just as he was about to climb to his feet, he heard a rustle in the bushes to his left. He slowly turned his head and looked in the direction of the sound. There was one of the bandits, smiling—with a knife in his hand. Gary decided that sleep was a better option!

In the morning when Gary awoke he noticed the others were already moving around camp. Some were eating while the rest were gathering up their gear. He thought, No need to expect them to feed me. He lay still, not wanting them to know that he was awake. Two men rose from the fire and started walking toward Gary. He did not know whether to pretend to be asleep or to sit upright. He decided it would do no good to pretend to be asleep he rose up onto his elbows as they approached. The men picked him up by his arms and walked him to the fireside.

After he was forced to sit down on a fire log he glanced around he could tell immediately which of the men was their leader—it was the man seated alone on the other side of the fire the look in his eyes was all Gary needed, yes this is the man, he thought. The leader! Next to Omar was a log with a machete stuck into it.

The man never looked up at Gary as the three men approached. The men grabbed Gary and forced him to his knees. One tied a small rope around his right arm just above his elbow he pulled the rope very tight, which caused Gary to scream in extreme pain. Still, no one talked. The leader never bothered to look up at Gary; instead he continued to probe the fire with a stick. The rest of the men continued to sit across the fire and were watching what was going on with a keen interest. Gary decided to say something, "What do you want of me?" Still no one spoke. One of the men pulled Gary's tied arm across the log while the other man held Gary down. My God, he thought, what are they going to do, break my arm? "If you will just ask me, maybe I could tell you what you want to know," he said again. The leader of the group stood up and pulled the machete from the log. Oh Jesus, he thought, he is going to cut off my arm! "Stop! I will tell you what you want to know!" he screamed. "Please," he begged, "don't do this to me!" The second man grabbed Gary around the neck while another man approached from the opposite side of the fire and helped hold Gary down. With one swift swing of the machete, Omar severed Gary's arm just below his right elbow! Gary screamed in agony!

Once Omar decided to return with Juan he directed his men to continue the hunt for the others. Three would follow the trail the tracker had taken and one would continue the search the area for sign of the Americans until Omar returned.

The three Muslim bandits followed the trail until they found the body of the van driver and the blood trail from the boy. "He has found him! Look, he has taken his head!" one of the bandits said excitedly. "Come! We must catch up with him and help find the others!"

"Get up, people, we have to get moving." John hated to wake everyone, but he knew that time was running out. He also knew they should not have stopped so early last night, but it had to be done.

Charlie lay next to Mila. For the first time since he had met her, he felt a sense of closeness. She had surprised him with her determination and drive. She could have gotten away several times after seeing the bandits at the port city, but she chose to stay with them. She moved her head from his shoulder and sat up beside him. He looked at her and said, "How are you doing, Mila?"

Mila could hear the affection in his voice and it made her want to cry. "I am fine, Charlie, just a little sore."

Jerry sat up and said, "When do we eat?"

Ramon looked at him in confusion and said, "Do we have time to eat, Mr. Jerry? Should we not get going?"

Jerry answered him, "We have to eat something, kid, or we will never make it. We have a long day ahead of us."

"He's right, Ramon. It may not be much, but we need to put some food in our bellies," John said. "What did you pack, Charlie? I never thought to ask."

"A bit of this and a little of that and more of this then he let out a weak laugh." They ate some fruit and a sandwich, drank some water, and headed into the jungle.

"I think if we head south for a couple of hours we will be on the other side of the village and back toward the main road. What do you think, Charlie?" John asked.

"It depends on how tough the jungle is, but if it is anything like yesterday, I think you may be right."

The jungle seemed to close in around them as they moved through the underbrush even though it was early in the morning the heat and humidity along with the dense jungle slowed the group's advance. The men took turns cutting away the jungle, but as the day wore on the heat again took its toll, especially Mila.

"John, we have to stop soon. Mila can't go on," Charlie said.

"Yes, I can, Charlie. I will be okay; let us keep going," Mila answered. "I am not tired; besides, they will catch us if we stop!"

"Mila, you are exhausted, and we all need a break anyway," Charlie responded.

The group had not made much progress the last couple of hours, but John realized that Charlie was right. They were aware that the bandits would catch up soon. The trail was a dead giveaway and helped the bandits move through the jungle. John and the others were literally cutting trail for the Muslims and at the same time leading them directly to them!

John looked over his shoulder and realized that Jerry had also fallen behind and was not able to keep up the pace. The group had to slow down to allow Jerry and Mila to stay with them. "All right, we will stop for a few minutes, but remember—if you need an incentive to keep going, think of the Abu Sayyaf!" he said.

You could see the terror in Mila and Ramon's faces when John mentioned the Abu Sayyaf! Ramon had taken the lead for the last couple of hours. It was amazing to the others how he continued to cut away the jungle and kept moving ahead!

Again they stopped to rest. "We have to come up with another plan, John," Jerry commented. "Mila and I cannot stay up with the rest of you. If we keep going at this pace, they will catch us before the end of the day. Besides, we all know that we are leaving a clear trail for them."

"Damn it, Jerry, what can we do?" John responded in frustration.

Jerry looked at him and said, "Listen, we need to decide what is best for all of us. I suggest that Mila and I head directly for the primitive village and hope we can get some help from the natives. The rest of you can continue toward the main road. When you reach the road, you can get help and come back to the village for us."

"Mila goes nowhere without me!" Charlie yelled. "If anyone is going to the village with her, it will be me!" John knew it was the right move even through at first he believed staying together would be best, but now------? He turned and to the group and said, "all right, Mila, Jerry, and Charlie will head for the village, and Ramon and I will move toward the main road. Will that satisfy everyone?"

"Please, I can stay up with you! We must all stay together!" Mila cried.

"No, Mila, it has been decided. We will head for the village. We will be there in a couple of hours," Charlie said to her. "Here, John, you and Ramon take the extra water canteen and a pistol. We will be okay with what we have, and you will need it; you still have a full day's walk to the road." Charlie handed the canteen and pistol to John.

The group walked another hour together until they crossed an open patch of ground. Finally Charlie whispered, "Stop." He continued, "Well, folks, this is it." He grasped Mila by the hand, motioned to Jerry and the three of them headed into the jungle, leaving Ramon and John standing in the makeshift trail.

Ramon felt a loss in his stomach. He had never gotten along with Mila; however, now, as they separated, he wished he had said something kind to her. He turned and looked at John. They now appreciated that they had lost something special. John paused and said, "Where did it all go wrong, my young friend, where did it go wrong?" And with that the two continued their journey through the jungle.

CHAPTER 23

Back at Camp

The warriors sent by the chief from the primitive village rounded the corner of the road and spotted the campsite. There were two men sitting under a tree next to the road. One of the warriors motioned to his companions to stop then slowly moved nearer to the two men, using the jungle as cover. Once closer, they realized that the men were asleep. While they were watching, another man emerged from the jungle and yelled. He was very angry and struck one of the sleeping men on the side of his head. The two men jumped to their feet and started talking to the third man. The warriors moved back into the jungle.

The lead warrior whispered to one of his companions, "I must go back to the village and tell the Honored One what we have seen. I will leave you and others here to keep watch." The other man nodded his head in agreement and the lead warrior started back in the direction they had come. The others moved back under the cover of the jungle. They would wait for the chief to decide on what to do with these men; however, they knew the answer. After all, they are at the site where the yellow metal is hidden, aren't they? They will die!

The lieutenant was standing in the clearing watching the men working at the tunnel entrance, "What are you doing! Omar will cut our heads off

146

if we have not cleared the tunnel by this day! Is that what you want?" The men looked down at their feet; they knew he was right. The clearing was not going good, not good at all.

One of the men who had been helping the miners said, "The miners have told us it will take another day—we will not have the tunnel open today!"

The lieutenant looked at them and said, "Do you want to be the one who tells Omar we cannot open the tunnel?" None of the men said anything; they continued to clear broken timber from the tunnel entrance. The two miners were digging just inside the tunnel. As the lieutenant approached, one of the miners said, "Where have you been? Your leader told us that you would help us—we cannot do this alone!"

The lieutenant looked at them and said, "Shut up or I will kill you. Now do you understand?" The lieutenant knew that Omar would kill all of them unless the tunnel was open. He was angry with his men for not helping the miners; however, he would not say this in front of them. "Everyone get back to work!" He held up his rifle and motioned toward the tunnel. He decided he would return to the camp and get the other two guarding the camp to help clear the tunnel.

The last thing Gary remembered before passing out was his arm lying on the ground with blood gushing from the stump, the fingers on the severed hand still twitching! As he fell into unconsciousness, he thought, *this is a terrible dream, this can't be happening!* Several minutes later he knew it wasn't a dream when he awoke and saw his severed arm lying in front of him. Omar was standing over him, the blood still dripping off the machete. Gary realized with horror, "it wasn't a dream!"

Omar motioned to the men to tie Gary's other arm. Gary was too weak to stop them and screamed, "Please, *no!*"

Omar raised his hand for the men to stop. In clear English he said, "Where are the others?"

"What do you mean?" Gary asked.

Omar motioned to the men to pull Gary's other arm across the log.

"Stop, I will tell you what you want to know!"

Again Omar motioned the men to stop. "Where are the others?" he asked again.

"They went upstream. They are going around the village!" Gary yelled then collapsed onto the ground.

"What village are you talking about?" Omar asked.

"There is a village a couple of miles from where we crossed the stream," Gary answered.

Anger crossed Omar's face. He kicked Gary in the ribs and walked away. "You three will take this American back to the camp. He pointed to one of the men and said, "We will return to the stream and find the Americans. Move!" he yelled.

The men immediately jumped at his command and one followed Omar back toward the stream, three men stayed behind with Gary.

The warrior returned to the village and told the chief what they had seen at the camp. They told him of the encampment near the old tunnel to the gold and the men working to open it.

The chief looked at the men and said, "This is why my nephew is dead? They have brought the curse upon us! They are seeking the yellow metal!" he yelled, and then called warriors to his hut. "Tomorrow we will kill them all!"

CHAPTER 24

Jungle Trouble!

Charlie, Jerry, and Mila continued toward the primitive village, not knowing what their fate might be—but realizing they had no choice it was the village or certain death! It was late in the afternoon and the jungle was hot and humid. Charlie held his hand up and said, "Let's take five. We are making good time and should be near the village by nightfall."

Jerry welcomed the break. "Charlie," he said, "what do you think will happen with the gold?"

"Well, Jerry, we had better concentrate on our lives for the time being. But I will tell you this, I'm sure as hell going to think hard, if we get out of this mess, before I go looking for it again!"

"Yeah, a man sure thinks about his priorities when he might lose his life!" Jerry answered back.

Charlie continued, "I can't figure it out yet, Jerry, but it just doesn't seem like it was greed to me; it was more of an adventure. Does that make sense to you?"

"If we were in Elko, Charlie, on this deal I would say greed, man, greed! But right now and right here, this whole thing is a great adventure. The gold doesn't seem to be important to me anymore."

Three hours later of hard travel it was clear to Charlie that something was wrong; they should have been near the village by now, but there was no sign. He didn't say anything to the others; Jerry was too tired and was not paying attention to what was going on he just followed Charlie and Mila through the jungle. Mila, however, was well aware of what was happening but chose not to say anything to Charlie. What good would it do to say anything, she thought.

Omar and his companion were back at the stream within an hour after leaving the campsite where Gary was being held captive. Once they had returned to the stream, he immediately started walking upstream searching for signs of the Americans. Once he crossed the trail the boy and driver had taken, Omar came stopped. He had sent three of his best men after the tracker. He thought, *well enough*. The other one was near they would continue to follow the other signs.

The American had said his people had headed upstream to go around a village. Again he asked himself, *what village was the American talking about?* Now Omar was frustrated. *I should not have injured the American; I should have taken him with us!* Just as he was about to move onto the trail the other Muslim emerged from the jungle. He stopped and looked at Omar and said, "I have found their trail Omar!" "Good we will go upstream and find the infidels!"

Omar and his man returned upstream . After an hour of tracking they found where the Americans had cut back into the jungle. Omar again thought of his manpower, I am acting like a fool! I must think more before making decisions. I have spread my men too thin. I was taught better than this in training. My men will start wondering if I am a deserving leader! Doubt now was creeping into the back of his mind causing him concern. Omar was angry not at his men but at himself. He thought; I will kill them! I will kill them slowly! He intensified his pursuit just as they were cutting away at the jungle his lead tracker emerged in front of them. Omar pushed around him and at the same time said, "Follow me, and follow me now!

CHAPTER 25

Back to the Camp

The men at the tunnel worked all night, and by morning they had opened a small hole into the cave. The lieutenant told the soldiers to stop working and directed the miners to open the hole and go inside. The two miners worked for another hour and finished opening the hole enough for them to crawl inside. They yelled back to the MILF leader, saying they would need a light. The warrior wrapped a shirt around a stick, lighted it, and passed it into the hole.

After crawling a few feet the men were able to stand up and began walking back into the cave, holding the makeshift torch ahead of them. Once they reached the end of the cave they were amazed at the sight of gold, stacked in rows up to the ceiling! They were not able to see everything since the torch was burning out, but they could still see the gold!

"Go, tell the bandit leader we have found the gold," one of the miners said.

"Wait, are we going to give all the gold to them?" the other asked.

The first miner looked at the gold and thought, if we tell them, they will kill us. "We will hide some of the gold inside the tunnel so they cannot find it," he suggested. "They will not come into the tunnel; they are afraid of the underground. They are not miners. Quick," he said, "start moving the gold. We will hide it in the tunnel!"

The two men started removing the gold from the floor and stacking it against the side of the tunnel. Meanwhile the leader of the bandits wondered what was taking the miners so long to come out of the tunnel. He squeezed his body through the entrance and started walking toward the dim light of the torch. Finally his courage gave out, he couldn't go any further. He was about to shout to the miners when he heard a tremendous cracking and thunderous noise come from inside where the miners were. Dust bellowed out of the small opening, the ground began to shake, and the man turned and ran from the tunnel. He quickly climbed through the small opening.

The miners never knew what had happened. They had removed the gold too fast, causing the ropes tied to the ceiling to slacken. The timbers above came crashing down onto the men. Once the ceiling began to fall, it was too late. Both miners were buried under the debris as the floor holding the gold and the two men crashed down onto the second floor. The second floor collapsed, sending the men and gold into the dark cave below.

The bandit was visibly shaken as he came out of the tunnel. The others had heard the tremendous noise and were standing near the tunnel opening.

"What has happened? What was the noise we heard?" one asked.

"It looks like the tunnel has fallen in," the lieutenant said. "We must go inside and open it up!"

The other men froze. They would not go into the death trap; no one could make them! Omar could kill all of them if he wanted, but they would not die inside the cave! They backed away from the tunnel.

The lieutenant pointed his rifle at the men. "Go inside, I say, or I will shoot all of you!"

Still the men refused to move; the men were visibly shaken. The lieutenant realized he would not be able to force the men inside; besides, if he killed them, who would dig for the gold? With the men ready to bolt for the jungle the lieutenant decided it could wait until tomorrow or he would end up being here alone when Omar returned and he didn't want that! He was sure Omar would understand once he realized what had happened. Yes, he thought, he would wait for Omar. He looked at the men and said, "Return to camp. We will continue the tunnel tomorrow while we wait for Omar."

No one argued with the lieutenant but they had all decided that they would never enter the tunnel—not now, tomorrow, or ever!

The three bandits Omar sent up the trail toward the village soon found the body of the driver. They wondered, "Where is the scout?" One of their men was missing now, and there was no sign of him. This bothered the men. They wondered if they should continue searching for their companion or return to Omar. The lead bandit said, "We cannot return without the Americans. Something is not right; we must find out what has happened." The three men continued moving up the trail searching for signs of the tracker and the Americans.

"This trail has been used for many years. Where does it lead?" one asked his companion.

After finding the boy and killing the scout, two of the village warriors had taken the boy's body back to the village while the others continued down the trail toward the stream looking for signs that would explain the death of the child. When they heard the three bandits speaking to each other as they moved along the trail, the warriors stepped back into the jungle to wait! The chief had made it clear, "Kill them all!"

The warriors were waiting in ambush as the bandits continued up the trail in search of the Americans. It did not take long. Within seconds the bandits were attacked and hacked to death with machetes. The primitive village warriors stood over the men, trying to decide what to do with them. Finally, one said, "We must show the chief that we have avenged his nephew's death. Cut one hand from each of these cowards, killers of children. We will take them back to the village," he continued. "Let the birds have their bodies!"

The men had done their deed, and they started back toward the village they would tell the chief what had happened.

The trail was almost too easy! Omar stopped several times, expecting an ambush—but nothing! *Why is this*, he thought. *Why do they make my job so easy?* After three hours of tracking, the two found where the Americans had split up. He took his machete and slashed at the jungle in frustration. "Again they have separated!" he screamed.

The two rebel bandits looked at Omar in fear; they had not seen their leader this way. The second in command thought, *this is not going as planned. What are we going to do? More importantly, what is Omar going to do? Does Omar know?*

Omar looked at the two trails and said, "You will follow this one," pointing in the direction Charlie, Jerry, and Mila had gone. "We will follow the other. If you find them, bring them to me!"

The bandit thought, I am only one; I will need help. He knew he could not tell this to Omar; if he did, he was not sure if Omar would not kill him on the spot! The bandit hesitated before he started into the jungle after Charlie's group.

"What are you waiting for?" Omar yelled. He raised his rifle and pointed it at the bandit. "Move!"

This was enough incentive for the bandit; he immediately began his pursuit!

Omar turned toward the trail and said to his last bandit, "We go!" He thought they will be no hostages; they will all die!

CHAPTER 26

Chief

The chief led his warriors to the campsite the next morning. The old man was determined to wipe this terrible curse from his tribe. All of them would pay for his nephew's death! When they arrived, they found his warriors waiting for him near the camp hidden inside the jungle brush, watching. The chief motioned to one of the men who had been there all night to follow him away from the camp.

Once they were far enough away so as to not to reveal their presence, the chief asked the warrior what was happening with the group inside the camp. He explained to the chief that the men were working at a clearing near the road and that some of the men were digging into the mountain. The chief and the man went back to the place where the rest of his men were waiting. After looking over the camp, he directed two of his warriors to approach the campsite and to be ready to attack. "However," he said, "Not now; we will wait for tomorrow's daylight!"

Meanwhile the bandits had returned to the clearing and were deciding what they would do next. The tunnel had caved in, and Omar was coming; this was bad very bad! The lieutenant was not sure if the men would enter the tunnel even if he directed them. He was in fear of his life—Omar accepted no excuses! He had decided if the men would not enter the tunnel in the morning, he would leave this place and return to his village; Enough! He thought. He turned to the men and said, "If we do not have the gold when Omar arrives, he will kill us all. We must enter the tunnel!"

One of the men asked, "Where are the miners? What has happened to them?"

The lieutenant could only answer, "I do not know; either they are dead or trapped, but we will find out tomorrow. I will go inside first and see what has happened. The rest of you wait here for me."

The next morning at dawn, while the rest of the bandits waited at the camp, the lieutenant took a flashlight and entered the tunnel. There was rock and debris lying along the tunnel. He advanced into the small opening and hollered, "Hello!" There was no response. Now he had to decide what to do—should he continue to crawl through the opening, or return outside and go back to the camp where the men waited?

Meanwhile, back at the camp, one of the men said, "I will not go inside the tunnel! We will all die!"

Another said, "We will die anyway if Omar comes back and finds out we have not taken the gold from the tunnel!"

The first man again spoke. "I am tired of this. We should not be here. We must leave this place!"

The three bandits looked at each other and started backing slowly toward the truck finally turning and running full speed toward the truck. None of them saw the warriors hidden in the jungle around the campsite. Just as the group approached the truck, one of the bandits saw the warriors and yelled, he raised his rifle and began shooting. The chief, seeing what was happening, yelled at the others, "Attack!" The first warrior in camp was killed immediately' however, the others were able overrun the Muslims. Before the bandits realized what was happening, a dozen warriors were attacking them from all directions. Within minutes they were either hacked to death or full of poison darts!

The lieutenant decided the cave was no place for him. He turned around and began climbing out of the cave. *I am leaving this place; Omar can do as he wants. I am going back to my village!* After climbing to his feet and brushing himself off, he started back toward the camp. Then he heard the rifle fire. He carefully crept near the campsite. As he got closer, he could hear shouts and more gunfire. He peered out from the cover of the jungle. What he saw terrified him—his men were being cut to pieces!

He knew there was nothing he could do to help them. He thought, *I must save myself!* He ran for the tunnel, crawled through the small opening, and crouched down, terrified of what might happen to him if he were found. *Omar*, he thought, *is a bad leader! What has he done to us?*

After the skirmish the chief led his warriors to the tunnel and directed them to cover the entrance. Soon, there was no sign that a tunnel had ever existed! He turned to his warriors and said, "We will return to our village!"

Gary was being led back to the camp by the four bandits; however, due to his loss of blood and being in shock, he was not able to stay up with them. They were forced to stop several times and wait for him.

"He is going to die, let us kill him now and return to the mine camp," one said.

"No, if we kill him, Omar will have us killed," answered the lead man.

The first bandit said, "We will tell Omar that he tried to escape and we had to shoot him."

"You are a fool! How can a man with one arm escape from us? We will take the American back to the camp!"

It took them until evening to reach the camp. What they found left them in shock! The dead bodies of their comrades were hanging from a tree near the van, the bodies been cut to pieces by machetes!

"What is this?" one cried in terror.

The lead bandit directed the others, "Go to the tunnel site. See if you can find the lieutenant, he is not among the dead here." He looked at Gary and said, "Never mind; I will go with you. This one is not going anywhere. Look at him; he acts like he is already dead!" and laughed sarcastically.

He was right. Every time Gary looked at his severed arm he became more depressed and had a difficult time dealing with it. Gary thought, what am I going to do the rest of my life with a missing arm? These men will never let me go; they will kill me once they have found the others and taken the gold! Then he thought good, good I want to die!

The Muslim bandits left Gary at the camp and headed toward the clearing and the tunnel opening. Gary stood in the middle of the camp staring into space. In his mind he could see the shocked look on John's and the others' faces when they saw his missing arm. He could see Mila shrinking back from him in horror. He could feel the sympathy of the others each time they looked at him.

Gary glanced over at the bodies hanging from the trees. It was odd; the rifles were still lying on the ground. Whoever had done this had not taken them. Then he realized, The savages from the village! That was the only explanation. They had discovered the bandits at the camp and assumed they were part of American party. He remembered what the chief had said, "We will kill anyone trying to find the gold!" Yes, that was it. They found the bandits here; they put two and two together—and came up with three.

That, however, was the least of his problems. He again looked at what was left of his arm. I will never be able to live with this! He thought. Gary walked over to where the men were hanging from the tree. The villagers had done quite a job; they had hacked the men's bodies but made sure there was still enough left to hang. They had done a thorough job of killing them. Gary sat down next to one of the weapons lying on the ground. He picked up the rifle with his good hand and placed the weapon between his knees. He put the barrel into his mouth and pulled the trigger!

The Muslims heard the gunfire and quickly returned to the clearing where they found Gary lying in his own blood with a bullet hole through the top of his head. They had found the tunnel closed, and now the American was dead! One said, "Omar!"

"Where?" the others said, turning in fear. "Where is Omar?"

"No, no, I did not mean Omar is here, I mean, what will Omar do to us? Look what we have done—we do not have the gold, the American is dead, and all our comrades are hanging from a tree! We are dead men! The lieutenant is missing or dead—very bad, very, very bad!" The soldier dropped his weapon to the ground dejectedly and stood looking into the jungle.

"Where is the lieutenant?" the other bandit asked. "What has happened to him? Where is the leader of this group?"

"He is gone; he must have gotten away," said his companion.

The lead bandit looked at his companions and said, "No more! We will return to our village. If Omar decides to kill us, so be it, but we will not stay here and be killed like our companions. Let us go!"

The men took one last look at the slaughter and slowly walked toward the two trucks parked along the road. They were going home; they were tired of this terrible place! This place is cursed!

CHAPTER 27

Caught!

"Did you hear that?" Jerry asked Charlie.

"Yes, I heard it." Charlie motioned to Jerry and Mila to hide behind a tree.

The bandit had been following the signs for about an hour. It was getting dark and he was having some trouble staying on the trail. He knew he was moving too fast but he also realized he wanted this to be over with; he was tired of this game. He thought, Omar must stop this pursuit. We will never find all of the Americans. We must go back to our village!

His rifle was hanging from his shoulder. He decided he did not need the rifle; after all he was looking for some Americans—what resistance could they give him? He thought The Americans are soft; they have no stomach for fighting!

The sound of the bandit moving through the jungle was still far off but Charlie realized that their trail was easy to follow. That could not be helped and Jerry and Mila could not travel through the jungle unless Charlie cut away the underbrush. So it was just a matter of time before whoever was following them caught up. Charlie looked at Jerry and Mila and said, "Listen, I don't know who is following us. It may be John and Ramon, it could be Gary, or it could be the bandits, but I will have to stay behind and find out; you both understand that, don't you?"

"Why you?" Jerry asked.

"Listen, I have the gun and besides, I have the best chance of shooting the bastards if it is the bandits, that's why."

Jerry looked Charlie in the eye and said, "Mila and I don't have a chance without you, Charlie. We won't last a day out here by ourselves, and you know that if you get killed, we are as good as dead anyway!"

Mila looked at the two men and said, "Let's just run! We can stay ahead of these people. We will be at the village soon!"

Charlie and Jerry knew this was not the case. They were lost, and it might take hours or even days to reach the village.

"No," Charlie said, "we will have to deal with what or who is following us and that's final."

"I agree," Jerry answered. Jerry grabbed the pistol from Charlie's belt and stood back from the two. "I'll wait for the bastards and shoot the SOBs if need be, but you two have to keep going—and that is the end of this discussion!"

Charlie stepped toward Jerry, but Jerry moved back. "We don't have time for this, Charlie, and you know it, so for Christ's sake, get going before it is too late!"

"At least let me show you what you need to do then," Charlie said.

"Okay, but make it fast!" Jerry replied.

"You have to get off the trail, Jerry. They will be following our trail. If this is the MILF and they are as good as I think they are, they will be ready for an ambush. Do you understand?" Charlie led Jerry back in the direction they had come. He took Jerry by the shoulder and said, "Here is a good spot. Hide behind the underbrush, Jerry. When they come around the corner of that tree, you will have a clear shot. Wait until they are right on top of you before you start shooting. If you shoot too soon, you will miss, and it will be all over for you, do you understand?"

"Yes, yes, I understand. Now get going!"

Charlie walked back and took Mila by the hand, saying, "Mila, we will not be able to cut the jungle away. If we do the bandits or whoever is out there will hear us, do you understand?"

"Yes, Charlie, I understand." Charlie pulled Mila next to him and squeezed, damn sometimes I wonder about me am I completely crazy?" Mila was confused when he let her go she looked up into his eyes and said, "Why do you talk like this Charlie?" Charlie had no time to explain and with Mila in hand started moving slowly through the jungle.

The bandit stopped in his tracks; had he heard something moving ahead? He slowed his pace and began to look at the surroundings and everything in front of him. He stopped every thirty feet or so to listen. He was in a deadly track, a killing mode!

Jerry lay in wait, the sweat running down the back of his neck, his heart pounding inside his chest. He knew whoever was out there could hear it beating! He thought back to when he was a young man. *I wasn't the smartest guy on the block, but hell, I wasn't the dumbest either!* He thought, *I was one of those guys that no one ever noticed. I guess I was kind of hard to get to know. I always wanted the big deal even when I was just out of high school. No real friends—I suppose that because I was always getting the few guys I did know into some screwball deal,* he laughed to himself. *I wonder what they would think of me now.* Jerry refocused on what he must do. He held the pistol with both hands against his chest; he would wait until they were right on top of him. He reminded himself, *don't shoot too soon!* He kept saying to himself, *Wait . . .wait!*

The bandit eased up behind Jerry. He carefully pulled out the knife from his waist and raised it over his head; he would wound this man with his knife.

"Watch out, Jerry!" Charlie hollered. Charlie had led Mila into the jungle a couple hundred yards and told her to wait for him. He had returned to where Jerry was lying in wait. He was just in time to see the bandit raise the knife.

Jerry rolled over on his back and pulled the trigger. A loud shot rang out, but it was too late; the bandit had aimed his knife at Jerry's shoulder. However instead of cutting his shoulder, he had cut deep into Jerry's chest. The bandit felt the bullet go into his chest. He looked at Jerry and thought, what has this infidel done to me! then he stood up and touched his chest with his hand, blood trickling from the bullet wound. He stood for a minute then fell on top of Jerry.

Charlie ran up to the two men lying on the ground. He pulled the dead man off Jerry. Jerry looked up at Charlie and said, "He cut me, Charlie, and he cut me bad!" Charlie looked at the blood starting to ooze from the wound and knew Jerry was dying. There was nothing he could do!

Charlie tore a piece of his shirt and covered Jerry's wound and said, "Yeah, he cut you, Jerry, but you got the SOB!" Jerry tried to get up but realized he didn't have the energy, and he lay back onto the jungle floor.

"Where is Mila, is she all right?" Jerry asked.

"She's alright, I left her in the jungle. I should have stayed, Jerry! Damn it, you didn't have a chance!" Charlie turned away from Jerry for a moment; he didn't want to look at his dying friend.

"Charlie, this was for the best. At least you and Mila have a chance now, so for Christ's sake, get going!"

Charlie turned to say something to Jerry, but he was gone! Charlie fell to his knees and began to sob. He thought, what has happened? What the hell have we gotten ourselves into? God, please help us!

Omar thought he heard a shot but he could not be sure; he had been pursuing his quarry and was concentrating on the trail the group ahead was leaving. He turned to the bandit and said, "Did you hear that?" The man could see the hate and fear in Omar's eyes; he stood looking at him but said nothing. Omar continued to stand still listening to the jungle. Finally, he made a slow step forward and stopped. He said out loud, "Our man got them, yes! He got them!" A cringing smile crossed his face. He turned again and said, "What is wrong with you? Move!"

The bandit had decided *Enough!* He would wait for Omar to sleep, and then he would run, yes, he would run away from this crazy man! Omar was no longer the powerful all knowing leader he was a frantic unpredictable man; the man knew he must get away from Omar or he was going to die, not from the Americans but by Omar's hands the man was crazy!

Omar had decided that he was after two people. The signs were clear; one very light, and one a man maybe two hundred pounds. He again stopped for a minute to listen for another shot or something that might tell him what had happened. The shot had not sounded like a rifle but more like a pistol, but he couldn't be sure; it was too far away. He thought, We are near, and said to his companion, "Sit. We will rest. Our prey is very near."

The look on Omar's face was pure crazed hate. As the two men sat next to a fallen tree, Omar kept twisting his knife over and over in his hand staring into the jungle. Finally, he lay back against a tree and allowed his eyes to close. He had not realized until this moment that he was exhausted. The chase had heightened his adrenaline, and now that he was close and could feel the prey he could relax, just a little! But yes, a short rest would clear his head and improve his ability to kill!

The bandit watched as Omar's eyes closed. He tensed as he watched this crazy man slowly fall asleep. Omar's chest moved in a slow rhythm up and down, up and down. After ten minutes the man slowly got to his feet.

He was fifteen feet from Omar. The sweat was unbearable; it ran down the front of his shirt, his hair was soaking wet. He stood watching the Muslim leader then began to move slowly away from the clearing toward the trail they had traveled.

He was leaving. He knew Omar would not follow him as long as the prey lay ahead; however, he also knew that Omar would track him down and kill him once he finished the Americans. But now he must run—this was a bad sign, a bad place. That was not his friend's rifle but someone else's pistol. He knew his friend was dead. He had decided, no more, no more!

Just as he turned and started back down the trail, he felt the knife go deep into his back! Omar stood behind him with his hand across the man's mouth, driving the knife deeper into the man's back. A whisper of agony escaped the man's lips as he felt his life slip away. Omar gritted his teeth and said, "You are a coward! You do not deserve to live! I will tell the others how you ran from the challenge like a little boy, a woman!" Omar let the man fall to the ground, pulling his knife as the body coiled and dropped into a fetus position below him. Now, Omar thought, the others!

John and Ramon were moving through the jungle, Ramon leading and cutting away the jungle trail. John said, "Did you hear that, Ramon?"

"Yes, Mr. John, it sounded like a pistol shot."

"Keep moving! We can't stop now—they must have caught up with the others, and that means they are on our trail also!"

An hour later, it was apparent that the two men could go no farther. It was dark, and they were worn out from fighting the jungle. John looked at Ramon and said, "We can't go on, Ramon; we are running blind!" Ramon hesitated. He knew that the bandits would not stop until they had found them—but he also knew that fighting the jungle at night was a waste of time.

Omar was close enough to hear the men cutting the jungle underbrush. As he tracked the two men, he became increasingly angry with himself for what had happened and at the men who were able to escape from him. He thought, I will make these men pay! We will have the others to hold for ransom, but these men will pay with their lives!" He quickened his pace, but at the same time he was careful not to create too much noise. No sense in letting them know that I am close," he thought.

He sighted John first. He was sitting next to a tree with his head down. He waited patiently until he saw Ramon. The boy was standing near John, but he was not resting—he was looking almost directly at Omar! But because of the dark, Omar was sure the boy could not see him crouching in the underbrush.

"Mr. John, I do not feel comfortable waiting here—we must keep moving!"

"Ramon, I understand, but it is a waste of time fighting the jungle at night. We will only go in circles, and that won't do us any good. You can stand watch for the first four hours, and I will relieve you until morning."

Ramon sat down next to John. They were both exhausted. After a few minutes John looked at Ramon and said, "Ramon, you have never said what you think about us coming here to find the gold."

Ramon sat silent for a few minutes. John continued, "What do the Filipinos think of us, Ramon? Do your people like Americans?"

Again Ramon sat in silence. "Ramon?" John waited. "Are you going to say something?"

Ramon finally responded, "Mr. John, I do not want to say."

"Ramon, I consider you a friend. We are in a lot of trouble, so I think we should be honest with each other."

Ramon hesitated and began to speak. "I am from a small village in Mindanao, Mr. John. I do not know for sure what other Filipinos think about Americans, all I can say is what I think. I see our young girls looking for foreigners to save them from our poverty. They do things that our people do not like. Our young women leave our villages and go to Manila; they find foreigners and try to trick them into marriage. But most of the foreigners do not want them as wives; they use our young girls for what they want and then tell them to go! I do not blame the foreigners, Mr. John, but it shames our people. Mila only wants to have a good life. She is a good girl, but she is desperate to find a man, Mr. John. The people came to my village and opened the mine, but they did not take care of Mother Earth, so our water is not good to drink, and our jungles have been destroyed. You have treated me with respect, Mr. John, and I also feel you are my friend—but I must say what I have said." Ramon again sat in silence.

"Thank you, Ramon. Now I understand how you feel, I will tell you this—if we ever get out of this, I will never harm you, the people, or your country."

Ramon stood and said, "I am going to search for the trail ahead to see if we can continue. You can wait here for me, but we must keep moving. I will come back if it is too dark to go on."

John was too tired to argue with Ramon. "All right, but don't go far—we do not want to get separated; we need to stay together."

Ramon began cutting away at the jungle, and it wasn't long before he was out of sight from John. One hundred yards from where he had left John, Ramon found a trail. He followed it another hundred yards, to where it began to open up into a clearing. He could hear a steam!

Ramon returned to where he had left John. He was very excited and had trouble telling John what he had found.

"Settle down, Ramon, take your time. What is it you want to tell me?"

After a moment, Ramon related what he had found.

"Okay," John said. "We will get some sleep and start early in the morning."

"But Mr. John, it is only a short distance to the clearing—we can keep going," Ramon answered.

"Ramon, if it is that close, a few hours will not make a difference. Besides, I cannot go any farther tonight. We must get some rest."

Omar sat in silence trying to hear the conversation and what the boy was saying. He realized that he must wait until morning; it was too dark and he did not want to make a mistake. He could wait—he had them in sight! Omar found a nearby tree and relaxed against it. It was difficult to sleep. He wanted these two men dead, but at last he fell into a deep sleep.

The next morning at dawn Ramon was shaking John awake; however, John was exhausted and continued to lie on his side and refused to wake up. "Please, Mr. John, get up we must go!" Ramon urged.

John raised his head and said, "You go ahead, Ramon, and check out the clearing again. I will be ready to go by the time you get back." John knew this was not a good idea, but he could not seem to get to his feet. He needed another few minutes then he would be ready.

Ramon stood over him for a few minutes and decided he would do as Mr. John had asked, although he did not like it! He grabbed his machete and headed for the clearing.

After waking up, Omar watched the two men. They were still where he had seen them the night before. *These men are stupid! Just as I thought; they have not tried to escape during the night. What fools they are! It will be easy for me. I am going to make them pay for causing me this trouble!*

Omar began to reflect on the last couple of days. *These Americans have destroyed me as a leader. My men question my decisions, they do not trust my judgment; why? The Americans! I will make an example of these men, and then no one will ever forget that I am the leader!*

John was still sleeping against a tree not fifty feet from where Omar was hiding. Omar had watched as the boy turned away from the sleeping man and walked into the jungle. Omar waited until the boy was well out of sight and started crawling on his stomach toward John. Finally, he was within ten feet of his prey. John was sleeping with his head resting on his elbow, breathing heavily. Omar eased up onto his feet and carefully pulled his knife from his belt. John moved slightly; however, he did not get up. Omar froze in his tracks.

John had heard Omar but knew he must not make a move too soon or it would be all over. He thought, I need to wait until he makes a move toward me. He eased out the pistol from his belt and waited.

Omar again moved toward John, holding his knife ready to strike. As he stood over the man with his knife ready, the man suddenly rolled over. Omar saw the pistol in John's hand and jumped back. John slowly stood up. He was holding the pistol in his right hand and was pointing it at Omar!

"Stop right there or swear I will shoot where you stand!" John had cold look on his eyes he meant every word.

Omar lowered his knife and stood looking at John. He said, "I have several of my soldiers waiting in the jungle. If you shoot me, they will hear."

"Well, you speak English," John replied.

"Yes, I speak English, but that does not mean I will spare you! You infidels come to my country and think you can change us! You take our land, rape our women, and steal our gold! Now you will die!" Omar moved toward John.

John raised the pistol and said, "If you want to live, you had better stop right there!"

Omar hesitated and said, with a smile on his face, "I am not afraid to die but you, my friend, will also die, so go ahead and kill me if you can."

Omar began walking toward John. John could not believe this man, was he crazy? Didn't he realize that he was about to be shot?

Omar got within five feet of John when John hollered, "One more step and you are a dead man!"

Omar ignored John and continued to move toward him. John pulled the trigger but nothing happened! My God, he thought, I forgot to load the pistol!

Omar drove the knife deep into John's chest. He again thrust the knife into John, and the more he stabbed, the more he became enraged. He kept stabbing John over and over. Omar was completely out of control. All of his frustration was being vented at the man in front of him! Again and again he sunk his knife into the man's body. John fell to the ground. Omar raised the knife again to strike John; however, he heard something moving behind him. He turned, but it was too late. Ramon swung the machete with all his might!

Omar's head was severed and fell to the ground! Ramon looked at the two men and sank to his knees. Mr. John was bleeding, a gurgling sound coming from his chest each time he took a breath.

John raised his head and looked at Ramon. "You are a good friend, Ramon; now you must go, I am through I'm dying run Ramon, run!"

"I will help you, Mr. John; we are near the trail, we can make it to the road!"

"No, Ramon, he told me that there are more of them. His men are coming—you must go." John lay down and closed his eyes; he was dead.

Ramon wiped the tears from his eyes and touched John on the shoulder. "I will never forget you; you will always be my friend." He turned and started toward the clearing, not looking back. He thought, I will leave this jungle and return to my home!

The next morning Mila woke Charlie as soon as the sun came up. "Charlie," she said, "We must go; it is daybreak, and the Muslim bandits will be coming soon."

For a split second, Charlie had forgotten what had happened the night before; however, it came back to him in a frightening instant! Charlie covered his eyes with his hands and began to sob. Mila wrapped her arms around him and comforted Charlie the best she could, but at the same time she realized that hesitating could end their lives. She again said, "Charlie, we must go!"

Charlie took a deep breath. He decided she was right; there was nothing he could do for Jerry. He looked at her and said, "I'm going to bury him Mila." She was going to protest, but the look in his eyes convinced her it would do no good to try to talk him out of it.

Charlie dug a small grave in the jungle, then laid Jerry's body into it and covered it with underbrush and dirt. He looked at the makeshift grave. He said something under his breath that she couldn't hear and finally said to her, "You are right, Mila; let's get moving." He looked one more time and said out loud, "I will get these sons of bitches, Jerry, if it's the last thing I ever do!"

After traveling for another two hours, Charlie said to Mila, "I'm going to climb a tree to see if I can find out where we are." Charlie climbed a large tree and looked over the jungle. At first all he could see was more jungle ahead of them. He was about to climb down when he spotted what he thought was smoke drifting above the jungle. It looked to be about a mile ahead. Charlie got his bearings and climbed down the tree.

"I see smoke ahead of us Mila, in this direction," he pointed toward where he believed the smoke was coming from the jungle. Charlie took Mila by the hand, and the two continued moving through the jungle. He again turned and looked back to where he had buried Jerry and said, "I'm going to get us out of this, Mila. We have Jerry looking out for us now."

The chief and his warriors had returned to the village, but before leaving the American camp he had told his warriors to hang the dead intruders up in the trees. Let everyone who comes here see and never return to this place! The men closed off the tunnel where the yellow metal was hidden. He again said to his men; now we go and never return!

While the battle was raging at the camp, the bandit lieutenant had climbed through the small opening into the cave. He had decided to wait inside the tunnel until Omar returned; he could not fight all these men. However he thought, *Who are these people? Why did they kill my men? What is happening?* Suddenly he could hear the men digging at the front of the tunnel entrance. He froze and pressed his body against the wall of the cave. *I will wait for Omar*, he thought. The lieutenant was going to wait a very, very long time!

Ramon returned to the trail he had found the night before. He continued following it all morning; by the afternoon, finally, the trail separated, one going toward the main road and one heading toward the primitive village. He said out loud, "I will go to the main road and find help I am afraid the villagers would kill me if I go to their village."

By late afternoon Charlie and Mila were approaching the village. The jungle had been cut away surrounding the village. They found a makeshift garden planted near a stream. Charlie turned to Mila and said, "This must be the same steam we crossed on the other side of the village." They moved on and encountered two women coming up the trail from the village to work in the gardens. The women, when they saw Charlie and Mila, dropped their baskets and ran back in the direction they had came. Charlie and Mila continued it the trail and soon entered the village.

The chief and his warriors were waiting for them as they walked into the center of the village. The warriors surrounded them and pushed them in front of the chief. One of the villagers approached them and said to Mila, "What are you doing coming into our village? You have brought the curse of the yellow metal upon us!"

Mila recognized the man from the fishing village that had translated for them once before. Charlie looked at Mila and said, "Tell them we were looking for the yellow gold, but I want them to know that you had nothing to do with it; you are innocent."

Mila looked at Charlie in surprise and said, "I will not tell them that, Charlie. I am also responsible for what has happened. If the chief decides to punish you, he will also punish me!"

Charlie said, "Mila, do as I say!"

"The girl does not have to tell us what you have said; I understand the English," the man responded. He turned to the chief and explained to him what the American had said.

Charlie continued, "We did not want anyone to be hurt; we only wanted the yellow metal. We made a terrible mistake, but we do not deserve to die for it!"

Again the man translated to the chief. The chief looked at Charlie and Mila. They were filthy and worn out; he knew they were not going to cause any more trouble to his village, but he also knew that no one must know where the yellow metal was hidden. Too many lives had been lost over this metal and they would never allow that to happen again. He spoke to his interpreter and motioned toward Charlie and Mila.

The man turned to Charlie and said, "The chief will not allow either of you to leave this place. He said there have been too many deaths already. He says you will stay with us."

"What does that mean?" Charlie asked.

"You will never leave!" the man answered.

"But we must help our companions!" Charlie yelled. Mila began to cry and looked at Charlie with tears running down her face.

She said, "Do not say anything more, Charlie; we must stay here it is the only option—other than death!"

Charlie stood in shock! "Stay here forever!" he yelled. He looked into the jungle and around the village in disbelief! He had nothing left. This was the final humiliation; his spirit was broken.

Mila looked up at him she understood he would never be the same! Mila had seen the Abu Sayyaf bandit hanging from the tree. The warriors had hacked him to death. The chief had decided that he did not need to ask the bandit why he had killed his nephew—the curse of the yellow metal was the blame!

The remaining Abu Sayyaf returned to their village in the mountains and never spoke to anyone of what had happened. They would never know what happened to Omar or did they care. They realized that the kidnapping was no more! They would find a new leader, but this was the end. There would be no capture and ransom of the Americans!

Ramon broke from the jungle onto the main road. He stood looking down the road waiting for someone to come along. He hoped it would not be the bandits, but he was too tired to care. He untied a small bag hanging from his waist and opened it. He pulled five gold coins from the bag and looked at them. *I can return to my village now—I have found the gold!* He also thought of all the terrible things that had happened and said out loud, "I understand now, Grandfather. I will never tell anyone where the gold is hidden!"

As for Charlie and the others, Ramon decided that would have to wait until another day. He was going home!

Dateline Manila—The Manila Times reported today that three Americans have been missing in the jungles of Mindanao for over a month. It is assumed they are being held by the Abu Sayyaf, however,

this has not been confirmed. The American embassy has refused comment. In other news—

END PART ONE

MINDANAO GOLD

Part Two

Back to the Treasure!

PREFACE

Part Two, the continued saga of *Mindanao Gold*. In Part One, a group of adventurers discover a hidden gold stockpile left by the Japanese army during World War Two. The Japanese, during their occupation of the Philippines, confiscated massive gold deposits and hid the treasure in caves throughout the islands. As of 2010, very little of the gold has been recovered. In the first book, our adventurers discover the treasure; however, they were not successful. *Mindanao Gold, Back to the Treasure*, is the continued story and the attempt to reclaim the gold. So let us continue the saga. Will the gold be recovered, or will the curse continue and more lives lost?

Author note: The story depicts the Muslim bandits as the cruel component in the story. Although the portrayal of these men is that of bandits, the majority of Muslims within the Philippines are peaceful and family oriented people. The bandit groups in the Philippines are like in most countries—diversified, and unrecognizable by any means as one particular group. However, in this setting in southern Mindanao, the Muslim enclave is burdened with a large faction of bandits until this day, this is fact of life in southern Mindanao.

CHAPTER 1

The Players

Six years have passed since Charlie and Mila entered the primitive village. The first two weeks in captivity, Mila realized that Charlie had lost his will to live. As time passed, Charlie became more and more distant, and, within six months, was more dead than alive. Each morning Mila would bathe, dress, and feed Charlie—he had no desire to do anything other than sit in front of his hut or aimlessly wander throughout the village. Mila spent most of her time with Charlie in the hope that he would regain an interest in life, but after several months nothing seemed to have any impact on him. The villagers no longer were concerned with Charlie trying to escape; it was obvious Charlie had no intention to run. The natives called him "the man with a lost soul"!

The young man from the fishing village, who had been the interpreter for the village chief when Mila and Charlie were taken captive, continued to speak for them. The interpreting had been necessary until Mila was able to understand the primitive dialect. After a couple of months Mila no longer needed the young man to interpret, but failed to mention this to anyone. Since Charlie no longer would speak, Mila needed some companionship, which the young man provided. At first she could not understand why she did not tell the young man that she no longer needed him to interpret; as time went on she began to realize why—she was falling in love with him!

Magellan was one of three children. His father was an adviser to the chief of the village. When he was ten years old, his father decided to send him to the fishing village to attend school so that he could help the villagers understand what was happening in the outside world. The village preferred to left leave alone; however, the chief and Magellan's father realized that the outside world would come to their village sooner or later. In 1992 their predictions came true with the arrival of John Barringer and his group.

Magellan continued to attend school in the fishing village until he was eighteen years of age. Once he had completed his education he returned to the village; however, his father decided that Magellan would serve the village better if he remained in the fishing village as a fisherman. At first Magellan did not want to stay in the fishing village; he missed his family and friends however as time passed, he became adjusted to living in the village and the life of a fisherman.

When Charlie and his group came upon the primitive village while searching for the gold, Magellan's father suggested to the chief that it was the time to send for Magellan to act as an interpreter.

Later after the capture of Charlie and Mila while acting as the interpreter, Magellan developed a personal relationship with the girl. He became more and more sympathetic to the young woman's plight and would find any excuse to talk with her. The longer they were together, the more Magellan wanted to be near her. Mila was also desperate for companionship. She needed someone to talk to, as Charlie had cut off all communication, leaving Mila alone facing an unknown. After the tragedy in the jungle, she was isolated within the village. The villagers did not trust the young woman and avoided her. Magellan was the only one who would speak to her; she depended on him. Each day she would seek out Magellan; if it were not for the young man's kindness, she was convinced she would end up like Charlie. It was only a question of time before the two became intimate after a year in captivity Mila and Magellan fell deeply in love. After marriage they eventually moved back to the fishing. Each week they would travel back to his village and check on Charlie and visit his family. Two years after the marriage Mila gave birth to their first child Stopie. He was the change in the direction of Mila's life she no longer yearned for the United States her love now belonged to her family and the confines of the islands.

CHAPTER 2

Charlie

During the monsoon season, the afternoons' heavy rains drenched the village. Water filled the nearby streams, flooding the village and the jungle. The villagers would prepare for the afternoon rains and move their belongings inside their huts. As the rains began to fall, they would automatically enter their huts and wait until the rains subsided. Within an hour the rains would stop, and the villagers would continue with their daily lives.

Charlie ignored the rain. He sat outside his hut in the downpour, the water soaking him, the wind blowing—but Charlie paid no attention to the rain and wind pounding him.

An old lady looked at him from her hut and shook her head in disgust. She turned to the others in the hut and said, "This man is evil! He must not stay here any longer! He will bring trouble to our village!" Her son nodded his head in agreement.

Over the past six years the village people had begun to fear Charlie. They had witnessed villagers of their own like Charlie in the past; once they were afflicted, they were taken from the village into the jungle and left to die. This was the law!

The old lady's son stood next to his mother and watched Charlie as he wondered from hut to hut. Charlie had no expression on his face he stared straight ahead as he walked around the village. The boy said to his mother, "I will talk to Val about this man. We will call a meeting of the council and have this man sent from our village. We will no longer have him in our village!"

Valisimo was the eldest son of the chief and had become chief after the death of the old man in 1994. The villagers called him Val, a nickname he had from childhood. Val's father had proclaimed that Charlie and Mila would remain in the village until their deaths; however, things had changed since the old man had died. Charlie sat in front of his hut day after day staring into the jungle. If it were not for Mila, the man would have starved to death! Each day Charlie had to be treated as if he were a child. But after six years, the villagers had tired of this and demanded that Val rid the village of the crazy man. As long as Charlie did not cause trouble, however, Val was obligated to follow his father's wishes. But today Charlie had given him a reason; this crazy man's time had arrived!

Charlie blinked his eyes and looked around the village. It was the first time in almost six years that he had shown any sign he was aware of what was going on around him. At first Charlie did not realize where he was or what was happening. He slowly looked around the village, trying to understand what was going on. The rain and the wind continued to drive against his face and he thought, *I have to get out of this rain what the hell am I doing!*

Charlie slowly stood to his feet. He looked around and realized he was standing in front of a hut. He pulled back the blanket covering the door and entered. Inside he found a bed and his belongings stored next to the back wall. Charlie was confused. He stood in the middle of the room for a few minutes trying to figure out what was happening. The last thing he remembered was when Mila and he had entered the village—but other than that he had no idea what had happened since.

Suddenly he remembered—Jerry! Charlie screamed and slumped to his knees, covering his eyes with his hands, and he began to sob. *What have I done? This miserable nightmare was my entire fault!* After a few minutes he stood up, thinking, *I have to find out what is going on.*

Charlie realized he was very cold; he was soaking wet from the rain and realized he needed a change of clothes. Charlie slowly moved toward his things stored in the back of the small hut. He leaned over and began rummaging through his belongings. Suddenly he stopped, stood back from the bags, and thought, Mila, where is Mila? My God, what have they done to Mila?

Charlie charged out the door of the hut and frantically looked around the village. The rain had slowed; however, water was running in all directions. Charlie had no idea of where to look for Mila, but he knew he must find her. He ran around the village, but as he approached each hut, the villagers closed their doors to him. He screamed, "Where is Mila?" but the villagers could not understand this crazy man's dialect.

"What is this crazy man doing now?" asked the old women. She turned to her son and said, "You must find Valisimo! This man is going to harm us; he is crazy!" The son waited until Charlie had run past their hut and down to the other end of the village. He pulled back the flap to his hut and ran, terrified, toward Val's hut.

He found Val sleeping on a grass mat near a small fire in the middle of the hut. The young man grabbed him and screamed, "You must stop him!"

Valisimo awoke in confusion; he had no idea what this boy was yelling about! He sat up in bed, rubbed his eyes, and asked in an irritated voice, "What are you talking about?"

The young man began to holler, "The crazy man is trying to kill our people! You must stop him!"

Val grabbed the boy by his arm and said, "Stop yelling, and tell me what you are talking about."

Meanwhile, Charlie had returned to his hut in frustration and was standing inside. He said out loud, "Why won't these people tell me what they have done with Mila?" Fear gripped his entire body—he had to find Mila! Charlie slowly removed his wet shirt and pants, dried off, then reached inside his bags and grabbed some dry clothes. He thought, First I have to get changed and then I will find her!

After listening to what the young man had to say, Val opened the curtain door of his hut and looked around the village. By now several villagers were outside and were frantically talking between themselves. As Val approached the group, several of them began to yell at the same time, "Stop this crazy man—he is going to kill someone!"

Val raised his hand and said, "Stop! I cannot understand what you are saying if all of you are talking at the same time!"

The villagers settled down somewhat but still continued to whisper among themselves. The old woman looked at Val and said, "This crazy man must go before he does something to us! You are our chief, and it is your responsibility!"

Val looked around the village and asked, "Where is he?"

One of the villagers pointed toward Charlie's hut and said, "There, he is there."

Val motioned with his hand to two of his warriors and said, "Follow me." Val pushed back the cloth doorway and entered the hut with the two warriors close behind. Charlie had just finished dressing which was a surprise to him as he had lost several pounds over the past few years while at the village. He was tightening his pants around his waist to keep them up. He turned around to see the three men entering the hut. He thought, finally, someone is going to tell me where Mila is. He stepped forward and asked, "Where is Mila?"

As Charlie stepped toward the three men, they immediately retreated toward the doorway. Val did not understand what Charlie was saying; he raised his hand toward Charlie indicating to him to not come any closer. Charlie stopped and waited for one of the men to answer his question, not realizing they could not understand him. He repeated his question, "Where is Mila?"

Val waited for a moment then he turned to the warriors and said, "Tie him up. I will send for Magellan and Mila; they can tell us what this crazy man is saying."

The two warriors carefully approached Charlie and grabbed his arms; this was a big mistake! Charlie was much bigger than the two men, and by using his weight he whipped his arms two men went flying through the air across the hut! Val stepped back, the men just missing him as they flew by! Charlie stood looking at them in anger but also deep inside with fear. Again the chief instructed the two men to restrain Charlie, but he realized this time he would have to help them. Eventually the three men were able to force Charlie to the ground while all the time they struggled to tie him down he kept screaming, "Where is Mila, where is Mila!"

Val and his men left the hut and returned to where the other villagers were waiting. The chief looked at one of the young men of the village and said, "Go to the fishing village and find Magellan and Mila. We will find out what this crazy man wants. Until then, no one will enter his hut!"

The young man turned and ran from the village. He would bring back Magellan and Mila; however, just as he was leaving, Mila and Magellan arrived. Mila could see that something was wrong; the villagers were standing in the center of the camp surrounding Val. They were all talking at the same time and seemed upset about something.

The young man ran up to them and said to Magellan, "You must come! The crazy man is trying to kill all of us!" Mila and Magellan looked at each other in confusion.

Mila asked, "What are they talking about?"

Magellan answered, "I do not know, but I will find out. Take the boy to my mother's hut; I will find out what has happened."

Mila lifted their young son into her arms and walked toward his mother's hut. She was very worried; she knew something was wrong, and it was about Charlie! She kept looking over her shoulder as she walked, thinking, I will leave the Shopie at the hut but then I must find out what is going on. Charlie had not caused any trouble in six years at the village; why now?

Magellan approached the villagers, stopping in front of Val and asking, "What has happened, my chief?"

"I am not sure, Magellan. The villagers tell me that this Charlie, as you call him, has tried to kill one of our villagers, but I cannot find out who he has attacked. We have tied him up in his hut until I can find out what is going on. I will need you and Mila to speak with him."

"I will go and speak with Charlie and find out what he wants."

"Take Mila with you. She understands this man and can help."

Magellan did not like this idea. If Charlie had tried to kill one of the villagers, he did not want his wife near Charlie. He did not want to challenge the chief in front of the other villagers, however.

Mila returned to find Magellan walking toward Charlie's hut. "What is going on?" she asked.

Magellan said to her, "Charlie has tried to kill one of the villagers!"

"No, this cannot be true," she replied.

"The chief has told me that you and I must find out from Charlie what he wants, so we must go to his hut. Mila, I want you to stay behind me until we find out what is going on. Do not get close to Charlie until we are sure it is safe, do you understand?"

Mila looked at Magellan and said, "Charlie has not said a word to anyone in six years. All he does is sit at the hut all day. Why, after all this time, would he try to kill someone?"

They continued toward Charlie's hut. As they approached the opening, Mila grabbed Magellan's arm and said, "Let me go in first! Didn't you say he was tied up?"

Magellan loved Mila and was determined that no one was going to harm her! "Mila, I cannot allow anyone to harm you. I know you feel that Charlie will not do anything to you, but I cannot take that chance! He has not been right with himself for some time and may not be the same man as you remember."

"Please," Mila begged.

Magellan looked at her. Since the first day he fell in love with her he could not say no, but still he hesitated. "All right, Mila, but I will be right behind you. If Charlie does anything THAT will harm you, I will kill him!"

Mila carefully opened the flap to the hut. Charlie was lying on his side, tied hand and foot, facing away from the doorway. Mila said, in a quiet voice, "Charlie."

Since the warriors had tied Charlie up, he had been lying there trying to make sense of what was going on. He could not remember much since Mila and he had entered the village, other that the constant nightmares about the others, especially Jerry. He couldn't get Jerry out of his mind. It seemed he was dreaming about Jerry every minute of his life. He kept seeing Jerry dying in front of him and thinking it was his fault! But other than that, he could not remember what had happened since they had entered the village!

Mila repeated, "Charlie?"

Charlie rolled over and saw Mila standing in the doorway. "Mila," he said, with panic in his voice, "are you all right?"

"Yes, Charlie, I am fine."

Charlie began to struggle against his bonds. Magellan moved forward but Mila raised her hand to stop him. "Charlie," she said, "don't do anything, just listen to me."

Charlie relaxed a little and said, "What is going on, Mila? Why have they tied me up?"

"Charlie, the villagers told us that you have tried to kill someone!"

"Kill someone? What are you talking about?" He again started fighting the ropes.

"Tell him to stop fighting. Mila, or we will leave," Magellan cautioned her.

"Charlie, settle down," she pleaded. Charlie again relaxed and looked at her. Mila bent down and began to untie Charlie.

"What are you doing?" Magellan yelled, "Leave him alone!"

Mila continued to untie Charlie. She said, "Charlie, I am going to untie you, but you must lay still, do you understand?"

Charlie nodded his head in agreement and stopped fighting the ropes.

"Mila, please do not free him," Magellan begged.

She turned to look at the man she loved and said, "He is my friend. He will not harm me."

After untying Charlie she said, "Charlie, you know that you have not spoken a word for six years!"

"What? What do you mean, six years?" After Charlie was free and sitting upright

Mila spent the next couple of hours telling Charlie what had happened since they entered the primitive village six years earlier. "After a few weeks in the village," she explained, you withdrew into yourself. I tried to bring you out of your depression, but nothing worked. Eventually, you stopped talking, eating, and cleaning yourself. Once you had given up, I began taking care of you. I would wake you up in the mornings; lead you to the nearby stream, bathe, and dress you. The first year I spent all my time with you, Charlie. Then I began to see Magellan more and more; I needed someone, Charlie." Mila explained that during the second year of captivity she and Magellan were married. A year later she gave birth to their son, Shopie.

After she had finished Charlie looked up at Magellan and said, "Does he speak English?"

"He can understand you," she answered.

"Young man, I am still very confused, but I want to thank you for taking care of Mila."

Magellan looked at them and at first did not know what to say. He nodded to Charlie.

"Mila, I need time to think. Do you suppose they will let me stay here for a while? I promise not to cause trouble."

Mila looked up at Magellan and he nodded approval, saying, "I will talk to our chief, but Charlie, you must not leave the hut!"

Charlie nodded his head in agreement then Mila and Magellan left.

After Magellan told the chief what had happened in the hut, Mila began to plead with the chief and promised to watch over Charlie. Val stood in front of the two for some time not speaking then finally said, "I have discovered that the man did not attempt to kill anyone; however, the villagers are still terrified of him. They do not want him in our village any longer. I will allow you to watch him, but he must not leave the hut until we decide what must be done, do you understand?"

Mila nodded her head and smiled at the chief and Magellan. "I will not disappoint you; he will not cause any further trouble."

With the approval of the two men she started to leave, but before doing so she motioned for Magellan to follow her. After they were a safe distance from the chief, Mila took Magellan's face into her hands and rose up and kissed him. She looked deep into his eyes and said, "I do not deserve such a man, and I love you with all my heart! I tell you this because I know what you are thinking. You are wondering if I will return to Charlie. That will never happen; you are my husband and the father of our child. I am yours forever!"

Magellan wrapped his arms around Mila and said, "Mila, go to your friend; he needs you. I will be waiting for your return."

Mila walked into the hut and found Charlie sobbing softly, sitting with his hands covering his face. "What is the matter, Charlie? They have told me I can take care of you, do not cry."

"Oh Mila, I can't get Jerry out of my mind! Every time I close my eyes I see him lying there in front of me dying! It's going to drive me crazier than I already am!"

"Charlie, let me fix you something to eat and then you need to try to sleep."

"I can't, Mila! If I close my eyes, all I see is Jerry!"

"Wait here, Charlie. I will be right back." Mila left the hut and returned to Magellan. She said to him, "I must have some herbs for sleeping; Charlie must sleep."

Mila entered her mother-in-law's hut and asked her for some of her sleeping herbs. The woman never questioned Mila; she only knew the Mila was her son's wife, and she therefore would never question her about the request. Magellan's mother walked over to a cupboard and retrieved a small bag from one of the shelves and handed it to Mila.

"Give him a half a handful of this in some warm water before he sleeps. This will allow him to rest."

Mila returned to the hut. She took Magellan with her because she wanted him to feel comfortable around Charlie. She prepared something to eat. Later she fixed Charlie the drink. He looked at her and said, "Mila,

I am afraid nothing is going to work. I'm sure I'll have terrible dreams about Jerry again."

"Please drink this, Charlie; at least let's give it a try," she answered.

Charlie raised the cup and drank down the liquid. The three of them sat in silence for a while until Charlie became drowsy from the drink. Mila moved to the back of the room and made Charlie's bed. She looked over at the two men and said, "Let us go, my husband, and allow Charlie to sleep." She had purposely called to Magellan as her husband. She wanted both men to know who she belonged to. Magellan rose to his feet and waited for Mila to return to him. She looked at Charlie as they left and said, "Get some sleep, Charlie. We will talk more in the morning."

All of a sudden Charlie was dead tired. He had a hard time climbing into bed; in fact, he didn't bother to remove his clothes, he just pulled the covers over him.

"Charlie, Charlie."

Charlie opened his eyes and looked up at Jerry standing over him. "Jerry, is that you?"

"Yeah, Charlie, it's me."

"But you're dead! I saw you die!"

Jerry smiled, "Charlie, I have been waiting for you to come to your senses for almost six years. I've been in your head every night trying to get you to come out of your stupor, and now that you have, I need to talk to you, so listen."

"But Jerry—" Charlie protested.

Jerry raised his hand and said, "Charlie, I said listen."

Charlie lay back down and looked up at Jerry.

"Charlie, this is the only time I can talk to you, so listen carefully. John and I have been waiting a long time for you to wake up. Charlie, it's time to get the gold. You are the only chance John and I have, so by God you had better wake up and smell the roses!"

"Jerry—" Charlie again said.

"Don't say anything, Charlie. I am running out of time. You need to understand as long as the gold stays hidden, John and I will never rest, so Charlie, you have to go back and get it! Did we die in vain? We need your help, Charlie, so get the damn gold!"

Before Charlie could answer him, Jerry was gone! Charlie sat up in his bed, sweat running down his face, his clothes soaking wet. The sun was streaking through the flap in the doorway. Charlie looked around and noticed a bowl of warm corn mush sitting on the table. Apparently Mila had been there. He rose to his feet and sat down at the table. He started eating, and the more he ate, the more he realized how hungry he was.

He finished the mush and sat back to reflect on what had happened during the night. The more he thought about it, the more confused he became. He thought; Jerry is dead. What in the hell is going on? This dream was different; he actually talked with Jerry, didn't he? Did it really happen?

Charlie was still at the table when Mila entered the hut. "I see that you have eaten, Charlie; how do you feel?"

"Better. I just can't believe that six years have passed, that's all!"

"Charlie, you have to try to forget the past. Those terrible days are over. We must move on and let the past be the past. Charlie, I want to show you something."

Mila left the hut for a moment and returned with a small boy about a year and a half old. "Charlie, this is my son Shopie."

The little boy reminded Charlie of Magellan. Charlie sat at the table looking at the boy. "He is a fine-looking lad, Mila; I am proud of you."

Mila picked up her son and moved toward the table where Charlie sat. She placed the boy on Charlie's lap. The little boy put his thumb in his mouth and looked up at Charlie with his big, brown eyes. With his other hand he reached up and touched Charlie's face. He kept rubbing Charlie's beard with his small hand.

Charlie laughed and placed his hand on top of the boy's head. "He sure doesn't seem to be afraid of me, does he?"

Mila smiled and said, "Who could ever be afraid of you, Charlie? You are a good man. I remember you saving my life, Charlie, and I know how kind you can be."

Charlie looked up at her and said, "Mila, why didn't I recognize how good you were when I had the chance?"

She placed her hand on Charlie's shoulder and said, "Charlie, I have changed. Remember all I wanted from you was a chance to go to the United States? I did not realize what was truly important to me until I married Magellan."

"Well, that's, as you say, in the past now. Both of us can look to the future."

Just as Mila finished talking, Magellan walked into the hut. At first he was concerned that his son was sitting in Charlie's lap, but after a few moments he realized that the boy was safe. He recognized the compassion in Charlie's face when Charlie looked down at the boy. In broken English Magellan said, "How are you feeling, Charlie?" "Much better, young man; again I want to thank you for taking care of Mila. She has told me how much you have done and how much she loves you. This embarrassing to Magellan it was not something someone talked about in front of others; in his culture love was a very private affair between a man and woman. Mila smiled at him and put her arms around the man she loved.

"I have returned from a meeting with our chief. I have told him that you have regained your senses and will not harm anyone in our village. He has seen it himself; however, he is still concerned and believes you should leave the village by tomorrow."

"Can I talk to the old man? I would like to thank him for watching over me all these years."

Mila looked at Charlie in confusion and then realized that Charlie did not know the old chief had died. "Charlie," she said, "the old chief died two years ago. His son is now the leader of the village."

"I'm sorry to hear that, Mila. I hope the son is as good as his father."

Magellan interrupted, "Val is a good man. He leads his people with honor."

Charlie looked at the two and said, "Can I meet him?"

"I do not know, but I will ask. In the meantime, do not leave the hut unless Mila or I am with you. There are some who would want to kill you. You are only safe if one of us is with you; it is best you stay in the hut."

The next day Magellan returned to Charlie's hut and told him the chief would meet with him in one hour. Charlie asked, "Where does he want to meet?"

"He will come to your hut. You must remember he is our chief and treat him with respect. Mr. Charlie, this meeting will decide what is going to happen to you, do you understand?"

"Yes, I do, thank you, Magellan."

An hour later Val and one of the men who had tied Charlie up entered the hut. Charlie looked at the young chief and said to Mila, "Tell him I recognize him from yesterday and want to say I am sorry for my actions."

Mila repeated to the chief what Charlie had said. The man showed little emotion and started taking to Mila in dialect. Mila turned to Charlie and repeated what the chief had said.

"Charlie, the chief says you must leave the village immediately. He cannot guarantee your safety. He says there are elders in the village who want to have you killed. They say you violated the curse of the yellow metal and must die!"

Charlie asked, "What else does the young chief have to say?"

Mila, Magellan, and the young chief spoke for a few minutes and then she turned to Charlie. "Magellan and I have told the chief we will take you from here and you will never return. He has agreed but has told us this must be done today."

"When can we go, Mila?" Charlie asked.

"Now, Charlie. The villagers are out working in the gardens and hunting. This is the best time to leave."

Charlie packed his bags and the three of them left the village. Magellan led the way, while Mila carried Shopie in her arms, Charlie following behind. Soon they were out of sight of the village. Charlie started to reflect on the past six years—the loss of the others, his loss of memory, and the fact that Mila was now a wife and mother. Things had definitely changed. Charlie reflected, I can only hope it's for the good!

CHAPTER 3

Back in the World

It took all day to reach the main road. Charlie was not used to walking; the group had to stop several times for him to rest. As usual, Charlie was amazed at how strong Mila was—she carried her son and was able to stay up with Magellan. The two must have made this trip many times, for Magellan rarely looked behind to check on them. He continued to set a fast pace and only stopped when Mila would tell him Charlie was falling behind.

As they passed the old camp, Charlie didn't look at the entrance; he continued to move forward. Traveling toward the fishing village, Mila told Charlie what she knew of the site and about the warriors, the death of Gary, and the Muslims. She told him about the cave; however, Charlie asked that she not say any more—he did not want to know what had happened. The only question he asked was what had happened to Ramon. She explained that Ramon was never found and it was assumed he had returned to his village.

After reaching the main road, they flagged down a Jeepnee and they were taken to the fishing village. Mila and Magellan led Charlie to their home on the outskirts of the village. As they approached Charlie saw the old van they had used sitting in front of the house.

He asked Mila, "Is that the van?"

"Yes, the van owner came looking for it, but after hearing about the Muslims he hastily left the fishing village and never returned."

"Does it work?" Charlie asked.

"Yes," she said, "Magellan is a good mechanic and has kept the van running."

Charlie paused for a moment and took a quick look into the van. Again his emotions began to surface; Jerry, Gary, and John, their all gone. God, he thought then continued into the house.

After storing his bags in a small room Mila had made up for him, Charlie sat down to rest. It had been quite a walk.

Magellan said to Mila, "I must go to the fishing village. I have been away too long—the others need my help to catch the fish." Mila unexpectedly leaned up and kissed him on the cheek, which embarrassed him for the second time. Magellan's expression told the story—warriors did not show affection in front of strangers! He regained his composure and left for the village.

Charlie was amazed at her Mila's energy as she immediately began to clean the house and fix something to eat. He said to her, "Mila, I am impressed; you are quite a woman. You have walked all day carrying your son, yet you still have the energy to clean your house and feed the boy and me."

"Charlie, this is not work for me; I am happy to do this. I have a man who loves me, and a child I love with all my soul. It also makes my heart feel good to see you living again!"

Charlie shook his head and smiled at Mila. He returned to his bags and rummaged through the contents; he needed to know what was still there. He found the bankbook in one of his coat pockets; it was important. He took a look and realized had almost $40,000 in the account. One problem solved!

After dinner Charlie asked if he could lie down for a while so Mila took him to the small room in back of the house. Charlie stretched out on the bed and in a few minutes he was sound asleep. Suddenly he awoke; he remembered what Jerry had said: "Get the gold, Charlie!"

The room was dark. Charlie got out of bed and walked into the main part of the house. He found Magellan eating his dinner and Mila holding the boy.

"Did you get some sleep, Charlie?" she asked.

"Yes, Mila, I feel a lot better. How were things at the fishing village?" he asked Magellan.

Magellan looked up at him and said, "There is much work to be done, but things are good!"

Charlie approached the table and sat down. He looked at the two and said, "I will be leaving in the morning. Mila, I do not want to interfere with your family any further."

"But Charlie, you have only been here one day! Please stay with us for a while," she answered.

Magellan surprised Charlie by saying, "Yes, Charlie, stay with us until you are feeling better."

Charlie knew Magellan did not have to say this. He realized he was in the way and should not take advantage of their hospitality. He also knew he must take care of some unfinished business for Jerry and John! He owed them, and he realized he would never rest until the business of the gold was taken care of—and neither would his friends he left behind!

CHAPTER 4

Davao

The next morning, Charlie found Mila setting at the table. She had cooked him breakfast and was waiting at the table for him. The boy was playing on the floor and looked up at Charlie when he entered the room. A big smile crossed the little one's face, and he reached out for Charlie. Charlie looked at Mila for approval, and she grinned. Charlie bent over and picked up the boy. Shopie giggled and started rubbing Charlie's face again. Charlie sat down at the table and began to eat, while Shopie pulled at Charlie's beard, Mila watched with a smile on her face. "Charlie, let me take him from you so you can eat."

"Please, Mila; let him sit here for a while. It's been a long time since anyone made me feel this good. I will give him back after breakfast." While he ate he asked Mila when the bus would come so he could catch a ride to Davao.

She looked at him in surprise and said, "Why would you ride the bus? The van is here, Charlie."

"Oh, I couldn't take the van, Mila; that is for you and Magellan."

"Charlie," she said, "we will never use the van—it reminds us of the tragedy. The only reason Magellan kept it running was to sell it if we could, but no one wants it. Everyone here knows of the deaths that it was involved with. You would do us a favor if you took it away and got rid of it."

"Are you sure, Mila? I mean, do you really want me to take it?"

"Please, Charlie."

"Listen," Charlie continued, I have some money in Davao. When I get there I will send some back to you for payment of the van."

"Please, Charlie; just take it away. We do not want anything to do with it."

Charlie realized that he was not going to convince Mila and decided to drop the subject. Two hours later Charlie said his goodbyes and was on the road to Davao but before he left he took Mila into his arms and said, "Mila, you are the daughter I never had. I will always love you for what you have done for me."

She looked up at Charlie and said, "Please come back to us, Charlie. Do what you must, but come back to us." The little one sitting on the floor playing looked up into Charlie's eyes and started to crawl toward him. Charlie picked the boy up, kissed his little hand and handed him to Mila. He walked out the door, climbed into the van and was gone. Tears rolled down Mila's cheeks; she wondered, "Will I ever see him again?"

First thing Charlie thought of while on the way to Davao was, got to get some new clothes! Christ, I lost fifty pounds and boy do I need cold beer!

Davao hadn't changed much, he thought, as he drove through the city. The place looked just the same as it did six years ago! Crowded streets loaded with vendors, trucks, tricycles, kids, and carts everywhere, dogs eating out of garbage cans along the road. Just as he was about to pass an old van loaded with bananas, a small girl not more than five years old darted across the road in front of his van. Charlie jammed the brakes on; within seconds it seemed every horn in Mindanao was blaring!

The sweat on Charlie seemed to explode from his body—every inch of him was drenched. He realized he had been gripping the steering wheel from the time he entered the city limits. He thought, Settle down, man; you're gonna kill someone! He continued to drive along General Santos, the main street of Davao, when he noticed a policeman signaling him to pull over. Charlie thought, now what?

The policeman walked up to the driver's window and motioned Charlie to roll down the window. "May I see your driver's license and registration, please? Do you realize that the license plate is out of date?"

Charlie began to panic, Shit, he thought, I forgot about the damn van.

"Officer, I just bought the van and haven't had a chance to get the paper work done."

The policeman began to write out a ticket. Just then Charlie spotted the bank across the street.

"Officer, if you will let me go to the bank for a few minutes, I am sure we can work this out."

The policeman looked at Charlie for a second and said, "That cannot be possible. I need to see your driver's license and registration."

"Tell you what, Officer—you can wait here at the van and I will return in a few minutes. I can't leave my van alone; would you mind watching it? Besides, you can see me when I go into the bank, right?"

The policeman looked at Charlie again and said, "I will give you five minutes to do your business. If you do not return, I will find you and arrest you for driving a stolen vehicle!"

Charlie climbed out of the van and headed straight for the bank. When he entered he noticed a stack of withdrawal slips on a counter near the door. Charlie realized that he was still sweating; his clothes were clinging to his body and sweat was dripping off his nose. A middle-aged woman standing across the room was staring at him like he was some kind of freak. Charlie tried to ignore her but she continued to stand and look at him. Finally, she walked across the room and started talking to the security guard. Oh no, Charlie thought, this is it! That's all I need is more misery from the cops!

The two continued to talk, and finally the guard pointed toward the back of the bank. The woman turned and started walking in the direction of the women's bathroom!

Charlie glanced down at his hands dangling next to his body—both his fists were clinched, the muscles in his forearms bulging. Charlie screamed inside his head, Settle down!

He walked to the table with the withdrawal slips and began to write down the amount he would need. He thought, would one hundred-fifty thousand pesos be too much? Hell, I don't have any idea! He went ahead and wrote it down; after all, if it didn't work he was screwed anyway!

Charlie approached the teller and handed the girl the withdrawal slip along with his account book. She looked at Charlie and said, "Good afternoon, sir; how are you today?"

"Fine, thank you, young lady," he responded. Charlie fought the urge to run. His stomach was churning, and again the sweat began to run down his face. The teller turned to her computer and began to enter the data.

A few minutes later she looked at Charlie and said, "Could you wait here for a moment, please? I have to check the account and confirm it with the bank manager."

Charlie froze. "What seems to be the problem, young lady? Isn't the account any good?" he asked.

She responded, "No sir, the account is good; I just have to check on something," and left the counter.

Charlie knew he was going to be sick; he was dizzy and light-headed. He thought, this is it they are going to put me in jail. I never got the money out of the account; it was always Jerry. Damn him! He told me I was on the account now what? What the hell is going to happen? Here I am driving a stolen van and trying to get into an account that isn't mine!

"Sir?"

Charlie looked up. A small man was standing next to the teller with Charlie's withdrawal slip in his hand. The man continued, "It has been quite a while since you have withdrawn from this account."

"Yes," Charlie replied, "I have been out of the country for some time and have just returned."

"Sir, are you satisfied with our service?" the man asked.

"Yes, I am," Charlie replied. "Is there a problem with the account?"

"Oh no sir! In fact your account is one of our best in fact the account has increased substantially since your last withdrawal. Did you realize that the account has increased to $61,000?"

Charlie took a deep breath and said, "My goodness, no; that's very nice to hear."

"Well, if there is anything we can do, please let us know," the man said, and walked away.

The teller asked, "Sir how would you like the money in small or large bills?" Charlie responded, "Oh, just break it up into different denominations if you would I'm kind of in a hurry."

Once outside the bank Charlie wanted to yell at the top of his lungs! He stood on the top step of the bank thinking, I'll never pull this off, guys, without your help. I'm tellin' ya, I am a wreck! I can't even buy a glass of beer or find a place to stay without fuckin' it up! Charlie looked across the street at the policeman and decided to return to the van. He found the policeman sitting in the driver's seat with his citation pad in his hand.

"Well, my friend—did you get your banking done?" the officer asked.

"I sure did," Charlie answered. "I wonder what we can do to take care of this problem. You see, I am on the way to the Department of Transportation to change the title and register the van. Can I pay you a fine here so I can get the van taken care of?"

The policemen looked at Charlie and said, "What do you mean?"

"Well, I thought if I could pay a fine with you and take care of the van, everyone would be happy. I know you are busy, and this way both of us would be satisfied."

The officer looked at Charlie and said, "How much do you think a fine like this is worth?"

Charlie had been in the Philippines long enough to know what to do about traffic citations, but he also knew he must be careful—if he was too pushy, he might scare off the policeman and end up in jail. "I was thinking if the same thing happened in the United States, it would cost me about 500 pesos—but of course that is in the U.S."

"Well, you are not in the United States, my American friend, you are in the Philippines, and we do not let anyone go at the price. This is very serious in our country," answered the policeman.

"What would you think about a thousand pesos, does that seem fair?" Charlie waited for a response.

The policeman leaned over the steering wheel and said, "What about fifteen hundred pesos? That seems more like a proper fine to me."

Charlie shrugged his shoulders and said "I have just taken fifteen hundred pesos out of my account and cannot pay more than a thousand pesos, so I guess we will have to go to the police station and take care of this." Charlie tried to look miserable and resigned to the fact he was going to jail.

The officer said, "All right, give me the thousand pesos. You must get this problem taken care of by tomorrow. If you do not, I will arrest you, do you understand?"

Before leaving the bank Charlie had separated the money. He pulled fifteen hundred pesos from his pocket and handed the policeman one thousand. The policeman handed Charlie a bogus ticket and walked away.

Fifteen minutes later Charlie traded the van at a used car lot for a Toyota pickup and fifty thousand pesos—he was on his way! He knew that the used car dealer would have a new title for the van before the day was out!

Now what? How much time do I need to develop a sensible plan? He thought of Jerry and John and said out loud, "Boys, we are going to get the gold!

First Charlie rented an apartment near downtown then he bought some clothes and a case of San Miguel, Philippine beer. It was time to tear the head off a couple. Good ole' Charlie was back!

After about three beers, Charlie felt the effect. He was half drunk and feeling no pain! He realized he had not had a beer in six years—he remembered drinking a half case without getting a buzz, but it sure in the hell was different now!

Charlie got up from his chair and decided to go down to his old watering hole and see what had been happening since he had been gone. Fifteen minutes later he entered the bar. He took a look around and realized that not much had changed other than a new bartender was standing behind the bar. He still was feeling the effects of the beer that he had at the apartment and decided he had better slow down, so he ordered a Coke. While he drank his Coke he casually looked around. There wasn't anyone in the bar that he recognized. An expat was sitting a couple of stools down from him with a young Philippine girl sitting beside him. Charlie thought, some things never change, same ole, ole!

Charlie finished his Coke, waited another half hour then decided to order a beer. While drinking his first beer, he took another look around and saw that two men had taken a seat at a table near the back of the bar. Charlie turned back to take another pull off his beer. He started feeling good again and ordered a shot to go along with his beer. After about an hour the beer and booze started working on him.

All along he could hear the two men at the back of the bar talking, and he continued to eavesdrop on their conversation. The more beer they drank, the more escalated the conversation became. The bartender had told them a couple of times to hold it down. Charlie heard one of them say, "Bullshit! I am telling you they will never mine in Diwalwal! I have been there and it is the most dangerous place in the Philippines!"

The other man responded, "Like hell! I've done some engineering for a small-scale mining company and they are ready to open up the whole area. All they need is a little money."

Charlie was well aware of Diwalwal. It had the highest grade of gold in the country but was controlled by small-scale miners. In the past ten years over 300 miners had lost their lives fighting over the gold. The first man was right; no one was going to get control of Diwalwal!

Small-scale mining was a hot topic in the Philippines. Most of it was illegal and the resulting chaos made the Old West look like child's play in comparison. People died almost every day at the mine sites. No, law, no order—just survival. The most dangerous small-scale area in the country was Diwalwal there were ten thousand miners fighting for a mountain of gold.

It had been a long time since Charlie had talked to anyone about mining. He needed something to take his mind off the last six years, and this might be that opportunity. He picked up his beer and started walking over to the two men. Charlie stopped for a second and thought to himself, Be careful, Charlie; don't go saying something that you will regret. Remember—just a little conversation!

"Excuse me, guys—do you mind if I sit down with you I've been listening to your conversation and would like to join in if possible been a long time since I talked with a couple expats."

The two men looked up at Charlie and said, "Hell no, partner; be our guest. We could use some company."

Charlie introduced himself, saying, "I couldn't help overhearing your conversation about Dawalwal thought I might join in if you two don't have a problem with that."

The man who had made the comment about not getting into Diwalwal said, "Then ya heard my friend say he can get in there eh—can you believe that!"

"Well, I have to agree. Diwalwal is a tough place to work. I've been in the Philippines more than ten years and have learned to stay away from there."

The two men became very interested in Charlie the minute he told them he had been in the Philippines for ten years. The man sitting to Charlie's left, said, "I'm Gil Martin, and this is my buddy Arnold James. What did you say they called you?"

Charlie looked at the two men and repeated, "Charlie Taylor."

"Yeah," the other man said, more than a bit drunk, "didn't ya hear him say Charlie Taylor? Hell, you're gettin' drunk, old son!"

Gil gave Arnold a hard look but continued. "Well, Charlie Taylor, it is nice meeting you. How about we buy you another beer?"

Charlie nodded his head in agreement. Gil got up from the table and headed for the bar.

"So Charlie, what kind of business are you in out here in the Philippines?" Arnold asked.

Charlie answered, "I'm a mining engineer. What about you two?"

"Well, isn't that a kick," the man said, "so are we!"

Gil returned to the table with six beers in his hands and said, "No sense in making too many trips to the bar, right, guys?" He started laughing.

Arnold waved his hand motioning Gil to quite down and said, "Gil, the guy's a mining engineer, isn't that somethin'?" his partner said, and slapped the table with his hand. "We've hit the jackpot!"

"Well, what do ya know about that," Gil responded, and sat back down at the table.

Three hours later Charlie realized he had drunk way too much. Besides he didn't feel comfortable with these two men. They kept questioning him about gold mines in Mindanao, and where could they get into something good. Charlie was in no mood to discuss business anymore he had had enough. He could handle little light-hearted conversation, but the two would not let up. Finally, Charlie decided it was time to call it a night.

He looked at the two men and said, "I am over my limit, boys, and have decided to head for home. Maybe I will get a chance to have a drink with you two down the road."

Charlie started to get to his feet but Arnold grabbed him by the arm and said, "Oh hell, Charlie, its early! Sit down and have another drink."

Charlie was immediately pissed by the way the man grabbed him and held him down. "Friend, I will ask you just one time to turn me loose. I hope for your sake you know what I mean."

Gil who was sitting on Charlie's right caught Charlie by surprise when he hit Charlie with a hard right cross in the side of his face. Charlie slid off his seat and staggered back from the table then fell to the floor. The two men were on him in an instant, kicking and punching while he lay on his back. Charlie coiled up in a ball the best he could to protect himself from the blows, but one of them was able to kick him in the head. Charlie started to pass out from the blow—the beer he had been drinking didn't help either!

All of a sudden the beating stopped. Charlie was not being kicked anymore but he was too dizzy to see what was going on or why they had stopped beating him. He felt someone apply a cold towel to his forehead. He carefully opened his eyes and looked up. He couldn't see the two men that had attacked him but seen the bartender was leaning over him. The man looked down at him and asked, "Are you all right, mate?"

Charlie had a difficult time answering the man at first but eventually said, "I think so, but I won't know until tomorrow for sure, that's when I'll really start to feel it!"

The bartender laughed and said, "Hell, you're all right—you still have a sense of humor."

Charlie got to his feet with the help of the bartender and took a cautious look around. He didn't see the two men in the bar but he wasn't taking any chances and backed up against the wall, just in case they were waiting to finish the job.

"Don't worry, mate; those two bastards are gone."

Charlie turned to see who was talking to him and noticed a man in a baseball cap leaning up against the bar, holding what looked like a Billy club. The bartender had returned behind the bar and was serving a couple at the other end. Charlie carefully walked over to the man and said, "I suppose I should thank you."

"No worries mate. I never have felt good about two blokes doing one in a fight just thought I would even up the match; if you know what I mean."

"Well, thanks anyway. I suppose if it wasn't for you and the bartender I would have ended up in the hospital."

"I wouldn't go to a hospital in this country, mate—you'd probably end up worse off than before the fight!"

Charlie laughed and said, "I guess you're right. The best medicine is just to not get the hell knocked out of ya!"

The man laughed and responded, "Can I buy you a drink?

"No! The last thing I need is another beer! What I need is something to eat and some sleep," Charlie replied.

"My name is Nels. What do they call you, my friend?"

Charlie looked at him and replied, "The last person who asked me my name beat the hell out of me!"

Both men started laughing at the same time. "Okay, if you don't want to tell me your name then let me buy you something to eat."

Charlie grinned and said, "The name is Charlie Taylor, and I am going to buy you something to eat; how does that sound?"

"Sounds good to me. Where can we get a decent meal?" Nels asked.

"I know a place downtown where we can find a nice North American breakfast if you're interested," answered Charlie.

"Wait a minute, what about a good old-fashioned Australian breakfast—can we get one of those?"

Charlie put his arm around the man's shoulder and said, "Absolutely. Let's get the hell out of here." Charlie gave the bartender a friendly wave and the two men exited the bar.

Half an hour later the two were sitting at a table in a small restaurant in downtown Davao. Charlie looked across the table and said, "So, Nels, you are from Australia? I would have never guessed."

"What ya mean, mate? Hell, any bloke can tell where I am from!"

Charlie laughed and slapped the table with his hand. Nels grinned ear-to-ear and bobbed his head, signaling Charlie that he had caught the joke. The men continued small talk until they had finished eating then Charlie stood up and said, "Nels, I can't thank you enough for what you did. You didn't have to get into that mess back at the bar. I won't forget it."

"No worries, Charlie—like I said, I don't like a deal where there is two to one."

The two men shook hands, and Charlie started to leave the restaurant. He hesitated and returned to the table.

"Listen," he said, let me give you my telephone number if you get back into town, give me a call." Charlie wrote his number down on a napkin and handed it to Nels.

"Good, mate. I'll do that."

Charlie returned to his apartment an hour later. He thought, *it's been quite a day! A couple more like this, and I won't have to worry about what I am going to do—I will be dead or in the hospital!* The beer, the fighting, and the meal had done him in—he was too tired to get up from the chair and fell sound asleep.

The next morning the sun cut through the blinds, hitting Charlie in the face. He woke up startled and covered in sweat. The first thing that entered his mind was, "What the hell did I say to those two SOBs?" "Why in the hell did they jump me?" Charlie tried to think back; did he say anything about the gold? Hell, he was drunk, but how drunk was he? He remembered about Diwalwal but thought, Shit that was early—I am sure I didn't screw up then, but what about later?

Charlie spent most of the day trying to remember what he had said. Bits and pieces would come and go, but he still couldn't put it all together. Then he stopped and a cold sweat hit him. I remember telling them that they had no idea about gold! He had told the two that he knew where there was more gold than a thousand Diwalwal's!

God, what have I done? He thought, Settle down! I am sure I didn't say anything else, so take it easy. Damn beer! Later that afternoon, Charlie decided to go into town and get something to eat right now he had had enough thinking especially with a hangover!

CHAPTER 5

The Plan

Charlie stayed close to home for a couple of weeks. He didn't want to get himself in a bind and decided the best way to do that was stay the hell out of town. Sitting at home wasn't the answer, though; he still couldn't come up with a decent plan on how he was going to get the gold. Charlie was at the kitchen table writing some notes, trying to develop a plan, when the phone rang.

"Hey, mate! What's going on?"

Charlie had no trouble identifying who was on the phone. "Nels, you back in town, eh?"

"Yeah Charlie thought you might want to have a beer with me."

"Sounds good how about meeting me at the bar about seven?"

"Seven she is," Nels answered.

Just before leaving his apartment, Charlie said out loud, "Keep your damn mouth shut, Charlie—and for Christ's sake, don't get your ass drunk!"

Charlie entered the bar and spotted Nels right away. He walked over and sat down next him. Once Charlie was settled, Nels ordered a couple of beers. Charlie asked, "What have you been up to the last couple of weeks?"

"I just finished a drilling job in northern Luzon, Charlie."

Charlie remembered that while they were eating breakfast Nels told him he was a diamond driller. Nels had come to the Philippines for an Australian mining company in '97 to do some drilling. After he had completed the job, he decided to stick around for a while and do something on his own. He had taken on a couple of small independent jobs but had spent most of his time having a good time.

"When are you going back?" Charlie asked.

"Oh, I don't think I will go back. Charlie. The job wasn't much and I didn't see any future in it."

"So what's the next move, Nels?"

"Nothing right now Charlie. Just wanted to have a couple of beers with ya mate."

The men talked a couple of hours and told each other about themselves. Charlie was careful not to bring up the gold to Nels and instead talked about the jobs he'd had in the Philippines and the states. Charlie looked up at the clock and it said ten. He thought a second and said, "Hell, it's ten already and I have drunk too much beer, Nels!"

"A half-dozen beers is not too much, Charlie—Christ, man we just got started!"

"No, Nels, this is what got me into trouble last time, remember?"

"Don't you trust me, Charlie? Remember, I was the one that got those bastards off you!"

"Yes, I know, Nels, but I'm a little gun shy, if you get my drift."

Nels laughed and said, "Okay, Charlie, but don't worry I'm not a hard ass. I'll shoot straight, my friend."

Charlie hesitated for a minute and said, " Okay, Nels, let's have another one! I'm buyin!"

"Charlie, what say we get us a couple of girls? There are two fine-looking things just down the bar."

Charlie had not been with a woman for six years and it was hard to turn Nels down. He nodded his head in agreement.

An hour later the four were sitting at a table talking. Charlie was having a good time. Nels leaned over to Charlie and said, "Charlie, do you have a place we can go? This young lady is ready to have a good time, if you know what I mean."

"Sure, Nels, let's go back to my apartment."

The next morning Charlie woke up with the woman he had come home with. She was asleep, so he eased himself out of bed. Once on his feet he staggered a bit and grabbed his head with both hands. He whispered,

"God, what a headache!" He went into the kitchen and poured himself a glass of water. He walked into the leaving room where Nels and the other woman were lying on the floor with a blanket half draped over them sound asleep. Charlie quietly eased his way outside and sat down on the apartment steps.

A few minutes later Nels opened up the door and sat down next to Charlie. "How was your night, Charlie? I hope you can remember—I sure in the hell can't!"

"I guess it was okay, Nels—I don't seem to have any bad thoughts."

Nels laughed and got back up. "I think I will make some coffee Charlie, if it's okay. I sure could use a cup."

Charlie nodded his head and said, "Sounds good. I'll make it, Nels; I know where everything is."

The girl had gotten up from the floor and went into the bedroom to lay down with her girlfriend. Charlie and Nels had a couple cups of coffee and decided to fix some breakfast. Just as Charlie was getting down the frying pan, one of the girls came into the kitchen and said, "We will cook something for us. You two can relax."

Charlie and Nels didn't argue; they were in no shape to be noble!

After breakfast the two women cleaned up the dishes while Charlie and Nels relaxed in the living room. One of the women approached the men and said, "We must leave now; we have to be at work in a couple of hours."

Nels stood up and said, "No worries; I will take you home."

"That is okay; we can catch a cab."

"No, I will take you. It will only take me a minute to get my bearing and then we can leave," answered Nels.

"You are very nice, but we will catch a taxi." And with that, the two women left the apartment.

Later on Nels looked at Charlie and said, "Mate, it is time for me to get out of your hair. I'm going to head back to my hotel and get some sleep." He got to his feet and started toward the door.

"Hold it, Nels—I want to talk to you about something. Sit back down."

Nels returned to the chair and sat down. "What's up, Charlie? You sound serious."

"Nels, what I'm about to tell you will sound like a cheap novel but believe me, all of it is true. After you hear what I have to say, you may not want to hear any more."

"Hold on, Charlie—I'm not sure I want to hear any more now."

"Nels, just give me fifteen minutes. If after that you don't want me to continue, just raise your hand, fair enough?"

Nels nodded his head in agreement, and Charlie began the story of the hidden gold. After about fifteen minutes Charlie hesitated and waited for Nels to make a move, but Nels said nothing so Charlie continued. He told Nels the story from the beginning, when Ramon first talked to him. Two hours later Charlie sat back in his chair and looked at Nels.

"Do you want a cup of coffee, Charlie?"

"Sounds good, Nels," Charlie answered. Nels got up from the table and poured the two men coffee. He did not sit back down at the table but instead began to pace around the apartment, sipping his coffee. Charlie could tell Nels was having a hard time understanding everything he had been told.

"Charlie, that's one hell of a story. I need time to think this over. Can you wait a couple of days?"

"Sure Nels. I know it's a lot to think about, especially on such short notice."

"Okay, Charlie. Let me take a couple of days and I will get back to you."

"Just one thing, Nels—keep this between the two of us, ok? I don't want trouble."

"No problem, mate—it's between you and me." Nels set his coffee cup down and walked to the door. He turned, looked back at Charlie, and said, "Charlie, stay close to home and I will call you, okay?"

"Sure Nels. I don't need any more headaches right now."

Nels left the apartment Charlie leaned back in his chair. God, I hope I am doing the right thing!

During the next two days Charlie waited at the apartment. The only time he left was to get something to eat. He wasn't able to sleep. He asked himself over and over, *did I do the right thing? What if Nels gets drunk and starts telling everyone about the deal? What if he doesn't call? Shit, maybe I made a big mistake!*

Charlie was just finishing dinner when the phone rang.

"Hello, Charlie, how are things going?"

Charlie recognized Nels' Australian accent immediately.

"Charlie, I'd like to talk with you about your set-up can you meet me at the place we ate the last time?"

"Sure. What time do you want to meet?"

"It's about four-thirty now; how about seven, Charlie?"

"Seven is fine, Nels. See you then."

Charlie was at the restaurant by six-thirty. He ordered a cup of coffee and waited for Nels. He had his back to the door and was surprised to hear Nels say, "How long have you been here, mate?"

"About 15 minutes. Sit down and take a load off."

Nels sat down at the table and said, "Have you had anything to eat, Charlie?"

"Yeah, I ate before I came over, how about you?"

"No, I'll order something." After Nels ordered dinner, he turned to Charlie and said, "I have a couple of questions, Charlie, before I can decide what to do but first listen, before I go on you need to know something. I came over to the Philippines to do a little diamond drilling. I wasn't looking for anything special, just wanted an opportunity to see what the hell was going on over here. I like the people and the culture. The Filipinos are good people, and I like the easygoing lifestyle that's why I stayed after my contract was done. Like I told you the other night I've been taking some small jobs to get by, but I really haven't looked for any big deals, if you know what I mean. So when this thing came up, I wasn't sure I wanted anything to do with it."

Charlie looked into his cup of coffee and said, "I understand, Nels. I know I'm asking a lot just by telling you this crazy tale. I can understand your reservations, so if you want out, I understand."

"Slow down, Charlie, I haven't said no yet. I just wanted you to know where I stood." The waiter brought Nels his dinner and filled the two coffee cups. The men sat in silence until the waiter left the table. "Charlie, I have a couple of questions before we go on, okay?"

"Shoot, Nels."

"How were you going to get the gold out of the country? And what were you going to do about the Philippine government?"

Charlie looked across the table at Nels. He hesitated for a minute and said, "Nels, we spent most of our time trying to find the gold; we didn't get that far. It was decided to cross those bridges after we found it. What sense would it make to ask the government or, for that matter, set up a way to get rid of the gold before we found it? All we had in mind was to find the gold; remember the whole deal was far-fetched, to say the least!"

Nels leaned back in his chair and looked at Charlie with a frown on his face. "Charlie, let's look at the two questions one at a time. If the Philippine government gets wind of this, they will be all over you. They will deport both of us, and take the gold. This is not the U.S., Charlie; don't expect any deals from these people. Second, if you dig up the gold, you have to get it out of the country, and after you get it out of the country, how do you dispose of it? The minute it shows up on the market, all hell is going to break loose!"

Charlie was speechless. He hadn't thought about any of this. Of course, Nels was right; if anyone found out what was going on, the deal would be finished and all the work and the deaths of his friends would be for nothing!

"I'm not saying it can't be fixed, Charlie, but God, man! It's not going to be easy!"

Charlie raised his hands up and said, "Nels, before we go any further, do you want in or out? You need to understand that I'm going through with the deal. I made a promise to someone and I'm not giving up! I have to know now, Nels I can't wait another couple of days or a month for you to make up your mind. I like you—but this has to be decided tonight."

Nels motioned to the waiter for more coffee and said to Charlie with a cautious smile, "I'm in, Charlie—if you still want me, mate."

Charlie reached across the table and shook Nels' hand and said, "We have a deal, mate!" Both men laughed at Charlie's attempt at the Australian, mate.

For the next two weeks the men stayed close to Charlie's apartment, planning how to get the gold and how to get rid of it.

"Charlie, we are going to need help, and we are going to need some cash to make this work. Where do we stand on these two issues?"

"We have about $60,000 American in the bank, Nels, and I think I have a plan to find some help. I don't think I want any more expats in the deal, Nels. Remember what happened the first time. The more people involved, the more chance someone will put a knife in your back, do you agree?"

"Yes, I agree, but if we don't get some expats involved, what is our alternative, Charlie?"

"Filipinos, Nels. The ones I'm thinking of will be loyal and won't screw us."

"Who do you have in mind, Charlie?"

"Remember Ramon and Magellan, Nels? The ones I told you about?"

"Yeah," Nels responded.

"Well, I think I can get both of them if we work it right and not because of the money, but because these people have a deep loyalty to me and me to them."

"All right, Charlie. What's next?"

"Nels, we made a big mistake by renting vans and drivers so I think we had better buy our own rig and equipment. Also, it fits that the less people who know about this the better."

Nels agreed with Charlie and said, "We have to keep a low profile, Charlie. We need a cover story. People might get suspicious and start asking questions when we start spending money."

"You're right, Nels. We're a couple of prospectors for a major mining company and are looking at possibilities in the Philippines. It's pretty common around these parts."

"Charlie, one more question. What about those two assholes that beat the hell out of you—can you remember what you said to them?"

"I've been thinking about those two, Nels, and the best I can remember is that I told them that they didn't know what real gold was—I knew where there was plenty!"

Nels raised his eyebrows at Charlie.

"I know, Nels. I probably said the wrong things, but there isn't too much we can do about it now—we just have to keep an eye out for them."

"Right, Charlie; we'll cross that bridge when we come to it." Nels leaned back into his chair and said, "the gold Charlie where do we get rid of the gold? A smile crossed Charlie face and he answered, "Malaysia!

It took the two men a week to get all they needed. They purchased a used van for $10,000 and the trade-in of Charlie's Toyota truck, and another couple of thousand to pick up the equipment and supplies. Charlie bought a used Bobcat and trailer. He figured the Bobcat would speed up the opening of the tunnel. They were sitting in Charlie's apartment when Nels said, "Mate, we've been busy all week. What you say we have a couple of beers tonight?"

"You know that's a good idea! I am ready to relax. We won't have another chance for a while. Let's just make sure we watch what we are doing, okay? You remember the last quiet evening I spent in a bar, don't you!"

The two men entered the bar and sat down. The bartender walked up and asked, "Where the hell you been, Nels—have you given up drinkin? Don't you know that's a cardinal sin for an Aussie?"

"May I be struck dead first, Mike!" The three men laughed. "Tear the head off a couple for us and we will see if I have given it up," Nels replied.

Charlie and Nels had just drunk their second beer when someone tapped Charlie on the shoulder. Charlie turned around and found one of the men who had beaten the hell out of him standing behind him. He jumped up from his stool and said, "Better be careful, partner—I'm not drunk this time!"

"Whoa, my friend I'm not looking for trouble," the man answered as he backed away. "I just wanted to apologize—we were all drunk that night, remember?"

Charlie relaxed a little and said, "Fair enough. Let's forget it and let bygones be bygones."

The man smiled and said, "Now that's what I was thinking. Can I buy you boys a beer?"

Before Charlie could answer Nels said, "Listen, mate, I was the one who pulled you two off my friend that night, and I am telling you now to get lost! I don't like you or your friend—and if that doesn't sit well with you then let's take it outside, mate!" Nels stood up and turned directly to the man in front of him. "You've got about five seconds to get moving!"

The man stepped back and said, "Who's your friend, Charlie—he seems a little hostile to me! Sounds like he's never made a mistake, eh?"

Just as Charlie was about to answer the question, the man's partner approached the bar. The four men stood facing each other—it was obvious that trouble was about to start. The bartender approached the foursome from the other end of the bar and said, "Listen, I don't want any more trouble in my bar with you two. So take a hike or I will have you thrown out! If you don't believe me then make a move!"

The two men took a cautious look around. There were four other men around the bar that had stood up and were obviously friends of the bartender.

The first man said, "Hold on —we were just trying to apologize to Charlie here, that's all. We're not looking for any trouble."

"All right then, clear out," the bartender added.

The two men slowly started backing up toward the door. The first man stopped and said, "Charlie, we'd like to have a chance to talk to you if we can, what you say?"

Charlie looked at the two men and said, "You heard him—take a hike!"

The second man made it to the door and said to his friend, "Piss on him, Gil." He looked at Charlie and continued, "We'll be seeing you again, partner," then walked out of the bar with his partner close behind.

Charlie and Nels sat back down at the bar and took a drink from their beers. Charlie was squeezing his glass. He looked down at his hands shaking and said, "I screwed us, Nels—those two are up to something!"

"Yeah, you're right, Charlie, but remember what we decided—we will take care of them when the time comes. For now let's have a few more drinks and have a good time. I'm not going to let those two spoil my night!"

Charlie didn't let Nels know but the confrontation bothered him. He wasn't afraid to fight the two men; he was concerned more with what they might do to get even, or worse, cause trouble with the deal!

Two days later they were on their way to the fishing village. Charlie had explained to Nels that this would be the best way to get started. They would recruit Magellan and Mila and then go on to Ramon's village.

CHAPTER 6

The Site

"I'm going to get that SOB, Gil!"

Gil turned to Arnold and said, "Shut your mouth! This bastard has something going on and we are going to get part of it, do you understand! We can't start trouble with him if we expect to get a piece of the action."

Arnold's muscles in his face tightened up and he looked down at his beer. "Yeah, well, I don't like somebody tellin' me to get lost!"

"You are an idiot sometimes, Arnold! You haven't got shit sense; now that we may have something here that might give us a break and you want to screw it up! I don't give a damn what you do after we get what is coming to us, but don't dick around until we have it, do you understand?"

"Listen, all the bastard said was he had more gold than we would ever see—what the hell does that mean? If he had so much, why the hell was he sitting in a bar with us, for Christ's sake! Far as I'm concerned, the guy's an a-hole!" Gil glanced at Arnold with a disappointed look on his face he shook his head disgustedly and mumbled, "a-hole!!

Gil continued, I'm not sure what it is but whatever it is, it's more than we've got."

"So what are we going to do, Gil?"

"We're going to keep an eye on these two, Arnold, that's what we're going to do!"

First on the agenda for the two was to find out where Charlie lived. For two days they kept an eye on the bar, watching Charlie and Nels come and go, to the hardware shop, to the car repair joint, all over town loading supplies. They followed the pair, being careful to not be seen.

"They're up to something. Arnold."

"They sure the hell are, partner—look at all the shit they're buyin'."

"They have money, that's for sure," Arnold continued.

Later in the week Charlie and Nels headed for the fishing village—not realizing that the two men were following close behind.

"Hello, Mila!"

Mila looked up from her small garden to see Charlie and a stranger standing over her. The boy was sitting between the garden rows picking at the vegetables. Mila jumped up and threw her arms around Charlie's neck. "Charlie, we missed you," she said as she squeezed his neck.

"Mila, this is Nels, a friend of mine."

Mila released her grip on Charlie and looked at Nels shyly.

"So this is Mila, eh, Charlie?" Nels held out his hand and Mila cautiously took it. Nels was impressed with her beauty. Her hair was tied back into a bun, but Nels could tell it was long and had a beautiful sheen to it—and her figure was magnificent! No doubt about it; she was an attractive woman!

Charlie picked up the boy and said, "This is Shopie, Nels." The little boy giggled and grabbed at Charlie's beard. Charlie laughed and said, "He doesn't forget, eh, Mila?"

Mila was aware of how she looked and self-consciously smoothed her hair and brushed off the dirt from her skirt. "You and your friend must be hungry, Charlie. Let me fix you something to eat." Charlie rolled his eyes.

Mila led them into the house he then hurried around the kitchen fixing a meal for the them. Charlie sat down at the table and began to play with Shopie while Nels sat across the table from him. Charlie looked up and said, "Magellan must be working at the fishing village."

Mila turned from the cupboard and nodded in agreement. "He will be home soon, Charlie, and will be happy to see you."

Charlie wasn't sure that was true; he didn't feel Magellan was too happy with him, and only tolerated him because of Mila. He pretended to agree and said, "Yes, I want to talk to him about something when he gets home."

Mila felt uneasy about Charlie's comment but didn't let Charlie or his friend see the concern on her face. "First you men need to eat; the talk can wait until later, Charlie."

Charlie could tell the uneasiness in her voice. "Sure, Mila—as usual, you're right again; Food first!" All three laughed.

Just as the two men were finishing eating Magellan walked through the door. He didn't notice them at first and asked Mila, "Who does the van belong to, Mila?" She was about to answer him when he spotted Charlie sitting at the table. Silence stifled the room. Finally Charlie spoke.

"How was your day, Magellan?" Magellan turned to Mila and waited for her to translate. Although he spoke some English, he depended on Mila to tell him what Charlie had asked. She translated and he nodded okay to Charlie and walked over to his wife. It was obvious to everyone that Magellan was not happy with Charlie and his friend being in his house.

"I have fixed something for you to eat, my husband," Mila said in Filipino. Mila became very nervous and began putting food on the table. Charlie sat the boy down onto the floor and Shopie immediately crawled to his father. Magellan picked him up and sat down to eat. While Magellan ate his dinner Charlie tried to have a light conversation with.

"How is the fishing?" he asked.

Again Magellan looked to Mila to translate. She told Magellan what Charlie had said and he responded, "It is not good these days. The fishing has been very bad for some time; we do not catch many fish."

"I'm sorry I haven't introduced my friend, Magellan; this is Nels."

Nels stood up and put his hand out. Magellan hesitated and slowly took Nels by the hand. Nels could never get used to the soft handshake of the Filipino; there was never any grip when they took his hand. He shook Magellan's hand and said, "Nice meeting you." Magellan immediately released his grip and glanced up at Nels for only a moment, nodded his head, and kept eating.

Charlie thought, this is going to be tougher than I thought. I will need help from Mila, that's for sure!

After Magellan had finished his meal, the three men stayed at the table while Mila cleaned the dishes.

"Mila, come and sit down for a few minutes. I need to talk to both of you," Charlie said.

Mila wiped her hands and walked over to the table. This was it, she thought—Charlie is going to ask for something. In the back of her mind she knew what it was! Carefully, she pulled a chair up to the table and sat down.

Charlie didn't know for sure how to start so he just said it. "Mila, I am going after the gold!" And I will need you, Magellan and his friends help us. There he had said it! He could see her cringe. She froze! Mila knew this was coming but did not want to hear it. Magellan was not sure what Charlie had said, but he could see by the look on his wife's face that it was bad! He turned to her and asked in dialect, "What has this man said that has frightened you?" Mila started to cry. Magellan stood up, looked at the two men, and said, "Leave my house, now!"

Charlie could not understand what he was saying but knew they were in trouble!

Magellan repeated what he had said and went to the door. He opened it and motioned for Charlie and Nels to leave.

"Wait, my husband—these are my friends! Do not make them leave our home!"

Nels was not sure what was going on, but he knew it wasn't good! He also realized this was between Charlie and the two Filipinos. Magellan stood at the door—he was not about to change his mind! Mila stood up from the table and walked over to her husband. She picked up her son who was crawling toward Magellan and cradled him in her arms. She took Magellan by the hand and led him back to the table.

"I will tell you what Charlie has said, but I want you to listen; please do not cause trouble."

Magellan purposely left the door open; but slowly allowed Mila to returned him to the table. Mila spent the next few minutes telling her husband what Charlie hand said. When she finished she sat back in her chair and lowered her head.

Magellan looked back and forth at the two men. He thought, I do not like these men—they have hurt my wife. They are not our friends! He turned to Mila and said, "These are bad men. They are not welcome in our home. When we wed, I made a solemn oath with God that no one would ever hurt you again—and I will not let this man hurt you!"

"I am your wife and will always obey you, my husband. But you must understand that this man is my friend; he saved my life, and I am obligated to him."

Anger crossed Magellan's face and he said, "How can you let this man come into our home and hurt you? He is evil! He does not care for you, don't you understand?"

"First, let me tell you what he wants, my husband; then you can make your decision. Is that too much to ask?"

Magellan folded his arms across his chest and sat back in his chair. He said, "Find out what they want us and our friends to do and then I will tell them to leave!" Mila turned to Charlie and said, "My husband what to know exactly what you want from us he is very upset Charlie." Charlie said I have a plan worked out that will allow us to get the gold and no one will get hurt. All I will need is some manpower to get it done."

Mila began telling Magellan what Charlie had said. The more she told him, the more upset he became. After she had finished, Magellan raised his voice and said, "No, no one will take the gold, no one!"

Charlie didn't have to understand what they were saying; Magellan's actions told the story! "Wait a minute, Mila," he said, "let's hold off until tomorrow. We will talk again after Magellan has time to think about this and calm down."

Charlie motioned to Nels, and the two men walked outside. Charlie stood by the fence and whispered, "Damn, why can't I learn this language? If I could only tell him about Jerry and John he would understand I'm not doing this for the gold—it's for them, it's to finish this thing!"

Nels wasn't sure of everything Charlie was saying to himself, but he had a good idea and said, "You're right, partner. Let's get some sleep and go at it again tomorrow, what do ya say?"

Charlie took a deep breath and said, "Yeah, Nels—tomorrow will be a better day."

The two men returned to the kitchen. Charlie looked at the two sitting at the table and said, "Tomorrow, okay?"

Magellan failed to look up. Mila said, "Yes, Charlie; you and your friend must get some sleep. We will talk tomorrow."

That night no one slept. Mila lay next to her husband and thought, *what does Charlie want from us? Doesn't he see that this will cause trouble?*

Magellan lay looking up at the ceiling. He was not going to let these men hurt his family. He did not care about this gold. He thought, this gold has a curse. It will destroy anyone who touches it!

Charlie was thinking over and over again, I made a big mistake. I am hurting the only ones that I really care about. Tomorrow Nels and I are getting the hell out of here. What was I thinking! Christ, look at the trouble I have caused!

Nels feel sound sleep; after all it had been a long day. He thought Charlie will handle this—and if not, we will do it on our own.

The next morning Charlie and Nels woke up around five. Charlie felt tired from the lack of a good night's sleep. Nels, on the other hand, felt refreshed and well rested! The two men entered the kitchen only to find Mila finishing breakfast. It was obvious from all the food she had prepared that she had been up for some time. Magellan had already eaten his breakfast and was pacing the floor. He was usually at the fishing village by this time, but Mila had asked him to stay until he could talk to Charlie. Charlie sat down at the kitchen table and said, "Good morning, everyone. It looks like we are the last ones up."

Mila smiled at Charlie and said, "Good morning, Charlie," and nodded toward Nels. Magellan stopped his pacing and nodded at Charlie.

"Should we get this over with Mila, or should we eat our breakfast first?" Charlie asked.

"If it's all right with you, Charlie, Magellan would like to go, so can you finish telling us what you want?"

Charlie knew this was difficult for Mila. He realized that Filipinos are usually very introverted and have a difficult time asking an expat for something. Charlie smiled at her and said, "You bet, Mila. Let's get this over with; it should only take a minute."

"Thank you, Charlie," she replied.

"I thought about this all night, Mila, and I have decided not to get you two involved. So why doesn't Magellan go fishing and we can have our breakfast?"

Nels was surprised at Charlie's comment but said nothing. He had decided whatever Charlie wanted was good enough for him. Mila translated to Magellan, who looked at Charlie in confusion but said nothing. He picked up his lunch from the counter and started toward the door—he didn't want Charlie to change his mind. Mila sat down at the table, took Shopie into her arms, and began to feed him. The little boy kept grabbing at the spoon each time she tried to put it into his mouth, which made the food run down his fat little cheeks. Charlie smiled at the boy and began to eat his breakfast. Nels sat down at the table and took a sip of his coffee.

"After breakfast Mila, Nels and I will head for town. We have a couple of things to pick up."

Magellan opened the door to leave. Mila got up from her chair and walked over to him with Shopie still in her arms. She reached up to kiss him on the cheek and told him; "have a good day, my husband." Magellan's face flushed; He grunted something and left the house.

A little later Mila looked at Charlie and said, "Charlie, are you sure we cannot help you? Magellan is upset, but if you want me to, I can talk to him again."

"No, Mila. I have decided that I have caused you too much pain already. We will be fine, so let's drop the subject. I want you to relax—don't let this bother you." Charlie could see the relief in her face and knew he had made the right decision.

Later on the two men left the house and continued to the fishing village.

"First, Charlie, I am fine with your decision. I think it was best for everyone, but we still have a problem. Remember, we were going to see if Magellan could help us dig for the gold, right?"

Charlie continued to drive toward the fishing village, looking straight ahead. "Yeah, Nels, but after I saw the reaction from the two of them, I realized that it was going to cause a problem, so I decided it was a bad deal all around."

"What is the plan now, Charlie?"

"Let's play it by ear, Nels; there may be someone at the fishing village we can use." Charlie knew this would not work, but he didn't want to talk about it now. The men in the fishing village would never keep a secret, and after they had dug up the gold they would tell everyone of the find. They would have to go after it alone or forget the project all together.

Nels decided to drop the subject and asked Charlie what they would find in the village.

"They have the basics, Nels—rope, shovels, and flashlights. We got everything else in Davao. This afternoon we will go out to the site and take a look; how does that sound?"

"Good, Charlie, I am anxious to see it."

Charlie dropped Nels off at the hardware store and said, "I'm going to get us something to eat for lunch at the restaurant while you finish picking up the equipment. Anything you want?"

"Beer!" Nels blurted out.

Charlie leaned back in the car and laughed. "I should have known!"

He parked the van, entered the restaurant, and walked directly to the bar to order a beer. He took a long drink then motioned to the waiter and began to order the lunch. After he had finished his order he turned on his bar stool and browsed the restaurant. He was about to turn back to face the bartender when he noticed two men sitting near the back of the bar. At first he did not recognize who they were and started to take a drink from his beer. Shit, he said to himself and turned back around. It's those two bastards! Charlie took a closer look as he eased up from his stool and started walking slowly toward them. He stopped a couple of tables away and stopped. Neither man noticed Charlie; they were deep in conversation and unaware of what was going on around them. Even though it was early in the morning, it was obvious that they had had several beers—the table was full of empty bottles. Charlie walked up to them and said, "What the hell is going on, boys?"

Gil turned in his chair and looked up at Charlie. He didn't act surprised and said, "Well, look who's here, Arnold—our old friend Charlie!"

A smile crossed Arnold's face and he said, "Yeah, ain't this a sight for sore eyes," then took a drink from his beer.

Gil continued, "And what can we do for you, my friend—can we buy you a beer?"

"No, I already have one, thanks. What I do want is to know what you two are doing here, if you don't mind."

Arnold stood and walked up to Charlie. He said in a sarcastic tone, "It's a free country, isn't it, Charlie? We might ask you the same thing. Since when can't a man have a couple of beers—or are you the one that decides that?"

Charlie put his hand on Arnold's chest and eased the man back from him. "No, I don't make those decisions. It seems odd that you two would end up here, that's all."

"Relax, Charlie," Gil interrupted, "we are just on a little vacation, if you know what I mean. We decided to take a drive down this way. People have told us how nice Mindanao is around these parts. You must agree, Charlie—you're here too, right?"

Arnold laughed and said, "Yeah, ain't it pretty?"

Charlie's temper began to rise. He still remembered the beating and said, "Let me make something clear to both of you. Don't get in my way, or I will put both of you in the hospital!"

"Sounds like a threat to me, Gil, what do you think?"

Gil got up from the table and said, "Take it easy, guys. We're only having a couple of beers; no need to get uptight about it." Gil moved closer to Charlie; now both men were within a couple of inches from him.

Charlie knew what was coming next. He set his feet and waited for one of them to make a move, but thought, What the hell, they got the first punch last time—now it's my turn! Arnold was standing to his right and Gil to his left so Charlie decided to take Arnold first.

Gil looked at Charlie and said, "Charlie, there's no need for trouble; why—"

Charlie threw a left punch that struck Arnold in the forehead. Charlie had lost fifty pounds in the last six years and was now all bone. His knuckles had little flesh on them—his hands were as hard as steel. He felt the blow in his hands and knew Arnold was going down.

Gil was caught completely by surprise, and Arnold never knew what hit him! Gil's mouth was wide open in surprise when Charlie tacked him. Down onto the floor the two men went with Charlie on top of Gil. He straddled Gil, drew back his fist, and hit him square in the face. Blood exploded from the man's mouth and nose.

Charlie got to his feet and turned to see Arnold trying to regain his senses. He was on his hands and knees, holding his head in his hands. Charlie walked over to Arnold then stepped back and kicked Arnold in the face. Down he went again! By this time Gil was sitting up with a bewildered look on his face. Charlie grabbed him by his shirt and raised him to his feet. He looked Gil in the eyes and said, "You know, Gil, this is my kind of fun! Now I know how you and that asshole felt when you were doing the job on me." Charlie smiled and hit Gil with a right cross; again the blood exploded across Gils's face and down he went.

Charlie took a look at the two men and waited to see if they were ready for more. It was obvious that they had had enough. He turned and walked over to the waiter and said, "Is my food ready to go?"

The waiter was frozen with fear and just looked at Charlie; he looked terrified!

"Is my food ready?" Charlie repeated.

"Ye-ye-s, sir," the waiter answered. He turned and ran into the kitchen. In a couple of minutes he returned with a box of food and handed it to Charlie, making sure he wasn't standing too close!

Charlie took one more look at the men on the floor, walked over to the bar, took one last look at the boys, through down 500 pesos and walked out. He didn't realize how good he felt until he was outside. He thought, I could get used to kicking the shit out of those two SOBs! He laughed out loud.

Charlie met Nels at the van. Nels had just finished loading the equipment and said, "I was just about to go looking for you, Charlie—did you get my beer?"

Charlie looked at Nels and laughed. He replied, "No, Nels. I got sidetracked and forgot it; ain't that something!"

"Well, we can't leave without it, Charlie—I wouldn't last half a day without some beer. No problem, mate; there's a small grocery store on the way out of town. We can pick some up there."

Charlie smiled and put his arm around Nels and said, "You know, this is turning out to be a great day!"

Nels was confused but didn't say anything. The two men got into the van and drove out of the fishing village, stopping long enough to pick up the beer. As they drove toward the site, Charlie was whistling a tune with a slight smile on his face. Nels looked over at him and said, "Well, are you going to tell me why you are so happy, or is it a secret you are going to keep from me?"

Charlie glanced over at Nels, waited a minute, and then started telling him what had happened. When he finished Nels said, "Why the hell didn't you come and get me? I would have enjoyed having some fun too!"

Charlie's smile disappeared from his face. He looked at Nels in concern and said, "Damn, Nels! It didn't come to mind. I'm sorry; next time I will let you in on it!"

Nels laughed. "Don't look so concerned, Charlie! Damn, mate—as long as you came out on top, that's the important thing!"

Still, it bothered Charlie that he had not found Nels before he confronted the two men at the restaurant. He looked back at Nels who was looking out the window and said, "Nels, I regard you as a friend. Damn it, I wasn't thinking!"

"Charlie, forget it mate; it's okay. I didn't think it would bother you that much."

"Nels, from now on we have to trust each other. I guarantee it won't happen again. I was wrong!"

Nels started to say something back to Charlie, but he decided enough had been said.

"This is the road to the site, Nels. We have about fifteen more minutes and we will be there."

As they approached the site, old memories started creeping back to Charlie. Sweat started running down his face and neck. Charlie stopped the van and got out. The old site next to the road was covered in jungle and it was hard to imagine the camp. Charlie stood looking—he could see all of them sitting next to the fire: Mila, John, Gary, Ramon, and Jerry;

yes, Jerry. Charlie couldn't move his feet—he was frozen in his tracks! He became dizzy and thought he was going to pass out!

"So this is it, eh, Charlie?" Nels was not paying attention to Charlie but was looking over the site. When Charlie did not answer him, Nels turned. Charlie was holding onto the fender of the van with his chin lowered. "Are you all right, Charlie?"

Charlie took a deep breath and said, "Yeah, Nels. Just give me a minute."

Nels rounded the van and walked up to Charlie. "You look bad, partner. What seems to be the problem?"

"Just some old memories, Nels, just some old memories I'll be fine in a minute or two."

The men sat down while Charlie regained his senses. Finally he said, "I'm ready, Nels. Let's take a walk; the tunnel is over this way."

"Are you sure, Charlie? We can wait a little longer if you want."

"No, let's get going, Nels. The sooner we get started, the better off we will be."

Charlie led Nels into the jungle, toward the tunnel. Charlie keep thinking amazing how fast the jungle grew back. It was as if no one had ever been here. In fact, Charlie thought, if I hadn't been here before, I would never be able to find the spot! He stopped and put his hands on his hips and said, "This is it, Nels!"

Nels looked around and had no idea what he was looking at. He turned to Charlie and said, "This is what, Charlie?"

"Nels, can you make out the slope of the ridge? Take a look over there."

Nels panned the area but still could not see what Charlie was talking about.

Charlie laughed and said, "Now you know what we were up against, Nels. This place looks the same as it did the first time I seen it. You just need to know what you are looking for."

"Hell, Charlie, I'm a diamond driller. What do I know about tunnels?"

"Let's unload the Bobcat, Nels. We can clear some of the jungle away; then you will see it."

Nels climbed into the Bobcat and drove it off the trailer. Charlie shouted, "Don't remove too much brush until you get to the tunnel site. Remember, we don't want anyone finding this place."

Nels lowered the bucket of the Bobcat and began cutting a road toward the tunnel site. He was careful not to disturb too much of the area with the bucket and soon was at the face of the mountain. Charlie tried to camouflage the entrance to the tunnel site; however, he knew that the damaged jungle would repair itself within a week as long as they left it alone.

The two men worked until dark then decided to set up a camp. "Not bad for the first day, Charlie; the Bobcat was a great idea."

Charlie looked at Nels as he set up the portable stove and said, "Get us a beer out of the cooler, Nels, what do you think?"

Nels face went ashen. "God almighty, mate—I haven't had a beer all day!" Nels ran to the cooler and opened it up. Staring down at the ice cooler he saw several soft drinks but no beer! He turned around and looked at Charlie who was standing behind him with a big grin. Nels said, "Charlie where the beer? Damn Nels I forgot to tell you once I was inside the store I figured we better stay off the alcohol until we finish this job no sense in bein drunk while we are at it." Nels was dumbfounded! He gasped for air, his mouth hung open he was devastated! " Charlie, he said beer ain't alcohol!" Damn man we got to go back! Charlie burst into laughter and fell to the ground the look on Nels face was all he could handle! "What, mate, what going on?" Nels said. Look in the other cooler in the back of the van partner there is lots of, Charlie frowned, non-alcoholic beer for you." Nels made a dash for the van, opened the door and dug down into the cooler and pulled two cold cans of beer from it. He trotted back to Charlie, and at the same time opened his beer and took a long drink. "Oh man, that tastes good! Damn partner you almost killed me off there!

Charlie watched Nels swallow his beer and said, "You never know, Nels—we may give up beer if we work every day as hard as we worked today. It will save us some time and money if we stop buying beer." Charlie made sure he was not facing Nels when he mentioned not buying any more beer; he couldn't keep a straight face.

Nels slowly lowered the beer from his mouth and looked at Charlie. "You can't be serious, mate! You can't keep the foolishness up you'll drive me nuts!"

Charlie turned around and laughed when he saw Nels. The look on the man's face was tragic! "Well, I guess we can afford a beer once in a while, Nels. What do you think?"

Nels could see the sly grin on Charlie's face and broke out into laughter.

Although the men accomplished clearing the open area in a couple of days, it was obvious they were going to need help when it came time to start supporting the tunnel. The Bobcat would be fine for removing dirt and debris but timbering took manpower!

While having dinner, Charlie looked over at Nels.

"Nels," he said, "it's time we went looking for some help. We will be opening the tunnel in the next couple of days and we can't get it done by ourselves."

"I agree, Charlie. But where the hell can we find someone we can trust?"

Charlie answered, "Ramon. Tomorrow we will drive down to his village and see if he can help us. He might have a couple of people to give us a hand; you never know." "Wait Charlie are you sure he is there?" Remember you haven't seen him in 6 years besides you told me he might be dead, remember? "Yeah I know Nels but I had Mila do some checking for me before I left for Davao. When we got back she told me that Ramon is back at his village with a wife and family."

"That's a good idea, Charlie, but do you think he will come in with us? Remember what happened with Mila?"

"He will help, Nels. I know the guy. He's a good man. But if not—at least we gave it a try, right?"

Nels nodded his head in agreement and took a long drink of his beer. He thought, At least we still have beer!

The next morning the two men camouflaged the site as best they could. They covered the Bobcat, cleaned up the tools, and hid them in the jungle. Charlie got behind the wheel and started driving down to the main road. As they entered the main road, Charlie thought he spotted something hidden in the brush. He stopped and took a look but decided there was nothing there. He again headed toward Ramon's village.

"Get back, you idiot! He's going to see us!" Gil grabbed Arnold by the shirt and pulled him back into the brush. The van stopped for a moment but continued onto the main road. "Jesus, that's all we need. If they know we are here, they will raise hell." He looked at Arnold in disgust and sat back down.

"I don't give a shit," Arnold replied, "I'm going to get even with that SOB no matter what it takes!"

"Yeah, yeah; I can see by the way your face looks that you are one tough bastard! And what will that accomplish? Do you think they will let us in on what they are doing just because you knock the hell out of him?"

Arnold lowered his head and said, "No—but damn it, I'd feel better!"

Gil answered back, "You know, sometimes I wonder why I keep you around. You are a hothead! One of these days it's going to get you in big trouble—and me along with you! Now let's wait a few minutes until they are out of sight and then we will take a little drive."

Fifteen minutes later, the men were driving up the road from where Charlie and Nels had come. After an hour driving back and forth on the road, Gil looked at Arnold and said, "This is getting us nowhere. Everything looks the same!"

Fortunately for the two men, the road became too rough to travel after a couple of miles. Gil backed up the truck and turned around. Little did they know that another hour of driving, and they would have ended up at the primitive village—that would not be a good thing! Gil pulled over, turned off the truck, and said, "We gotta get out of here. We can't stay any longer. If they catch us here, we are in deep shit!"

"Then what are we going to do Gil?"

"Wait, Arnold. Wait until they come back and then we will follow them. That's what we are going to do. I have a feeling they won't be gone long."

CHAPTER 7

Ramon

Four hours after leaving their camp, Charlie drove the van around the last curve entering Ramon's village.

"My God Charlie! It's like you said; there was one heck of a mine here— amazing!"

Although a lot more jungle had grown up around the mine site since Charlie's last visit, it was still impressive with the mill and mine buildings still standing. There was no longer a guard at the gate; it hung on its broken hinges, ready to fall to the ground. Charlie drove the van into the parking lot and got out. Nels climbed out and stood looking at the main office. Charlie approached the office and walked through the door. No one was in sight. He was about to walk out of the office when a boy about ten years old peered into the office, shyly looking at the two men.

Charlie looked at the boy and said, "Hello there, young man. Can you tell me where everyone is at?" The boy bolted down the stairs and disappeared down the main road away from the office.

Nels said, "Well, that didn't work, Charlie; what's next?"

"Let's find Ramon," he answered.

The men climbed back into the van and drove toward Ramon's house. As they approached, Charlie was surprised to see a new house sitting in place of the old one. Charlie looked at Nels and said, "Wait here, Nels; let me go in first. Something is going on, and I am not sure what it is."

Charlie walked up to the door and knocked. He waited a few minutes and knocked again. The door opened a slight crack and a young woman with a small child in her arms peered out.

"Is Ramon home?" Charlie asked.

The woman did not answer and tried to close the door. Charlie placed his foot inside the door, preventing her from closing it, and repeated, "Is Ramon at home?"

The woman realized that she could not shut the door with Charlie's foot blocking the way. The baby began to cry and she rocked the child in her arms. Charlie looked over the shoulder of the young woman in hopes of spotting Ramon. He saw two other small children playing on the floor; they were about two or three years old. Charlie could see that the woman was very frightened so he removed his foot and she immediately closed the door.

He stood at the door for a few minutes deciding what to do, when he heard someone say, "Mr. Charlie?" Charlie turned around and found Ramon standing behind him with an amazed look on his face. The two men didn't say another word. Ramon rushed Charlie and threw his arms around him.

"Mr. Charlie, Mr. Charlie, I thought you was dead!"

Charlie answered him, "Not yet, Ramon!" He released Ramon and stood back. "Damn, boy—am I glad to see you!"

Although Ramon was six years older he didn't seem to have aged a day. Charlie motioned for Nels to get out of the van. Nels quietly walked over to the two men standing in front of the house; he had learned to be careful around these people—they seemed to frighten easy.

"Ramon, this is Nels," Ramon shook Nels' hand, and again Nels felt uneasy with the soft handshake from Ramon, but didn't act as though it bothered him.

He grinned and said, "Charlie has spoken a lot about you, Ramon; I am glad to finally meet you." Ramon had a shy look on his face and only nodded in reply.

"I see you have a new house and maybe a new wife, Ramon," Charlie said.

At first Ramon beamed and smiled, but all of a sudden he seemed ashamed. He lowered his face to his chest and turned from Charlie.

"What is wrong, Ramon?" Charlie asked. Ramon didn't respond. Charlie took Ramon by the shoulder and gently turned him around to face him. Ramon looked up at Charlie tears were running down his face. "Ramon?" Charlie repeated with concern on his face.

Ramon raised his head and looked into Charlie's eyes and said, "I did not know, Mr. Charlie. I thought the bandits killed you, I did not know!"

Charlie took Ramon back into his arms and said, "Ramon, how could you know what happened to us? You had to save yourself from the bandits."

Ramon continued to cry and apologize to Charlie over and over again. Finally Charlie released Ramon and said, "Believe me, Ramon—you done the right thing. Now let's forget this foolishness!"

Ramon finally regained his composer and said, "Come into my house and meet my family, Mr. Charlie."

The three men entered the house. Once inside Ramon's wife, still holding the baby, backed away from the men and stood rocking the child. "This is my wife, Anna, Mr. Charlie, and my three children." Charlie put his hand out to the woman but she backed away and looked at Ramon for support. "Forgive her, Mr. Charlie, she does not speak English and is afraid of strangers."

"Where is your grandmother Ramon?" Charlie asked.

"She is no longer with us. One year after I returned home, she passed on," Ramon replied. He talked to his wife in his dialect and she handed the baby to Ramon and proceeded to the kitchen. "I have told her to fix something to eat and make some coffee for us."

"You don't have to do that, Ramon, we are fine," Charlie answered.

"This is my home, Mr. Charlie, and you are part of my family. You must sit and eat with me, please."

Charlie took his hand and ruffled Ramon's hair, nodding in agreement. "Can I?" Charlie said, pointing to one of the children playing on the floor. At first Ramon was not sure what Charlie meant until Charlie reached down and picked the little girl up in his arms. Ramon's face beamed with pride. The little girl looked up at Charlie, reached up with her hand, and caressed his face in wonderment.

Charlie started laughing and said, "What is this thing with my face? Every time I hold a child, they want to touch my face!"

Ramon looked at Charlie smiling and answered, "The children have not seen a man with a white face with hair growing on it, Sir Charlie. They do not understand this."

Charlie thought for a minute and realized most Filipinos with a beard were the Muslims—no wonder they were curious! The little girl continued to grab at Charlie's rough beard with a perplexed look on her face.

An hour later the three men were busy eating dinner while Anna continued to maintain her distance from them. She only approached the table to deliver more food or to fill their coffee cups.

"You still haven't told me about the new house, Ramon. Where did you get the money for it?" Charlie asked.

Ramon sat in silence with his head down and did not answer.

"Let's not go through this again, Ramon. What is bothering you now?"

Ramon looked up at Charlie and said, "The gold, Mr. Charlie. I built the house with the gold from the tunnel." Ramon tensed up and waited for Charlie to say something.

"What do you mean the gold?" Charlie responded.

"I know you will hate me now, Sir Charlie, but when I was in the tunnel I took a small bag of the gold, not much, just a small bag."

Charlie slapped his hand down on the table and started roaring with laughter. Nels, Ramon, and Anna all jumped back, all had had a look of fright on their faces.

Nels said, "Jesus, Charlie! Are you tryin to scare us to death?"

Charlie couldn't stop laughing. Ramon continued to stare at Charlie with an amazed look on his face. Anna gathered the children up and sat them all together in the back of the room. The baby began to cry. Charlie finally was able to stop laughing and looked around the room as he wiped the tears from his eyes.

He said, "Relax everyone." He looked at Ramon and said, "Ramon, I am glad that someone got something out of that nightmare I'm happy for you."

Nels returned to his meal and started eating again. He looked over at Charlie. "Damn, man! Don't do that again; it's going to take a week for me to get over that!"

Ramon still was not at himself; he was very confused. He expected Charlie to yell at him or do something to him—he did not expect Charlie to be happy about what he had done.

Charlie looked at Ramon and said, "Believe me, Ramon, it is okay. I am telling you, you did the right thing. People died over that damn gold so feel good you were able to take advantage of it—at least their lives were lost for something good!"

Ramon remained cautious; however, he decided to not pursue the matter any further.

Charlie took a hard look at Ramon and said, "Ramon, what if I told you I was going back for the gold?"

Ramon tensed. He stared at Charlie. He could not believe what he had just heard!

"Mr. Charlie, you cannot get the gold—the villagers will kill you!"

"No, Ramon, I spent six years in their village. I am sure they will let us take the gold. The old chief has died and I am sure his son will not cause us any trouble. If I can get the young chief to let us dig up the gold, would you help us?"

Ramon had not thought about the gold for some time. He had decided never to think about what had happened to him six years ago. After he had returned to his village, he had given a few of the gold coins to his uncle. When he was asked about the gold, Ramon told them that the others had found a small amount of gold and that they had shared it with him. He told his people that he had gotten an equal share of one bag of gold and the others had decided not to look for more. At first, his neighbors continued to question Ramon about the gold. However, after several months they no longer cared, and the matter was dropped. No one in his village had mentioned the gold for over three years, which made Ramon happy. As far as he was concerned, it was over. Now Mr. Charlie had returned and was talking about the gold again!

"Listen, Ramon, it won't be different this time. We can get the gold without worrying about the villagers or the Muslims! Besides we know where it is. Nels and I have bought equipment that will help us dig for the gold."

Ramon sat in silence for a few minutes and finally said, "But the Muslims, Mr. Charlie; what will we do?"

"What about the Muslims? Ramon, I can tell you that the primitive warriors killed most of them and the rest went back to their village."

"Yes, I understand, Mr. Charlie, but the Muslim terrorists are killing people in my province. We lost two of our men just in the last week!"

This was a surprise to Charlie; he was not prepared to hear about the Muslims.

"What do you mean, Ramon? The Muslim terrorists have never bothered your village before?"

"Mr. Charlie, things have changed. The Muslim bandits are much trouble. The government troops have been fighting them in the south. There is much killing on both sides. The Muslims are now spreading throughout the island of Mindanao to run from the government troops. They have small camps everywhere in Mindanao, Sir Charlie. Every month they come to our village and take our food and what little money we have. Did you not see what our village looks like now? Everyone is terrified of them Sir Charlie. Some of our people have left the village in fear of their lives!"

Nels looked across the table at the two men and said, "Ramon, this doesn't make sense. The MILF never killed anyone from what I remember; they only kidnapped for ransom."

"No, Mr. Charlie, the group called the Abu Sayyaf—they are very dangerous. They do not only kidnap Filipinos, but also foreigners. If anyone tries to free the hostages, the hostages are killed—their heads are cut off and stuck onto a post!" Wait Ramon remember I know the Abu Sayyaf very well! But I agree with Nels they don't usually hang around this part of Mindanao this is NPA country." Nels said, "NPA?" Yeah Charlie answered, the National People's Army, communist to you Nels." Nels said, "Now we got Commies eh mate?" "Yep answered Charlie what do ya think of that my friend!" Well get in line might as well tackle the whole bunch while we are in this thing!" Nels pushed his cap back and shook his head in amazement.

Charlie continued, "Listen, Ramon, I don't know about these Muslims, but your people cannot just sit back and wait for them to kill you and take all your valuables. Forget the gold for a minute. You must stand up to these people. If you help us find the gold, you can pay for protection from the bandits. By the way have they taken your gold, Ramon?"

"Not yet, Mr. Charlie; they only take from my uncle, he is the leader of our village. The bandits tell my uncle what they want and he gives them the gold. I have been giving him some of my gold so they will not kill him. The bandits do not know or care where the gold comes from as long as they get what they want."

"Ramon," Charlie said, "sooner or later they will ask your uncle where the gold comes from and then they will come looking for you!"

"No, Sir Charlie, my uncle will never tell these men about me!"

"I hope you are right, Ramon, but I doubt it. Either way—when the gold runs out your uncle will be forced to find more. If he does not then the bandits may kill him. You must understand that?"

Ramon sat in his chair, upset by the conversation. It was apparent to the two men that Ramon had not considered this possibility. "Sir Charlie I must think about this. I would like to talk with my uncle. He must help me decide."

"Sure, Ramon you don't have to make a decision right now. Go see your uncle and have him help. All that I ask, Ramon, is that you do not tell him where the gold is or how much is there; is that fair?"

"Yes, Mr. Charlie," Ramon replied.

Later that day, while Ramon visited his uncle, Charlie and Nels waited for him in Ramon's home. Once Ramon left the house, however, his wife took the children to her family's house she did not want to stay in the house while the strangers were there.

While they were gone, the two men continued to discuss the plan. "Charlie, if we can't get Ramon to help, it doesn't mean the end of the world, you know. We can get it done ourselves—it's just going to take longer."

"I know, Nels, but the longer it takes the more chance someone is going to find out what we are up to. Besides, I want Ramon to get his fair share of the gold."

"Well, whatever you and Ramon decide, Charlie is good enough for me. Like I said, I'm not making a big deal out of the gold. Sure, I'd like enough money to live comfortably, but too much and it can be more trouble than it's worth!"

"Are you saying that you might not want to dig up the treasure, Nels?"

"No, no, Charlie, don't jump to any conclusions! I'm only saying if we get it fine, but if not, I'm not going to worry the rest of my life about not being rich."

"Nels, I don't know if it's the gold or if it's the dream I had about Jerry, but one thing is for sure—I will never rest until this thing is done."

"Alright Charlie like I told you before in Davao, I'm in!"

Just as Charlie got up from the table, Ramon and his uncle entered the house. Charlie introduced Ramon's uncle to Nels and the four men sat down at the table. The uncle began the conversation.

"You are back, my friend. Ramon tells me that you can help our village, but he would not tell me how."

Charlie said, "We believe there may be more gold at the site than what we found the first time. We are not sure how much, but we expect it to be more than the few coins. I know that Ramon has given you some of his share from the last search and would give you more if we can find it. Ramon also tells us that the Muslim bandits have been taking all your valuables, and you're concerned about what they might do if you don't have anything else to give them, is that true?"

Ramon's uncle squirmed in his chair and said, "Yes, we are very concerned about what these rebels may do to us. As you can see, they have taken almost everything we have. We are able to mine a small amount of gold from the small-scale mining near the village, but it is very little. And the rebels demand more! They have killed several of our people over the last two years and are threatening to kill others if we do not give them what they want. Can you help us, Sir Charlie?"

"I'm not sure. But it's a cinch if you do not have something to give them next time—there will be trouble. I cannot guarantee what we will find, but whatever it is, it will help you."

Nels had been listening to the conversation and said, "I don['t know you personally but I will tell you this. If you continue to give these bandits what they want, they will never leave you alone. You are going to have to stop them sooner or later even if some of you will die, do you agree?"

Ramon's uncle looked at the two men, a concerned expression on his face, and said, "Of course you are right. We cannot continue to pay these bandits. But you must understand that we are a poor people; we do not have the resources to fight these men. We have asked the government to help us but they ignore our pleas. They are fighting the rebels in southern Mindanao and do not have the time or enough soldiers to help us. Therefore we must pay the Muslim bandits." Remember we are farmers and miners not fighters.

"How many bandits come to your village for the gold, Ramon?" Nels asked.

"Because we are far from the Muslim stronghold in Jolo, there are only a few that come to our village. Most of them are farther south, fighting the government troops."

"When do you expect them to come back to the village?" Nels asked Ramon's uncle.

"They will be here any day. That is why I am here. You must leave the village. If they find you here, they will take you hostage."

"Let us worry about that," Charlie answered.

The uncle looked at the two men and said, "You must understand—if they find you here, they will not only kidnap you, they will punish our village for letting you stay with us!"

Nels glanced at Charlie and said, "Why don't you let us have a little privacy; maybe we can come up with something to stop these people from terrorizing the village."

Ramon's uncle looked at them and said, "Please, you must leave our village. We do not want any trouble with the bandits."

Charlie realized how frightened the man was and said, "Okay, we will leave tonight. We did not come here to bring you trouble."

Nels started to speak, but Charlie motioned him not to say anything. Ramon and his uncle stood up from the table. The uncle shook hands with the two men then walked to the door and said, "I must return to the village and tell the people what you have told me."

Ramon asked his uncle, "Do you want me to go with you, Uncle?"

"No, Ramon, you must stay with your guest. I will tell our people what has been said." With that he left the house.

The moment the door closed, Nels stood up and said, "Bullshit, Charlie! We can't let these people be terrorized by the bandits! Hell, if there are only a few, we can run them off!"

"Settle down, Nels—"

Nels interrupted, "Settle down? How can you let these people be terrorized and not do something?"

"Nels, I agree, but let's not fly off the handle here, okay?" Charlie turned to Ramon. "Is there someplace else we can stay, Ramon? We don't want to cause you and your family any more trouble."

"Sir Charlie! You are my friend you must stay at my home!"

Nels said, "No, Ramon; Charlie is right. We can't stay here; we will endanger your wife and children. You must find us a place to stay outside the village."

"Don't argue, Ramon—we are right," Charlie added.

Ramon was dejected. He wanted to make up for what he had done to Charlie years earlier. He did not have enough of the gold to give to Mr. Charlie; the only thing he could offer was his home for the two men to stay. Ramon started to say something, but Charlie raised his hands, indicating the conversation was over.

"All right, Sir Charlie. I know of a place outside our village that the rebels will not find."

"Let's get some grub together and get out of here, what do you say, mate?"

Charlie agreed with Nels, and the three men prepared to leave Ramon's house. An hour later they arrived at an old mine office outside the camp that was hidden from the main road.

"No one ever comes here since the big company stopped operations, Mr. Charlie.

"This is great, Ramon. It will do just fine," Charlie answered.

"I must return to my family, Mr. Charlie. My wife is very upset and I must comfort her."

"Good, Ramon, you go home to your family," Nels replied.

After Ramon had left the office, Nels said, "We have to help these people, Charlie. Remember what the uncle told us; there are only a few of the rebels. It sounds like we can handle them, what do you think?"

"I was thinking the same thing, Nels—but first we need to decide what we want to do. If we get involved it could get real ugly. Remember, the last time I tangled with these bastards three of my friends ended up dead!"

"I understand, mate if you want, we can pull out of here right now. I just hate to see these people getting kicked around, that's all."

Anger flushed across Charlie's face. "I didn't say I wanted to go, did I? Christ almighty can't a man say something without being accused of being a coward!"

Nels raised his hand above his head, turned, and left the office. He walked outside the building and sat down on the steps. Damn, he thought, a month ago I was sitting in a pub having a drink—now look at the fix I'm in!

"Nels."

He turned his head and saw Charlie standing behind him. He hadn't heard him walk up.

"I'm sorry for losing my temper. This thing has been building up inside me for years. I'm not sure we are doing the right thing. If something happened to you or Ramon, I don't think I could handle it." Charlie was not looking directly at Nels but out to the walkway, his hands in his pockets.

"No worries mate. Sometimes I forget what you've been through. It's just that I don't want to think about what will happen to these people if we don't help them."

"If you're still with me, Nels, I'm willing to do whatever we can. Is that fair?"

"Good enough mate. Let's forget that and start thinking of something we can do."

A few days later the two men walked back into the village. Ramon's uncle saw them approaching and ran up to them.

"Please," he said, "you must leave our village! The Abu Sayyaf has been seen in the next village! They will be here any time!"

Charlie asked, "Where is Ramon? We want to talk to you two."

"Please leave our village! There is nothing you can do! If the rebels find you here, they will kidnap you and punish our people—so go!"

Charlie grabbed the man by his shoulders and said, "No! We can stop these men with a little help from your village, but you must be willing to help! If what you have told us is true—that there are only a few—we can stop them." Charlie could see the fear in the man's face, but he continued, "These men will never let you go. They are bandits and have no sympathy for your people. Sooner or later you will not be able to pay them off, and they will punish all of you, don't you understand?"

The man looked at the two men and said, "What can we do? They have guns; we have none! These men are killers like I told you our people are only farmers and miners."

Nels interrupted the man and said, "They are men just like you. If we show them that you are willing to fight for what is yours, they will ask themselves if it is worth a fight. Believe me; they do not want to die any more than you do!"

The old man could see that these men were not going to leave the village and said, "If I allow you to talk to Ramon and he agrees with me, will you then leave our village?"

Charlie stepped back from the man and said, "If Ramon agrees with you, we will leave the village and never return."

"Wait in my office. I will find Ramon and bring him to you. But you must not waste time—the rebels will be here soon."

Fifteen minutes later, Ramon and his uncle arrived at the office. Ramon nodded his head at Nels and said to Charlie, "My uncle has told me what you have said. I will listen to you, Sir Charlie, because you are my friend, but I do not know how we can stop the Abu Sayyaf from taking our gold—so you must tell me."

Charlie turned to Nels and said, "How many weapons do we have, Nels?"

"After you told me about your first run-in with these bastards, Charlie, I decided we needed a little more firepower, so I bought half-dozen rifles and four pistols. I figured if they caused us trouble at the site again, we were not going to run!"

Charlie motioned to the table in the office and said, "Let's sit down and talk. First you must understand that the rebels only go after defenseless or harmless groups; they like having the odds on their side. The only time they get tough is when they know they have the upper hand. That's how they work, so here is what I have planned. Tomorrow—or whenever they show up—your uncle and I will confront them in front of the office. I don't want Nels to be there. I don't want them to know how many expats are here—we want them to guess. If we can convince them that there are several of us then that will give us an edge. How many of the villagers can handle a weapon, Ramon?"

"Sir Charlie, most of our miners can use a rifle. They have been trained since they were small boys to hunt and also to protect their claims. But you must understand that they have never had to kill anyone."

"If we are damn lucky, Ramon, they won't have to kill anyone this time either! Ramon, I want to see these men here within an hour so we can get ready for the rebels. Can you do that?"

"I will try, Mr. Charlie. How many men do you need?"

"Six will do, Ramon."

One hour later Charlie was standing in front of six very scared men! The men were timid and stood in a bunched group behind Ramon. Nels whispered to Charlie, "They don't look like much, Charlie; I doubt they will use the rifles if we need them."

"Filipinos are a very quiet bunch, Nels, but when it comes to action, you can depend on them as long as they trust you." "Remember World War Two. These people were the most courageous in the entire south pacific conflict."

"I hope you are right, mate!"

The plan was simple. Three of the Filipinos, along with Charlie and Ramon's uncle, would be waiting for the rebels at the uncle's office. Nels and the others would be hidden behind buildings near the office. If, after confronting them, the bandits left the village, the others would not interfere; they would stay hidden. However, if it looked like trouble, Nels and his men would step out into view of the bandits and show them that the villagers meant business.

One of the villagers waiting outside ran into the office and yelled, "They are here!"

Charlie jumped to his feet. "Damn! I don't know if that's good or bad—what does he mean they are here"?" He looked at Ramon's uncle and continued, "You told us tomorrow!"

All of the Filipinos except Ramon started toward the door. Nels hollered, "Damn it, stop!" The men froze in their tracks; each one had a look of pure terror on his face. Nels yelled, "If you don't stand up to these men, I will kill you myself, and I mean it! The first man out that door will get a bullet! Ramon, you better tell them what I said because I mean it!" Nels face was red with rage!

Ramon quickly told the Filipinos what he'd said. The men looked into the Australian's eyes and knew he meant it. Nels waited for Ramon to finish and then continued, "Are they with us or not, Ramon? I don't have time to wait for them to grow balls!"

"They will help, Mr. Nels."

Charlie could see the terror in the faces of the men. He wasn't sure if it was because of Nels or the rebels, but it was there!

"Okay, settle down!" Charlie looked at the group and said, "Nels, take your men out the back door and get them in position. Ramon's uncle and I will go down and meet these SOBs. I will stall them until you get where you need to be." Charlie and the uncle headed out the front door as Nels and the rest of the men went out the back.

The Muslim bandits were just crossing the road heading for the office. Charlie counted six men dressed in shabby clothing holding automatic weapons across their chest. It was obvious who the leader was; he was a tall man for a Filipino, with a belt full of ammunition crossing his chest, surrounded by three others.

The uncle whispered to Charlie, "The tall one is the leader, Mr. Charlie. He is very dangerous—you must be very careful!"

Charlie whispered back to the uncle under his breath, "I figured he was the man just by the way he walks. Let me do the talking, okay?"

"Yes, you must do the talking! I do not believe words will come out of my mouth if I try!"

The minute the rebels spotted Charlie, they slowed the pace. The men raised their weapons to ready position, but the leader motioned to lower them. He approached Charlie and Ramon's uncle and said in clear English to the uncle, "Good morning. I see you have company today."

Ramon's uncle tried to answer but nothing would come from his mouth, his throat was so tight!

Charlie stepped forward, put out his hand and said, "It's nice to hear English. It will make things a lot easier for us to talk. He continued, I suppose you are wondering what I am doing here."

The leader smiled and said, "It has crossed my mind."

"Well, I work for an international mining company and we're thinking of opening the mine. We've been here a couple of days looking the place over. It's quite a site, I have to say."

The leader of the bandits carefully looked around and said, "We? How many are there of you?"

Charlie answered, "Enough to get the job done, if you know what I mean."

The leader understood what Charlie meant! He looked toward Ramon's uncle while still talking to Charlie and said, "This man and I are in business together. Has he told you?" The rebel leader had a fierce expression on his face. "We protect these poor people from terrible bandits who try to take their valuables. There are many bad people in this part of the Islands."

Charlie knew this was it; he had to make a stand now! "From what this man has told me, you have done an excellent job of protecting their village and he appreciates it. However, now that we are here, we no longer need your help. But you are welcome to visit the village any time you like." Sweat was running down Charlie's face, the muscles tightening as he gripped the pistol in his belt and waited for the rebel leader to respond.

The rebel leader tuned to his men and told them what Charlie had said. They all began to laugh.

"Did I say something funny?" Charlie asked the bandit leader.

"No, no my friend, something happened on the way to the village that we found amusing, that is all." Again the rebel leader turned to his men and said something to them under his breath. The men raised their weapons in the ready position. He turned to face Charlie and said, "I don't think we should leave these poor people to the bandits; I believe we will still take care of them. What do you think of that?"

Charlie walked up to the leader and leaned toward him as though he wanted to whisper something. The rebel leaned forward to hear what Charlie wanted to say. Before he knew what was happening, Charlie had grabbed him by the neck and twisted him in his grip. Charlie had already drawn his pistol and had it up against the man's head.

The rebels were taken by surprise; they were confused and didn't know what to do! Charlie had been waiting six years for this; he was ready to kill this man on the spot. Nels had misunderstood Charlie a couple of days earlier when they argued at the mine office—Charlie wasn't afraid of the rebels, he was afraid of himself! He knew once he confronted these cowards that killed his friends he was going to get some payback—and now it was payback time!

Charlie said, in a cold demanding voice, "If your comrades decide to do something stupid, I will blow your head off, is that clear?"

The rebel leader answered, "I would suggest that you put the pistol down. There are six of us and only one of you."

Charlie replied, "Let me correct you. There are five of you—you won't be around after the shooting starts!"

The man in Charlie's grasp tried to squirm but Charlie had a death grip and held him firmly. "Nels, why don't you show yourself?" Charlie hollered.

Nels and the other five men stepped from behind the buildings, their weapons at the ready. Charlie twisted the man's head so he could see Nels and the others. The rebel said, "I see that you have prepared yourselves for our visit, but you must know that these villagers are only miners and will not have a chance against my men."

"Maybe you are right, but again that's something you will never know, because I guarantee you that you will be the first casualty!"

At that moment one of the rebel bandits aimed and fired his automatic weapon at Nels and his men! Charlie struck the leader's head with his pistol and turned the weapon on the man that had fired. The bullet struck the man in the chest and he fell to the ground. Nels and his men opened fire; three of the bandits were hit and went down the other two bandits dropped their weapons and raised their hands above their heads. The Muslim leader was on his hands and knees holding his head.

Charlie hollered, "Hold it, Nels!" He turned to find Ramon's uncle lying on the ground. At first he thought the man had been shot, but further observation indicated the man had passed out cold! The leader slowly got to his feet still holding his head and carefully looked around. He no longer had his weapon in his hands; he had dropped it when Charlie struck him with his pistol. Nels and the others moved in around the rebels, holding their rifles ready to fire if necessary.

Charlie grabbed the leader by the front of the man's shirt and said, "We can finish it right now, but I would suggest that you consider the alternatives. Do you understand?"

The man assessed the situation and said, "I believe you have us in a disadvantage. We did not come here for this; we came here as friends and protectors of the village. I am sorry for the misunderstanding."

Nels walked up to the leader and raised his rifle as if he were going to strike the man then said, "Don't give us that bullshit! We know why you are here! If I had my way, we would finish you off right now!"

Charlie interrupted Nels. "As I see it and if I were you, I would take you're wounded and clear out. That's what I would do—but again, that's your call."

The rebel leader spoke to his men and turned back to Charlie. He said, "I see that the village no longer needs our protection. If you will allow us, we will leave in peace."

Nels grabbed the man by the shirt collar and said, "Sure you will, and in a week you will be back!"

"You misunderstand us. We do not want trouble. One of my men made a mistake and has paid for it with his life. We do not want any more trouble."

"That's enough," Charlie said. "You will leave this village and never return. Our company is hiring a security force from Manila with three expat managers. They will be here next week. If you or any of your people show up here again, they will kill every one of you, do you understand?"

The bandit leader took another look around and said, "Again, I apologize for the misunderstanding. We will not return to this village." With that the leader told his men to pick up their weapons.

Charlie raised his pistol and said, "Leave them! You won't need them anymore!"

Nels turned to Ramon and said, "Escort these gentlemen from the village, and make sure they are far from here before you let them go."

Ramon answered, "Yes, we will take them far from our village and make sure they never return!"

Charlie hesitated and was concerned. He motioned Ramon to one side and said, "Ramon, if you kill these men then you will be no better than they. Do as we ask—take them from here and let them go."

Ramon had a confused look on his face and started to say something to Charlie but decided to keep quiet. Ramon also remembered what these rebels had done to John and the others but he obeyed. He had three of his men circle the bandits and finally directed them toward the road. The bandits did not resist and started walking in the direction they had come; they were in no mood to continue this nightmare! They had no problems with the poor villagers, but they had not bargained for this!

After Ramon and the bandits were out of sight, the villagers came out from their houses and began to shout, jumping up and down in joy. Ramon's uncle grabbed Charlie around the waist, hollering, "Thank you, thank you, my friend!"

Nels stood with a huge grin and yelled to Charlie, "You are a hero, mate!"

Charlie just shook his head, raised his hand up and mopped the sweat from his brow then took a deep sigh of relief.

Three hours later, Ramon returned to the village and told Charlie that the rebels had been turned loose many miles from the village. Charlie looked at Ramon and said, "Good, Ramon. We are not killers and again emphasized. If you had killed those men, you would have been no different from them; do you understand?"

With a concerned expression Ramon answered, "Yes, Sir Charlie, I understand, but—"

Charlie said, "But—?"

Ramon looked down at his feet and said, "Nothing, Mr. Charlie I was thinking of Mr. John is all."

Charlie hugged Ramon and said, "I know, kid, I know."

Tears welled up in both of the men's eyes. It was difficult—and each one knew in their hearts it wasn't over yet, not by a long shot!

Two days later Charlie, Ramon, and Nels were headed to the site.

CHAPTER 8

Back to the Site

Arnold sat at the table picking at the label on his beer and said, "They ain't coming back, I tell you!"

Gil looked at Arnold and said, "Will you knock it off! I have been listening to your bullshit for over a week, and I am tired of it! They would never leave all their equipment alongside the road if they didn't intend on coming back, for Christ's sake!"

Arnold started to say something to Gil but froze. Gil looked at him, wondering. "Now what's wrong?"

Arnold leaned over slowly and whispered to Gil, "They're here!"

"What?" Gil exclaimed!

"Damn it, man, they just walked into the restaurant!"

Gil started to turn around, but Arnold grabbed his arm and motioned for Gil to get up from the table slowly. The two men eased up from their table and moved out of sight of the doorway.

Charlie walked into the restaurant and took a quick look around. He turned to Nels and said, "Let's find us a table and get something to eat."

Nels nodded and started looking for an empty table then said to Charlie and Ramon, "There's one, mate." He immediately walked over and sat down.

Ramon followed the two men and sat down next to Nels. Since the run-in with the rebels, Ramon had become close to Nels, who reminded him of Jerry. He considered Nels his hero. He was looking at Nels with admiration when Nels said, "Ramon, any good man would have done what we did back there. You don't owe me anything. I appreciate your friendship, so let's leave it at that, okay?"

"I am sorry; Mr. Nels, but you are a good man just like my Sir Charlie. You helped my people, and I will never forget it." Nels took what Roman said about Charlie and a major complement Charlie was his hero any comparison was something else!

Nels smiled at Ramon and shook his head. He realized that nothing he could say would change Ramon's mind. Besides, he liked this young man! Ramon had stood up to the rebels and had proven to Nels that he was a real man—more than Ramon realized himself. "Okay, kid, let's eat."

A grin crossed Ramon's face. The men had just received their food and started eating when they heard a commotion behind them. Arnold and Gil were attempting to leave the restaurant when Arnold tripped over a chair. He was watching the three men at the table while at the same time trying to sneak out the back door. His foot had gotten tangled up in the chair and caused him to sprawl out onto the restaurant floor!

Gil stopped in his tracks. He was at the door when Arnold had taken the fall. He thought, What's next?

Charlie was on his feet in an instant. He started running back toward Arnold, whose legs were still tangled up in the chair. He frantically rolled around the floor trying to get free of the chair. Gil quickly ran to Arnold's aid and pulled the man to his feet. They ran through the back door of the restaurant, disappearing down the alley.

Charlie stopped half way back to the door and returned to the table. "I guess we still have those two to worry about, guys. We will have to keep an eye out for them."

"Yeah, I guess you are right, Charlie," Nels replied, "but next time maybe I will get a shot at kicking the piss out of them!" Charlie and Nels started laughing. Ramon looked at the two men in confusion but laughed anyway.

That afternoon the three men decided to pay Mila a visit. Ramon had not seen her since he had left them in the jungle. He had mixed feelings about Mila—he remembered her resentment over Charlie, but he also remembered her compassion while the bandits were chasing them through the jungle. Charlie knocked on Mila's door and waited for her to answer it.

The minute she opened the door she threw her arms around Charlie and said, "Oh, Charlie, I have missed you!"

Charlie said, "Take a look at what I brought with me!"

Mila turned to Ramon and yelled, "Ramon!" She let go of Charlie and grabbed Ramon around the neck.

This took Ramon completely by surprise, and he was shocked by her gesture. She hugged him so tight that he was having difficulty breathing! Ramon looked at Charlie for help, but Charlie only laughed.

Finally, she stepped back and took a look at Ramon and said, "My, you are a handsome man!" This immediately embarrassed Ramon and he lowered his head, his face turning red hot!

Nels said, "Careful, Mila; he's a married man!"

This further embarrassed Ramon. He had the look of a lost child on his face and turned to Charlie for help. Mila laughed out loud at Nell's comment. Charlie smiled and said, "We had better leave poor Ramon alone before he has a heart attack."

"Come into my house, Sir Charlie. I will fix you something to eat," Mila said with a big smile on her face.

Nels said, "Every time we come here, Mila, you want to feed us. Do you want to make us fat?"

Mila frowned at Nels and lowered her head.

Nels wrapped his arms around her and said, "I'm kidding, sweetheart! We've just eaten at the restaurant."

After he released her, Mila smiled again and said, "The food at the restaurant is not good for you, you must eat my food!"

The three of them sat down at the table and Mila poured some coffee. Charlie picked up Stopie and held him in his arms. Ramon watched Charlie as he played with the boy. He thought, this is a good man!

As Charlie and Nels drank their coffee, Ramon and Mila began to talk in their dialect. Ramon explained to Mila what had happened to him and John in the jungle and told her about his family.

After Ramon had finished she said to him, "You must bring your family here so I can meet them, Ramon." Ramon was pleased to hear her say this. He did not want to stay away from his family long. If Mila would allow his family to stay here then he could visit them while they were looking for the gold.

He turned to Charlie and said, Sir Charlie, can my family come here and stay while we dig for the gold?"

Charlie looked at Mila and said, "What will your husband say, Mila?"

"My husband will not mind. Besides, Stopie will have someone to play with. I have talked to my husband and told him he must help you, Charlie—you will never get the gold without him. He will talk to his people and they will help you dig for the gold. If you do not use the men in my husband's village, they will never allow you to dig."

"Mila, we did not come here to get your husband's help. We do not want to cause any more trouble for his people. If they will let us search for the gold then we will not need their help," Charlie replied.

"No," she said, "he will help you!"

Charlie was surprised at how firmly Mila had made the comment. Two hours later Magellan returned from the fishing village. He was disappointed to see Charlie, Nels, and Ramon at his home but did not say anything to them. It was obvious to Charlie and Nels that Mila and her husband had argued about them. Mila forced Magellan outside to talk. The three men could hear them talking, but in a few minutes the two entered the house and Mila said, "My husband will help you." She turned to Magellan and gave him a hard look!

Charlie sat at the table in silence for a few minutes with his hands folded in his lap. Leaning back in his chair, finally he said, "Mila, are you sure your husband wants to help us?"

Mila answered immediately in a tense voice, "We will not talk of this again, Charlie. It has been decided." She turned from the table and walked into her kitchen.

Again the men sat in silence. Nels glanced over at Charlie and whispered, "Mate, that is one tough woman—I see why you spent time with her!" A hint of a grin crossed Charlie's face; all he could do was nod his head in agreement. He was not about to say anything in front of Magellan; he did not want to embarrass the man any farther.

Without warning Mila returned to the kitchen and said to Charlie, "Charlie, you will go back to Ramon's village and bring his family here." Ramon's eyes widened in surprise but remain silent. Again Mila glanced at Magellan, turned, and left the kitchen.

Gil and Arnold sat at around the campfire sipping their coffee. Arnold looked across the fire at Gil and said, "Why the hell did we run! I wanted a part of the SOB, damn it! I owe him!"

"You owe him, ha! He kicked the hell out of us! What were you gonna do, fight him like a turtle, on your back? If I hadn't helped you to your feet, he would have done another number on you!"

Arnold looked down into his coffee cup and replied, "Bullshit. Next time I'll show you what I can do." His sincerity, however, was suspect.

"There isn't going to be a next time, Arnold. We are going to find out what these guys are up to and that means we stay clear of them, understand! Now, I expect them to show up at their camp in a couple of days and then we will find out what is going on. Until then we stay here in camp and mind our own business!" Gil looked at Arnold—his face was still covered with yellow bruises where Charlie had hit him; in fact, Gil too was carrying a few scars from his encounter. Both men had the look of a raccoon; it would be several days before the bruises would clear up.

CHAPTER 9

Back to Camp

"Are we ready to go, Nels?" Charlie asked.

"Yeah, Charlie, I just loaded the last of the equipment and food."

"Well, let's get moving, guys. We have some gold to dig!"

This was a happy day for Ramon. Charlie had driven him back to his village, loaded his family and returned to Mila's home. Within a few minutes after arriving the two women were talking nonstop as they worked in the kitchen. The children were playing, everything was working out to everyone's satisfaction—even though Magellan was still moping around the house. He thought, I love my wife very much, and if it was not for her, I would not help these men. I cannot lose her! From the first time he had met her at the primitive village he had been in love. He respected her pride and strong will, but most of all he was stricken with her beauty! Every day when he came home from work, he couldn't help but watch her with the child, working around the house. She was amazing, and nothing would get in the way of his love, nothing!

It was decided that Charlie, Nels, and Ramon would return to the camp near the site and begin reopening the tunnel. Magellan would return to his fishing boat and wait until Charlie needed him. Charlie knew that the opening of the tunnel was only a three-man job as long as they used the Bobcat equipment. If necessary, Ramon could find a couple of extra men to help, but for now Magellan could return to work. Once they started timbering the tunnel opening; that would be the time they would need him.

When the three men were in the van and settled in, Charlie drove out of the fishing village and headed toward the site. Nels was the first to speak. "Charlie, has Magellan talked to the chief of the village yet?"

"Yeah, he was there yesterday. He told Mila that the young chief was not happy but would help if necessary. The chief's only stipulation was that we did not bring any more white people to the site, and not to bring any of the gold to his village; that's all right with us!"

Nels smiled and nodded his head in agreement. Just as they finished their conversation, Charlie turned off onto the dirt road, they were back in business!

"Get up, damn it, they're back!" Gil walked over to where Arnold was bent over digging in a food sack and kicked Arnold in the ass. Arnold abruptly straightened up and turned around. Gil threw out the coffee in his cup and set it on the table. Arnold placed his hands on his hips, leaned back, scratched his head, yawned, then took a look around and said, "Who is back?"

"Jesus, I wonder why I keep you around! Who the hell do you think is back?"

Finally, it dawned on Arnold who Gil was referring to. He pulled his baseball cap down over his forehead and walked over to where Gil was crouched in the jungle brush next to the road. As he stepped over a log they were using as a seat, his foot tangled and he tripped. Arnold sprawled face first into the fire. Although the flames had been doused, the coals were still very hot. The coals began to burn his face and forearms and he immediately began to struggle to his feet, screaming in agony!

Gil turned to the campsite to find Arnold jumping around, slapping at his clothing! Arnold was yelling, "Help me, damn it, I'm on fire!" Gil ran to Arnold's aid and began to knock the hot ashes off his burning clothes. After knocking off the hot ambers Arnold started to settle down. He was standing in the middle of the camp with a fearful look on his face and said, "Thanks, partner I thought I was a goner for a minute."

Gil did not respond but immediately returned to his hiding place near the road. He was concerned that the men in the van may have heard the commotion. As the van passed, he could see the three men. There was no sign that they had heard the noise created by Arnold's battle with the hot coals. Gil relaxed and thought, Will it never end! He again turned and looked at Arnold who was still brushing off the coals. This is turning into a nightmare! It will be a miracle if he doesn't kill himself before this is over—and maybe me with him! Arnold was quite a sight—along with his raccoon face, he now was covered with ashes from the fire. He reminded Gil of a tragic circus clown!"

Gil took a deep breath and walked over to Arnold. "We'll give them a few minutes and then follow. Maybe we can find out what they are up too."

Arnold nodded in agreement and said, "I need a few minutes, Gil; I have to change my clothes. Christ, man! I burnt myself pretty good!"

Gil shook his head in disgust and began removing the brush hiding the truck from view. He had just finished when Arnold returned from the tent and said, "Do you need some help, partner?"

Gil looked at Arnold in frustration. The truck was clear and ready to go. He replied, "Just get into the truck, for Christ's sake—and tie your boots!"

Arnold looked down at his boots and grinned. "That's all I need, is to trip on the laces, eh?" He climbed into the truck and Gil began driving in the direction of the other vehicle. They had gone about two miles when he spotted the van parked alongside the road. Gil immediately jammed on the brakes and stopped the truck he put it in reverse and began backing up as fast as the rig would move! Arnold was not prepared for the sudden change in direction and as soon as Gil hit the brake, Arnold's face struck the dash board, no seat belt!

Arnold let out a holler, "Damn it, man! Are you trying to knock my brains out?"

Gil only glanced at Arnold for a second. He continued to drive the truck backward until he was out of sight of the camp. He stopped and climbed out. Arnold was tenderly inspecting his throbbing nose and forehead. Gil walked on the side of the road staying near the jungle overgrowth until he could see the camp. He was peering through the underbrush when Arnold walked up behind him and said, "Do I have a bruise on my forehead partner?"

Gil grabbed Arnold by the shirt collar and pulled him into the brush and said, "Are you nuts? Stay out of sight, for Christ's sake! Do you want them to see us? And by the way, keep your voice down!"

Ramon thought he had heard something and turned to look down the road; he noticed the brush along the road moving. He walked over to Charlie, who was unloading the van, and said, "Sir Charlie, someone is watching us."

Charlie stopped unloading the van and answered, "What do you mean, Ramon?"

Ramon said, "Do not look down the road. I'm not sure if they are still there, Sir Charlie, but I saw the brush move, and there is dust above the road."

"Okay, Ramon." Charlie walked back to where Nels was standing near the van and said in a whisper, "Nels, let's take a walk into the jungle toward the tunnel."

Nels responded, "Okay, mate, but let me finish unloading the van."

"No, leave it until we get back."

"But it will just take a minute, Charlie."

"Nels, we have visitors!" Nels started to turn around, but Charlie whispered, "Don't look, Nels; just follow me." Charlie turned to Ramon and said in a loud voice, "Ramon, we are going to check out the tunnel site. You continue to unload the van." Ramon was not certain what Charlie was up to but nodded his head in agreement. The two men disappeared into the jungle.

After they were out of sight of the camp, Charlie turned to Nels and said, "Let's circle around and find out who the hell our friends are hiding down the road; I've got a pretty good idea!"

Gil and Arnold watched as Charlie and Nels disappeared out of sight into the jungle. Gil turned to Arnold and said, "Better get the hell out of here—I don't like the looks of this."

Arnold responded, "What do you mean, Gil?"

"I mean I think they are on to us, damn it!"

"Oh, I don't think they know we are here. Shit, man, we're fifty yards from their camp!"

Gil hesitated for a few minutes and finally said, "Okay—but if something happens, we'll have to get out in a hurry!"

"Nothing is going to happen; they aren't smart enough to catch us!"

Just about the time Arnold finished , Charlie and Nels stepped out from the jungle behind them. Charlie hollered, "Hold it right there, boys!"

The two men were taken completely by surprise! Gil hollered at Arnold, "Run!" Arnold turned and looked at Charlie and Nels, his mouth hanging wide open. He had no idea where to run and ran directly into Gil! The two men bounced off each other and headed in opposite directions. Gil was first into the jungle, ducking his head as he ran. Arnold began running toward the main road and at the same time looking behind him at Charlie and Nels. As he crossed the road and entered the jungle he turned to face the direction he was running just in time to see a large tree branch in front of him. Too late! it struck him across his forehead, knocking him cold! He was lifted off his feet about two feet in the air by the force of the blow and hit the ground, flat on his back.

Gil ran into the jungle a couple hundred yards then stopped and hid behind a large tree. He was still hiding when someone said behind him, "You must return with me." Gil turned to find a young Filipino man holding a machete in his hand. Gil leaned up against the tree, a look of fright across his face, and said, "Okay, son—just don't do anything with that knife!"

Charlie walked up to where Arnold was lying on the ground. A large lump was forming across the man's forehead. With the added bruises and burns from his other escapades, poor Arnold was quite a sight! Charlie thought, The guy looks like the elephant man!

Arnold began to groan. He rose up onto his elbow and with his right hand he rubbed his now-swollen forehead. The branch had added another prominent knot next to the one he got from the windshield incident.

Charlie leaned over, grabbed Arnold by the collar of his shirt, and said, "Get up, Arnold. Let's take a walk back to the truck; you know it seems you spend a lot of your time on your ass!"

Arnold turned his head and peered up at Charlie. He was in no mood to argue and struggled to his feet. The two men returned to where the truck was parked alongside the road and found Gil leaning against it with his hands folded across his chest. Ramon and Nels were on either side of him, Ramon holding the machete ready.

Charlie said, "It's nice that you two gentlemen have paid us a visit. Now why don't you tell us why you are here?"

Arnold stopped rubbing his forehead and said, "What do you mean a visit? You don't own the Philippines! We have as much right here as you do!"

Gil could not control his anger. He shook his head in disgust and said, "Shut the fuck up Arnold! Don't act like a complete idiot!"

Arnold's mouth dropped open in disbelief but he said nothing. Charlie said, "Let's take a walk back to our camp we can talk about this over a beer." Nels was surprised at Charlie's invitation but decided to wait until they were alone to ask him what he had in mind. Ramon continued to hold the machete over his right shoulder, ready to take action if needed. Charlie motioned with a hand directed at Ramon to relax, which made Gil much more comfortable, to say the least! Ramon hesitated but eventually lowered the machete to his side and followed the group back to camp.

After arriving at camp Charlie told Ramon to get four beers out of the cooler. He directed Gil and Arnold to take a seat next to the campfire. Ramon reluctantly handed Gil and Arnold a beer each then gave Charlie and Nels theirs. Nels looked at Charlie and said, "Can I talk to you for a minute, Charlie, in private?"

"Sure, Nels," Charlie answered. "But first let's get some info from our two friends. Gil, why don't you start? Maybe now you will give us some straight answers."

Gil began, "I'm not going to bullshit you. Arnold and I have been watching you for a couple of weeks and I'm sure you already know that. You said something back in Davao that we were interested in, concerning gold. It was too bad that we had the little run-in before we could find out what you were getting at, but that's another story. I don't know what you have going, but I would like us to forget the past and start over. I know you don't trust us, but I'm tired of the deception and all the horseshit that's been going on the last couple of weeks."

Charlie replied, "Well, at least I feel better that you're being straight and not giving us a line. It makes it easier for us to make a decision on what to do with you two. Nels and I have to talk this over for a few minutes. You two can finish your beer. We'll be right back." Charlie motioned to Nels with a nod, and the two men walked away from the camp.

After walking a safe distance from the others, Nels began, "You sure are treating those two SOBs nice, Charlie. What's going on?"

"Nels, here's the way I see it. If we turn them loose, they are just going to keep watching us and eventually give us more trouble. I guess we could shoot them and bury them in the jungle, but let's face it—we are not the type to murder anyone. At first I thought we could send them to the primitive village and have the natives hold onto them until we are done here, but that could take months. I'm not sure what problems that may cause at the village. I think the best thing to do is bring them in. At least we can watch them closer. Remember, Nels—there's enough gold to satisfy us for a hundred lifetimes!"

Nels removed his hat and ran his fingers through his hair. He finally turned to Charlie and said, "Mate, I don't trust either one of those two, but Arnold bothers me the most. He doesn't seem to be too bright and will screw us eventually if he gets the chance. I believe this Gil guy might end up being okay, but again, I don't know." He paused for a minute and continued, "Well, Charlie, it's up to you. I will go along with whatever you decide."

The two men returned to the camp. Gil and Arnold had finished their beers and were waiting to hear what Charlie had decided. Charlie spoke to Ramon first.

"Ramon, I want you to go to the village and have the chief and ten of his warriors come back to camp with you."

Ramon was not sure why Sir Charlie made this request but nodded his head and started walking toward the village. Nels said, "Wait, Ramon. I'll drive you to the village; it will take less time." Charlie agreed, Nels and Ramon climbed into the van and drove off. After the van was out of sight, Gil asked Charlie what was going on.

"Gentlemen, about five miles from here is a primitive village, with about fifty warriors. When the chief of the village returns with some of his men, I am going to tell him that you are going to help us. But listen close, boys—I am also going to tell him that I do not trust you. I will instruct him to leave some of his warriors here to watch every move you make, and if you make the wrong move, I will have them cut your heads off!"

Arnold jumped to his feet, clenched his fist, and said, "You dirty SOB! I'm going to knock hell out of you!" He jumped over the campfire and drew back his fist. Gil attempted to grab Arnold's arm to prevent him from swinging, but was too far away from the two men to do any good.

Gil had nothing to worry about; Charlie had anticipated Arnold's move and was ready. Arnold took a wild swing with his right fist at Charlie's face. Charlie leaned back and let the fist miss by several inches. He grabbed Arnold by the hair and pulled down at the same time raising his right knee to meet Arnold's head. As Charlie's knee connected he let go of the man's hair, and Arnold went flying backward, landing on his back. He was out cold before he hit the ground.

Gil looked at Charlie and said, "I don't suppose he will ever learn, Charlie. Believe me; I don't want any more trouble. If you want, I will get rid of Arnold—he's been nothing but a headache ever since I met him!"

Charlie answered, "Let's wait for Nels to get back. I'm sure when Arnold comes too he won't give me any more grief."

Gil walked over to a water bucket and soaked a handkerchief then leaned down and wiped Arnold's bleeding face. He thought, God, what a mess! The guy never learns! Arnold came to and began to struggle to his feet, but Gil held him down and said, "Arnold, damn it, that's enough!"

Arnold replied, "Damn, man! This asshole is going to have our heads cut off! What are you going to do, stick your head over a log and let them do it?"

Gil continued to wipe Arnold's face with his wet handkerchief and said, "No, Arnold, I'm not going to let them cut off either of our heads, and I am sure Charlie is not going to let it happen—so settle down!"

Fifteen minutes later Nels returned to camp with the village chief and several of his warriors. He took a quick look at Arnold and thought, Is there another knot on that nitwit's face?

Gil and Arnold stared at the men in terror—the warriors were carrying their machetes, spears, and blowguns. They were ready for action! Charlie took Nels, Ramon, and the chief aside to discuss the situation, while the warriors surrounded Gil and Arnold. After a few minutes the men returned to the campsite, and the chief directed his men to get in the van. Nels climbed into the van and began driving back to the village.

Once the van was out of sight, Charlie turned to Gil and Arnold and said, "The chief wants to kill the both of you, but I persuaded him to let us handle the situation. He has agreed to let you stay and help; however, he is going to keep six of his warriors near the sight. Either one of you decide to make a run for it, they have been told to finish you off. Do you understand?"

Arnold jumped up and yelled, "You can't do that—it's murder, plain and simple!"

Charlie responded, "You are absolutely right, Arnold; that is exactly what it is. And another thing—no one would ever find your bodies. How does that sound?"

Arnold started to say something, but Gil grabbed him by the arm and said to Charlie, "Okay, Charlie, whatever you say—we are in!"

"But Gil—"

Gil squeezed Arnold's arm and said, "We are in, and that's the end of it!"

Charlie told Ramon to bring him the map. He took it, laid it out in front of Gil and Arnold, and said, "Once I tell you what is going on, you will have two choices. One, help us, or two—"He didn't have to say anymore!

Charlie was just finishing telling the two men about the gold when Nels returned from the village. Charlie stopped discussing the plan and said to Nels, "Did you drop off the warriors near camp, partner?"

Nels replied, "Yeah, mate. There are six of them setting up a camp about a half-mile from here. They will keep an eye on us from now on."

"I have explained to the boys about the gold and what we plan on doing. Do you have anything to say?"

"Yep, Charlie; let me say a few words." Nels walked up to Gil and Arnold and said, "As far as I am concerned, I would just as soon give you to the warriors. But Charlie's decided to let you in. Let me make something very clear—one false move on either one of your parts, and I guarantee I will help the warriors finish you off!"

Gil raised his hands in a defensive posture then held one out to shake and said, "There will be no reason for the warriors to get involved. We aren't going to be any trouble—this is too good!"

Nels took Gil's hand and shook it but he was still not convinced he could trust either one of them.

CHAPTER 10

The Tunnel

The next morning the four men worked on the tunnel, and by the end of the day they had re-supported the opening and were removing loose material from inside the tunnel. Charlie was pleasantly surprised with Arnold's ability—he was a skilled Bobcat operator and was able to remove the loose material from inside the tunnel with astounding speed. After clearing the loose rock from the front of the tunnel, the Bobcat continued further into the opening again everyone was astonished on how Arnold ran in and out of the tunnel removing the additional rock. The others stood along the edge of the tunnel watching Arnold dig the rock. He returned from inside the cave with the bucket of the Bobcat empty then jumped down from the machine and ran up to Charlie, yelling, "There's a damn body in there!"

"A body?" Charlie responded.

"Yeah, I was about to fill the bucket again when I seen this damn skeleton lying over a pile of dirt!

"Okay," Charlie replied, "let's take a look."

The men re-entered the tunnel, Arnold leading the group to where the remains were stretched across a mound of dirt. Charlie leaned over and examined the remains. He stood up and said, "I have no idea who this person might be. When we closed the tunnel, there was no one inside. We were the only ones here all of us left the site when the Muslims were seen heading toward camp."

Nels interrupted Charlie, "He sure in the hell isn't going to cause us any trouble, Charlie. My suggestion is to remove the body and get back to work."

Charlie replied, "And that's exactly what we are going to do." After removing the skeleton, Arnold continued to dig and clear the tunnel toward the main cave.

Gil also proved to be an asset to the group. His engineering ability allowed the men to reinstall the timbers at the opening to the tunnel. It was clear Gil had some major background in underground mining.

A couple hours after they removed the body, Arnold returned from inside the tunnel with a full bucket of material. He signaled to Charlie and said, "That's the last of it, Charlie. I have cleared the tunnel back to the main cave area."

"Good, Arnold. What does it look like?"

"Charlie, there is a huge pile of rock and timbers at the cave. It must be twenty feet high."

Charlie hollered to Nels and Gil, "Guys, it's time we take a look at the cave."

Arnold climbed out of the Bobcat, and the four men entered the tunnel on foot. Nels yelled at Ramon, "Come on, kid—you need to see this too."

Ramon hesitated. He was apprehensive about entering the tunnel—the memory of his first time inside still bothered him. He had had a difficult time forgetting the skeleton of the dead Japanese soldier he had found during the first trip . There were times Ramon had nightmares seeing John dying, the soldier's and Omar's decapitated heads lying in front of him and the skeleton in the cave. He took a deep breath, however, and followed the others.

As the men approached the cave area, Charlie stopped and began looking along the sides of the tunnel where Arnold had used the Bobcat in cleaning the tunnel. Approximately fifteen feet from the main cave along the side of the roadway, Charlie leaned over and started cleaning dirt from what seemed to be part of a gold bar that was sticking out of the loose material. The other men stood over him as he continued to clear away the dirt.

Finally Charlie stood to his feet, holding the bar in his hands. He said, "Let's go outside and get a better look at this."

They exited the tunnel into the sunlight, where Charlie held out the gold bar and said, "Nels, bring me that bucket of water, will you?" Nels walked over and picked up a bucket of water the men had been using to wash their hands and brought it to Charlie. Charlie submerged the bar into the water and began to wash off the loose dirt. Finally he pulled the bar from the bucket and held it in front of him.

Gil leaned forward and said, "My God, it's gold!"

Nels ran his hand over the bar as though it were a delicate silk pillow and said, "I've seen gold bars before, Charlie, but I never thought I would be touching one that belonged to me!"

Charlie put the bar down onto the ground in front of the men, placed his hand onto his chin, and said, "Why the hell did we find the bar along the wall in the tunnel? We never moved the gold when we found it the first time. Something isn't right, guys. The only thing I can come up with is the body we found was someone who went into the tunnel after we had gone—but who in the hell opened up the tunnel?"

Gil really didn't care about the history of the tunnel he was more concerned in finding more of the gold. He was anxious to get going again and asked, "What do you want to do, Charlie?"

"First, we had better find out if there is more gold along the walls of the tunnel and we need to see if there are any more bodies inside. Do you all agree?"

He turned to Arnold and said, "Arnold, while the rest of us are inside, why don't you dig through the rock you brought out from the tunnel? You might find some bars that you brought out with the loads."

Arnold nodded his head in agreement and climbed back into the Bobcat as the others returned inside the tunnel. Within an hour the men had located ten additional bars. After digging along the tunnel wall, Nels finally stood up and said, "I don't see any more, Charlie. Let's take the ones we found outside and see what Arnold has come up with."

When the men exited the tunnel, they found Arnold putting another gold bar next to the one Charlie had found earlier. There was an additional six bars stacked alongside the first bar for a total of seventeen.

The men stood looking at the gold in front of them. Arnold said, "What do you think their worth, guys?"

Charlie scratched the back of his neck and said, "I would guess it's probably worth $550,000 at today's prices—but that's only a guess. We'll need to assay and weigh them first. My biggest concern right now is how the damn stuff ended up alongside the tunnel walls. We sure in the hell didn't put it there last time we were here—am I right, Ramon, all the bars were in the main room."

Ramon didn't say anything but nodded his head in agreement. Charlie turned to the group and said, "All right, we can't do anything about this right now. The answer is inside the tunnel. Let's get back in there and see if we can find out what happened."

The men all nodded their heads in agreement then Charlie led the way back into the tunnel. As they started walking toward the tunnel, no one noticed Gil standing over the stacked gold. He had a strange look on his face. He leaned over and picked up one of the bars and began rubbing his hands across the top of the bar over and over again.

"Gil!" Arnold hollered from the tunnel opening, "Are you comin', partner?"

Gil turned and looked at Arnold, a glazed look in his eyes. He didn't answer him right away; instead, he stood in a daze looking at the gold in his hands. Arnold repeated, "Gil, let's go! There's more where that came from!"

Gil was not listening to Arnold. He was deep in thought, Christ, I'm a millionaire! I can't believe it—I'm a millionaire! No one, and I mean no one, is going to take it away from me! I will kill the first man that tries! Let's see, he continued, seventeen bars at about 120 ounces each at $400 an ounce; damn, that's eight hundred thousand bucks!

Arnold was tired of waiting for Gil. He shook his head and ran to catch up with the others, who had disappeared inside.

Finally Gil set the bar back onto the stack and walked toward the tunnel, still with the strange look in his eyes.

"Nels, why don't you take a look around and see if you can find any signs of other bodies? The guy we found could not have moved all the gold; there had to be more than one."

"Good idea, Charlie. I'll take a look in the back of the cave and see what turns up."

"Be careful—this place looks pretty shaky no need in anyone getting buried!" "No problem, mate, I don't intend on getting killed in here!"

CHAPTER 11

Where's the Gold?

Charlie stood looking at the massive rock pile, which reached to within five feet of the top of the cave. He directed his high-powered light overhead and carefully examined the roof above him. The area where the floor had covered the top of the cave was now gone; a massive hole was in its place. He turned to the others and said, "Someone or something tripped the trap, boys! The entire flooring above the cave is missing. Take a look over there—see where the water has been turned loose? From what I can see, someone started removing the gold and released the ropes holding the floor from above. Once the floor collapsed and fell onto the gold, everything went. Then the water was turned loose from behind the second wall and filled the entire cave."

Arnold asked, "What does that mean, Charlie?"

"Well, Arnold, the gold is now buried under all the rock you see here. Remember I told you that there was a large hole under the floor the gold was on? When the roof collapsed it took out the lower floor. Once that happened everything—including the wall holding back the water—turned loose."

Nels returned from the back of the tunnel and said, "I can't see any bodies, Charlie. The only other explanation is that if they were in here, they're now under the rock and debris."

Charlie replied, "We can't do anything about it now, Nels. Let's decide how in the hell we are going to remove all this rock and support the cave. We can't get much done until we cover the hole above the cave and stop the water from running in. Best thing for us is to go outside and figure out this mess."

Everyone agreed and the group returned to the clearing outside the tunnel. Arnold was the first one to speak.

"Let's take five and get something to eat. It's getting late and I am beat!"

"Beat?" Gil replied, "We're almost there—this isn't the time to quit!"

Arnold was surprised at Gils's comment. He looked at him and noticed that he seemed upset and anxious. "Hey, the gold isn't going anywhere, partner. We have plenty of time to dig it out. Relax. Let's get something to eat."

Charlie responded, "I agree with Arnold. If we don't get some rest and something to eat, we might end up getting someone hurt."

Gil started to say something but thought better of it. He didn't want to start something he couldn't finish; he didn't want trouble with the others.

As the men began to eat dinner, Nels suggested that they come up with a plan. Gil suggested that, since Charlie and he were engineers, they would work together and come up with a plan to support the work site, while the others hid the gold that they had already recovered. Everyone agreed.

Ramon had been silent for most of the day. He had noticed the way Gil was acting and had an uneasy feeling—the same feeling he experienced with Gary! Gil had changed dramatically since the discovery of the gold. Ramon thought, I must tell Sir Charlie of my feelings. I do not want the same thing to happen as before with Mr. Gary.

Charlie was cleaning up the dishes with Ramon. Ramon said, "Sir Charlie, I do not feel right with this Gil person. He is acting like Mr. Gary—the gold has made him change."

Charlie stopped washing and said, "What do you mean, Ramon?"

"Well Sir, when you held the gold bar in your hands, Mr. Gil was watching you with a strange look on his face. He reminded me of Mr. Gary!"

Charlie stood in silence and said, "Ramon, I want you to keep an eye on Gil. If you see anything, and I mean anything suspicious, I want you to tell me. I will have the village warriors keep an eye on him also. I agree with you; we don't want trouble. We've seen enough and don't need any more! From now on don't let this guy out of your sight!"

Ramon nodded his head in agreement and the two men returned to the campfire where the rest of the men were finishing their coffee. Nels stood up, stretched, and said, "That's enough for me. I'm headed to bed."

Gil and Arnold stood. Gil asked, "What time do we plan on starting in the morning, Charlie?"

Charlie was deep in thought and didn't answer right away. Gil repeated, "Charlie, what time in the morning?"

Charlie turned to face Gil and said, "I'm sorry—what did you say? I wasn't listening?"

Gil repeated again, "What time in the morning?"

Charlie was looking into Gil's eyes and answered, "Daylight, Gary, daylight."

A surprised look crossed Gil's face and he said, "Gary?"

Ramon froze. Charlie answered, "I'm sorry, Gil—I was thinking of Gary when you asked me. Forget it—let's hit the sack."

Charlie headed for his tent; however, Gil did not move. He stood watching Charlie pass by. Gil felt uneasy; he didn't like the look on Charlie's face.

The next morning during breakfast Nels suggested they have a meeting each day before starting work. All agreed finally, Charlie said, "Okay, Nels, why don't you get us started?"

Nels stood up, began to pace back and forth in front of the group, and finally said, "Listen, we have about $850,000 worth of gold already and I expect there is going to be a lot more—"

Arnold interrupted Nels with a loud shout, "Yeah, you can say that again, partner!" Everyone turned to look at Arnold, who seemed a little embarrassed with his outburst. He lowered his head and began to pick at the fire with a stick he was holding.

Charlie smiled and said, "Go ahead, Nels—I think Arnold agrees with you." Everyone laughed, and Nels continued.

"Like I was saying, we have started finding gold but my biggest concern is after we get it, what in the hell are going to do with it?"

Arnold could not hold back and said, "First thing I'm going to do is get me a new truck, by God!"

Charlie smiled again and said, "That's not what he means, Arnold. We have to find a way to get the gold out of the Philippines. The government will never let us keep the gold if they find out we have it."

Arnold's face turned crimson and again he began to dig into the fire with his stick.

"We have to decide what to do with the gold once we find all of it."

Gil understood what the two men were talking about, but he wasn't sure Arnold was on board and decided he had better say something.

"Listen, Arnold—if we start trying to sell the gold here in the Philippines, the government will take it from us. There's a law that says any treasure found in the Philippines must be turned over to the government. That means we are supposed to tell them we have found the gold—and then give it back to them. The government is required by international law to give us 10 per cent of the total value, but that usually doesn't happen. They find some chicken-shit reason not to give the 10 per cent, or they delay the payment. If I know government, it will take a couple hundred years! Another thing—if anybody finds out what is going on here; we will have half the country on our backs and will be pushed out—or worse, killed for the gold!"

Arnold scratched his head and said, "You mean to tell me if anyone finds out we have the gold, they are going to take it from us?"

Gil nodded his head and said, "You got it, partner!"

Charlie decided he had better say something. "Listen, I have known about the gold for over six years. Nobody other than us and the villagers know about it, so as of now we are safe. If anyone here thinks that they can get away with telling anyone about the gold, they are mistaken. Once the cat is out of the bag, we are finished—does everyone understand that?"

Arnold was the first to answer. "Yeah, now that I think about it, you're right. If the word gets out about the gold, we're done." Everyone looked at Arnold for a second and wondered if he'd even been listening. "My question is what do we do now?"

Nels answered, "That's why I felt we needed to talk about it. We have to come up with a plan. Once we have recovered all the gold and valuables, we have to move it in a hurry. The longer we hold on to it here, the bigger the risk. I've been worried about this since Charlie and I got together, and the only solution, in my mind, is to get the damn stuff out of the country! If we can hide the gold and store it somewhere out of the country then we have some options. First, if we can't sell it internationally, at least we can bargain with the Philippine government and make a deal. As long as it's not here, we got them by the balls, right?

We might offer them all the gold for 20 per cent. If the gold is not in the country then we have the leverage, do you see what I am getting at?"

Arnold jumped to his feet and said, "We can't give them all the gold for a measly 20 per cent! The hell with them!" Arnold was agitated and started walking in circles, he continued out load, Dirty bastards, dirty fuckin bastards!"

Gil held up his hand and said to Arnold, "Do you know how much 20 per cent could be Arnold? Let's just say we find twenty million, okay? Twenty per cent of twenty million is four million dollars; not bad for a couple of months' work!"

Arnold ignored Gil's comments and yelled again, "Bullshit! If we find twenty million, then damn it, I want the twenty million!" He kicked the dirt with his foot and walked away from the campfire.

Charlie wasn't surprised at Arnold's reaction. Greed has a way of changing people for a moment, and he thought of Gary. Everyone sat in silence. Finally Charlie said, "I have been working on this for a while. I believe there are too many risks dealing with the Philippine government. I believe our best bet is to get the gold out of the country and try to trade it on the black market. It will probably take some time, but it will be safer than trying to hide it from the Philippine government. We probably can get rid of it for fifty cents on the dollar, so if we find twenty million, that's ten million for us."

Arnold turned around and said, "Good idea, Charlie. I like that a hell of a lot better than the four million Gil's talking about!"

Charlie had to smile. A month ago Arnold would have jumped through his ass if someone had offered him $10,000—much less four million. But again he thought, Greed does strange things to people.

Nels spoke up, "All right, all right, this isn't getting us anywhere. All I wanted to do was bring it up. My suggestion is we find the gold first and continue to figure out a way to sell it."

Ramon threw his remaining coffee into the fire and paused for a minute, thinking, I do not understand all of what these men are talking about, but the gold we have already found is enough for me. Why do they want more? This is bad, what they are talking about! I am a Filipino and do not want to lie to my government. They will put me in prison if I help take the gold from my country! These men do not understand that I do not want to leave my village—I do not want to go to another country I must think about this!

For the next two weeks the men continued to remove the loose dirt and rocks from the cave and support the ceiling above. Charlie, Gil, and Ramon had found where the water was flowing into the cave the Japanese had diverted a small stream on top of the mountain into the cave below which caused a deep pool above the cave holding the gold. The bottom of the pool was sealed to prevent the water from entering the cave unless someone tripped the trap! The three men diverted the stream back to its original flow, which stopped the water from going into the cave. Once the entire pile of rock and dirt had been removed from the cave, the men started digging the rock from the hole under the floor; however, the deeper they dug with the Bobcat, the more difficult it became to back the machine out of the hole.

Arnold was attempting to back out of the hole while working the controls of the Bobcat back and forth, with very little success. The engine whined, the tires were spinning, but the Bobcat failed to move from the pit. Finally Charlie hollered, "Hold it Arnold you are just going to tear up the Bobcat!"

Arnold shut down the machine and climbed out. "You're right, Charlie. That's about as deep as I can go!"

Charlie continued, "Listen, the last time I looked at the hole under the floor, it was at least a hundred feet deep. We can't go down that deep with the Bobcat, so we need to come up with another plan. Let's find the others and see if they have any ideas."

The two men exited the tunnel. Gil, Ramon, and Nels had built a hiding place for the gold outside the tunnel and were just finishing the camouflage when Charlie and Arnold entered the clearing. Gil turned, and seeing the two men, he hollered, "Well, how does our hideout look to you, Charlie? Can you see anything more we need to do?"

Charlie looked over the site and said, "Looks great, Gil—no one would ever suspect that there is anything there except jungle. Good job."

Gil seemed pleased with Charlie's comment and said, "How about you—how's the mining going?"

Charlie answered, "Not worth a damn, Gil. We can't go any deeper with the Bobcat. The only way we can go deeper is to do it by hand—and that will take us a year!"

Nels said, "Charlie, I'm no mining engineer, but I have been asking myself how in the hell would the Japanese dig a hole that big in the first place. It seems to me that it would have taken them a year at least to dig one that big; am I right?"

"You're probably right, Nels," Charlie responded. "The only other way they could have dug the hole is if they came up from the bottom. It's what we call in the mining business 'driving a raise.' They would have driven a tunnel underneath the one we are working on and then mined a hole from below up under the cave inside our tunnel."

Nels scratched his beard and said, "That makes more since to me, mate. From what you told me about the Japanese and the primitive village, the Japanese were not here long enough to dig down a hundred feet from the top, so the hole from the bottom might be the answer."

Charlie and Arnold caught it right away—Nels had something.

"Yes," Arnold said excitedly. "They had to have driven a raise, right, Charlie?"

Charlie looked over at the men and said, "Has to be, damn it, it has to be! Tomorrow we start looking. Yep—as Scarlett said, "Tomorrow is another day!" Arnold scratched his head and thought, "now who the hell is Scarlett and how'd she get into the deal, damn it how many more Is out there getting a share!"

Later that afternoon while the group ate their lunch, Gil mentioned that they were running out of supplies. He said, "Nels, how is the beer holding out?" Gil knew that the Australian was a beer drinker and this was a good way to get him to listen.

Nels responded, "Hell, I've been so busy I haven't thought about it!" He walked over to the cooler, lifted the lid, and said, "Christ, there're only three beers left!"

Gil continued, "Yeah, that's not all we're running out of. Just about everything is down. I need a break from this place. Who wants to go into the fishing village with me and get some supplies?"

Arnold looked around at the group and said, "Not me; I'm going to stay here until we get the rest of the gold. I'll eat grass if that's what it takes, but I'm stayin'!"

Gil was not pleased about Arnold's comment; he was counting on Arnold coming with him. He had decided that the two men needed to talk in private and start making their own plans. He said, "Damn, Arnold, the gold isn't going anywhere. You might as well come with me; you need a break."

"Bullshit partner! I'm staying here! You can do what you want, but I'm going to find the gold. Besides, I wouldn't do you any good at the village—my mind would be here the whole time!"

Charlie interrupted, "I'll go with you, Gil. I want to stop by and see Mila and Magellan. It's time we brought him into the plan. You never know, he might have an idea on how to get rid of the gold. Besides, Ramon needs to see his family."

Ramon smiled. "Yes, I must see my wife and children!"

CHAPTER 12

The Fishing Village

Later that afternoon Charlie, Gil, and Ramon drove to the fishing village. Before leaving the site Charlie suggested that Arnold and Nels look for a possible place the Japanese would put a tunnel under the existing one. Before Nels could say anything, Arnold said excitedly, "Great idea, Charlie! Let's get moving, Nels; we'll find the damn tunnel before these people get to the fishing village!"

Arnold headed for the work site at almost a full run; Nels laughed as he followed Arnold and hollered over his shoulder to Charlie, "If we are not at camp when you return, don't worry—Arnold will probably have a hole dug halfway to New York!"

Charlie laughed and hollered back, "Hog-tie him if you have to; we'll be back tonight about nine." By the time Charlie and his group had climbed into the van, Nels and Arnold were out of sight!

Charlie turned the van onto the road to the fishing village. He glanced into the rearview mirror and saw the excitement on Ramon's face—it was obvious that Ramon was anxious to see his family. Speaking to no one in particular, Charlie said, "We'll stop by Mila's place first and give Ramon a chance to see his family—any objections?"

Ramon grinned. "Thank you, Sir Charlie. I would like to see my family very much!"

Gil waited for Ramon to finish and said, "No need for me to go with you guys. It might be better if I start getting the supplies. By the time I get done, it will be time for us to go back to camp. Besides, if I do the shopping, you two will have more time to visit." Charlie thought about this for a minute. He still was not comfortable with Gil and didn't want to leave the man alone—but on the other hand he would like to spend more time with Ramon and Mila's families. He turned to look at Gil and said, "You sure you don't want to meet the families, Gil? They're great people."

"If we had more time, Charlie, I would, but we need to take care of business. There will be other opportunities. Why don't you let me off in town on your way through?"

"All right, if that's what you want. When you finish with the supplies; just give me a call on my cell phone and we'll meet you at the restaurant." Charlie smiled, "You know the restaurant I'm talkin don't you, Gil?"

Gil looked over at Charlie and said, "Yeah, I know the one!"

The van drove slowly through the main part of town. Charlie pulled over next to the hardware store and let Gil out. Before driving away, he leaned out his window and said, "I will expect a call about seven. I figure we'll need to be out of here by then."

Gil waved his hand in agreement and entered the hardware store. Charlie pulled away from the curb and drove to Mila's home. The minute the van pulled up in front of the house, Ramon's wife came running up to the vehicle. Ramon jumped from the van and the two embraced. Mila walked up to Charlie and gave him a hug around his waist.

"Why do you stay away for so long, Charlie? We miss you! Look at those two!"

Charlie turned to see Ramon and his wife still holding each other, tears streaming down their faces. Mila said, "You cannot keep these love birds apart for so long, Charlie, it is not right! Let's go into the house; I will fix you something to eat."

Charlie raised his hand in exasperation and said, "Mila, we don't come here to eat all the time—we come here to visit you!"

She glanced over her shoulder at him while she walked toward the house and said, "You will have something to eat, and that is that!"

After dinner, Charlie explained to Mila what had been happening back at the campsite. He was explaining about Gil and Arnold when she stopped him.

"Magellan has told me about these two men, Charlie. They have made trouble in our village—they do not pay for their food and the place they are staying. The fishing village does not want these men here."

This didn't surprise Charlie; he had no idea what Gil and Arnold had been up to before they started working at the camp—but not paying their bills sounded reasonable. Charlie pulled out his wallet, took out 10,000 pesos, and handed them to Mila. Mila took the money with a confused expression on her face, asking, "What am I going to do with this money, Charlie?"

Charlie leaned forward and took her by the hand, saying, "Pay the bills for those two if you will, Mila. I don't have time right now to tell you why, but do this for me."

Mila threw the money onto the table angrily and said, "No, I will not help those two men!"

Charlie, again, was not surprised at Mila's reaction. He was becoming accustomed to the new, stronger-willed woman. He said, "Okay, Mila. I will have to tell you something about these two before you say no to me." For the next half-hour Charlie explained his concerns to her. He finished by saying, "Now do you see—if we throw them out, they will come back with others, and we will have more trouble. If they are with us, at least we can keep a close watch on them."

Mila placed her hands on her hips and looked at Charlie and said, "Only for you, Charlie; I would not do this for any other!"

He responded, "Thank you, Sweetheart," and gave her a big hug.

Two hours later, Magellan entered the house, wrapped his arms around Mila and kissed her. He turned to Charlie and shook his hand. After Magellan finished his dinner, the group sat around the table while Mila related to Magellan what Charlie had told her. After Mila had finished, Magellan spoke to her in dialect. They talked for several minutes, and finally she turned to Charlie, saying, "My husband tells me that your friend was at the dock today asking about a boat. The man wanted to know if there was a cargo ship nearby that he could look at, but no one knew of such a boat."

Charlie folded his arms across his chest and sat back in his chair, thinking, what the hell is this guy up to? Now I can't leave him alone for one day! He turned to Ramon and said, "Ramon, you stay here for a couple of days and see what else our friend has been up to. I will tell him you want to stay with your family; how does that sound to you?"

Ramon grinned and said, "That is a very good idea, Sir Charlie. I would like to be with my wife."

Charlie smiled back at Ramon and said, "Then it's settled!" He glanced at his watch and realized that it was almost eight o'clock. He thought, where's Gil?

"Listen," he said, "I am going to have to take off now, but I will be back next week for sure, so Ramon, you and Magellan need to find out what this guy is up to." Charlie stood up from the table, crossed over to Ramon and Magellan, and shook their hands. Before leaving the house, he kissed Mila on the forehead and started out the door then stopped and turned around. Charlie walked over to where the children were and kissed each one on top of their heads. As he kissed each one of them they giggled and ran to their mothers. Finally, the last thing, he grasped Ramon's wife's hand and gave it a gentle kiss. Her mouth dropped open and her face flushed scarlet—but everyone knew that she was very happy with Charlie Taylor!

Charlie entered the restaurant about eight-thirty and looked around the dining area then looked across at the bar. Gil was leaning up against the bar with a beer in his hand. It was obvious that he had been drinking for some time; several empty beer bottles were sitting in front of him. Charlie walked over to the bar and said, "Did you get everything we needed, Gil?"

Gil slowly turned toward Charlie. He had a confused look on his face, as though he had no idea who Charlie was or what Charlie was talking about. Finally, Gil began to speak; however, his speech was slurred and what he was able to get out didn't make much sense. Anger crossed Charlie's face; he considered knocking the man on his ass but decided it would do no good—he probably wouldn't feel it anyway! Charlie thought, Better get some food and coffee into him; he'll never make it back to camp in his condition. He wrapped Gil's arm around his shoulder and started walking him toward a nearby table. Charlie remembered to grab what money was left on the bar, but as he grabbed the money, he noticed something strange. When he first walked up to the bar he had noticed several beer bottles in front of Gil, but now he realized that some of them were of a different brand. Why would someone change beer brands? Most people I know stay with one. Did Gil have some company tonight?

Charlie sat across the table from Gil, watching him attempt to eat his food. It ran down his face as he tried to find his mouth with the fork. He kept trying to order another beer but Charlie motioned to the bartender with his hand, indicating no more. Charlie walked outside while Gil attempted to finish his meal. He dialed Nell's cell phone. When he answered, Charlie told him, "I made a mistake and left Gil alone for a while. He got drunk. We won't be in until tomorrow so don't wait up for us."

"No problem, mate. I have some news for you if you can take it—we might have found where they put the lower tunnel, but we have to remove some jungle first. More about that tomorrow—you better take care of your friend."

"My friend, eh? Okay, Nels, I needed some good news right now." Charlie gave a big sigh and said, "good night."

"Good night, Charlie. Make sure you bring back lots of beer!"

Charlie returned to the restaurant and found Gil passed out with his face buried in his food. Charlie rented a room above the restaurant and dumped Gil onto the floor near the bathroom. He wasn't about to babysit the asshole—if he got sick, so be it, but he was on his own!

The next morning Charlie woke up at dawn. He turned over on the bed and looked near the bathroom door where he had left Gil the night before, but Gil was no longer there. Charlie started to get up but settled back down when he heard Gil vomiting from inside the bathroom. After a couple of minutes Charlie got up and put his pants on then walked over to the bathroom. He hollered through the door, "Let me in there—I need to take a piss!"

Gil took a deep breath and answered, "Can you give me just a couple of minutes, partner? It seems I got a bit of the flu or I ate something bad; do you know what, I—"

Before Gil could finish, he started vomiting again. Charlie realized he wasn't going to get into the bathroom for a while so he put on his shirt and left the room, looking for the public toilet. After taking a leak, he headed downstairs to get some breakfast. He had just finished eating when Gil walked up to his table. Charlie looked up and said, "How about some eggs, Gil? I just had some sunny side up, mixed in with some toast all slimy ya know what I mean? They were great!"

Gil's face turned a pale gray and he replied, "No, thanks, Charlie. I ate something bad last night. I don't feel so hot—I'll just have some coffee." After the waiter poured the men some coffee, Charlie asked Gil, "Did you get the supplies, Gil?"

Gil looked at Charlie for a minute and finally said, "Yeah, I left them at the hardware store with the other things we needed. I told them we'd pick them up last night, but you never showed up, so I guess we can get them this morning."

Charlie thought, This SOB isn't going to admit he was drunk as hell last night! Unbelievable! He decided that it was more important to get back to the camp rather than argue with Gil about being drunk the night before. He stood up, pulled some money out of his pocket for breakfast, and headed out the door.

Charlie had loaded almost all the supplies by the time Gil was able to make it to the hardware store. It was obvious that Gil wouldn't be much help! Charlie thought, Poor guy—he has to get over the flu! Gil climbed into the van and Charlie started driving out of the village, thinking, He's going to remember this trip for a long time! As they turned onto the main road, Gil said to Charlie, "Charlie, do you mind turning on the air conditioner? I'm sweating like a pig—this flu has really got me down!"

"Sorry, Gil; the damn thing is on the blink—can't get it to work," Charlie answered. It was summertime in Mindanao; the temperature during the day was about ninety degrees with 90 per cent humidity— which made things very difficult for Gil, but Charlie was willing to suffer the heat if only to make things miserable for Gil! Before arriving back at camp Charlie had to stop the van several time to allow Gil to "get rid of" the bad food he had eaten the night before!

Charlie pulled the van into camp and climbed out. Gil remained inside; he didn't seem to have the energy to get out of the van. Arnold ran up to Charlie, his eyes wide, and said excitedly, "Charlie, I think we might have found something—" He hesitated and an expression of disappointment crossed his face when he noticed Gil still in the van with his head resting on the dashboard, but he continued. He again took a look at Gil in the van and was pretty sure of what had happened. Nels had said something to him the night before. He continued talking to Charlie, "Nels wanted to wait for you to come back, but I think the two of us could have handled it." Arnold became more excited and started talking fast, walking back and forth in front of Charlie.

Charlie grabbed Arnold by the arm and said, "Settle down, Arnold! We'll take care of things a little later on, but first let's unload the van."

A sheepish grin crossed Arnold's face and he replied, "I guess I'm a little excited. All right, Charlie; I'm sorry. I'll start unloading." He headed for the van. When he noticed Gil still sitting inside, Arnold turned to Charlie and said, "What's up with Gil?" However he was well aware!

Charlie grinned and answered, "I think he has a case of the flu, but you might ask him how he is doing. By the way, where is Nels?" It was the first time that Charlie had seen Arnold grin at Gil's expense—usually he defended his buddy to the end.

"Shit!" Arnold said, "I was supposed to bring another machete and some water back to him. Damn it! I forgot when you drove up!"

"Don't worry about it, Arnold. You go ahead and take back what you need. Let Nels know we are here unloading the van."

"By the way, Charlie, where is Ramon?"

"I'll tell you when you get back. Better help out Nels for now, Arnold."

Arnold waved his hand in agreement, grabbed the water and machete, and headed into the jungle.

It took some prodding, but Gil finally climbed out of the van and began to help Charlie unload. Because of his flu, he was in the way most of the time. Finally, Charlie said, "Take five, Gil—I'll finish up." He had just finished unloading the van when Nels arrived back at camp. Arnold wasn't with him.

Nels was covered in sweat and had to sit down for a minute to rest before updating Charlie. He said, "Like I told you last night, Charlie, we might be on to something. Arnold and I found a gully about 30 feet below the upper one yesterday afternoon about six o'clock. It looks like it runs toward the main tunnel, but we will have to clear some jungle to make sure. I found some old cans and boxes like the ones you found near the main tunnel. They were buried under some jungle cover, but when I cut away the vines I found one. I kept clearing away the jungle and came up with about half dozen or so cans, bottles, and other debris, but it was late and we had to come back to camp. Japanese writing," Charlie, Japanese! I had quite a time getting Arnold to leave and come back to camp. Damn, Charlie—he's a workaholic!"

Gil spoke up for the first time since they had returned. "Well, I got the flu or something back at the fishing village. I don't know how much help I will be today but tomorrow I think I'll be fine."

Nels gave Gil a sarcastic look and said, "Yeah, mate, Charlie called me last night and told me how sick you were!"

Gil didn't respond, instead he lowered his head and began to shuffle his feet while he pushed his hands deep into his pockets. It was obvious he did not want to continue this particular conversation any further!

Charlie looked at Nels and said, "What's next? Do you want to fix something to eat or go back to the new site?"

Gil interrupted and said, "I can fix something to eat. Why don't you two go and help Arnold? In fact, send the crazy bastard back to camp—he won't stop working unless you tell him to!"

"That makes sense, Charlie. Let me take you to the site. I'm sure you want to see it. Anyway, Gil is right—you have to run Arnold off or he will work himself to death!"

The two men left the camp and headed toward the new site. After about a half-hour, Charlie could hear someone breaking brush ahead of them. They walked down a steep slope where they found Arnold hacking away jungle underbrush. He was so involved in his work that he did not hear the two men approach.

Charlie hollered, "Take five, Arnold, before you kill yourself!"

Arnold turned around he never bothered to say hello; instead he said, "It's here, guys—look at what I found." He handed Charlie a rusted bolt and said, "This is what they used for hooking the rail together."

Charlie looked at the bolt. Arnold was right; it was used to connect the rails. Charlie raised his eyes from the bolt to say something but was taken by surprise at the look on Arnold's face. The man was glistening with sweat; it was obvious that he was near exhaustion. Charlie noticed the muscles in his face were taut. Arnold was breathing heavily and walked back and forth in front of the two men in an agitated state.

Nels took hold of Arnold's arm and said, "Gil wants you to go back to camp. He has something to tell you. Arnold, you need to get away from here for a while."

Charlie interrupted Nels and said, "Yeah, Arnold, we can't afford for you to end up sick like Gil. You're the best man we've got. Who would run the Bobcat if you end up sick?"

Arnold stood looking at the two men. He thought, "Christ, I'm ready to go to work. We are almost there—I don't need to rest!"

Nels repeated, "Go on, Arnold, and go back to camp. It's going to be at least a couple of days before we get this place cleared out."

Charlie said, "He's right, Arnold. Now go on!"

Arnold knew he was not going to win the argument and slowly turned toward camp, but before he left the site he said, "If you need help, come and get me. I'm ready to work all night if necessary!"

Nels responded, "If we need some help, we will come and get you, Arnold—I promise." With that, Arnold gave up and headed toward camp.

After Arnold was out of sight and hearing range, Charlie turned to Nels and said, "Jesus Christ—is this guy for real?"

Nels smiled and answered, "Charlie, I've started to like him. He doesn't sit on his ass, and he'll do whatever you ask of him. He's been great the last couple of days."

"Your word is good enough for me, Nels. If you say he is okay, then he is okay."

Arnold walked up on Gil, who was boiling vegetables and frying hamburgers on the camp stove. Gil did not hear Arnold until he said, "Need any help, partner?"

Gil had just placed the spatula under one of the hamburgers. With his hangover in high gear and the surprise comment from Arnold, Gil threw the hamburger high into the air and let out a scream! He turned to face Arnold, his face was ashen, and said, "Damn, man, don't do that! Ya tryin to finish me?"

Gil was still shaky and Arnold's surprise visit didn't help! His face was still chalk-white, but he finally relaxed enough to say, "What in the hell is the matter with you? Are you completely nuts? You don't walk up on a man out of the blue and say something like that—especially in the damn jungle!"

Arnold stood looking at his partner. The man was a wreck—his body was covered in sweat, and his face was covered with splotchy red spots. Arnold said, "Shit, you look like you've been on a week drunk!"

"Damn it! Didn't they tell you I had the flu?"

"Yes, they told me but it don't look like the flu to me—it looks like an old-fashioned hangover."

"Oh, forget it! I have something more important to tell you, and I don't want the others to hear what I have to say."

Arnold replied, "It still looks like a hangover to me."

Gil shook his head in disgust and decided not to continue this ridiculous conversation. Instead he said, "I think it is time we made our move, partner." A confused look crossed Arnold's face, but Gil didn't wait for Arnold to respond.

"I met someone at the fishing village that's going to help us get what's coming to us. He has a boat big enough to carry the gold and will take us across to the Malaysian coast. From there we are home free!"

Arnold could not believe what he was hearing. He looked at Gil and said, "What gold are you talking about? We only have about $850,000 worth; it's going to be at least a month before we have more."

Gil sat the spatula down, walked over to Arnold, took his finger, and began tapping it against Arnold's forehead. "How much money do we have, my friend?" He didn't wait for an answer but continued, "None! Do you really believe there is anymore?"

"We know there is $850,000! I don't know about you, but that's plenty for me!"

Arnold was about to continue when he heard Charlie and Nels approaching from the jungle. He whispered, "We need to talk about this later, but I want you to know that I am not ready to walk away from this deal!"

Gil was unable to respond to Arnold; Charlie and Nels were within hearing distance. He turned toward the stove just in time to see black smoke bellowing from the burnt hamburgers.

Charlie hollered, "Gil, you didn't have to send up a smoke signal—we made it back safe!"

Nels and Arnold started laughing. Gil ran to the stove and pulled the frying pan away from the flame—it would be vegetables and cold cuts tonight!

CHAPTER 13

Tunnel Number Two

Each time Gil approached Arnold to discuss his plan Arnold would walk away. In fact, when they retired for the night, Arnold placed his bed next to Nels, making it impossible for Gil to get Arnold alone. The next morning was more of the same. Arnold kept his distance from Gil until the group headed back to the new site.

After arriving at the new tunnel site, the men sat down for a minute and started discussing the best approach to open the lower tunnel. Charlie was first, saying, "If we try to do this by hand, we will be here for quite a while. I don't know about the rest of you, but I want to get this over with. We still haven't decided how we are going to cash in, so tell me—do any of you have any ideas?"

Arnold leaned against a tree and said, "I have one, Charlie."

"Okay, Arnold, what do you have in mind?"

Arnold continued, "I can break a road into the place in four hours with the Bobcat. Once I get in, I will have the place open by tomorrow."

Nels nodded his head in agreement and said, "You got to admit he's good on the Bobcat, Charlie. I think he can do it!"

Charlie turned and looked at the steep bank behind him and said, "Arnold, are you sure you can get in there? If you're not careful, you can roll the Bobcat over and break your neck!"

Arnold walked halfway up the bank and kicked his foot into the loose ground. "Give me four hours and we'll have a road into this place."

Charlie looked at Gil and Nels for their comments. Both men nodded their heads in agreement. He turned to Arnold and said, "You've got it, Arnold. Let's get to work. We'll try to clear some of the smaller stuff while you concentrate on the road. I don't know how much help we'll be, but we'll give it hell!"

Within a couple of hours, Arnold had cleared a road from the main camp to the steep embankment leading to the second tunnel. The bank was very steep. The Bobcat slid sideways as the machine moved closer to the edge of the ravine. Nels stopped cutting away the jungle ahead of the excavation and watched as Arnold again moved closer to the edge. He hollered, "Watch it, Arnold! You're sinking into the loose dirt on the left side!"

Arnold ignored Nels and forced the machine ahead. Without warning the left wheel disappeared into the loose dirt, the Bobcat swung wildly to the left, and teetered over the bank. Arnold tried to reverse the machine; however, the angle was much too steep. The Bobcat was like some trapped animal screeching and groaning. The machine's rear axles rose up off the ground, the nose dipped deep into the soft dirt, and in slow motion the Bobcat started rolling end over end down the steep embankment. It ended on its top at the bottom of the ravine.

Everyone ran toward the machine. Arnold was crumpled up in a fetal position inside the cockpit. Gil hollered "Arnie! Are you all right partner?"

Nels peered into the cockpit then turned to Charlie and said, "Give me a hand, Charlie—I think we can pull him out if we move his legs over."

The two men carefully eased Arnold from the Bobcat and laid him down on the ground. Arnold was out cold; however, once they laid him down he began to groan with pain. The men stood over Arnold and Nels said, "I've had a little first aid; let me check him out."

Nels leaned over Arnold and began to run his hand over the man's body, starting from his feet and carefully moving toward his head. As he touched Arnold's left arm, the man again winced in pain. Nels stood up and ran his right hand through his hair. He said, "The best I can figure, boys, is he has a broken left arm, but I have no idea if he is injured internally."

Arnold opened his eyes and looked up at the men standing over him. He said, "What happened?" He attempted to stand up but Gil crouched down and placed his hand on Arnold's chest, saying, "Hold on, Arnold—you've taken quite a tumble. Just lay still for a minute. You rolled the damn Bobcat over on top of you!"

Arnold relaxed onto his back and said, "My left arm hurts; can someone take a look at it? I think I broke the SOB."

Nels answered, "I think you are right, Arnold. Do you have any other pain?"

Arnold slowly moved his legs then carefully sat up with the help of Gil and said, "No, just my left arm."

Charlie leaned down next to Arnold and said, "Arnold, we need to get you out of here. Can you walk if we give you a hand?"

Nels interrupted, "Let me put some kind of splint on him before we move him, Charlie; we don't want to cause any more injuries to that arm." Nels cut two strips of wood from the underbrush and placed one on each side of Arnold's left arm. He cut some strips of cloth from Arnold's shirt and tied the two wood splints together. Each time he would tighten the cloth strips around Arnold's arm, he moaned in pain. "I'm sorry, Arnold, but I have to make sure the arm doesn't move, mate."

Arnold nodded his head in agreement and bit his lower lip until Nels had finished.

"Give me your shirt, Gil," Nels said. At first Gil hesitated then Nels said, somewhat irritated, "I have to make a sling, damn it, so give me the son of a bitching shirt!"

Gil pulled off his shirt, handing it to Nels. Nels wrapped the shirt over Arnold's shoulder and around his left arm, then carefully cinched it up and said, "He's as ready as I can make him. Let's try and get him to his feet."

Charlie moved around to Arnold's left side and placed an arm under his left shoulder. Gil did the same on the right side, and the men carefully raised Arnold to his feet. He stood unsteadily for a couple of minutes and finally said, "I think I'm okay, guys. Let's try and get me out of here."

It took the men a half-hour to get back to camp. Arnold seemed to improve as they approached camp. The men attempted to lay Arnold down onto his sleeping bag; however, Arnold insisted, "I feel better sitting up, guys; just let me sit down for a while."

Nels looked at Charlie and said, "Charlie, he needs a doctor. The arm is broken, but who knows what else is wrong? I don't have the training to do any more. We'll have to take him into Davao."

Arnold interrupted, "Bullshit. I will be fine in a couple of days. Just let me rest here at camp. Hell, just because I have a broken wing doesn't mean I can't help!"

Gil shook his head and said, "No, partner—you are going to see a doctor and I'm going to take you and that's the end of it!"

Charlie agreed, "He's right, Arnold—you have to see a doctor. We can't take the chance you may have internal injuries. Besides, you'll need a cast for that arm."

Arnold started to protest again but Nels said, "They're right, mate. You are going to the doctor—so get used to it!"

Charlie said, "Listen, Gil, you stay here with Arnold. Nels and I will go back to the site and take a look at the Bobcat. We may have to get some repair parts in Davao. We might as well pick them up while Arnold is there getting his arm taken care of."

Nels looked at Charlie in surprise but didn't say anything.

Gil said, "Good idea, Charlie. I will take care of my partner. You two better make sure we have a machine left to work with. We'll be fine here for a few minutes."

Charlie nodded his head in agreement and started walking back to the second tunnel site. Nels hesitated for a minute and eventually followed. After the men were out of site from the camp, Nels grabbed Charlie by the arm and pulled him to a stop. He said, "Jesus, mate—the man is injured! We need to get some help for him!"

Charlie took a deep breath and said, "I know, Nels, but I needed to talk with you alone for a minute. I just don't trust Gil. There is no telling what he will do once he gets into Davao. Christ, man, he knows too much!"

Nels hesitated for a minute and said, "I will go in with Arnold and Gil can stay here with you, Charlie. That way we'll keep an eye on him. How does that sound?"

Charlie answered, "Nels, I'm damn concerned about the project. Every day we are delayed, there's a chance that someone will find out what we're up to. Gil isn't worth a shit—I need you here!"

The two men stood in the jungle facing each other. Finally Nels said, "Let's send Ramon in with them. He can watch the SOB."

"That's not a bad idea, but I was planning on Ramon helping us at the site. Remember, we're down to two of us. We'll need extra help."

"I don't know the answer, mate. All I know is that we need to get Arnold into Davao."

Charlie looked off into the jungle then turned back to Nels and said, "We don't have a choice. We will have to send Mila with them."

"I don't know, mate—can Mila handle Gil?"

"Mila may not be able to—but Magellan can," answered Charlie.

Nels looked at Charlie, a sly grin crossing his face. "Maybe we give Gil a little pep talk before they leave. We'll tell him what Magellan will do to him if he gets out of line. What do you think?"

Charlie answered, "Oh, you can bet I will give him a little pep talk!"

The two men laughed Charlie said, "Better get back to camp."

"This is our chance, Arnold!" Gil had waited until Charlie and Nels were out of sight. "We couldn't have planned it better!"

Arnold raised his head and looked at Gil with a concerned look on his face and said, "What are you talking about?"

"Didn't I tell you I talked to a guy in the fishing village that's got a boat?"

Arnold still wasn't sure what Gil was talking about and said, "What guy?"

Gil threw his hands in the air in frustration and said, "Don't you ever listen! I met a guy in the village that has a boat! The man told me that he travels throughout the islands and trades with the villages along the coast. I asked him if he would be interested in taking a trip to Malaysia in a couple of weeks and he said, 'No problem." I got his number says he'll be in Davao for the rest of the month! Don't you see, Arnold—this is the perfect set-up were in! We'll go into Davao, get your arm taken care of and while we are there, I'll find the man and set us up for a little trip—get my meaning?"

"Gil, what in the hell are you talking about, a little trip?" Arnold asked.

Gil lost his patience. He grabbed Arnold by his broken arm and yelled, "You had better wise up, buddy! I am taking the gold and getting out of here—with or without you!"

Arnold almost passed out with pain; he became dizzy and started to fall. Gil pulled on the sling and kept Arnold upright. Sweat poured down Arnold's face. He took a deep breath and was about to say something when he heard Charlie say, "What the hell is going on here?" He had returned from the tunnel site with Nels.

Gil backed away from Arnold, visibly shaken, and said, "Charlie, he was ready to pass out and started to fall, so I grabbed him, that's all."

Charlie was very angry. He grabbed hold of Gil's arm, pushed him back, and said, "I'll bet you were helping him; is that why you grabbed him by his injured arm, you SOB!"

Nels asked Arnold if he was all right. Arnold nodded his head and said, "Thanks, Nels; I'm okay. Gil was just trying to stop me from falling. I guess he forgot about the bad arms is all." Nels didn't believe it for a minute; he knew something was going on, but if Arnold wasn't going to say anything, he couldn't say or do anything to Gil.

Gil walked back over to where Arnold was sitting and said, "God, I'm sorry! I completely forgot what I was doing. I just seen you falling and grabbed on. Are you sure you're all right, partner?"

Arnold looked up into Gil's eyes. What he saw frightened him—the man's eyes were filled with hate, his teeth were clenched, and his fists were doubled up in tight balls. Nels and Charlie were standing behind Gil and could not see the look on his face. Arnold said, "Let's forget it. My arm is hurting to beat the band. I need to see a doctor—it's worse than I figured." Although his arm was hurting from the accident, he was more concerned with the look from Gil. He thought, the son of a bitch looks like he wants to kill me!

An hour later Arnold was ready to go to Davao the arm now was swelling and was numb. Gil said, "I will drive him straight to Davao. I should be there in about four to five hours."

Charlie stepped forward and said, "Gil, I want you to follow me with the truck into the fishing village. I want Mila to go with you, and I'll bring Ramon back to the site to help Nels and me."

Gil looked at Charlie. He seemed surprised at the suggestion and said, "Hell, Charlie, there's no need to have the woman go with us. It's at least four hours of driving. If I take Arnold in by myself, we can be back here by tomorrow night."

Arnold turned to face Gil and said, "Gil, I think it's a good idea. The girl knows the city and can interpret for you if need be." Arnold didn't want to be alone with Gil. He realized if He went alone with Gil into the doctor he may not make it! He no longer trusted his partner! He said to Charlie, "Yeah, that's a good idea. Maybe she can help me with this pain, huh? "

Nels decided that he should say something. "Gil, Charlie and Arnold are right. You'll need help. Mila can take care of Arnold while you drive. It just makes sense that she goes along."

Gil realized that he was losing the argument. He stood looking at the three men and thought, Damn, I need to get Arnold alone—the girl will be in the way; however, Gil knew he was not going to convince the group to allow him to take Arnold to Davao without the girl. Finally he said, "Yeah, I suppose you are right she can keep an eye on Arnold and line up a doctor when we get to Davao."

Charlie responded, "Good then. Let's get going. We don't want Arnold to wait any longer than he already has. Nels, you might as well ride into the fishing village and help Gil pick up a few things for their trip. I'll meet you at the house."

Gil started to object to the plan but thought better and started walking toward the truck. Once he was out of sight, Charlie grabbed Nels by the arm and said, "Keep an eye on him, Nels. We don't want him talking to anyone, understand?"

Nels smiled and said, "He won't get two feet from me, mate—even if he wants to take a trip to the crapper!"

Fifteen minutes later they were on their way to the fishing village; Arnold in the van with Charlie, Nels and Gil following.

CHAPTER 14

Davao

Gil pulled the truck into a parking spot in front of the hardware store while Charlie continued toward Mila's house. As Nels and Gil climbed from the truck, Gil said, "Why don't you take a look around for some supplies? I'm dry as dirt—I'm going to get a beer."

Nels answered, "A beer! Now that sounds good. I'll go with you—we have plenty of time; Charlie will be a while, I'm sure. He'll want to update Mila on what's happened." Nels thought, Christ, we haven't been here two minutes and the SOB is trying to get rid of me!

Gil stood looking across the van's hood at Nels. There was disappointment in his look, but again, he did not challenge Nels suggestion. As they headed for the bar, Nels said, "Better be careful, Gil; we don't want to get the damn flu again!"

Gil stopped and looked at Nels. He was going to say something but thought better of it and just answered, "Yeah, right." The two men walked to the bar.

As soon as the van pulled up in front of Mila's house, she walked out the door, waved, and said, "Hello, Charlie—we didn't expect to see you so soon." But when Arnold got out of the van she hollered, "Oh my! What has happened?" She took Arnold by the arm and helped him toward the house. Charlie followed them inside and in a few minutes had explained the accident.

"Mila," he said, "I have some things in the van I need to give you. Have Ramon's wife get Arnold a cup of coffee; we'll be right back." As soon as the two left the house Charlie turned to Mila and said, "Mila, I need to ask a big favor of you. I need you to go into Davao with Gil and Arnold and find a doctor to check him out." Mila hesitated, concerned. Charlie took her by the hand and said, "I know this isn't something you want to do, but we have no choice, Mila. Nels and I still don't trust these two, and we need to watch them while they are in Davao. If you want, you can take Magellan with you."

She again hesitated but then said, "I will do as you ask, Charlie, but my husband is out on his fishing boat with Ramon and will not be home for some time."

Charlie stood looking at the young woman. He thought, I can't take the chance with these two and Mila we have to come up with another idea. He said to her, "Mila, I can't take a chance. Gil and Arnold are not to be trusted, and if they decide to do something to you, I can't stop them. Maybe I will go into Davao with them and Ramon and Nels can handle the camp."

She answered, "Charlie, if these men try to hurt me, my husband and the village men will kill them. I can go into Davao—I am not afraid!"

Charlie thought about what she had said and answered, "Mila, if anything were to happen to you, I would never forgive myself. I am not so concerned with Arnold, but Gil is bad news!"

"Charlie, don't worry. No one will harm me. All you have to do is mention my husband and what he will do if someone hurts me."

Charlie asked, "Are you sure, Mila? I can change my plans without any problem."

"It is settled. I will go with them to Davao. I know where we can find a good doctor; that is the final word!"

Charlie was still hesitant but realized that he was not going to win this argument and said, "Okay, Mila, but I want you to take my cell phone. If anything happens, you must call me right away. I will give you Nels phone number. Now we must get back to the house. Arnold will get suspicious if we are out here any longer."

Gil realized that Nels was not going to leave him alone. After drinking the first beer he said, "Better get those supplies; it's getting late and Charlie will be showing up any time."

Nels took a last drink from his beer and said, "Yeah, all we need to do is start drinking too much. Charlie will be pissed!" Then he hesitated and added, "But again so will we!" Nels let out a wild laugh and said, "Get it? We'd be pissed too!" Without saying anything further they headed for the door. Gil remembered the earlier comments concerning the flu and didn't see anything funny about those either!

As Gil and Nels approached the door, a fat man dressed in dirty clothes and wearing a ship captain's cap walked in. He grabbed Gil by the arm and said, "Hey, buddy—are we going to finish our conversation or what?"

A look of look of distress crossed Gil's face; he had no idea what to say. Nels looked at the fat man and said, "Do we know you, mate?"

The man answered, "I don't know you from Adam, pal, but I sure as hell know this guy."

Gil said, "Listen, I'd like to talk with you but I'm on my way to Davao and we just don't have the time." The man started to answer, but Gil pushed past him and walked outside. Nels hesitated for a minute, left the fat man standing in the doorway and followed Gil onto the street. The fat man looked confused. He hesitated, scratched his beard, pushed his cap back, and finally walked over to the bar and sat down. He watched Gil and Nels through the window head down the street, thinking, what the Christ is going on? One day the bastard wants to rent my boat, and the next time I see him he gives me the brush off! He ordered a beer and thought, well, if he is going to Davao, maybe I will leave a day or two early and head back myself. I'll find out what the prick is up to!

Walking down the street, Gil knew that Nels would not let the encounter go. He was going to ask questions, and Gil knew he better have the answers! More importantly, he hoped the ship captain caught the message about Davao. If he were smart enough, he would find him in Davao.

Finally Nels said, "Okay, Gil, what was that all about?"

"That? Oh, I met the guy last week when Charlie and I were in town. He has a boat I was thinking maybe we could rent if we need to, that's all."

Nels continued, "What did you tell him, Gil? Does he have any idea what we are up to?"

"No," Gil replied. "I told him we might need some equipment shipped in and that we were doing some prospecting near here. He has no idea what we are doing, Nels."

"Why the fuck didn't you say something last week?" Nels was getting pissed off again; he thought; more surprises!

"I only talked with him for a minute. I just forgot; that's all."

The men arrived at the hardware store, and fifteen minutes later they had bought the supplies. Charlie showed up in the van and asked, "Are we ready to travel?"

Before Nels could reply, Gil answered, "Yeah, we're ready. Better get going. The sooner we leave, the sooner Arnold sees a doctor." He hurried to the van and opened the back door to load the supplies.

Mila was sitting in the back seat, Arnold in the front. Gil looked at the girl and said, "Hello, young lady. It's nice to finally meet you." Mila nodded her head but remained silent. Gil walked around the van to the rider's side and peered into the window at Arnold. "How are you feeling, partner?" Arnold started to answer but Gil was already walking around to the driver's side.

Arnold thought, "Damn, I'm glad the girl is with us!" After Gil had climbed into the van, Charlie walked over to the driver's window and said, "Listen, Gil. Mila is very important to me. I don't want anything to happen to her, do you understand?"

Gil felt a chill run down his spine. The look on Charlie's face scared the hell out of him!

Charlie continued, "She is married to one of the warriors of the primitive village. If something were to happen to her, I'm not sure what they would do with you. They can be very dangerous, so for your sake, take good care of her!"

Gil had a sick feeling creeping into his stomach. He hadn't thought much about the girl until now and was starting to realize what Charlie was telling him. He thought, Jesus Christ, these bastards are on to me! Sweat ran down Gil's face. He took a deep breath licked his dry lips and to settle down and said, "Don't worry Charlie—I will treat her with kid gloves. You don't have a thing to worry about." Gil tried to smile, but the fear of what might happen to him grew in his stomach—which prevented him from smiling. In fact, he was now thinking of not taking the trip at all.

Charlie stood next to the van for several minutes. He did not respond to Gil but gave the man a fierce look. Finally he stood back from the van and waited a minute for Gil to say something, but it was clear to Charlie that he had made his point.

Gil eased the van away from the curb and drove away. After the van was out of sight, Nels walked up to Charlie, who was still watching the van, and said. "I didn't want to say anything until after they left, Charlie, but there is something you should know. Gil talked to some fat bastard with a ship captains hat on while we were at the restaurant but I have no idea what it was all about. Gil told me the guy had a boat and they had talked last week about renting it."

Charlie slowly turned to Nels and said, "What was that, Nels? I was thinking of Mila. Did you say something?"

It was obvious to Nels that Charlie was very concerned about the girl. He waited a minute and then repeated what he had said.

Charlie looked at Nels and said, "I don't like the looks of this. Suppose we take a walk down to the restaurant and see what this guy is up to."

Nels replied, "Good idea, mate. I'd like to ask a couple of questions myself."

The two men entered the restaurant. The man was easy to spot; he was standing at the bar. Nels took a better look this time. The guy was about 5'6", 200 lbs, wearing a dirty T-shirt, with a worn-out ship captain's cap cocked on the side of his head. It was obvious that the man wasn't fond of bathing. His beard was rough; he looked as though he hadn't shaved in several days.

Charlie and Nels walked up to the bar and stood next to the man. Nels said, "Say, buddy, I'd like to ask you a couple of questions if I might."

The fat man turned to look at Charlie and Nels and said, "I don't believe I know you boys." He raised his hand and offered to shake with Charlie and Nels.

Charlie slowly took the man's hand and gave it a shake.

The fat man continued, "Well, what can I do for you gentlemen?"

Charlie was sizing the man up. Not exactly a man about town, he thought. His clothes were filthy, as well as his yellow, chipped teeth. Nels said, "We were just wondering about our partner. He acted like he knew you this morning when we met you at the door."

The fat man took a long drink from his beer and said, "How do I know that this so-called partner is really one of you; you might be giving me a line of bull just to get me to talk to you." I think I'll keep my opinions to myself boys if ya don't mind." With that the man turned his back on the two and faced the back bar.

Charlie looked at Nels, raised his eyebrows, and said, "It's no big deal if you don't want to talk to us. That's fine. We were just curious, that's all."

Nels grabbed Charlie by the arm and said, "Better get going, mate; we're running out of time." Charlie hesitated and finally the two men left the bar.

The fat man watched as they disappeared. He thought, I wonder what this is all about. This Gil fellow wanted to rent my boat, but it seems there is more to this—and now that these other two have made it a point to visit me, where is the other one? Not much of a partnership, if ya ask me. All Gil had asked him was to rent him his boat. He had hinted that the fat men meet him in Davao in a week, but the fat man hadn't decided to go into Davao—until now! He thought, I think I had better take a little trip—this set up could get very interesting! He made up his mind. He finished his beer and headed out the door, he thought, Davao here I come baby I'm comin home!

The fat man's name was Nick Peaks. He had been in the Philippines for the last ten years, since his dishonorable discharge from the navy in 1973. Nick had been a riverboat captain during the Vietnam War and was into the black market trade in Southeast Asia. During one of his illegal runs into Cambodia, he was picked up by a navy escort vessel—along with a boatload of contraband—and thrown into the Saigon brig. Six months later he was released and scheduled to return to the U.S. While waiting to board a plane for San Francisco, he was able to slip away during an attack on the airport and been hanging around Southeast Asia since.

Nick had spent time in Manila on his recreation leave in 1972 and, after escaping the MPs, decided to return to the Philippines. From 1973 to 1983 he had operated a charter boat for vacationers from Japan and Australia, After several illegal run-ins Nick was fired by the charter company. He eventually scraped and hustled enough cash to buy a boat. It wasn't long before he was running anything he could get his hands on. Didn't matter who the client was as long as the cash was available he was available. Every crook and illegal outfit from Hong Kong to Manila knew Nick, yep, "No questions asked Nick!"

For the last two years Nick had used his boat for several different questionable deals. He had developed a risky partnership with the MILF— they were paying him big bucks to bring in guns and ammunition from outside the Philippines. Most of his trade was between Indonesia and Malaysia. He would pick up the illegal contraband and transport it to the island of Jolo in southern Mindanao. Nick knew that the relationship with the MILF was chancy but he also understood it was a moneymaker.

As he headed out the door he again thought, Yeah, I think I will take a little trip over to Davao tonight. The more I think about it, the more I like it. I'm sure my friends in Jolo would be interested in what these boys might be up to! A smile crossed his face and he yelled at the bartender give me my bill buddy I'm travelin south tonight!"

Mila sat quietly in the back seat of the van. No one had said much since they left the fishing village. She looked at the two men in the front seat and thought, *Charlie worried about these two. I will keep watch over them. They better not do bad things to Charlie!*

Arnold's arm and ribs were killing him; he was in terrible pain, but Gil seemed not to notice or care. He was driving over the rough roads without any consideration of Arnold's injuries. Gil was focused on the road and never bothered to ask Arnold how he felt. Finally Arnold said, "Partner, could you slow down a little? The bouncing is killing me!"

Gil stared to say something to Arnold but hesitated. He wanted to reach over and bust him across the mouth! Things were not going according to plan; he was pissed and wanted to take it out on Arnold, but he simply said, "I'm sorry, partner. I wasn't thinking. I'll slow er down a bit."

Gil also had been thinking about the gold and the boat captain. The only good thing about the trip to Davao was the chance of talking to the fat man about his boat. He hoped that he would show up in Davao. He didn't have a chance to talk with him in the restaurant; Nels had shown up and put a stop to his plans. All he was able to say to the man was that he would be in Davao for a couple of days. He paused in thought, then again began to consider the situation. Damn, I hope he got the message back in the bar! Gil was worried that the man would not show up—but there was nothing he could do about it now.

The road to Davao was terrible. The only decent road took them near the small villages along the way, 500 feet of concrete through the village, then back onto the dirt road. Arnold, who was dying with each pothole, gritted his teeth and thought, its crazy how this country built roads—a little here, a little there.

And he was right—the government had used a system to keep the small villages happy, especially during elections! The government would give each town leader an amount budgeted for roads. By the time the mayor and other officials grafted their share, there was almost nothing left for roadwork. Each community would build a road through the center of the village, leaving the main highway outside their respective village for someone else to worry about. Consequently very little happened to the main road—which meant the roads throughout Mindanao were in terrible shape. There were sections of road thirty kilometers long that had been neglected for years—which slowed traffic to a crawl. Each time the van would pass through a village, Gil would increase his speed; however, as he exited the village he would have to slow the van to avoid the massive ruts and boulders in the middle of the road.

The constant braking was beginning to irritate Gil. He finally said, "Christ, why in the hell can't somebody fix the damn roads in this country?"

Mila started to answer Gil but thought, why do these people come to our country if they do not like our roads? Why don't they stay in their own country? She too was irritated—she did not like leaving her family and was tired of this man complaining!

"Charlie, why don't you fix something to eat and I will unload the van?"

Charlie had just climbed from the van. He turned and said, "Good idea. There's still some daylight and I would like to check out the Bobcat before dark."

Nels nodded in agreement and began to unload the supplies. An hour later, after eating and a couple of beers, the two men headed for the new site and the Bobcat. As they walked along the trail Nels said, "Charlie, we are going to have to do something about Gil. I guess you already know that, mate."

Charlie stopped and turned around to face Nels. "Nels that dirty bastard is up to something! If he gets in our way, I will kill him! I had the same thing happen the last time and didn't do anything about it—and two of my friends ended up dead! It won't happen a second time!"

Nels scratched his head and said, "Murder, Charlie?"

"Self-defense, Nels," Charlie answered.

Nels looked at Charlie and did not like the expression on his face. The man seemed distant and showed no concern about what he had said. Nels waited a moment and finally said, "Charlie is the gold worth killing someone for? For God's sake, Charlie—we are not murderers!"

"Nels, I wish I could say we aren't going to have to kill anyone—but it might come down to us or them. I have a feeling that Gil would kill us in a heartbeat if he thought it would serve his purpose. I am willing to give the man the benefit of the doubt, but I am not going to allow anyone to lose their lives because of him—and that's the end of it!"

Nels stood looking at Charlie for some time and finally said, "Let's let it go for now, Charlie. We can deal with the problem after they get back from Davao. Right now we need to see how much damage there is to the Bobcat." The two men looked at each other then Charlie turned and walked down the trail toward the new site.

Once they arrived at the site, the men approached the Bobcat and began to examine the machine. Nels said, "She's a little banged up, Charlie, but I don't see any major damage. How about you see anything bad?"

"No. Same over here, Nels," Charlie replied. Nels placed his hands on the upper frame of the Bobcat and gave it a slight push. The Bobcat rocked a little and he said, "Mate, I think we can push it over onto its wheels; what do you think?"

Charlie crossed over to Nels side of the machine and said, "Sounds good to me; let's give it a try." They rocked the Bobcat back and forth until it started to move. It rolled over and bounced onto its wheels, almost making another rotation, but then stopped and righted itself. Nels climbed into the operator seat and examined the controls. He turned the starter button. The engine belched black smoke and tried to start.

Charlie hollered, "Wait a minute, Nels! It's probably flooded. Give it a chance to clear out."

Nels waited a few minutes and pushed the starter button again. The Bobcat engine coughed and tried to start. Charlie hollered, "Keep going, Nels—I think you've got it!" The third time Nels pushed the starter button, the Bobcat engine began to run black oil spoke belched from the exhaust. Charlie clapped his hands together and yelled, "There she goes!"

Gil was fuming It took seven hours to reach Davao Arnold and the damn roads kept him on edge the entire drive and two extra hours didn't help!

Once inside the city limits, Mila gave directions to the hospital. After admitting Arnold, Gil said to Mila, "Why don't you relax here for a while? I know the trip was hard on you. I have to pick up some supplies for camp."

Mila was convinced that Gil had other ideas; however, Charlie had cautioned her not to question Gil but to keep an eye on him while they were in Davao. She answered, "Yes, I am a little tired. I will lie down for a few minutes and then check on Arnold. Where can I reach you if something comes up?"

"Don't worry; I will only be gone a couple of hours. I will call the hospital in an hour or so to check on things," he replied.

Gil knew of only one place where a guy like Nick would end up in Davao—Goldfield Lounge and Entertainment Center. Yeah, he thought, entertainment center! Not quite as fancy as Manila, but then again it was a standard girly bar. The Goldfield was tough, real tough. Nothing but bad apples here—and here is where he would find Nick!

By the time he reached the bar he was afraid the man would not be there, and he felt nervous as he walked through the door. Gil looked around the tavern and at first he could not see the captain. Three girls grabbed him by the neck and tried to kiss him. One of them said, "What's your name, handsome? Are you looking for a good time?"

Gil was in no mood. He was here for business and had no time for this. He looked at the girl for about a second and pushed her roughly away from him then walked away. The girl was angry and said to her partner, "These are the kind of men I have no use for—they are pigs!"

Again Gil was starting to feel his trip might be for nothing; however, as he headed for the bar he noticed the man sitting at a table at the rear of the room. Relief passed over him. He thought, "Well, something is going right."

Gil walked over to the man's table and said, "Good evening, my friend. I wasn't sure you would be here; how did you get here before me?"

Nick pointed to an empty chair and motioned Gil to sit down then said, "You forget, I have a boat. It's only 3 and half hours from the village to Davao by sea. Now let's stop the small talk why don't you tell me what the hell is going on and why your partners were asking me questions back at the fishing village?"

Gil was disturbed at the comment and said, "What do you mean, my partners?"

"Don't act dumb with me! I don't have the time or the patience! Why don't you come clean and tell me the whole story before I get up and walk out of here?"

"I don't know what you are talking about, I swear," Gil replied.

The fat man took the last swallow of his beer and stood up to leave.

"Wait; give me a few minutes to explain. I guarantee it will be worth your time," Gil pleaded.

Nick sat back down and said, "You have five minutes. If what you say doesn't make sense or isn't worth my time, I'm out of here!"

Gil replied, "Can I at least get us a beer? Christ! I've been driving all day and could use a drink."

The fat man nodded in agreement and Gil called to the bartender, "Hey, bring us a couple of beers." After the bartender had delivered the beers Gil bowed his head and grasped his beer by both hands. He thought, what should I tell this bastard? I don't want him in on the gold, but hell—I need him. Finally he spoke. "First, don't worry about the other two. This is just between us. I have a deal that will make you a rich man if you listen and be patient."

The captain replied, "Like I said, five minutes."

Gil had an urge to get up and leave. He wasn't sure he was making the right decision, but again he thought, what choices do I have at this point? He looked across the table, and leaning forward he said, "What if I told you I have some valuable Philippine artifacts worth a lot of money and I want to sell them at a profit? I am talking about treasure, my friend!"

Nick took a drink from his beer and said, "What do you mean valuables?"

Gil answered, "Portraits, goblets, jewels, and some ancient artifacts, that's what I mean." The fat man was about to say something but Gil raised his hand and continued, "My friends and I have been opening a tunnel to do some exploration work and found a cave full of treasure. When I suggested that we sell it, they told me it wasn't worth the time and that we were looking for a gold mine. Besides, they said, it belonged to the Philippines. Can you believe it, the Philippines! I tried to convince them that the stuff was worth a lot of money but they still weren't interested. Finally I gave up and decided to go it alone."

Nick waited until Gil finished and said, "Why don't you sell it back to the Philippine government? I'm sure they would be happy to have it back."

Gil replied, "I thought of that, but if I know the government, they will confiscate the stuff and I will end up with nothing. My best bet is to get it out of the country and sell it on the black market."

The fat man took a deep breath and said, "What makes you think I would do something illegal? Maybe I will turn you in—the Philippine government might appreciate the gesture and pay me a little finder's fee; did you think of that, my friend?"

A chill ran down Gil's back. He thought, have I misjudged this guy? He continued, "Okay, let's say you turn me in and they give you a little something for your trouble but what if they don't? If you work with me, we both can make some dough. I am guessing the stuff is worth about a hundred thousand on the black market, and I'm sure the government won't even come close to that."

The fat man laughed out loud and said, "You took a hell of a chance with me! If I were you, I wouldn't have even considered a deal like this—I don't trust anyone!"

Gil replied, "Well?"

Nick looked at Gil and said, "Let's have another drink. Maybe we can work something out. I have a few connections in Malaysia and Indonesia that might be interested in what you have."

Gil relaxed. God that was close—I was beginning to think this was a big mistake!

The two men continued to drink for the next four hours until Gil learned over to Nick and said, "Christ! I have to get the fuck out of here! I was supposed to be back at the hospital two hours ago!" Gil stood up and took the last drink from his beer. He looked at the fat man and said, "Okay, then—I will meet you at the fishing village a week from now with the stuff. You need to be ready to take off right away. In the meantime you can start arranging a meeting with your black-market friends. By this time next month, we will be rich!" Gil raised his glass and said, "Salute!"

The two men stepped outside the bar into the dark night/ Gil rubbed his eyes and looked around. He couldn't see very well, but as his eyes adjusted to the dark he spotted Mila standing across the street. He froze! He rubbed his eyes again and took another look across the street—but there was no sign of the girl. He thought, Was that Mila? He looked again, but there was no one there.

Nick looked at Gil; who had an odd expression on his face. "What's the problem? You look like you're having a heart attack."

Gil was still trying to see across the street. He narrowed your eyes, placed his hand over his brow and looked again—nothing! He hesitated for a minute and absent mindedly said, "Nothing, nothing. I just thought I seen someone I knew."

"Ah, hell—you're drunk. Better get some sleep," Nick responded. The fat man flagged down a taxi and climbed inside. He rolled down the window and said, "Are you coming?"

Gil still was looking across the street. The man repeated, "I said, are you coming or not!"

Finally Gil realized the fat man was talking and said, "No, you go ahead. I'll catch another taxi."

"Fine with me—I need to get some sleep!" The taxi pulled away from the curb and was out of sight in a few seconds.

Mila lay flat on the ground; her heart was pounding in her ears! She thought, *Did he see me? Oh my goodness, I'm afraid he saw me!"* Carefully she raised her head slightly and peered across the street. Gil was still standing in front of the bar with his hand covering his brow, looking directly at her. She watched as he stepped from the curb and started walking across the street toward her. Terror ran through her body! She thought, *He's coming over here! My God, he's coming across the street!* Just as Gil was halfway across the street a car horn blared. It surprised Gil, and he jumped back. The taxi driver leaned his head out of the taxi and yelled, "It is very dangerous walking in the streets at night, my friend; you look like you need a ride."

Gil looked at the taxi driver and hesitated for a minute. He was deciding whether he should cross the street or climb into the cab. He stood in the street still looking but he couldn't see a thing. Finally he opened the door to the taxi and said, "Take me to the Davao hospital and get there in a hurry! I have a friend there I need to see."

After the taxi pulled away from the curb into the night. Mila jumped up. She knew where Gil was headed! Mila knew Davao very well, and she knew Gil's taxi driver was going to take the long way to the hospital. After all, Gil was a foreigner—and taxi drivers in the Philippines never take the short route when they have a foreigner on board! Mila flagged the next taxi down and told the driver to take her to the hospital and hurry, please hurry!

Gil leaned forward and looked out the front window of the taxi. He couldn't recognize the area and said, "Where the Christ are we? I want to go to the hospital, and I mean now!" Ten minutes later his taxi pulled up in front of the hospital. Gil climbed out and said, "How much?"

The driver answered, "One thousand pesos."

Gil smiled and handed the driver one hundred pesos. The driver started to protest but Gil was gone. He was running up the stairs of the hospital thinking, I'll catch that bitch—and when I do— Two minutes later he was on Arnold's floor and headed for his room. He was half running by the time he entered the room. Arnold was asleep and did not hear Gil come into the room. Gil walked over and shook Arnold by his broken arm. Arnold woke up with a moan. He looked up at Gil and said, "What the hell are you doing? For Christ's sake, I have a broken arm!" Can't ya see the cast?"

Gil replied, "Never mind. Where is the girl?"

Arnold was confused and half asleep. He said, "What are you talking about?"

"The girl! Where is the girl?" Gil repeated.

Arnold was about to answer Gil when Mila appeared from the balcony outside the room. Before Gil could say anything, Mila said, "Where have you been? I have been worried! You were supposed to call me three hours ago!"

Gil had a cold look on his face and said, "Yeah, I got busy and forgot. How's Arnold been doing?"

She answered, "Fine. He has been asleep most of the night."

Arnold looked at them. He knew something was going on but wasn't sure why Mila was lying. The doctor had given him some pain medicine, but the arm was throbbing; he wasn't able to sleep. So when Mila made the comment, he wasn't sure what was up. He had had a bad sleep; the pain kept him awake until the nurse had given him a sedative about a half-hour ago. But one thing was for sure—he had not seen either Gil or Mila for at least three hours!

Mila felt as though she was going to be sick. She was terrified that Gil would find out she had followed him. She prayed that Arnold had been asleep the entire time they were gone, but she had no way of knowing!

Gil wasn't satisfied with Mila's comment. He continued to stare at her and at the same time he asked Arnold "Is that right, Arnold? Have you been asleep all night?" He never took his eyes off Mila.

Arnold said, "Matter of fact, Gil, I was awake for a while until the nurse gave me a sedative, but Mila took care of me until I got the shot."

Mila felt faint. Why did this man lie for me?

Gil relaxed and said, "Well, partner if you are all right, the girl and I need to get some sleep. I would like to head back tomorrow if you are up for it."

Arnold answered, "I'll be fine by tomorrow afternoon, Gil. The doctor set my arm and taped my ribs. I guess I cracked a couple." Besides he gave me some pain pills."

"Okay, Arnold. See ya in the morning," Gil replied.

As Mila and Gil walked toward the front door of the hospital, Gil asked, "Do you have a place to stay tonight, or do you want me to get you a room?"

She replied, "No, I will be fine. I have a room for tonight. I will meet you here tomorrow morning."

Outside, Mila flagged down a taxi, waved to Gil, and was gone. Gil stood on the sidewalk and watched the taxi drive away. He thought, I know that was her, damn it!

CHAPTER 15

Nels had made his second trip from inside the tunnel when Charlie stepped up next to the machine and hollered, "Let's call it a night, Nels—we don't need you busted up too!"

Nels turned off the engine and climbed out of the cockpit, dusted off his clothes, and said, "Yeah, I'm tired, mate. Let's go back to camp and get something to eat."

"Eat?" Charlie said, "No beer?"

Nels smiled and answered, "Well, mate—maybe just one."

They started walking toward camp. Nels said, "Charlie, I think we are close. The last trip inside, I noticed the tunnel was changing; It looks like I am at the caved area but it was too dark to tell."

"We'll know in the morning, Nels, but I think you're right. I measured the distance into the cave and it's pretty close to the one above."

"Charlie, if we're right we had better decide what we are going to do if we find the gold. Remember, we have those two blokes coming back later tonight or first thing in the morning—and I still don't trust either one of them!"

"I agree, Nels. When we get back to camp we can work on a plan."

The men arrived at the camp and began preparing something to eat. Charlie set a bucket of water onto the gas stove and began peeling potatoes. Without looking directly at Nels, he said, "Where are the guns, partner?"

Nels was in the process of opening a couple of beers; he stopped and looked at Charlie, hesitated for a minute, and said, "I've got them in my pack sack. Why?"

"Better give me one and you take the other. No telling what our friend Gil has done while he was in Davao. If I have him figured out, he's probably picked himself up a gun or two for himself."

Nels stood still for a few minutes with the two beers in his hands, looking at Charlie. Finally he said, "Charlie, I don't want any trouble with guns. If this SOB has a gun then we are going to have a problem."

"No, we're not,' Charlie answered, "because I'm going to frisk him the minute he turns up. And if I find a gun, I will break his neck!"

Nels walked over to the stove and handed Charlie his beer. "Charlie, what if he has a gun—are you planning to kill him?"

Charlie didn't answer for some time. He took a drink from his beer and stared at Nels. "Nels," he said, "I'm not sure what I will do, but one thing is for sure—that bastard will never tell anyone what we are doing here because, to tell you the truth, I'm in this deal until it's finished—and no one is going to stop me! You need to understand something. Two close friends of mine are dead and I am responsible for it. And no one, and I mean no one, is going to prevent me from finishing what we started six years ago!"

Charlie had gotten all worked up; sweat was running down his face. He could see Jerry's face staring at him as though he was looking into his soul!

Nels noticed Charlie was shaking and said, "Charlie, we have to ask ourselves if the gold is worth more lives. For Christ's sake, man—we are talking about killing a man, and I can't go along with it! Now promise me no one is going to die, or I walk right now, mate!"

Charlie did not answer but stood looking at Nels. He thought I need Nels; I can't do this alone. If he leaves, I am finished. Charlie finished his beer with one swallow and said, "Okay, Nels—no one is going to die. If they give us any trouble we will turn them over to the tribe and have them held until we are out of the county. Is that good enough for you?"

Nels hesitated. He looked close into Charlie's eyes and thought, is he telling me the truth, or has Charlie gone beyond reason?

Charlie turned back to the stove and began adding potatoes to the water.

Nels kept staring at Charlie but finally said, "Charlie, I mean what I say. If you plan on killing anyone, tell me now. I can't go along with murder."

Without turning to face Nels, Charlie answered, "No killing, Nels. Now let's forget it and eat something."

If Nels could have seen Charlie's face, he would have known immediately that Charlie was willing to do whatever he felt necessary—including murder! There was a cold hard gleam in his eyes. Death meant nothing—absolutely nothing!

CHAPTER 16

Back to Camp

Charlie and Nels were sitting next to the fire when the van pulled into camp. Gil stepped out of the driver's side of the vehicle and walked around to the passenger's door. He opened the door and helped Arnold from the van. Charlie stood up, put his coffee cup down and said to Gil, "Do you need some help?"

Gil had cradled Arnold under his shoulder and was carefully walking him toward them. He answered, "Thanks, partner, but I've been taking care of this SOB for some time now; we'll be fine."

Perspiration ran down Nels back. He looked into the fire. He could sense trouble! If Gil was carrying a gun then all hell was about to break loose!

The two men arrived at the campfire and Gil helped Arnold sit down. Charlie said to Gil, "Where is Mila?" Charlie was tense—if anything had happened to Mila, he was going to finish both of them here and now!

Arnold answered, "She's at the fishing village. It was late and she wanted to go home, Charlie."

Nels looked up from the campfire at Charlie and noticed the gun pushed down into his belt behind his back. Charlie reached around and felt the gun, keeping his back to Gil. Nels slowly stood up and approached Charlie from the rear. He put his arm around Charlie's shoulder and removed the gun from Charlie's belt. He could feel Charlie stiffen, but he had made up his mind there would be no gunfire tonight!

Neither Gil nor Arnold suspected what had happened Arnold said, "How about a cup of coffee, boys—it's been quite a trip."

Charlie stood frozen at the fire site. He was evaluating what had just happened. he thought, Jesus, now what? Am I alone? Has Nels turned on me?

Nels said, "Hell, yes, mate—you look like you both need a cupper!" Nels leaned over and poured two cups of coffee. At the same time he slid the gun under his shirt. Making sure no one saw what he was doing. After handing the men their coffee he said, "Well, what's the verdict it looks like you are pretty well banged up, Arnold."

Arnold took a slow drink from his coffee. He looked up at Nels. Sweat was running down Nell's face. It was hot, but not that hot! He felt uneasy but couldn't put a finger on it—something was wrong! He set his coffee down and said, "Couple of cracked ribs and a broken arm. Other than that, I'm ready to go dancing!"

Everyone nervously laughed, but the tension was still evident. Gil finished his coffee and said, "Guys, I'm beat. It's time for bed. Hours of driving have done me in."

He began to walk away, but Charlie grabbed him by his arm and said, "Don't get the wrong idea, Gil, but I'm going to frisk you."

Gil froze and said, "What the hell do you mean, frisk me!"

Nels started toward the two men, but Charlie looked at him; there was hate in his eyes. Nels realized he better back off. He knew that if he took another step, something real bad was going to happen!

Charlie looked Gil dead in the eyes and continued, "We are talking about millions of dollars worth of gold, Gil, and I'm going to make sure that nothing—and I mean nothing—is going to go wrong! You have two choices—let me frisk you, or end up in the primitive village for the rest of your life. You can make the choice!"

The two men stood facing each other. Gil's eyes narrowed, and he thought, I'm in a bad spot! If I don't let this SOB frisk me, I'm done—the villagers will hold me, and it will be over. Arnold can't help me and Nels will side with Charlie. Finally Gil said, "Go ahead and frisk me. I don't have anything to hide, for Christ's sake! I thought you trusted Arnold and me!"

Charlie ran his hands down both sides of Gil's body, between his legs and down his back. After he finished Gil looked at Charlie with a sneer on his face and said, "Satisfied?"

Charlie never said a word. He turned from Gil and walked directly to the van the two men had arrived in and began to search it. Gil stood for a moment, shook his head, and walked to his tent.

Arnold had been watching from the fire. He felt as though he was going to be sick. He carefully stood up and said, "Let's call it a night." He looked at Nels and said, "Can you give me a hand, Nels? I don't think I can make it on my own."

Nels was in a trance and did not respond immediately; however, he finally walked over to Arnold, put an arm around his shoulder, and began walking the man toward his tent.

Charlie searched the entire van but found nothing other than some supplies the men had brought back from Davao. He returned to the campfire and emptied the coffee pot, poured water onto the fire, and went into his tent. The dirty bastard's got a gun, and I'm going to find it if it takes me all day tomorrow!

Gil lay on his cot looking up at the ceiling of his tent. He was thinking about the piss stop half a mile from the campsite. Arnold was asleep and didn't have any idea what was going on. Gil was hiding two guns he had bought in Davao. A smile crossed his face, and he whispered, "The dumb bastard; did he think I was stupid enough to bring the guns into camp?" He rolled over and fell asleep.

Arnold sat on the edge of his cot and thought, Should I tell Charlie about the guns? Damn it, what a mess!

No, Arnold had not been asleep; how could he sleep with the pain and the way Gil was driving? Arnold ran his good hand through his hair and eased himself down onto the cot, but he did not sleep. The pain was getting to him—and the confrontation tonight wasn't helping!

CHAPTER 17

Mila

Mila did not sleep; she was worried about Charlie. Something was going on and she would have to talk to Charlie, but last night had not been the time. She was too tired, but most of all she did not want to cause suspicion. When Arnold asked her if she wanted to go home or go to the campsite, she had said, "I am very tired; I will go home." But by morning she wasn't sure she had made the right decision.

During breakfast she told Magellan what had happened and said he must take her to the campsite right away. Magellan sat listening to her. He was tired of this gold; he wanted things as they were before Charlie had came to their home. He said, "Can we not let these men alone, Mila? I am tired of this gold. We do not spend any time together; the children miss their mother—are you not also tired of this thing?"

Mila knew he was right, but she could not allow these men to hurt Charlie! "My husband," she said, "I agree the gold is a bad thing, and I want to do what you asked. I love you with all my heart and will do whatever you ask—but please, one last time, help me!"

Magellan clasped his hands together and lowered his head, looking into his breakfast plate. Finally, he looked up with tears in his eyes and said, "Will this be the last time, Mila? Can we again be the family, as before?"

Mila's heart was ready to break when she saw his tears. She leaned forward, put her hand on Magellan's face and wiped the tears. "Yes, my husband—this will be the last time." She rose from the table and walked across the room where her son was playing. She picked up the child and returned to the table. "This is our family, husband, and I will not allow anything to hurt us!"

Magellan leaned over and kissed the child and Mila. He said, "We will have my mother watch over Stopie while we go to the campsite."

Before leaving for the campsite, Mila walked to the small house next door where Ramon and his family had taken up residence. She could hear Ramon playing with his children inside. She knocked on the door and Ramon's wife answered. A smile crossed the woman's face and she said, "Hello, Mila, please come in."

Mila spent the next hour explaining what had happened in Davao and what was going on at the camp. After she finished, she waited for Ramon to say something.

Ramon sat in silence for some time and finally said, "I am worried for Sir Charlie and Nels. This man Gil is a bad person."

Mila answered, "I too am afraid of these men, Ramon. What can we do?"

"Mila, I will go to the campsite with you and make sure these men do not harm our friends."

Mila leaned over and kissed Ramon on the cheek. "Thank you, Ramon. I do not know what I would do without you."

On her way back to her house she stopped and looked up at the bright sunny sky. She whispered, "Please make this the last time. No more trouble." She was not a religious person, but this time she meant it; she meant it with her very soul!

Two hours later Mila, Ramon, and Magellan who had rented a vehicle drove into the campsite and realized at once that the men were not there.

Mila turned to the two men and said, "They must be at the dig site," and started down the path toward the new tunnel, her husband and Ramon close behind. As they approached the tunnel, Mila caught sight of Charlie standing on a mound of dirt next to the tunnel. Arnold was sitting next to him, while Gil was leaning against a tree smoking a cigarette.

Gil noticed the three Filipinos first. He pushed himself erect, dropped the cigarette to the ground, and crushed it out under his foot. Mila hurried to Charlie's side and touched him on the shoulder. A smile crossed his face; he said, "Mila! How is my little girl doing this morning?"

Mila reached up and kissed Charlie on the cheek. "Good, Charlie. How is the digging going?"

"Good! Last night we managed to dig close to the location of the cave above where we figure the gold is buried. Nels is inside with the Bobcat digging now. Mila, I think we are there!"

Arnold looked up at Mila and said, "Good morning, young lady."

Mila looked down at the man. It was obvious he was in pain from the expression on his face. She said, "Good morning, Arnold; are you feeling okay?"

"Yeah, I'm fine; just a little sore is all."

For a moment Mila was silent. She was thinking about the lie Arnold had told Gil in the hospital. Finally she said, "I hope you start feeling better."

Arnold nodded and remained silent. Mila was about to ask Charlie to take a walk with her and Magellan when Gil approached the group. Instinctively she moved closer to Magellan and took his hand into hers. Magellan moved between Mila and Gil and looked at Gil with anger in his eyes but said nothing.

Gil did not notice the gesture and instead said to Charlie, "Charlie, I'm going back to camp to get some more water. We're just about out." He turned and started back to the campsite. He glanced back at the group, his eyes meeting Mila's, and she immediately looked down, avoiding any further contact.

"Charlie," she said, "can you show Magellan and me the tunnel? I am excited about the gold!"

"Just a minute, Mila I want to talk with Ramon for a while." Charlie walked up to Ramon and grabbed him around the shoulders, giving him a big hug. "How's my little friend doing this morning?"

Ramon had not expected the hug and was taken aback by the gesture. He stepped back with an astonished look on his face. Charlie noticed the look and laughed out loud. He said, "Ramon, why don't you give Nels and Arnold a hand? Mila wants to talk to me for a while."

Ramon nodded his head and started walking toward Arnold. Charlie turned to face Mila. He noticed a look of fear on Mila's face. He hesitated for a minute and finally said, "Come with me. Let me show you what millions of dollars worth of gold looks like!" He laughed and headed for the entrance to the tunnel while Mila and her husband followed close behind.

Just as they approached the tunnel, the Bobcat was coming out. The three stood to one side as Nels drove the machine out onto the level ground. He turned the machine around, raised the bucket, and dumped the material he had dug onto the ground. Charlie waved at Nels and motioned him to shut down the Bobcat. After shutting it down, Nels climbed out, dusted off his clothes, and approached the group. He walked over to Magellan, shook his hand then turned to Mila, hugged her and said, "Good morning, Mila! You sure look good to a working man!"

Mila was used to men making similar comments to her from the time she was in Manila; however, her face flushed. It had been a long time since anyone other than her husband and Charlie said such a thing. Besides, she knew Nels liked her and she considered him a friend.

"What have we got Nels?" Charlie asked.

Arnold had struggled to his feet when Ramon approached, and the two men walked over to where the others were looking through the material Nels had just dumped onto the ground. Everyone at the site was picking through the dirt, looking for anything that might be gold.

Again Mila said to Charlie, "Charlie, I would like to talk to you for a few minutes. if you don't mind."

Charlie was busy sifting the pile of debris. He stood up and brushed off his pants. "Sure Mila; let's take a walk."

Arnold was standing next to Nels and looked over at Mila. He knew she was going to talk to Charlie about Davao, but he wasn't sure what she might tell him. Arnold knew it wasn't going to be good! Something had happened in Davao, away from the hospital. He wasn't sure what it was, but he knew that if it had something to do with Gil, it was bad.

Mila and Charlie walked toward the entrance to the tunnel. Once the two were far enough away from the others, she gripped Charlie by his wrist and stopped. She looked up and him and said, "Charlie, something is very bad!"

Charlie recognized the fear in her eyes and said, "Mila, what has happened? You look terrified!"

For the next few minutes she explained to him what had happened in Davao. After she finished she stood still, waiting for Charlie to answer. Charlie pulled off his hat and wiped the sweat from his brow, placed his hands on his hips, and looked into the tunnel. Finally he said, "Mila, Gil is a problem. Nels and I are well aware that something is going on. We are not exactly sure what he is up to, but we know it isn't good. If he tries to pull anything, he will end up in the village for the rest of his life—or he will end up dead!"

Mila took a step back and covered her mouth with her hand then lowered it and said, "Please, Charlie, do not kill this man! You will never forgive yourself! The gold is not worth killing for!"

"Mila," Charlie said, "don't you understand—it's not just the gold! I made a promise to John and Jerry that I would finish this thing, and no one will get in my way!"

For the first time, Charlie scared her. She stepped back from him with a frightened look in her eyes.

Charlie realized he had terrified the girl. He took a deep breath and said, "Mila, I love you like a daughter and would never do anything to hurt you or your family. I want you and Magellan to leave and never come back here, do you understand?"

"Oh Charlie," she said, "Please, I beg you! Do not do this thing! Leave the gold! Don't you understand God will never forgive you if you kill this person!"

Charlie took the girl into his arms, tears running down his cheeks. He placed his hands on her shoulders and looked deep into her eyes. She was also crying. Charlie said, "Mila, sometimes a person has to do things that are not right in the eyes of God, but you must understand—I cannot allow this man to get in the way of my destiny. I will do everything I can to not kill him, but there may be no other choice. I will talk to Val at the village and see what can be done. Can you accept that?"

Mila wiped her eyes and said, "Charlie, Magellan and I will go to the village and talk to Val. We will arrange for them to take this man."

"No, I don't want you to do any more. I will deal with Gil!"

Mila took Charlie by the hand. A tender smile crossed her face and she said, "Charlie, I will do this thing and that is the end of it." She turned before Charlie could say anything and walked back toward the men sifting through the dirt.

Charlie stood looking at the girl. He thought, Man, what a fool I was! She was the best thing that ever happened to me, and I let her go!

CHAPTER 18

Trouble!

The second Gil was out of sight from the others, he began to run toward the camp. All morning long he had been planning his getaway. Gil had it all figured out. First, he would move the gold at the camp into his van; second, he would stop and pick up his guns; and third, he would head for the fishing village. He would call the boat captain and they would be off the island by dark, heading for Malaysia!

Gil was having a hard time controlling his excitement, however. He continued to make plans as he ran down the path. He thought, The hell with Arnold! He was no good to Gil all beat up anyway; besides, he was sure Arnold was playing games with him. The SOB acts like he is one of them—so he can kiss my ass!

It only took a few minutes to reach camp. Gil got into the van and backed it up to where the bars of gold were stored under the tarp. He loaded the gold into the van and placed some boards under the tarp in an attempt to give the appearance the gold was still there. He walked over to the second van, opened the hood, and began to tear wires out of the engine compartment. He thought, Try and drive this baby! He laughed out loud, jumped into the van, and roared out of the camp.

A half-mile from camp he stopped at where he had hidden the guns. Gil pushed back the brush and reached down. "Where the hell are they?"

he said out loud. Frantically he pushed back more brush and pulled debris away from the site—but still no guns! Gil stood up, sweat covering his entire body. He clenched his fist and began looking in all directions. "Damn it! This is the spot! For Christ's sake, where the hell are the guns?"

Time was running out; he knew sooner or later someone was going to come back to camp. He had to make a decision. Again he said out loud, The SOB wasn't asleep! He clenched his teeth and whispered under his breath, "I'll get even! No matter what it takes, I'll get even!"

Gil ran to the van, jumped into the driver's seat, and headed down the road toward the fishing village.

Mila felt uncomfortable as Magellan and she approached the camp. Gil would be there; she did not want to talk to him. She had decided to tell Gil that she and Magellan were going to the village and had no time to spend at camp. As they entered the camp, Mila looked around to see where Gil was, but they found the camp deserted. At first she was relieved; she thought, *I will not have to talk to this evil man.* She relaxed and continued toward the main road leading to the village; however, something was not right.

She stopped and looked around the camp. Magellan said, "What is wrong, my wife?"

She answered, "I am not sure, but I do not feel right. Something has changed, but I do not know for sure what it is." Then she realized that one of the vans was missing. She walked around the camp then noticed the tire tracks leading up to the tarp where the gold was hidden. Mila carefully raised the tarp and looked at the pile of boards stacked where the gold had been. She dropped the tarp and backed away. She thought, what should I do? If I tell Charlie, he will go after Gil and kill the man. If I don't tell Charlie, he will never forgive me! What should I do?

Mila made her decision. She turned to Magellan and said, "Go to the village and tell Val that he must come here now. I will go back to the tunnel and tell Charlie what has happened. Now go!"

Magellan did not hesitate; he turned toward the road to the village and began to run. Mila started running down the path toward the tunnel.

Nels backed out of the tunnel with another load of dirt then turned the Bobcat around and raised the bucket. Charlie and Ramon were standing next to the pile of dirt and watched as it fell. Nels angled the machine to dump and Ramon noticed something sticking out of the dirt in the bucket. Ramon grabbed Charlie's arm and motioned toward the bucket. Charlie raised his hand and hollered at Nels, "Don't dump the load just yet, partner."

Charlie approached the Bobcat and took a closer look at the object protruding from the bucket. He reached up into the bucket and pulled it out. There was no question—it was another bar of gold! Nels and Ramon watched as Charlie began to wipe the dirt from the gold bar. Nels was still not sure what Charlie had in his hands, but he could see the look of excitement of Charlie's face. Charlie tuned to Nels and motioned him to dump the bucket.

Nels rolled the bucket over and the dirt began to fall to the ground. Several gold bars hit the mound as the bucket emptied. Ramon bent over, picked up a bar, and looked at it. He was more curious than excited. He thought, the bar is heavy is this what we have been looking for?

Arnold had been sitting under a tree; his arm and ribs had been hurting him for some time. He realized he had been doing too much and was paying the price, but when he heard Charlie scream, he immediately jumped to his feet and started walking toward the pile of dirt. Nels and Ramon could also hear Charlie's screams over the roar of the Bobcat.

Charlie began to jump around. He threw his hat into the air and hollered, "Shut her down, partner—we hit the mother lode!"

Nels climbed from the equipment and stood next to Ramon. Arnold got to the pile of dirt and watched as Nels, Ramon, and Charlie pull gold bars from the pile. The entire bucket must have been full of gold bars—at least twenty lay in the dirt pile next to the three men! As they dug through the dirt, the mound of bars continued to grow!

Charlie began to shake; the exhausting work and the heat were starting to get to him, but more than that, the emotional impact was too much. He stood back while the others continued to stack the bars. Charlie turned from the work site, walked away, and sat down. He began to weep uncontrollably. He dropped his face into his hands and continued to sob. Finally, he looked up at the blue sky and whispered, "Guys, we done it!"

Charlie stood up and for the first time realized that the other three men were standing over him. Without a word, Nels grabbed Charlie around the shoulders and hugged him. The two men stood holding each other for some time before Nels said, "You done it, Charlie! I don't believe I ever met a man with your determination, but damn it, mate—you done it!"

They turned to face Arnold and Ramon. Charlie found Ramon grinning from ear to ear. Arnold said, "Man, I never seen anything like this in my entire life! I never believed it was true, Charlie, but by God—you were right!"

Arnold walked over to the cooler and pulled out three cold beers. He returned to the men and handed each a beer. Nels raised his beer and said, "Charlie—one hell of a man!" All of a sudden he stopped and turned to Ramon and said, "Ramon, I'm sorry—do you want a cold beer?"

Ramon sheepishly looked down and his feet and said, "Oh, Mr. Nels, you know I do not drink the beer." Everyone laughed.

Mila was running down the path toward the tunnel. She knew that once Charlie knew what had happened, he would go after Gil and kill him. She stopped to catch her breath just before she entered the tunnel site and thought, *I must convince Charlie not to go after this man. Too many lives have been taken because of the gold!*

As she entered the site, Arnold was the first to see her. He hollered, "Mila, take a look at what we found!"

Mila noticed the gold but walked directly to Charlie. She grabbed his arm and said, "Charlie, I must talk to you." Charlie started to say something to her but she reached up with her hand and gently placed it over his mouth. She shook her head side to side, indicating he shouldn't speak.

Nels knew by the look on Mila's face that something was terribly wrong. He started to approach her and Charlie but decided against it. He thought, If this is as bad as she looks, I don't want to hear it!

The only words she said to Charlie were, "He is gone." Charlie was still smiling and wasn't sure what she meant. He took his cap off and ran his fingers through his hair. He asked, "Mila, what are you talking about?"

"Gil, Charlie. He is gone and has taken one of the vans."

Charlie stood looking at the girl. He still did not quite understand what she was saying.

Mila shook Charlie's arm and repeated, "Charlie, Gil has taken the gold and the van! He is gone!"

Anger crossed Charlie's face. He turned from the girl and started walking toward the trail back to the camp. Mila ran toward him and tried to stop him, but it was no use; Charlie pulled away from her and continued to the trail.

Nels could see the anger in Charlie's eyes as he walked by. He asked him, "What's going on, mate? Is there a problem?"

Charlie pushed passed Nels and continued toward the trail. Mila stopped for a moment next to Nels and said, "Gil has taken the gold and one of the vans. He is gone!"

Nels could feel the panic in his throat. He thought, Charlie is going to kill the bastard!

Charlie was on the trail and was half-running toward camp, still gripping his hat in his hand. The veins were standing out and his knuckles were white with strain.

Ramon took a deep breath. He had known this man for many years now and understood him. He was going to take the life of Gil—and there was nothing anyone could do or say to stop it!

Arnold heard what Mila had said to Nels and began to follow the others up the trail. It was difficult to keep up due to the pain but he knew that he had to arrive at camp with the group and prevent the two men from killing each other. Arnold was well aware of what Gil was capable of if he had the chance, but he had been convinced that he could talk Gil out of stealing the gold. After all, he thought, there is plenty for everyone! How could Gil be so stupid?

Nels caught up with Charlie as the group continued toward the camp and attempted to settle Charlie down. "Charlie, he's not worth it! If you kill the dirty bastard they will put you away for the rest of your life, don't you understand that?"

Mila also pleaded with Charlie as they moved up the trail. "Charlie, please don't do this thing! Nels is right you will regret this killing for the rest of your life!"

Ramon remained silent. He knew that nothing people said would change Charlie's mind. He also knew that he would give his life before anyone could harm Charlie!

Arnold was still struggling as he walked up the trail. His arm hurt and his leg was beginning to throb with pain; he continued to fall behind. He thought, Charlie gave us a chance, and this is the thanks Gils gives in return! Charlie's right, wanting to finish off Gil. From this moment on, he's not my partner. In fact he's not my friend!

Mila again pleaded with Charlie, "Charlie, you mustn't do this—"

Charlie suddenly stopped in the middle of the trail. Mila, directly behind him, ran into him, bounced off Charlie, and fell into Nels, who was following her up the trail.

Charlie turned around and faced the others. With intense anger etched across his face, he said, "Damn it! Don't any of you understand what has happened here? I won't deny that I want to kill the bastard, but it is a hell of a lot more than that. If he gets away, don't you think he will be back to take the rest of the gold from us? He's going to bring an army! If the word gets out on what we are doing here, every son of a bitch will be down our backs! For Christ's sake, haven't any of you been thinking of how bad things might get?"

Arnold finally caught up with the others and was listening to Charlie. He spoke up, "Charlie's right."

Mila and Nels turned to face Arnold as he continued. "I have known Gil for about five years and I know how he thinks. He's going to come back, folks—and when he does, he will bring plenty of help. We won't have a chance. We have to catch him before its too late—or it just won't be the gold we lose!"

Charlie pushed his hat back on his head, put his hands on his hips, and said, "Well, someone else is using their head at least."

Arnold looked down and his feet and continued, "I agree with Nels and Mila, Charlie. You can't kill him, but we have to stop him, and soon. Like I say, Gil probably has a plan already in place so time is running out. We have to find him and the sooner the better. I'm not sure what we'll do when we catch up with him, but we have to stop him."

Nels wiped the sweat from his face with a handkerchief and said, "All right then, let's get the bastard! But Charlie, promise me you won't do anything drastic. If we have to, we'll tie up the prick and drag him back here before we do anything else, agreed?"

Charlie turned back toward the camp and started walking. He said over his shoulder to the others, "Whatever happens to the son of a bitch, there's one thing for sure—I'm going to kick the hell out of him!"

The group entered the camp. Charlie headed directly toward the site they had hidden the gold. He threw back the tarp and looked at the blocks of wood stacked under it. He picked up a piece of the wood and threw it across the campsite and muttered under his breath, "I'll break his fucking neck!"

Nels looked around and asked Mila, "Mila, where is Magellan?"

"I sent him to the village to get Val, Nels.

Nels answered, "Good idea. We can use some help."

Arnold walked over to the van and looked inside. He got in and was going to start the vehicle when Nels asked him what he was doing. Arnold said, "If I know Gil like I think I do, he has done something to the van. He wouldn't leave without screwing it up, Nels."

Arnold started the ignition. The engine turned over but would not start. He tried again, but again the engine failed.

Nels hollered, "Hold it, Arnold! Pull the hood latch; I want to take a look at the engine." He raised the hood and started looking around the engine compartment. Charlie walked over to look over Nels shoulder. Nels breathed a deep sigh and said, "There it is, Charlie. The prick ripped out all the distributor wires."

Charlie leaned into the engine compartment and asked, "Can we fix it?"

Nels answered, "I'm no mechanic, Charlie, but it doesn't look good, mate."

Arnold had gotten out of the van and was standing next to the two men looking at the damaged wiring. He felt terrible and thought, I wouldn't blame these guys if they kicked the hell out of me. I should have warned them about Gil but I didn't." He said to Charlie, "Charlie, I wouldn't blame you if you kicked the hell out of me and sent me to the village for the rest of my life, but first I want to say something. I can get the rig running again. If you give me a chance, I'll do everything I can to help find Gil. You won't have to kick his ass—I will!"

Charlie stood looking at Arnold and thought, what should I do now? Can I trust Arnold, or is this part of their plan? He continued to think things over. Arnold would probably know where Gil may be heading and can give us an advantage; however, if he is in on this with Gil, he can be setting me up.

Charlie paced around the camp considering his options. Finally he said, "Are you sure you can get the van running?"

Arnold answered, "Yeah, Charlie. It will take me about an hour, but I will get her going."

Nels said, "Charlie, let me talk to you and Ramon alone for a minute." He turned to Arnold and said, "Get her going, Arnold. We're depending on you."

Nels led Charlie and Ramon away from the van and motioned for Mila to follow them. When they were far enough away that Arnold could not hear their conversation, Nels said, "Charlie, we have to trust him for now. We don't have any other choices. Besides, Arnold knows what can happen if he plays games with us."

Mila had decided that she had said enough and remained silent while Nels talked with Charlie.

Finally Charlie turned and hollered to Arnold, "How does it look, Arnold? Can you get the damn thing going?"

Arnold stepped back from the vehicle, wiped his good hand with a rag, and said, "Well, Charlie, we're lucky he didn't have more time to do damage. It looks like I can get her running in about an hour if things go right."

Charlie answered, "Okay, Arnold. The rest of us will start getting the van loaded. As soon as you're done, I'll head out."

Nels grabbed Charlie's arm and said, "Charlie, I've been thinking, mate. You better take Arnold along with you. He's going to have a better idea where to find Gil—but it's up to you."

Charlie hesitated for a minute and finally said, "We'll decide that when the time comes, Nels. Right now let's get started on loading the van."

CHAPTER 18

The Deal

"Yeah, yeah, I know it's short notice, but damn it! I need you and your boat now!"

Gil had been talking to the boat captain for ten minutes; the man wasn't happy about the idea of running up the coast to the fishing village on such short notice.

"It will take me a couple of hours to get there from here. And the weather is getting bad! Don't you realize this is typhoon season?"

"I don't give a shit about typhoon season! I told you I would pay you damn good for the boat, now get your ass in high gear and get up here!"

The captain didn't reply for some time. He was thinking, what's the rush? Can't this asshole wait a day or two? Finally he said, "All right, I will be there in two hours. You wait for me at the dock."

Gil hollered into the phone, "No, I don't want to meet you at the fishing village! There has to be another dock somewhere else near here."

The captain could hear the tension in Gil's voice and said, "What the hell is going on, buddy? What's the big hurry? And why can't I pick you up at the fishing village?"

Gil replied in anger, "Find another place near here, or the deal is off. I can find someone at the fishing village if I have to. I'm not in the mood to discuss this any further, do you understand?"

"All right, all right," the captain replied. "Easy, friend—let me think about this for a minute."

Gil was ready to hang up the phone. He realized that his time was running out. He also realized he had not had the time to do enough damage on the van, and if they were able to get it running, they would be at the fishing village within a couple hours—and he did not want to be here!

Gil spoke into the phone with in a desperate tone and said, "You have got thirty seconds to make up your mind—or I'm gone."

The captain replied, "Don't get in an uproar; I'll be on my way in five minutes. There's a small cove about two miles from the fishing village. I've used it a couple of times. It's not the best place to put in, but it will do. Take the dirt road on the east end of the village near the ocean and follow it. It will lead you to the cove. I'll be there in 40 minutes."

Gil replied, "That's better. I'm on my way." He did not wait for a reply. He hung up the phone, climbed into the van, and headed down the road. As he pulled away from the phone booth he glanced up into the sky. Dark clouds were forming and the wind was picking up. He hesitated for a moment and muttered, "Damn, I can't catch a break! Now the weather is giving me shit!"

Charlie was pacing back and forth in front of the van while Arnold worked on the wiring to the distributor. Working with one hand was difficult however Ramon and Nels handed him tools and help with the wiring as Arnold feverishly put the distributor back together.

Ramon walked up to Charlie and said, "Sir Charlie, I will go with you to find this man!"

Charlie looked down at the Filipino and realized again how much Ramon meant to him. The two of them had survived a terrible ordeal and yet his little friend was still with him. He smiled and said, "Ramon, you have done more than enough. I could not live with myself if anything happened to you. You stay here with Nels until I get back." When he finished he gave Ramon a tight hug.

Ramon pulled back from Charlie and said, "I will go with you!"

Anger crossed the little man's face and Charlie knew it was no use arguing with him. He smiled, raised his hands, and said, "You are beginning to sound like Mila, my dear friend—so I guess there is no use in arguing with you. You will go with me."

Ramon smiled and walked away. Charlie turned and hollered, "Christ, Arnold, you told me an hour! It's been almost two! Let's get the damn thing going—time is wasting!"

Arnold was about to reply when Mila said, "Here comes Magellan."

Everyone looked across the road to see Magellan returned with Val— and six of his warriors. Nels said to Charlie, "I've been thinking the best bet we have is for you to take Arnold and Magellan with you. I'll keep the rest of the natives with me and continue removing the gold at the site. If you don't find him and he comes back with help, at least we'll have enough gold to get out of here! We can move a lot of gold from the cave in a couple of days. I don't expect Gil back here before then; what do you think?"

Charlie started to answer then he heard the van's engine start up. Instead of answering Nels, Charlie headed toward the van. Arnold stepped back from the vehicle; he had a wide grin on his face and said, "There she is, Charlie! She's running smooth!"

Charlie could see the pride in Arnold's eyes and knew the man was sincere; he was happy he had done something for Charlie. Charlie looked at Nels, "Is everything ready?"

Nels nodded his head in agreement and Charlie climbed into the driver's seat of the van. He looked at Arnold and said, "Well, don't just stand there partner—let's get movin!"

Mila approached the van on the driver's side and said, "You will take Magellan and his warriors with you, Charlie. I will not let anything happen to you!"

Charlie answered, "Mila, I don't have time to argue. He has at least a three-hour start on us, so whatever we are going to do, let's do it!" Charlie didn't have to wait for Ramon he had been sitting in the back since Arnold started the engine!

Mila walked over to Magellan and spoke to him. Magellan stood back from her and a look of disappointment crossed his face. It was evident that Magellan was not happy about what Mila had said.

Charlie began to back the vehicle onto the road. Arnold was only half into the vehicle and was almost thrown to the ground. Mila said something else to Magellan that the rest of them could not hear. Magellan's mouth dropped open; he turned to Val and said something to the chief in dialect. Without hesitating, Magellan and three warriors climbed into the back seat. Charlie spun the tires of the van and headed down the road toward the fishing village.

Once the vehicle was out of sight, Nels turned to Mila and asked, "Mila, what did you say to your husband?"

Tears were running down her face. Finally she said, "I told my husband if he did not help Charlie, I would no longer be is wife!"

Nels shook his head. A look of concern crossed his face as he turned and walked away.

Ramon sat silently in the back seat of the van and thought, Mr. Charlie will not kill this man. I will!

CHAPTER 19

Boat

Gil had smoked two packs of cigarettes and still no boat. It had been almost two hours since he had talked to the captain. He thought where the hell is the son of a bitch? If he isn't here in the next five minutes, I'm out of here!

Gil put out his cigarette and started toward the van. He hesitated and took one last look down the coast. He started to turn back toward the van when he spotted the boat entering the cove a half-mile away.

It had been a rough trip from up the coast; the seas were getting bad. The captain had considered turning back several times as the waves continued to grow in height and strength. The wind had almost capsized the boat several times but he continued, cursing Gil, the weather, the boat, and his men. He could see Gil standing on the dock waiting. He thought, By God, wait until I get ashore! I'm going to tell this bastard what I think of him! However what the captain didn't realize was that Gil had picked up another pistol at the fishing village—and he would have no problem using it!

After tying up, the captain jumped from the boat. Gil could see the anger in the man's actions—he was yelling at his crew and had his fists clenched. He approached Gil with hate etched across his face and said, "God damn your soul, I almost lost my boat you son—"

Gil grabbed the man by his collar and looked him dead in the eyes. "Another word out of you, and I swear I will put a bullet into your head!"

The captain looked down and saw the pistol in Gil's hand. He thought, Jesus, he means it! He continued to evaluate the situation, thinking, I'm not sure what is going on, but this isn't the time to push the bastard! The captain stepped back and wiped the rain from his face with his hand and said, "All right, let's not get crazy here! But you need to understand that the seas are too bad to put a boat out right now. It's plain suicide! We're gonna have to wait until things clear up a bit."

Gil looked at the man like he had not heard a word and said, "Let's load the cargo."

The captain stood looking at Gil with a confused look on his face and said, "Didn't you hear me, man? We gotta tie down the boat and wait a while for the weather to clear!" "Bullshit Gil hollered, the sea is fine now let's get moving!" Nick answered, "Yes is quite here in the cove but it's a bastard out to sea!"

The wind had picked up and the rain had increased. The crew was still on the boat while Gil and the captain were standing on the dock.

Gil hollered, "You two come with me!" The two crewmembers looked at the captain.

The captain looked at Gil and thought, this guy is ready to kill someone! I can feel it—he's crazy! The captain hesitated for a minute and finally motioned for the men to follow Gil.

Gil had placed the gold into five wooden boxes he had bought at the fishing village. He opened the back of the van and picked up one of the boxes and handed it to one of the crewmen. The man grabbed onto the box but wasn't ready for the weight; he immediately dropped the box to the ground. Gil raised the pistol over his head and struck the man on top of his head with the barrel. He clenched his teeth and yelled, "Get the goddamn cargo on board and do it now!" He then pointed the pistol at the second man and said, "Pick it up, you son of a bitch!"

The man was terrified but knew he had no option but to pick up the wooden box from the mud. The men struggled to load the gold onto the boat as the wind rocked the vessel back and forth. Each time they attempted to step into the boat from the dock, the boat would rock violently back and forth, dropping two feet below the edge of the dock and then rising two feet above. The waves continued to crash against the dock, rocking the boat back and forth. The captain was aboard the boat and was attempting to grab the boxes from the two men. When he finally was able to get a decent hold of the box and felt its weight, he knew immediately what was inside.

Gil was busy trying to help load the other boxes and did not see the look on the captain's face. If he had, he would have seen the sly grin on the man's face. Suddenly the rain and wind didn't seem so bad to Nick after all!

By the time Charlie and the others had reached the fishing village, the rain was coming down in a heavy downpour. The wind was blowing, and the shops and restaurants had closed their doors. The villagers knew what was happening—there was a typhoon on the way!

Charlie was frustrated. He realized that Gil had a good four-hour head start on them—and he had no idea where the bastard was. He turned to Arnold, hollering over the deafening wind, "Take Ramon and check the restaurant and the rest of the town. See if you can find out anything." He turned to Magellan and with some difficulty told him to check the fishing docks and see what he could find out. Magellan nodded his head in agreement and headed toward the main dock.

Charlie started toward the hardware store. He knew Gil would be looking for some supplies before he left the village. Charlie had to bang on the door several times before the owner answered. The man opened the door enough to look at Charlie, but before he could say anything, Charlie forced the door open and walked into the store. The wind and rain blew into the shop with such force that it ripped the door from the shop owner's hand and slammed it into the wall, almost tearing it from its hinges. The man grabbed the door and with much difficulty closed and locked it.

Charlie was soaking wet. He stood in the middle of the room; water was running off of him down onto the floor. The shop owner handed Charlie a towel and said in broken English, "We closed—the typhoon coming!"

Charlie acted as though he hadn't heard a word the man said. He looked him in the eyes and said, "What did he buy?"

A confused looked crossed the man's face. Charlie walked up, stood no more than a couple of inches from him, and repeated, "I said; what did he buy?"

The man answered, "The American?"

"Yes, damn it, the American!"

"He buys many things! I not remember everything!"

Charlie grabbed the man by his shirt and said, "This is the last time I will ask, and you had better give me a good answer!"

The shop owner was terrified. He did not like these white men and did not want anything to do with them. But he also understood if he did not give this man what he wanted, things could get very bad!

Charlie loosened his grip on the man and the shop owner backed away from him. He continued to back up until he felt the counter against his back. Using his hands to guide him, he moved around the counter and stood looking at Charlie. He reached under the counter and pulled out a ledger and began turning the pages. Finally he stopped turning the pages and looked up at Charlie. He leaned forward against the counter, pushed the ledger across to Charlie, and stood back.

Charlie began to read the list. He wasn't interested in the list of materials until he read the last two lines: pistols/four boxes of ammunition. There was no sense asking the man why he sold Gil the pistols. Charlie knew anything was for sale in the Philippines if the price was right. Without saying anything, Charlie dropped the ledger onto the counter and walked over to the door.

The shop owner never moved a muscle; he stood transfixed as Charlie opened the door. Again the wind and rain exploded into the shop. Charlie took one last look at the man and closed the door behind him as he stepped onto the wooden sidewalk.

Arnold was waiting inside the van as Charlie climbed in. Both men were drenching wet. "Well," Charlie said, "what did you find out?"

Arnold hesitated before he answered then said, "I'm sorry, Charlie I couldn't find out a thing, but Ramon is still talking to people. These people wouldn't even open the door for me!"

Charlie started to get angry but then remembered that Arnold was in terrible pain. He had completely forgotten about Arnold's injuries. He said, "Don't worry about it, Arnold, I got some information. Now all we need is to find out what direction he headed."

Arnold was about to say something when Magellan tapped on the window. Charlie motioned for the man to climb into the back seat. Magellan opened the door and sat down. It took some time but eventually Charlie understood what the man was telling him. Gil had been to the fishing village several hours earlier and had spent about an hour buying supplies, which included a gun and ammunition. He had left the fishing village heading east along the oceanfront dirt road.

Charlie turned around in his seat to start the van but Magellan grabbed Charlie's shoulder. Charlie turned back around, looked at Magellan, and said, "We don't have any more time, my friend. We must catch him before he gets away."

Magellan shook his head, indicating they should not follow the direction Gil had traveled. He climbed out of the van and walked toward the hardware store.

"Damn it," Charlie said, "What the hell is he up to now?"

A few minutes later Magellan returned with the shop owner and both men climbed into the van. Magellan talked to the shop owner in their dialect for a few minutes. Finally, the shop owner looked at Charlie and said, in clear English, "Magellan wants me to interpret for you. He wants to tell you many things but cannot say them in English."

A smile crossed Charlie's face and he asked, "How did you learn to speak English so well in the last fifteen minutes?"

A shy smile crossed the man's face and he said, "I am the uncle of Magellan. I do not speak with whites unless I have no other choices. If the whites do not know I can speak their language then it is better for me."

Magellan again began to speak to the shop owner. After a few minutes, the man turned to Charlie and started explaining what he had been told. "Magellan has found out many things. First, he has said that the man you are looking for has been picked up by a boat two miles from here; they have been at sea for almost an hour."

Charlie's heart sank, he thought, now what? Although the rain and wind pounded the van, the silence inside was deafening. Charlie grabbed onto the steering wheel with both hands, his knuckles white. Finally he said, "Well, he's got us, guys. The only thing we can do is go back to the site." With that Charlie took a deep breath and started the van. The shop owner climbed from the vehicle and headed toward the hardware store with his hands over his head, trying to protect himself from the rain.

Arnold suddenly said, "Wait, Charlie—I know where Gil is going!"

Charlie turned to Arnold with a surprised look on his face and said, "What?"

Arnold was nervously rubbing his arm and looking out the side window.

Charlie continued, "Arnold, what do you mean, 'you know where he is headed'?"

"Malaysia. Charlie; he's headed for Malaysia. Way back, Charlie, when Gil and I were watching you at the camp, we planned to steal whatever you guys were trying to get and sell it in Malaysia. We didn't have any idea what you were up to, but we figured whatever it was, it would be worth money. I doubt he has changed his mind, Charlie—especially if he is aboard a boat."

"Get that shop owner back here!"

A few minutes later the owner was back inside the van but did not look too happy. After explaining to him what Arnold had said, Charlie had him translate the information to Magellan. Magellan and his uncle talked for several minutes; the uncle translated their conversation to Charlie.

"There is only one way to get to Malaysia—from here they must cross the Straits of Sulu. If that is the case, we can catch up with them—if they have left from the place we have been told of."

Charlie looked out his window to check the weather; it was bad, real bad! Charlie sat in the van; the frustration was unbearable. He turned to Magellan and said, "We can't follow him—it will be too dangerous, my friend."

The uncle translated the message to Magellan. Magellan sat back onto the seat for a few minutes and finally said something to the translator. He turned to Charlie and said, "Magellan says he will catch this man."

Charlie looked at Magellan with surprise and said, "No! It is not worth the risk!"

Magellan did not wait for the translation. He looked at Charlie and said in broken English, "We go, we go now!" He did not wait for an answer. He climbed from the van and motioned to everyone to follow him.

Arnold looked at Charlie and said, "I think the man means it, Charlie!"

Charlie started the engine and was backing out of the parking spot when Arnold said, "How about Ramon, Charlie—are we going to leave him?"

Charlie immediately turned off the engine and said, "There is no way in hell I would leave Ramon. Thanks, Arnold, for reminding me. If we have to wait all night that's what we will do—we will wait!"

Just as he finished, Ramon appeared, crossing the street in front of the van. He ran to the van, opened the back door, and climbed in. An excited look was on his face, and he said, "I know where he has gone, Sir Charlie!"

Charlie reached back and touched Ramon on the arm. He said, "So do we, my little friend, so do we!"

Fifteen minutes later they were aboard Magellan's boat, headed out to sea. The waves picked the small boat up and tossed it like a stick of wood! Charlie, Ramon, and Arnold were holding on for dear life; however, Magellan and his crew seemed hardly to notice the raging sea. Lightning flashed and thunder rolled across the sky. Each time the lightning flashed, Charlie could see the faces of Ramon and Arnold, both men's expressions masked in fear.

Ramon had tied a rope around Arnold and attached it to a cabin railing. It was evident that Arnold could not hang on to the craft because of his broken arm. Magellan turned to face Charlie and was yelling something, but because of the wind and rain Charlie could not understand what the man was saying. He wanted to go forward and talk to Magellan, but the typhoon made it virtually impossible to move around the deck. Finally Magellan motioned to one of his men to take over at the wheel. The man struggled to reach the front of the boat, and eventually he grabbed the wheel from Magellan. Magellan cupped his hand over the man's ear and said something to him then began working his way along the side of the boat toward Charlie.

He was within ten feet of Charlie when a massive wave lifted the small boat into the air. Magellan was tossed overboard! Charlie could not believe his eyes—as the boat dropped down into a swell, he could see Magellan ten feet above him, trapped on top of a massive wave! Charlie was in total shock, frozen against the rail of the boat, helpless.

Again the small boat rose high into the air on top of a monstrous wave, and Magellan disappeared. Charlie screamed above the wild wind, "No, my God, no!" He turned to see where the rest of the men were. Arnold was still tied to the railing, but Ramon was no longer next to him. Charlie looked back to the sea in time to see Ramon attempting to swim toward Magellan. He had a rope tied around his waist and was kicking his legs frantically, trying to close the gap between him and Magellan.

Charlie's mind was racing. I'm going to lose both of them! What have I done! Just as Charlie had given up all hope, another giant wave picked up Ramon and flung him next to Magellan—it was a miracle! Ramon grabbed onto his friend but the wave was pulling them away from the boat. The only thing preventing them from being swept away was the rope around Ramon's waist.

In an instant, Charlie came to life and started pulling himself along the railing toward the tied rope. He grabbed the rope, and with all his strength he began to pull. Each time he would gain some ground, the sea would shift and pull the rope from his hands; he knew he could not give up—these two men meant too much! He had made his mind up—either he would pull them back on board, or he would die in his attempt!

Charlie felt someone pulling on the rope behind him and took a quick glance back. It was Arnold! The man had taken off the splint from his broken arm and was pulling the rope with everything he had! Charlie grabbed the rope with renewed strength, and the two men pulled. Little by little the rope began to coil onto the deck.

Suddenly Ramon was next to the boat with his arms still around Magellan's waist. A sudden change in the sea pushed the two men aboard the boat. Charlie grabbed Ramon and pulled him next to him at the same time Arnold grabbed Magellan. It was truly a miracle both men were on board and alive!

Charlie could barely hear Arnold above the sound of the wind. "Magellan's not breathing, Charlie."

Charlie took the end of the rope and cinched it tight to the railing to prevent Ramon from being swept overboard. He rolled Magellan over on his back and began to push down on the man's chest. The boat continued to toss high into the sky making it almost impossible for Charlie to revive Magellan. Suddenly Magellan coughed and began to spit up water from his lungs. Eventually he sat up and looked around.

Before Charlie knew what was happening, Magellan was on his feet and heading toward the wheel of the boat. Charlie was astounded with the man—he could not believe how quickly he had recovered!

Magellan took control of the boat and sent the crewmember back to his post. He turned and faced Charlie and the others sprawled on the deck and motioned for Charlie to come forward. Charlie was amazed at the strength of the man and felt a tremendous respect for him. He thought, if this man can come back from death, the n I sure the hell can climb to the front of the boat!

Charlie inched his way toward Magellan until he was standing next to him. Magellan grabbed Charlie by his arm and pointed toward the sea ahead of them. Charlie wasn't sure what the man was doing until he saw a faint light out in front of them. Just as he was straining to make out the light, another wave picked up the boat and dropped it into another swell. Charlie grabbed on for dear life, losing sight of the light ahead of them!

As the sea raised the small craft again, he could see the light floating in front of them about two miles off the boat's port bow. Charlie turned to look at Magellan and saw the grin on the man's face. Neither man needed to say a word; they both knew it was the ship they were looking for!

Charlie put his arm around Magellan and gave him a hug. There was no question the ship ahead of them was Gil—no one else was crazy enough to be out here during the typhoon! At that instant Charlie and Magellan became a part of each other. If nothing else happened, these two men had bonded forever!

Gil woke up. He felt the ship rocking side to side; the erratic movement tossed him along with it. He tried to right himself but realized his hands and feet were tied. Each time the savage sea would radically shift the vessel from side to side, Gil's body bounced against the walls. Water had seeped into the hold and was splashing around inside at times Gil had to struggle for air as the water splashed over his head. He again tried to right himself but realized it was no use—they had done a thorough job in tying him to the hull. Above in the wheelhouse, the captain of the small ship was frantically fighting to keep it afloat.

Gil braced himself against a corner of the bulkhead as best he could. He fought to keep from being tossed and tried to remember what had happened to him. After the crew had loaded the last box of gold onto the ship Gil attempted to board the vessel. Just as he stepped onto the deck, a wave struck the boat, causing the craft to roll on its side. Gil attempted to right himself but was knocked off balance. He tried to catch himself from falling, but he landed on his hands and knees. The gun he had in his hand skidded across the deck. The last thing Gil remembered was reaching for the pistol.

The captain cursed under his breath, "If I lose my boat because of that dirty bastard, I will personally castrate him! If it weren't for the gold, he would be a dead man by now!"

The sea was as bad as he had ever seen it in fifteen years. He had already lost one of his crew to the storm and now he was short-handed. The bastard was staring at the gold bar when a massive wave hit the side of the boat knocking him overboard, the captain thought again, Damn fool overboard I hope the rest of them learned something from this! Once I get to the island then we will see what our friend has to say! Nick figured if the weather continued to raise hell he still had about an hour to the island. He had to laugh to himself. How could this idiot think he was going to load gold onto my ship and expect me to kindly take him to Malaysia, shake his hand, and politely walk away?

The rain was as bad as it could get. The only time the captain could determine his location was when the lighting struck. As it flashed he was able to make out the small island just off to starboard. He thought, once I get into the cove, the seas will settle down a bit and I can tie my recently rich friend to the dock. He had to laugh at his joke, recently rich! Then we'll haul our friend into the village and find out the rest of the story. Jargo has a way in getting people to talk—and it doesn't take very long! The captain was thinking of the Muslim bandit who everyone called Jargo.

Jargo was a wanted man on the main island of Mindanao, but the authorities hesitated to go after anyone in the south. His hideout was Jolo—Muslim country! Muslim bandits controlled the small islands off the southern tip of Mindanao and no authority in the entire Philippines was interested in going after them! The official position of the Philippine government was, "The Philippines are a free democratic government. Anyone is allowed to travel anywhere in our country." However, the unofficial position was, "If you travel to southern Mindanao and beyond Zamboanga; do it at your own risk. We cannot guarantee your protection or your safety"!

There was no question to anyone that southern Mindanao from Zamboanga to the Malaysian coast line was Muslim territory. The people living in Mindanao would tell strangers, "If you do not want to be kidnapped, or worse, do not go south!"

Again the heavy seas lifted the ship high into the darkening sky and again the lightning flashed. The captain yelled above the savage wind, "Yes, there it is!"

In the bow of the ship, Gil continued to struggle. The seawater was now splashing over his head as the ship tilted on its side. Each time he would hold his breath until the ship rolled back and the water ran to the opposite end of the cargo hold, allowing him to gasp air. Gil had managed to lap the ropes tied around his hands behind his back over a cargo rail, which prevented him from rolling back and forth as the ship twisted and turned in the typhoon.

Charlie was standing next to Magellan, holding onto the boat's wheelhouse with both hands. Each time the small fishing boat was tossed into the sky by the enormous waves, he would wrap his arms around the railing with all his strength. He could not believe how Magellan was able to stand on his feet! The man seemed to know what the wave was going to do before it slammed into the vessel!

For the next two hours, both vessels fought the savage seas, however as the crafts entered the island cove, the sea began to flatten out and the fierce storm's impact began to subside.

The captain grinned said out load to know one in particular, "Within an hour we will be at the village and the fun will begin. Jargo will get the information from our friend and that will be that!" He could see the landing just ahead of him. He had tied up to it many times and knew the cove well. Even in a typhoon he could handle the landing.

Meanwhile Magellan had turned the small fishing boat away from the main landing dock. Charlie hollered into his ear and said, "Where are you going, Magellan? We are not heading for the dock?"

Magellan did not answer. He raised his hand and pointed to a small eddy 500 yards south of the main dock.

Charlie immediately understood. He realized that if they attempted to dock next to the other ship, they would be seen. He turned and found Ramon and Arnold standing behind to him. He hollered over the wind, "We are going to put into the small cove about 500 yards from the main dock." Both men nodded their heads.

CHAPTER 20

The Island

"Get the damn ship tied up!"

Even though the seas had settled down, the waves were still crashing into the dock—making it almost impossible to secure the craft. In frustration the captain jumped from the vessel and grabbed the tie-down rope from one of his men, pushing the man away. As the wave retreated away from the dock and the ship was level, he wrapped the rope around the dock piling. After tying down the bow of the boat, he headed to the stern. The man holding the robe immediately turned it loose and backed away. The captain, in a rage, struck the crewman in the face with his fist. He grabbed the tie-down rope off the dock before the wind had a chance to pull it back into the sea. He again waited for the wave to roll away from the dock. Once the ship was level, he tied it down to the stern.

He hollered, "Get the cargo and the son of a bitch off the ship." The crew did not hesitate; they jumped back onto the small ship and began unloading the gold. Once the gold was safe on the dock, they headed down into the cargo bay. Gil was lying on his side; the seawater was just under his chin. Another three or four inches and he would have drowned! Two men untied the ropes, grabbed him around the waist and carried him up onto the deck.

The captain yelled again, "What the hell are you waiting for? Get him onto the dock!" The two crewmembers looked at each other, one shrugged his shoulders, and they lifted Gil up by his head and feet then tossed him onto the dock. Gil's body hit the dock with a thud. He landed on his back and realized immediately that his left shoulder had dislocated from the impact. He screamed out in pain.

"Pick him up, what are you waiting for?" Nick turned to one of his crew and said, "I will be back and when I do the gold better be right here. Do you understand!" The deck hand had been working for Nick for about 6 months and realized what the captain could do. He had watched as Nick ignored everyone when his friend fell overboard. The captain ignored the man struggling in the high sea and done nothing he simply complained losing another man to the sea! The deck hand had already decided the first chance he was given he was running, to hell with this man!

The captain stormed up the trail toward the bandit's encampment. As he walked through the heavy rain he thought, *No sense in showing the boys the gold until it's necessary.* A slight grin crossed his face as he pulled his coat tight around his shoulders and moved on. The two men carrying Gil followed close behind. Meanwhile the man left at the ship was already running in the opposite direction down the beach from the dock.

Charlie and Ramon jumped from the fishing boat as it ran against the beach. Charlie had grabbed the tie-up rope from the bow of the boat and now was running toward a palm tree anchored into the beach thirty feet from the craft. After securing the small boat, the men ran into the nearby jungle.

Charlie gathered everyone under the jungle canopy and began to talk to Ramon. "I'm not sure what is going on, guys, but we are going to have to follow the men from the ship if we expect to find out what Gil is up to." Ramon turned to Magellan and translated Charlie's message. Magellan nodded his head in agreement and started walking in the direction of the dock. After a minute, Magellan stopped and turned around to face the others. He spoke to Ramon in dialect then stood waiting for Roman to translate to Charlie.

"Charlie, Magellan tells me that he will take his warriors to the dock and find out what is happening. He says he is not being disrespectful, but you must understand, this is what they do very well!"

Charlie hesitated briefly then said, "I understand, Ramon, but tell Magellan not to confront them; just come back and let us know what is going on." Ramon passed on the information. Magellan nodded his head in agreement and headed into the jungle with the warriors.

As the men approached the landing they realized that the ship had been abandoned. Magellan carefully climbed aboard the vessel and began to search. It was not long before he discovered the boxes of gold stored on the deck. Magellan motioned to his two men to unload the gold from the ship. Within a few minutes the gold was sitting on the dock.

Magellan looked around the dock area; he knew that they could not carry all the boxes back to where Charlie and Ramon waited. He noticed a washed-out hole next to one of the dock support pilings anchored into the beach sand and directed his men to drop four of the five boxes into the hole. The four heavy boxes of gold dropped immediately out of sight. After washing their tracks from the sand he had the men carry the fifth box back into the jungle covering the footprints as they retreated.

Fifteen minutes later they arrived back at the hideaway where Charlie, Arnold, and Ramon were waiting. After explaining to Ramon what had happened, Magellan waited while Ramon translated to Charlie. A grin crossed Charlie's face. He walked over to Magellan, grasped his hand and forearm, and shook vigorously.

"Magellan has told me that there is a trail leading into the jungle from the dock, Mr. Charlie. He believes that is where the men have gone."

Charlie walked over and sat down on a large rock. He was thinking. We might be able to grab the gold and get the hell out of here—but what good would that do? Eventually Gil would be back at the camp with reinforcements. We wouldn't be any better off than we are now! "Ramon, tell Magellan that we have to get to Gil before he can cause us more trouble."

Magellan motioned toward the dock and started back into the jungle.

Captain Nick, his men, and Gil entered the bandit camp. The only light was from a small hut near the center of the camp. Nick knew that this was Jargo's hut. The only electricity in the camp was produced by a small generator the bandits had set up. The rest of the village used oil lamps or fire for their lighting. The typhoon had made it impossible for any fire around the camp; therefore it remained dark and deceptive.

The rain continued to drench them as they stood looking across the camp at the lighted window of the hut. Finally Nick motioned to the crew and they continued forward. The captain was just about to hammer on the door to the hut with his fist when two bandits appeared from behind them. They were pointing rifles at the group.

The captain raised his hands in defense and said something to one of them. Gil was not sure what was said, but the men lowered their weapons and one of them stepped between Nick and the doorway. With the point of his rifle he motioned the captain and his crew to step back from the door. After he was satisfied the men were far enough away from the doorway, he opened it and disappeared inside, closing the door behind him.

The door slowly opened into the hut, and a man peered out into the downpour at the group. He motioned for them to enter. As they did so, Gil carefully looked around. A large table was sitting in the middle of the room and several men were seated. The remains of half-eaten food lay scattered around the table. A bottle of rum sat in front of one of the men, half empty.

Nick walked up to the table and said, "My friend, you look in good health."

Gil realized that the captain knew these men, and an uneasy feeling came over him. The ship captain had been in no mood to talk to Gil from the time they docked until now.

The captain continued, "I brought something you might be interested in." He pointed to Gil. "He's an American!"

The man he was talking to did not answer; instead he picked up the bottle of rum and poured into his glass.

Gil glanced up at the captain. Even though the Nick was drenched with rain, he could see beads of sweat forming on his upper lip and brow.

The captain stood nervously in front of the table waiting for the man to say something. He nervously said, "Jargo, you know me! Damn it, man—say something!"

Finally Jargo set his drink onto the table and said, "Yes, I know you— you are a useless dog!" He jumped from his seat and struck the captain across his face with a small whip he was holding in his other hand.

The captain jumped back from the table and gripped the side of his face where the whip had stuck him. A trickle of blood oozed from between his fingers.

Jargo continued. "You must realize that the Americans do not pay kidnapping ransom, so why are you here?"

The captain regained his composer and answered, "Yeah, you're right, but you didn't let me finish. How does gold sound to you?"

Jargo leaned across the table and looked directly into Nick's eyes. "Gold? So now you have gold! So tell me—why would you risk the typhoon? Why do you come to me?"

The captain realized he must take a risk; he had no other choice. "You are right again, my friend. My plans were not to come here but the typhoon would not let me reach my intended destination. That, however, is to your advantage; don't you agree?"

Jargo stood looking at the captain and finally sat back down into his chair. He motioned to one of his men and said, "Give this dog a chair and put the American in the corner until I decide what we will do with him." After the captain had sat down Jargo picked up his glass again. He gazed down into the glass and said, "Now tell me about the gold."

The Nick reached over and grabbed the bottle of rum and pour himself a drink. He smiled and said, "My companion over there in the corner was kind enough to give me some gold." The captain leaned back in his chair, turned his head, and looked at Gil in the corner; a slight grin still on his face.

"So tell me, Captain—where is this gold?"

The captain took a drink from his glass and said, "You don't expect me to bring the gold here. I have hidden it, my friend, in a very secure place."

Jargo smiled and said, "Dear Captain, you know I have ways to make men talk. You should know better by now that no one keeps secrets from Jargo!"

"Again you are right; I know that you have ways to get information—and that is why I have brought this man to you. If you want the gold I have brought, I suppose you can get it from me—but what if there is more?"

Jargo smiled and said, "If that is the case, what do I need you for if the man you have brought me has the information?"

Nick began to sweat again he wiped his face with a rag he had in his back pocket. "Are you sure of that? What if the man fails to give you the answers you ask? I have known men who would give up their lives. Remember, this may be a lifetime dream for him. Isn't it better to have two men with the answers you seek?"

Jargo stood up from his chair and said, "Let us see, dear Captain. Let us find out how brave this man is. Bring the American to me!"

Gil had been listening and knew this was the end! He also realized if he told them about the tunnel and the whole story, they would kill him anyway. Two bandits grabbed Gil under the arms and lifted him to his feet. He attempted to walk but the ropes around his lower legs caused him to fall as he tried to step forward. The men dragged Gil across the room and sat him next to Nick.

Jargo looked across the table and said, "What do you think of your friend Captain Nick?"

Gil slowly turned to face the captain. He looked deep into the man's eyes and without warning spat into his face. There was no reaction except for the captain reaching into his back pocket, pulling out his handkerchief again, and methodically wiping away the spit.

Jargo and his men began to laugh; Jargo yelled, "I do not believe this man is your friend, Captain." Then suddenly Jargo became very serious. He walked around the table and grabbed both men by the hair and viciously jerked backward. The men fell over onto the floor. He stood over them and began to whip them across their faces. The beating continued for what seemed eternity for the two. The captain was able to somewhat protect himself with his hand; however, the blows struck Gil directly on his face.

Jargo backed away; sweat was running down his face, his shirt was soaked from the collar down. Breathing heavily he said, "I will give you ten minutes alone. Then you will tell me everything you know. I would suggest that you grant my wishes. I never ask the same questions twice!"

Jargo turned to his men and motioned them to drag Gil and the captain to the back of the room. Once they were lying on the floor next to each other, he walked over and said, "ten minutes!"

Magellan carefully approached the hut. He could hear men talking inside as he eased up next to the widow and peered in. The only person he recognized was the man called Gil. He was tied hand and foot and lay next to the back wall. A bandit stood over him with a whip in his right hand. Magellan could see blood across Gil's face. He looked around the rest of the room and counted six others watching the man with the whip. Magellan backed away from the window then crawled away from the hut.

Charlie and the others were waiting under cover of the jungle. Magellan told Ramon what he had seen then Ramon explained to Charlie what was going on inside the hut. Arnold began to pace back and forth; although he was upset with Gil, he was concerned with his safety. He realized what the bandits were capable of and it made the hair on the back of his neck stand on end.

"Charlie," he said, "I know how you feel about Gil, but damn it, man—these guys will beat him to death if we don't do something!"

Charlie turned around and looked at Arnold. "What do you expect us to do, Arnold? Didn't you hear what Magellan said—there are at least eight others in there, and—if you haven't noticed—we have one gun between us! Gil is in there because he made a decision—and right now it looks like it was the wrong one!"

Arnold turned away and walked toward the beach with his hand in his pocket. His arm had been hurting since he had helped pull Magellan and Ramon from the raging sea, but right now he didn't give a damn. He thought, they're going to kill him—and I can't do a thing about it!

Magellan grabbed Ramon by his arm and began talking to him. Ramon turned to Charlie and said, "Magellan, me, and his warriors will take care of the men in the hut, Sir Charlie." Charlie started to say something but Ramon continued, "We can take care of these bandits, Sir Charlie, but you must guard the door and prevent anyone from escaping."

"What do you have planned, Ramon? There are eight men in the hut, and they have rifles, for God's sake!"

"Sir Charlie, the rifles are no good to them if there is no light. If they cannot see who they must shoot then we will have a chance."

Arnold stepped forward and began to speak. "Listen, I probably know better than the rest of you what an asshole Gil is, but all I ask is if we can at least try to save his life? I know he has been a pain in the neck, but he was my partner for five years and I don't think I could live with myself if I didn't at least try. All I'm asking is that I go in with Magellan and his people Charlie, and try to save the guy; what do you say?"

Charlie never hesitated and said, "I have lost some good friends over this gold, Arnold, and you may be surprised at what I am about to say but, yes, you can try to save him. Just remember, these men here are my friends, do not jeopardize their lives! Do you understand?" Charlie turned to the others and asked, "What is your plan? What do we need to do to get this thing done?"

Ramon glanced around then answered, "We have decided this, Sir Charlie. We will barricade the door; you will shut down the generator supplying the light for the hut. When the lights go out, we will enter through the two windows into the hut."

The rain and wind had died down somewhat; however, the night sky was still pitch dark—which to Charlie made the plan seem plausible. Finally he turned and said, "All right then—let's get this over with!"

While Charlie and his men had been planning their attack inside the hut, Gil and the captain had been tied and were sitting back onto their chairs. Jargo sat his chair in front of Gil and leaned forward. He was smoking a large cigar. "Now, my friend. What have you got to say to Jargo?"

The sweat was running down Gil's face. He gritted his teeth and said, "What do you want to hear?"

Jargo took a deep drag from the cigar and the tip turned bright red. He knocked off the ashes and looked at the glowing tip.

Panic gripped Gil's entire body. He thought, This SOB is going to burn me!

Jargo was going to burn Gil all right, but not where any man would expect. But again—Jargo was a Muslim bandit! Without warning, Jargo jammed the hot cigar into Gil's right eye! The captain's mouth dropped open and he leaned away from the man sitting next to him. Gil screamed as Jargo continued to push the cigar farther into his eye. The pain was more than the man could stand and he passed out.

Jargo removed the cigar from the man's face. A black hole appeared where Gil's right eye had been. Gil's body was in convulsions, twitching and jerking. Jargo turned to the captain and repeated, "What do you want to tell me, my friend?"

The captain never hesitated, and yelled, "There is gold! There is gold aboard my ship! It is tied to the deck! Please, you can have the gold! Don't hurt me; I am your friend!" The captain was pulling away from Jargo but the ropes binding him held him to his chair.

Jargo carefully stood up, turned to one of his men, and said in his dialect, "Go to this swine's boat and bring me the gold." The man motioned to two of the other bandits and left the hut. Jargo sat down and poured himself a glass of rum.

Gil was regaining consciousness. The pain was almost more than he could stand! Jargo walked over and grabbed Gil by his arm and said, "What do you have to tell me, my friend?"

Gil was confused; the pain was unbearable, and he could not concentrate. He looked up into Jargo's face and said, "I don't know what you want. Why did you do this to me?"

A sadistic sigh escaped Jargo's lips and again, without warning, he jabbed his thumb into Gil's other eye! Again Gil screamed with agony; his head fell back onto his neck, his mouth gaped open!

The captain was terrified. His mind was racing, My God, I'm doomed! What the hell have I done?

For the next ten minutes the rest of the bandits inside the hut passed the time talking between themselves and occasionally laughing. Suddenly the door to the hut opened; the two men from the ship had returned. One of the men walked over to Jargo and whispered in his ear.

Jargo stood looking at the captain and Gil. Finally he said, "How much gold is aboard the ship, my dear Captain?"

The captain answered him immediately, "Five boxes, five boxes!"

Jargo turned to his men and said, "Get some more rum we are going to have some more fun with our two guest."

The captain hollered, "You have the gold! Let me go! I know where the rest of the gold is and I can bring it to you!"

Jargo walked over to the captain, raised his fist high into the air, and struck the man across the face. The captain was knocked cold!

Charlie and his men had seen the two men enter the hut. They waited until the door was closed behind them. Charlie carefully wedged a pole against the door while Magellan and the others worked their way around the hut and were hidden outside the two windows. Charlie eased away from the door to the hut and crept across the compound to where the generator whined. He took one last look at the hut then reached over and turned off the switch to the generator. The hut and the surrounding area was engulfed in darkness.

At first the men inside the hut began to panic then Jargo hollered above the commotion, "Stop your talking and go outside and see what has happened to the generator." This was not the first time the generator had shut down; it had been a common problem especially during a storm. The men settled down.

Inside the hut it was pitch dark. Charlie returned to the front door, pulled the pistol from his belt, crouched down, and waited. Magellan, Ramon, and tow of Magellan's men slipped into the hut through the window. At the same time Arnold and the other man followed from the other side. Charlie could hear some of the men still talking from inside but suddenly the hut became very quiet! Although some noise came from inside, Charlie could not tell what was happening.

Suddenly someone was frantically attempting to open the door. The door bowed from the impact. The door vibrated with another impact then finally collapsed, and a man jumped from the opening. At first Charlie could not see who it was, and he hesitated. The man began to run toward Charlie. Charlie realized that he was not one of his people, and he aimed the pistol and fired. The bullet struck the man in his chest. He stood for a moment, raised his hand to his chest, then slowly collapsed to his knees and fell face first into the dirt.

Charlie stood in front of the door waiting for someone else to exit. The hut was in a dead silence; nothing moved. Charlie's heart felt like it was going to jump from his chest!

"Charlie! Charlie, are you out there?"

Charlie recognized Arnold's voice and answered, "Yeah, I'm here! What's going on?"

"I'm not sure, Charlie, but I think it's all over. Better turn the power back on."

Charlie raced to the generator shack, turned the switch on, the hut lit up. He ran back toward the hut with the pistol still raised in his hand. Charlie stepped through the door and stopped in his tracks. Magellan stood over the bodies of two Muslim bandits, their blood streaked across the wall of the hut. Magellan had severed both their heads with one blow of his bolo knife. It was obvious that the two men had been caught off guard and never knew what happened.

Now that the lights had been turned on, Arnold walked over to where Gil was lying on the floor. He stood up the man's chair and looked into his face. Arnold began to sob—his face was a mess! Arnold shook Gil and said, "Gil! Damn it, Gil, talk to me!"

It was no use. Jargo had driven his thumb into the man's eye with such force that it had killed him instantly.

"Help me, someone, help me!"

Arnold turned around to see who was crying for help. The captain was lying on his side still tied to the chair. Arnold walked over and looked down at the man. The captain said, "Thank God, the crazy bastards were going to kill the both of us!"

Arnold looked back at Gil. He turned again to the captain and raised the bolo knife above his head. Before anyone could stop him, he struck the man across the face!

The captain saw the blow coming and strained to avoid the knife; however, it was no use! Charlie ran across the room and grabbed Arnold by the arm. "What the hell did you do that for?"

Arnold turned to face Charlie. Tears ran down his face and he said, "I know this SOB is the reason Gil is dead, Charlie! The only way I could help make things right for Gil was to finish off the bastard."

Charlie let go of Arnold's arm. Suddenly he realized that he had not seen Ramon. He began to yell, "Ramon! Ramon, where are you?"

Bodies were lying throughout the hut. Charlie walked around the hut pulling bodies back, frantically looking for his friend.

Magellan yelled, "Here, here is Ramon."

Charlie turned to find Magellan standing over a body. Charlie ran across the room and bent down. Blood covered the man's upper body. Charlie could see a terrible wound across Ramon's chest. Panic gripped him; he thought, Oh, my God! I have killed him!

Magellan crouched and carefully pulled Charlie away from Ramon. He started wiping the blood from the young man's body. Suddenly Ramon moaned, opened his eyes, and looked up at the two men leaning over him. Charlie immediately cradled Ramon in his arms and looked into his friend's face.

Ramon struggled to say something but had a difficult time getting the words out. Tears ran down Charlie's face. He took his free hand and began to wipe the blood from Ramon's face then said, "Ramon, no matter what it takes, I'm going to take care of you. But damn it—you stay alive!"

A slight grin crossed Ramon's face, and in a faint whisper he said, "You are all right, Sir Charlie, you are all right!"

"Don't say anymore, Ramon—we are going to get you a doctor!" Charlie turned to the others standing over him and said, "Let's get the hell out of here! Someone give me a hand with Ramon!"

Magellan leaned down and gathered Ramon into his arms. Charlie started to take him from Magellan; however, he looked into Magellan's eyes and realized that the man was not about to give up his friend too anyone, including Charlie!

As they left the hut, Charlie took one last look at the butchery that had taken place. He thought, Gold! The damn gold!

CHAPTER 21

Back From Hell!

"How bad is he, doctor?" Charlie stood staring into the man's face, waiting for an answer.

"Let's put it this way. I used 200 stitches just to close him up—and you ask me how is he? I don't know what happened to this man, but he is very lucky to be alive."

"Can I see him?"

The doctor nodded his head and said, "In most cases I wouldn't allow anyone to see him yet, but for some damn reason the minute he woke up he insisted he talk with you. In fact, we had to restrain him before he tore out all his stitches!"

Charlie brushed past the doctor and headed for the recovery room. It had taken them all night to get to Davao, only to find that the hospital closed due to the storm and didn't have a surgeon available. Charlie had threatened every person in the hospital to get a doctor.

The bleeding had been bad during the trip to Davao; the storm had not helped Ramon had passed out and didn't regained consciousness the entire trip. His breathing was shallow and there were times that it seemed he had died, but just before docking in Davao he had moaned, opened his eyes, and smiled faintly at Charlie. Now, nearly ten hours later, he was alive!

It was a miracle they had run into the American naval medical officer when they were at the hospital. The doctor was visiting one of the sailors from his ship that had been hospitalized while on leave in Davao. The sailor had been stabbed in a local bar and the doctor was summoned from the ship to sew him up. He was just leaving the hospital when Charlie spotted the insignia on his vest and had asked if he was a doctor.

Charlie entered the recovery room and walked over to Ramon's bed. Ramon's eyes were closed and as Charlie looked down at the frail Filipino, tears welled up in his eyes. He whispered, "Ramon?"

Ramon slowly opened his eyes and looked up at Charlie. A meek smile crossed his face. He said, "Sir Charlie, are you are okay?"

Charlie reached down and touched Ramon on his shoulder. "Don't worry about me, Ramon; let's concentrate on you."

Ramon took a deep breath before he spoke. "We have your gold, Sir Charlie. Now there will be no more killing?"

Charlie's face turned pale and he answered, "Ramon, the gold means nothing to me anymore. I have almost caused the death of one of the most important people in my life over the gold. I am convinced that the gold is a curse—your grandfather was right."

"No, Sir Charlie; I am the one who is to blame. I was the one who came for you, don't you remember?"

Charlie ran his hand through Ramon's hair and said, "I am going back to the fishing village to bring your wife and children right now. The most important thing is to get you well—then we will talk of the gold."

"But Sir Charlie—"

Charlie placed his hand gently over Ramon's mouth and said, "No more talk now, my little friend. You rest. I will come back with your family."

Ramon attempted to speak, but Charlie turned from the bed and headed toward the door. Outside the others waited. Charlie walked up to Magellan and said, "We will go back to the fishing village; Ramon will be okay until we return."

Magellan looked into Charlie's eyes, lowered his head, then turned toward the door and walked away.

Charlie's heart sank. He knew Magellan held him responsible for everything that had happened. If it hadn't been for me, he thought, this whole thing would never have happened!

Four hours later the small fishing boat tied up to the dock at the fishing village. A few minutes later, Charlie pulled the van up in front of Mila's house. Magellan immediately jumped out and ran to the front door. Mila opened the door before Magellan had a chance to and jumped up into his arms. Tears ran down her cheeks as she exclaimed, "Oh my husband! I have been worried! I feared for your safety in the terrible storm!"

The two held each other until Charlie approached them. Mila let go of Magellan and grabbed Charlie around the waist. Charlie held the small Filipina and whispered into her ear, "I almost lost Ramon, Mila. I don't know what I would have done if he had died. The gold is a curse and I am a fool. I should have listened to you."

Mila stepped back from Charlie and asked, "What has happened to Ramon? Where is Ramon? And Arnold, what about Arnold!

Charlie answered, "Ramon is fine Mila. He is in the hospital in Davao." The doctor also checked Arnold in he needs to recast the arm guess he dislocated the damn thing in all the excitement."

For the next few minutes Charlie explained what had happened in the Muslim compound. Mila did not interrupt him but stood frozen, looking into Charlie's eyes. After he had finished she said, "You are right, Charlie. The gold is a curse. You must finish this thing."

He responded, "It is finished. I don't want anything more to do with the gold, Mila. It has caused nothing but death and misery." Charlie's hands were dangling by his sides; Mila could tell all the energy had left the man's body.

She caressed his face and said, "Charlie, you must rest. You are exhausted and are not thinking right. I will return to Davao with Ramon's family and you must go back to the camp and rest."

Charlie started to resist but Mila placed her hand over his mouth and said, "Go!"

It was eight o'clock in the evening before Charlie arrived back at the campsite. The fire had died down so Charlie took his flashlight and walked around camp. He peered into a tent and found Nels sound asleep. Charlie stepped away from the tent and stood up. He thought *the hell with it; I will talk to him in the morning.* Charlie was exhausted and whispered, "Mila was right—I need some sleep."

Charlie laid his head down on the pillow and fell sound asleep. He was just getting comfortable when someone began to shake him awake, saying, "Charlie, wake up mate," over and over. Finally Charlie opened his eyes and saw Nels standing over his cot with a cup of coffee in his hand.

Charlie said, "Nels, I just got to sleep. Give me a couple of hours and I'll be ready to go."

"What time did you get in, mate?" Nels asked.

Charlie rubbed his eyes and said, "Oh, I don't know—about eight, I guess."

"Eight! Hell, mate, it's seven-thirty in the morning. Christ, you've had eleven hours of sleep!"

Charlie sat up and looked at his watch then peered outside at the sunlight. "My God! Mila was right! I must have been exhausted! It seems like I'd just gone to bed when you woke me!"

"Well, get out of the sack, mate, and I will have a cuper waiting for you at the fire." Five minutes later the two men were sitting together drinking their morning coffee. Charlie stood up and said, "Nels, I'm going to fix breakfast. I'll bring you up to date on what the hell I've been doing."

For the next hour Charlie explained what had happened to the gold and to Gil. Nels sat listening throughout breakfast without saying a word. When Charlie finally finished, Nels asked, "Is that about it, mate, or is there more?"

"No, Nels—that is it."

Nels dropped his breakfast plate into the dishwater and turned to face Charlie. "So what now, Charlie? Are we through with all the killing and the bullshit that goes along with it?"

Charlie could see the anger in Nels' face. He could almost read the man's thoughts. We told you not to go after this guy. We begged you not to kill him! Charlie hesitated for a minute then walked over and dropped his plate into the dishpan. He put his hands on his hips and looked out into the jungle. "I suppose it wouldn't do any good to apologize for what happened, would it, partner."

"No, it sure in the hell wouldn't!" Nels answered.

The two men didn't say another word until they had finished cleaning up after breakfast and putting out the fire.

"Well, are we going to dig some gold out of the hole, or stand here sulking all day?"

Charlie turned to answer Nels, but the man was already headed for the dig site. Charlie took a deep breath and followed him down the trail toward the tunnel. Charlie approached the dig site with his head down. He did not look up until he entered the level cut-out near the tunnel. When he did, he stopped dead. His mouth dropped open and his eyes bugged out. In front of him stood neatly stacked piles of gold bars. Each stack was at least five feet high and ten feet across. Charlie slowly began to count the piles.

When he finished he realized he had not looked at Nels until now. He faced his partner and found the man grinning from ear to ear with his hands on his hips. "Well, what do you think?"

Charlie slowly walked closer to the gold stacks. He ran his hand over the bars as he walked along the piles. Finally he turned to Nels and said, "My God, man! How did you do this?"

Nels pushed his hat back and said, "Charlie, after you left for the fishing village, I went back to the site and decided to dig a little with the Bobcat. I couldn't relax and had to do something. I drove into the tunnel and ran the bucket into the dirt pile, but when I tried to raise the bucket it wouldn't move an inch. I thought the damn thing had broken down, so I backed her up and tried again but it was no good, the bucket wouldn't make a move! I climbed out of the machine and took a look. Hell, mate—the pile was full of gold! I didn't waste any time, Charlie! I had the two warriors from the village go and get me fifteen more men and for two days we pulled gold from the tunnel. I had to bring out a half a load each time; that's all the Bobcat could handle!"

Charlie was still stunned. He kept walking around the gold touching the precious metal with his hands.

"Charlie, that's over six hundred million and there is still more inside!"

"Six hundred million?" Charlie could not believe his eyes. He walked over to a pile of dirt and slowly sat down. He began to rub his hands together; he couldn't decide what he wanted to do. He stood up again and began to pace back and forth, thinking, six hundred million!

"Charlie, I figure there is still plenty inside, but the place is a little scary. The walls are starting to cave in and I don't know if it is worth getting the rest; what do you think?"

Charlie was not listening to Nels; he kept thinking, six hundred million!

"Charlie, are you listening to me?" Nels asked.

"What, did you say something, Nels?" Charlie answered.

"Yes, mate, I did. I said it's too dangerous in there. Do we want to try to get the rest?"

"Oh," Charlie said excitedly, "I think this is plenty, don't you?"

Nels laughed and answered, "Yeah, I think we have enough!"

Charlie walked over, wrapped his arms around the Australian, and the two men began to dance around in a circle, yelling at the top of their lungs. When they were too exhausted to continue, they dropped to the ground breathing heavily and trying to catch their breaths. Charlie raised his head and a look of panic crossed his face. He said, "How in the hell do we get this out of the country, Nels?"

Nels responded, "One step at a time, Charlie; that's how you learn to walk, mate!"

CHAPTER 22

For the next six months the men used the fishing boats in the village to transport the gold to Malaysia as they had planned. Each day one of the fishing boats would load the gold and head for the island of Pulau Balambangan, off the coast of Malaysia, stopping to fish during the day and unloading the gold at night. Charlie and Nels had established a hideout inside the jungle and carefully concealed the gold. Once all the gold was stored on the island the two men began to open several accounts in the states of Sabah, Pulau, Kangar, and Johor, and eventually Kuala Lumpur. Within a year, the two men were very rich!

CHAPTER 23

The End?

Charlie pulled up in front of Mila's house. He climbed out of the van and walked toward the front door then gently tapped and waited. The door opened and Mila peered outside. She immediately opened the door wide and grabbed Charlie around the neck, squealing, "Charlie, where have you been?"

Charlie grinned and said, "I've been busy, Mila, how is everyone?"

"We are fine, Charlie; but do not stand in the doorway, come in!"

Charlie was about to say something when he heard a baby cry. Mila immediately turned around and walked over to a crib and picked up a baby. Stopie, who had been playing on the floor, jumped up and ran to his mother. He grabbed her by her leg and began to suck on his thumb. Mila began to gently rock the child in her arms until the baby was quiet.

Charlie walked over to her and kissed her softly on the forehead. "You and Magellan have been busy; I guess I should have come sooner."

Mila looked up at Charlie and said, "I have named my baby little Charlene after you, Charlie." Mila laid the baby back down into the crib and said, "Come, I will fix you something to eat."

Charlie laughed and said, "Some things never change, sweetheart!"

Mila's face flushed and she gave Charlie a light slap on his shoulder. "Where is Nels, Charlie? Did he not come with you?"

"No, Mila, Nels and Arnold have become very good friends. They are in Australia right now having a good time."

"How are they, Charlie? Are they over the terrible times that we have had?"

"I guess so, Mila, we don't talk much about it, but I'm sure they think about it once in a while."

Mila fixed Charlie something to eat and they small-talked until Magellan entered the door. Magellan stopped, looked at Charlie with concern on his face.

Charlie immediately got up from his chair, walked over to the man, and wrapped his arms around him. Magellan froze; his eyes widened, and he looked at Mila in confusion and surprise. Charlie felt Magellan tense as he hugged him and said, "Oh, come on, Magellan! With what you and I have been through together, you must understand that I consider you a dear friend!"

Magellan wasn't quite sure what Charlie had said until Mila had translated. He finally relaxed and gently put his arms around Charlie, but he still felt very uncomfortable! The two men separated and sat down at the kitchen table. Mila brought food for her husband and filled Charlie's coffee cup.

Charlie took a drink from his cup and said, "Mila. I have some good news for you I have put some money into an account in Manila for you and your husband. Any time you need more, just let me know. There is plenty more where it came from!"

Mila stood looking at Charlie with concern on her face. "Money? Why do you give us money?"

"Why did I give you money? For Christ's sake, Mila, it's yours!"

"But Charlie, we did not help you for the money! It would be an insult to our family if we took money from you!"

Charlie realized that it would be no good to argue with Mila; once she made up her mind, it was useless to continue. He handed her a bankbook without saying a word.

She opened the page and looked at the figure. 500,000,000 pesos! The book dropped from her hands and she began to cry! Charlie stood up and pulled the girl into his arms, comforting her. Magellan stopped eating and began to talk to Mila in their dialect. Mila stopped crying and began to laugh.

Charlie asked, "What did he say, Mila, what makes you laugh?"

Mila backed away from Charlie, wiping the tears from her eyes, and said, "My husband believes you want us to help you again!"

Charlie let out a roar and slapped Magellan on the back. "Tell him, Mila, that I'm not here for his help—the poor guy has been through enough! Now I must leave. I am going to see Ramon."

Just as he started toward the door, Mila took him by the arm and handed him the bankbook.

"What's this?" he asked.

"Look around, Charlie; this is my family—do we look like we need money?"

Charlie peered at Stopie and Magellan then back to Mila. He took in a deep breath and said, "Okay, okay! But if you need anything—and I mean anything—you call me, do you understand?"

She smiled again, pulled him close to her, and laid her head on his chest. Charlie could feel her tiny heart beating inside her breast and had an urge to squeeze her inside him. "Mila, you are the biggest loss in my life! I will never, never understand how stupid I was to lose you. Now I must go find Ramon in the fishing village."

"But Charlie, Ramon is no longer in the fishing village—he has returned to his home in the mountains."

"How long has he been gone?" Charlie asked.

"He left the fishing village more than six months ago," she answered.

Charlie sat back down and said with a sigh, "Get me something to eat, Mila—looks like I'll be staying tonight!"

She again laughed and turned toward the kitchen.

Early the next morning Charlie was on his way and finally pulled into Ramon's village in the late afternoon. Charlie pulled up to the front door of Ramon's hut and climbed out. Just as he was attempting to knock on the door, it opened and a small child about six years old was standing in front of him.

"Well, hello there, my little friend. Is your daddy home?"

The little boy immediately turned around and scampered back into the hut, leaving the door wide open. Charlie let out a loud laugh and hollered, "Ramon!"

Before Charlie realized what was happening, Ramon had jumped from a chair inside the house and slammed into Charlie, wrapping both arms around Charlie's waist. The impact knocked both men to the ground!

Ramon stood up with a look of shock on his face, looked down at Charlie, and said, "Please forgive me, Mr. Charlie—I am so happy to see you!"

Charlie pulled himself to a sitting position and wrapped his arms around his knees. He looked up at Ramon with a wide grin across his face and said, "That's the best greeting I've had in twenty years, Ramon!" Charlie climbed to his feet with Ramon's help. Charlie stood looking at Ramon with a grin on his face and said, "Are you going to invite me inside, or are we going to stand outside the rest of the day?"

"Please, Mr. Charlie, come inside! You are welcome in my modest home."

After they entered Ramon's house, Charlie asked, "Where is your wife, Ramon?"

"She is fixing the children's meal, Mr. Charlie."

"Well, let me see her, I have something good to tell the both of you!"

Ramon hollered to his wife in dialect and the small Filipina woman appeared in front of the two as though she had materialized from nowhere! Charlie reached down and grabbed the woman around her waist and began to swing her around in a circle! She screamed, and Charlie continued to dance around the room with her in his arms. Ramon began to laugh; he wasn't sure why Charlie was so happy, but he knew it was good! As soon as Charlie turned the girl loose, she ran to Ramon and threw her arms around him, burying her head in his chest. Ramon kissed his wife on the forehead and whispered into her ear. He gently pulled the woman's arms from around his neck and she slowly walked away from Ramon, staying clear of Charlie. She backed away from the two men and disappeared into the kitchen.

"My wife is getting us something to drink, Mr. Charlie. Are you hungry?"

"Ramon, if I stay near you and Mila, I will weigh 300 pounds! I don't need anything to eat!"

Ramon had a shy grin on his face and said, "Let us sit down, Mr. Charlie; the coffee will be ready soon."

Once the children were fed and the dishes put away, Charlie explained to them about Ramon's share of the money and the account Charlie had set up in Manila. Ramon, much like Mila, could not understand and said, "Mr. Charlie, I am happy, my family and I are simple people and do not need much money. This is my home, and I do not want to leave ever again. I will raise my children and never think of the gold! I am happy for you and that the gold has given you what you want, so keep it and be happy, Mr. Charlie."

Charlie handed Ramon the bankbook. Ramon opened the book and looked at Charlie in confusion. He asked, "What does this mean, Mr. Charlie?"

"Ramon, it means you have five hundred million pesos in the bank in Manila."

Ramon asked, "How much is this amount, Mr. Charlie? I do not understand."

"Ramon, there is enough money for you to buy the Philippines!"

Ramon's mouth flew open, his eyes widened, and he said, "But I told you once, Mr. Charlie; I do not want to buy my county!"

Charlie laughed and said, "I understand, Ramon. I just wanted you to know that the money was there. If you ever need it, find Mila and have her help you, okay?"

"I guess, Mr. Charlie—but I do not believe I will need this money."

Charlie realized that, like Mila, he wasn't going to have any better luck with Ramon concerning his share of the money. The next morning after breakfast, Charlie stood up from the table and walked over to Ramon. He said, "Stand up, my friend. I want to say good-bye for now."

Ramon slowly stood up. Charlie reached out and pulled the small Filipino man to his chest. He thought, I don't deserve a friend like this. He is a man among men. Tears streamed down both men's faces as they stood holding each other in the middle of the room. Finally Charlie stood back and said, "I am going to say something, Ramon that I have never in my life said to another man. I love you as a son. I will never, ever forget you. You are a part of me—you are in my soul!"

Without waiting for a response from Ramon, Charlie walked out the door. Before Ramon could regain his composure, Charlie had driven away.

Two days later, Charlie was on a plane to Perth to meet Nels and Arnold.

CHAPTER 24

Final Good-Bye

Charlie walked into the airport lobby and was greeted by Arnold and Nels. Arnold looked pretty tough, as though he was hung over, but Nels looked as though he was in great shape. Charlie said to Arnold, "Damn, man! You look like hell! What have you been doing? You look terrible!"

Arnold never responded; he just dropped his head and began to walk toward the exit. Charlie turned to Nels and said, "What's wrong with him, Nels?"

A sly smile crossed Nell's face and he said, "Well, mate, it seems that you Americans can't hold your drink very well!"

Charlie started laughing and hollered ahead to Arnold, "Say, partner, what is this Australian trying to say? He claims we can't hold our liquor—is that right?"

Arnold just dropped his head a little more and continued to walk toward the exit with his hands in his pockets. Nels smiled, shrugged his shoulders, and patted Charlie on the shoulder as they entered the street. Twenty minutes later they were in the penthouse suite at the Harvard Hotel.

"Pretty nice, guys!" Charlie exclaimed as he toured the rooms.

"Well, ya see, mate we haven't had a chance to stay here very much since we've been in Perth on business; you know what I mean."

Arnold rolled his eyes at Charlie and said, "Business! You ought to see what ole' Nels calls business! We haven't left a pub since we hit town! I can't believe the beer these bastards drink—they go on and on and on!"

Charlie said, "Sounds like things are going good for you two, but right now I need to shower and get some sleep. Why don't we meet down stairs in about five or six hours and talk a bit about our futures?"

Nels looked over at Arnold and said, "Come on, mate—we can take care of some business while Charlie settles in, what do you think?"

Arnold raised his hands with the palms toward Nels and said, "No way, no way! There ain't going to be any business tonight! I'm with Charlie, a shower and a bed for me!"

"Okay for you, my friend, but I had a couple of Sheila's waiting for us. But if you want to sleep then so be it!"

The two men were still arguing while walking down the hallway; an hour later Charlie was sound asleep.

About eleven PM the phone rang in Charlie's room. He sat up in bed and rubbed his eyes. The phone kept ringing. Charlie finally picked up and said, "Hello?"

"Charlie, it's Arnold."

"What's going on, partner?"

There was a hesitation on the other end. Arnold was caught off guard; Charlie rarely called him partner. Arnold finally regained his composure and said, "I'm afraid I have some bad news, Charlie—Nels is in jail!"

"Jail? What the hell did he do?"

Arnold took a deep breath and answered, "Charlie, you got to believe me. I tried to stop him, he just wouldn't keep his mouth shut."

"Arnold, just tell me what happened."

"We were doing some drinking at a little joint downtown and Nels starts to argue with some South Africans about who are the best miners in the world. Well, one thing leads to another and before I know it, they start kicking the shit out of each other! Ya know something, Charlie—the little bastard can fight! I thought you could hit, but damn it, man—he knocked out two of them before the cops got 'em!"

"Where are you now, Arnold?"

"I'm downstairs in the lobby, Charlie."

"Wait for me; I'll be right down!"

Charlie walked out of the elevator and looked around the lobby. Arnold was standing next to a bank of phones lined across the far wall. When he saw Charlie coming toward him he pushed his hands into his pockets and lowered his head. Charlie walked up to Arnold and said, "I thought you were going to bed?"

Arnold's eyes widened and he said, "Hey, Charlie that is exactly what I was going to do, but that damn Nels grabbed hold of my arm and just wouldn't let go!"

A smirk crossed Charlie's face and he said, "Yeah, I'll bet!"

Twenty minutes later the two men were at the local police station.

"Sir, I wonder if you could help me?"

The man behind the desk looked up and replied, "What can I do for you, mate? Are you lost in our big city?"

Charlie glanced back at Arnold and turned to the man, "No, sir; just trying to locate one of your residents."

"Why don't you tell me the mate's name, friend," the man answered.

Charlie started to say something when he realized he had never asked Nels his last name! Shock crossed Charlie's face and he stood looking at the man in silence.

"Well, are you gone mute? Say something, tell me the man's name!"

Charlie stuttered and said, "His first name is Nels."

A disgusted look crossed the man's face and he began to look into a book in front of him. He raised his eyes to meet Charlie's and said, "I have one Nels O'Connell in here for disturbing the peace; would that be the man?"

"Sounds like our boy. Is there some way we can get him out, do you think?"

The cop leaned back into his chair, folded his arms across his chest, and said, "Do you have any idea what Mr. O'Connell has been up to this night, mate?"

"No, but I can guess."

"No, I don't think you can, but I'm not going to spend the next hour or so telling you! If you are nice to me, I might let the bugger go for $2,000—and that doesn't include the damage to Paddy's Bar!"

"We can do that, sir. Where do I pay?"

"Just give me the money and I'll bring him out."

Charlie could see that the man wasn't very happy. Ten minutes later Nels walked through the doorway from the cellblock. His face was a mess. His right eye was closed and it looked as if his nose was broken. His shirt was pulled out from his belt and the shirt tails were hanging over his stomach. Charlie folded his arms across his chest and said, "It looks like you came in second best, my friend."

A hurt expression crossed Nell's face and he said immediately, "That's a crock! You ought a see them other two! Why don't you go back and take a look at them!"

"Let's get out of here, Nels. It looks like you need something to eat."

"Eat, hell—I need a beer, mate!"

Charlie shook his head, and the three men walked out the door. The man at the desk was watching and hollered, "Stay out of trouble or I will keep you six months the next time!" Nels turned around to say something but Charlie grabbed him by the arm and forced him into the street. Nels was still looking over his shoulder at the man but the door closed behind them before he could speak.

"Where were you at, Arnold, when those blokes jumped me?"

Arnold started to say something but Charlie raised his hands and said, "Damn it, it's over! Let's get out of here!"

When they returned to the hotel, Charlie said, "Let's get some sleep. We'll meet in the restaurant in the morning." Nels started to protest, but Arnold headed toward the elevators; it was evident that he had had enough! Charlie waited for the elevator doors to close; they would take the next one! He didn't want these two together until morning!

The next morning the three met for breakfast. Arnold looked better with a night's sleep but Nels looked like a hideous monster. His face had turned a sickening yellow and large bumps covered his face. His left eye was completely closed.

"I guess I shouldn't ask, but—how do you feel?" Charlie said.

Nels was eating eggs with some difficulty but answered, "No worries, mate, no worries."

Charlie asked, "Arnold, have you ordered?"

"Yeah," he responded.

"Are you to going to ignore each other all day, or are we going to forget last night?"

Arnold took a deep breath and said, "Listen, Nels, I'm sorry I didn't get into it with those guys, but I figured one of us should stay out of it. No sense in both of us endin' up in jail!"

Nels continued to eat, but finally he said, "Forget it, mate. I started the whole thing. Just don't have much use for those Africans, know what I mean?"

"Good," Charlie said, "now let's get down to business. I checked the accounts and we are worth about a billion and a half considering the interest we are getting right now. My question is, what do you two want to do about the money?"

Neither man said anything. Charlie waited but again the men ignored him.

"Damn it, guys! Did you hear what I said? We're worth over a billion dollars!"

"I heard you, mate," Nels answered.

Arnold just shook his head and looked away from the table.

"Well?"

Nels dropped his fork into his plate, wiped his mouth, and said, "Charlie, my friend Arnold and me done some talking the last few days and decided that you can have the dough."

"What the hell are you talking about, Nels? The money is all of ours!"

"Charlie, remember when we met and talked about this deal? I told you then that I wasn't interested in a lot of money, remember? Well, I haven't changed my mind!" Charlie sat back and looked at Nels. Bewilderment crossed his face. Finally he turned to Arnold and said, "And you, what is your story?"

"Charlie, last week you put ten million into my account. Hell, I'll never spend that if I live 500 years! Besides, I don't have a family. Christ, Charlie, even if I took the money, what would I do with it?"

"You two mean to tell me that we are sitting here with over a billion in the bank and you don't want it!" Again, neither man spoke. Nels began to eat his breakfast again and Arnold folded his hands across his lap.

Charlie threw his napkin onto the table, stood up, and said, "By God, if you think I am going to let you get away with this, you both are crazy! Don't you realize what we have been through to get where we are today?" Charlie's face was crimson, his teeth were clenched; however, neither man said a word.

The waiter walked up to the table and said, "Here we are now, who ordered the pancakes?"

Charlie knocked the man back from the table, and the food went flying across the floor. Everyone in the dining room turned to see what was happening. The waiter stood looking down at the food scattered around the table, horror written across his face!

Charlie stormed from the table and headed toward the elevators. Arnold looked up at the stunned waiter and said, "I think I ordered the pancakes." Nels smiled and took a sip of his coffee.

A week later Charlie stood at his balcony looking out over the city. He thought, *You were right, old man—the gold is a curse! Here I am, one of the richest men in the in the country and nobody wants anything to do with it! The only people I can trust or care about have told me to kiss their asses!* Charlie sighed a deep breath of resignation, turned around, and walked into the apartment. He stopped, turned again and looked across the Seattle skyline and thought, damn I'm missing Davao! He had decided he needed some time away from the Philippines and the difficult memories. He had tried to convince himself that the farther he could get away the better and Seattle seemed to be the place, he thought, *"Who am I kiddin I couldn't get the past out of my head if I traveled to the moon!"* Charlie drove his hands down into his pocket in frustration looked once more to the skyline. "Sure in the hell isn't home he said out load, it's too damn quite, it's just too damn quite!"

Dateline Manila: Today four wooden boxes of gold were discovered off the southern coast of Mindanao on a small island. Two fishermen brought the gold bars into Zamboanga and turned them in to the proper authorities. It has been speculated that the gold bars are part of the hidden treasure left by the Japanese army at the end of World War II; however, this has not been confirmed by the government of the Philippines; Further details to follow as they become available.

THE END

Epilogue

The book was loosely based on fact. The Japanese did confiscate large amounts of Philippine treasure while occupying the islands during the Second World War, and for the past sixty odd years treasure hunters from across the globe have searched the islands for the hidden riches. This is a fact: This year (2010) I was contacted by one of my Filipino friends who informed me that he aware where thirty-six bars of hidden Japanese gold were being kept. He wanted to know if I would help him and his friends dispose of it here we go again; Mindanao Gold III?

AFTERWORD

He has all the money he will ever want, has satisfied his debt to his friends lost in the jungle—so why is Charlie still looking out his window and wondering? There is no doubt that the gold exists in the Philippines, but is the gold the real issue here? Is it the chase, or is it reaching the goal? Maybe it's both—but only Charlie can find the answers. Ramon, Nels, Arnold, Mila, Magellan, and the rest have found their peace and are moving on with their lives, but Charlie? Let's hope he can find some satisfaction; after all, what sense does it make to risk it all again?

CONCLUSION

I have lived in the Philippines for several years and find it an adventure in itself. If you are ambitious enough and want to "time travel," come to the islands—you can move from the 21st to any century of your choice in just hours. Are you the type of person that wonders if you were born in the wrong time? Do you sit and daydream and think about the past and its challenges and rewards of adventure? Even today the Philippines is in constant transition; one day it's peaceful—you are on the beach; the next you have a frantic escape from bandits and/or extremists. In 1997, I was held hostage for a week by a group of radical miners, and I wasn't sure from day to day what was going to happen especially during their nightly drinking sessions! No need to relate the details other than what I have asked above: Are you ready for adventure and willing to take the risk? The majority of the time the islands are peaceful and a wonderful place to live; just be aware on the rare occasion when things tend to change direction.